ANANKE'S HAND

ANANKE'S HAND

A NOVEL

KD Hart

Ananke's Hand
PAPER ALCHEMY PUBLISHING

EIN: 30-1114815

Printed in the United States of America

First Printing, November 2018

ISBN 13: 978-1-7320988-0-0

For those who not only believed in this dream
but helped make it come true. Your time, love and
support mean more than you'll ever know.

ANANKE'S HAND

CHAPTER 1
Charlie Modern Day

I TRUDGE THROUGH MY DAYS in an exhausted zombie like haze, eager to return to the hurried heart beat and churning stomach that keeps my nights restless. The same bittersweet dream haunts me night after night; a lover I have never known feeds my starved soul in a way I thought existed only in drug store romances.

In love so true, penance must be paid and blood is the only currency accepted by fate. The beginnings we covet must always end, a certainty as inevitable as death. Roads twist and wind through the unforgiving hands of time where the destined and cursed collide.

THE OVERSIZED MOON GRABBED HOLD of me. I had never seen the her in such a way, the largest she'd ever been. I reached out, thinking I may touch her. She was shades of blood and amber, a ball of fire illuminating the night's sky. It was beautiful and terrifying.

Enchanted by her pull, I watched as she crossed the night sky, till she sank below the western hills. Her lover, the sun, rose in the east, chasing away the darkness in which she shines. His radiant rays fed her soul and she mirrored his devotion. Such as their curse, a love of beautiful ruin. For only brief moments in time, may they share the same sky.

A CURDLED SHRIEK AND FLASH of steel plunging through soft belly flesh jolt me awake. A tingling wave passed through my body and rang between my ears forcing my eyes open revealing the familiar security of the obnoxiously overpriced, eighteen hundred thread count, Egyptian cotton sheets that covered my plush California King.

For once, the saw mill sound escaping my husband's nightly breath was a comforting nuisance instead of its normal range inducing torment. My hand fell against the hardened toned abs I had spent countless hours crunching and planking and carving to perfection; searching for a baby bump I knew was not there before exhaustion grabbed hold and I immediately returned to a life in which time forgot.

My eyes snap wide awake and my heart raced as beads of cold sweat and hot salty tears stream down my face. The full moon's rays shimmered and danced across the wall, sneaking in through the shutter slats as I raced down the dark hall to my study. The antique Tiffany desk lamp's luminance was soft and warm as I manically flipped through the pages of my monogrammed, leather bound, journal; desperately searching for a clean sheet to vomit senseless words, not my own across the pages, the only relief for my weary soul.

Grasping at straws
Clinging tightly
to the memory

My skin tingled and goose fleshed
as the trail of your lips linger
long after the dream is broken and swept away

I feel you lost
in the tug and pull
on the fullest of moons

Every moment that has been, and what could be
in the pits of my heart
guiding my way

The light in your eyes
haunts my nights

A tortured soul
buried deep within
secrets untold

Haunted and cursed
without just cause
two paths fated to cross.

CHAPTER 2
Charlie Modern Day

WIND WHIPS THROUGH THE OPEN windows as rubber slaps the cracked and potholed highway at seventy miles per hour. The vastness of drought stricken Northern California wetlands felt eternal cruising up the deserted one lane highway.

Jack White screams across the radio but the wind, the road and my thoughts drown him out. Snippets and flickers of a time long passed cross my mind's eye. Nothing sticking long enough to make heads or tails of it, half the time they're gone before I realize what I've seen. It's so fucking frustrating.

I float between background noise and the static of my mind, staring through my reflection in the passenger side mirror; the wheels in my mind churn as Jack's ghostly voice barely anchors me here.

"Charlie."

I don't think it's a spirit. Actually, I know it's not. That's a completely different feeling.

"CHARLIE."

Maybe a past life trying to show itself? A scar on the land? I don't fucking know. It's never more than flashes of fire, glimmers of sails, galloping horses, or glimpses of a familiar stranger that in the depths of my bones I feel I have known for eons.

"Earth to fucking Charlotte!" Irritated fingers snap so close to my face, they stung my nose, pulling me from my thoughts back to life in front of me. Instantly I was annoyed. "Are you serious right now?" His booming voice agitated. "I've been talking to you for like five minutes!"

"Just in my own world I guess," my indifference angered him more.

"I'd fucking say so." His rant started to blend in with the rest of the static. "I have a shell for a wi-"

"Jesus Christ Michael," He pushed the right button and the fight bell rang. "I zoned out, what's the big fucking deal?" I crossed my arms in a huff.

To say my husband and my communication skills were lacking was a severe understatement. We were never the best couple, but things had been slowing coming to a boil for the past two, maybe, three years.

Lately, we had just been existing with one another. If we weren't ignoring the other's presence entirely; we were either struggling to make small talk or in a full blown argument. There was no middle ground anymore.

In one of our most recent arguments he demanded to know what he ever did to make me hate him so much. I need to preface this with; I do not hate my husband. People say things they don't mean when they argue. I should have replied, "I don't hate you. But here are reasons A - ZZ24 I am unhappy." as calmly and collected as possible. My actual reply was, "breathe" with a scathing venom that threw me off kilt. I had no idea such cruelty dwelled in me; it echoed in my head for days.

One would think if your actions made you feel so shitty, one would apologize, right? But it was just another mark in the tic for tac we had been accumulating and there was no way I was apologizing first.

Michael Walker was not some horrid fiend, philanders cheat, or physically abusive. We had been engaged in combative mental warfare for at least the past eighteen months, so it's impractical to say he isn't mentally abusive, but I'm not innocent in that either. So, let's move on.

On paper, he's a catch: Tall, every muscle in his body chiseled to perfection, dark hair, smoldering dark eyes with a heavy strong brow. Classically handsome with a bass-y baritone voice, that I have to admit, still got my panties wet when he wasn't being a total prick.

His string of gas stations and delis throughout wine country provided us a, not exactly glamorous, but a substantially comfortable life. With his success came the modern concrete monstrosity of a house plopped right in the middle of a ten acre vineyard. It doesn't match the vibe of the area and stuck out like a sore thumb. It's cold and soulless and I can't fucking stand it.

He designed the house he wanted, my opinion was not wanted or welcome. It boiled down to his money, his house, his choice. The fact that he refuses to let me work didn't carry any weight.

I feel like a whiney twat. I should be grateful. He did build me a beautiful studio with south facing windows. I have valley sun all day with plenty of space to paint. A nice little corner carved so I could focus on writing; though it didn't see much use. I had been blocked for years, never churning out more than a few incoherent scribbles in a journal. We turned the proposed walk in closet into a darkroom. I still used film, even in this digital age. It's an art that's being lost and I am utterly obsessed with the daunting beauty of it.

I know, I know. I sound like a spoilt brat. But here's the thing a lot of people don't understand; If you're not happy, you're not happy. Sometimes there's a void that money and things just can't fill. Sometimes, a soul needs more and as of late, my soul felt starved.

Looking back, I kinda think the house was the beginning of the end. The straw that broke the camel's back. The moment when every thought, fear, dream, premonition, what-have-you started to bubble to the surface.

I felt like *Sleeping Beauty*, but in reverse. Like I had been stuck in this trance, going through the motions, then one day, the fog cleared. I was awake, seeing everything for the first time. This whole life was false. Not my path and I have been struggling with it ever since.

Depending on your perspective, one could say I am the villain of this story; a 'bored housewife throwing everything away in her selfish pursuit happiness'. I wish I could remember the day I woke up a complete and total cliche.

I've communicated with spirits long enough to know that for the most part there are no villains, no heroes, just people walking the path they were destined. The hurt we cause one another is mostly unintentional, collateral damage to fate. But who knows? Maybe I'm using that to excuse my behavior. Maybe I'm a fucking nut case. Maybe I really am a horrible person ruining a perfectly good marriage. Only time will tell.

By the time the song ended I was so lost in the music, I couldn't see past the end of the microphone. A gravelly voice boomed over the speaker, "Fuck me, that was steamy Doll." while the tattooed blonde to my right spoke.

As the crowd in front of my came in to focus, I felt my body flush and the urge to run, but he caught my wrist before I could flee. "Now just where do you think you're going?" He pulled me in to his protective chest and I instinctively gravitate to the brown fleck in his sea green eyes. "You are the love I have waited a lifetime for." A wave of safety and home washed over me as his intense gaze burned through me and his lips inched closer to mine.

"Are you going to stay out here all night?" Michael popped his head in the car door.

Shit.

"It's been hours." he continued.

Hours? "I'm coming." I found myself still in the the passenger seat of the brand new, shiny, freshly leased Mercedes G Wagon.

Do you know how obnoxious I find this car? Everything about it just oozes douchebag. Sometimes I think he brought it home just to piss me off. He was always leasing something new and more over the top than the last.

I had been driving the same 1969 International Scout since I got my license at sixteen. I rebuilt her with my dad. It was he, who named her Scout. The obvious answer would be because her model when really she was named after "Scout Finch".

It was my father who instilled in me reading and art and the magic of it all. I wish he could have lived long enough to see her in the pristine condition she was today.

She was my most prized possession. Michael hated everything about her. It reminded him of who I was and me of who I could become. Neither thought sat well with him.

CHAPTER 3
Thomas Modern Day

SOME WOULD SAY MY RELATIONSHIP with my guitar, is if anything, an intriguing one. When I play her, she becomes an extension of my soul. My fingers glide up and down her neck the same as you would caress the curves of your lover. The Les Paul moans from chord to chord and I become lost in her. Phillip says you can see everything around me sink away; there is nothing but me and those six strings. I'm inclined to believe him, hours pass as if minutes.

It must be terribly difficult being my bandmate. Music and art flow through my veins, but it feels more like a curse than a blessing. One minute I am lost in her and the next I'm tossing chairs and cursing in an inaudible jumble of British slang not even I have any hope of trying to decipher.

Olivia has stated on multiple occasion, 'The only reason I've stayed as long as I have is because you that touch of genius about you. Something big is on the horizon, and I want a front row seat.'

All the greats flirt with the line of sanity. Well at least that's what I tell myself to rationalize being an insufferable knob.

"I promised my mom, I would draw the line at dismemberment; yours or mine." Olivia added in recent weeks as a fresh bit to her stock answer when I ask why she suffers the brunt end of a miserable twat.

Her voice faded as I cut her off, releasing an audible breath through my gritted teeth, "Where the bloody hell is that degenerate drummer?" My blood bubbles and jaw clenches as the countless scoldings I have issued on the respect of others time play on repeat in my mind. This might be a short rehearsal. "Have you talked to him at all today Liv?"

She ran her hand over her freshly buzzed, soft, prickly, head, searching for an answer. I'm sure, *how the hell did I let him convince me to shave my head,* ran through her mind as she cautiously answered "No, not today."

My annoyance erupted into anger and she the only target in sight. "What use are you then?" My accent made the words sound exponentially more degrading. "If you're going to be shaggin' Phillip, can you at least bother to keep tabs on him."

Her lily pad eyes instantly welled, all she could muster was, "Fuck you" as she snatched her bass and stormed out the door. She stopped at the open threshold, "You know, you don't have to be such a fucking dick, all the time." and slammed the door before I could reply.

CHAPTER 4
Phillip Modern Day

EVER SINCE WE WERE WEE lads, Thomas had a hole about him. Most people were unable to tell, but if you knew him long enough you could almost see it, right there, in the the middle of his chest. I don't even think he knew what would fill it. Whatever it was, it sure wasn't going to be found at the bottom of a whiskey bottle or shagging every tart that threw a look his way.

"Piss off Phillip." Thomas hissed as he swallowed the last gulp of bourbon, then without provocation slammed his low ball in to the brick wall.

Olivia was right, he's going of the rails. Thomas was stumbling drunk roaming around his flat barefoot and shirtless. His unbuttoned leather pants hung low off his hips and his eyes were glazed and crossed. He was at best, useless for the evening and at worst a danger to himself.

I phoned Olivia to tell her I'd be missing our date as I fetched a broom to clean up my cock of a cousin's mess while he dangled over the patio's banister. His flat is only three flights up, if he fell over, it wouldn't kill him, just fuck him up proper. Reckon it might be what he needs to knock some sense in to him.

I love my cousin, but he can be a third rate prick at times. The fact I made it the thirty some odd years without smothering him in his sleep is a a testament to my unyielding familial duty.

Thomas' entire upper body was limp flailing over the rail. He looked like a wet bath towel draped over a clothes line. "What are you doing?" I demanded, pulling him back over the banister, and guiding him to the chaise.

"I was going to toss myself over." Thomas paused as he drunkly shifted his attention to me. Sweaty chunks of blonde draped across his glazed eyes, "But then I realized the fall wouldn't kill me. I'd break a leg or something, and that would just piss me off." I couldn't help the chuckle that slipped. Which made him laugh, and soon we were both in hysterics. "You wanker, you thought of tossing me over?"

I thumbed the corner of my eye between bouts of laughter "Yes. Yes, I did."

"Twat." He played hurt.

"Seriously Mate," I paused a moment to ensure I had his attention, "there's a fine line-"

"I know." Thomas sobered. "I'll apologize to Liv tomorrow."

I kicked my feet up on to my footrest, looking up at the stars. If the thoughts running through Thomas' head were any louder I may actually hear what he was thinking, but I wasn't going to push. It wouldn't matter, he would only burrow deeper into himself.

It was an unusually warm evening in the city. The night air was refreshing as my thoughts circled and eyes fluttered to sleep. Just as I was drifting, I heard under his breath. "I just know she's out there."

"She?" I questioned darting to a seated position, but he was already in a whiskey induced slumber.

CHAPTER 5
Charlie Modern Day

I HAVE KNOWN MICHAEL THE majority of our lives. We met in the fifth grade when I moved to the rolling hills and sprawling vineyards of Napa County from my beloved little seaside Seattle suburb. It was the mid nineties; Kurt Cobain had crossed over from local hero to newest member of the 27 Club, Dave Grhol was a drummer god, Doc Marten's, flannel, and dirty hair was socially acceptable where I was from. At this new school it made me the; dirty, weird, alt, girl. Michael was the best liked of four Michael's in our class of twenty.

For five years that was the dynamic. We knew each other by name, well, I knew who he was. I probably wan't even a blip on his radar. Which I was more than okay with, we were at opposite sides of the spectrum. To say I was a pompous, judgmental, angsty teenager is, well, to be honest, an understatement. To say I thumbed my nose at the whole lettermen society was more accurate.

The summer between freshman and sophomore year he sprouted from five-foot-eight to six-foot-two making the basketball coaches fall over themselves. As we entered into our senior year, he topped off at six-foot-five and packed thirty pounds of muscle on to his previously spindly frame. By the end of his high school career, he had lettered in basketball, football and baseball.

I was still the grungy, little, alt, girl; now engrossed in art, photography and writing. I wandered the school like a vagabond; paint splattered clothes, talking to myself, compulsively scratching pen to paper. Writing consumed my soul, keeping me up all hours of the night. I somehow lost that along the way and it hurts my heart.

But that's a sad song for another day. Let's get back on track. Essentially, I had known Michael Walker for seven years, and we may have said maybe ten words to one another. Like I said earlier, completely different worlds.

Not like it mattered to me. Granted, he was pleasing to look at, but I always had a weird disdain for him. Dahlia, my best, well, only friend since the day we got paired together on a science project in the sixth grade, always poked fun, insinuating I had some sort of subliminal crush on him. "I mean look at him. How can your body not tingle when he's around?"

"I get it, but for me, it's more like he makes my skin crawl." I answered with a shrug.

She jumped down my throat, catching me off guard, "That's right. Everyone on this earth is soooooo much more materialistic, vapid and no where near as artsy and cool as the ever so deep Charlotte Bower." Apparently I struck a nerve. She didn't stop for breath, "The only way a guy can be cool enough for you to give the time of day is if he has tattoos. Or is a musician. Or a poet. Or something equally pretentious."

"Kinda sounds hot, when you put it like that." I goaded.

Scrunching her nose, she shakes her head. "No, because he'll have some god awful douche strip down his chin or something." A smile glazed across her eyes and we both laughed. "I'm just saying, you have a pretty ridged set of standards. They're kind of impossible."

"I dunno. You live up to those standards." I played.

"Yeah. And I'm like, your only friend." She snarked. Her playful tone softened. "You have these walls and it's this Sisyphean feat to scale them." Her concerned eyes forced my gaze to hers as she tenderly tucked one of many wild curls behind my ear. "It seems lonely."

It was far too serious a moment. I did the only thing I could think of. I pressed my lips in to hers. Not because I had some deep longing urge to kiss her. (And there's nothing wrong if thats what floats your boat. It's just not my cup of tea.) It was a means to an end. Here's one thing to know about girls. They talk. Incessantly. Sometimes, to shut one up, the only thing you can do is kiss her. I say this with thirty five years of experience being a girl. So I say it on safe authority.

"Jesus Christ Charlotte!" She stepped back laughing as she brushed the violation from her lips. "Don't you take anything seriously?"

It was easy to ruffle her feathers. I pouted. "You mean, you weren't professing your love to me?" Unable to contain my laughter, "How disappointed those bimbo cheerleaders will be to find out we never consummated our obvious lesbian feelings for one another." I dramatically batted my lashes at her.

"Shut up!" She playfully pushed me off the desk I had been sitting on. Four years later, we could only laugh at the ridiculousness of the rumor that lingered since freshman year. I mean, the ones who started it were the ones; binge drinking, making out with one another and stripping atop coffee tables, all to gain the attention of some date rape-y jock. How could you not laugh at the irony?

As my ass hit the ground, Captain America himself entered the empty classroom and lifted me to my feet. "You alright?"

"I got it." I snapped annoyed. Fucking Dahlia, she was right. My teenage body was betraying me. He is gorgeous and every nerve ending in my body noticed. I wanted to lick his abs so fucking bad. What? Where did that come from? You don't think he can tell right? God. Could you imagine; me, with him. How hypocritical could I be, before it turned into a punchline.

He tilted his head, forcing my gaze to his. I immediately resented how quickly my body mutineered against my brain. The sly smile from the corner of his mouth, gleamed across his large espresso eyes. "You sure about that?"

The bass of his voice vibrated through me. "I'm good." My body ran so hot, I couldn't convey the cold disdain I was aiming for. It came out more swoon-y.

He stood upright, crossing his arms, evaluating me. He shot

me that half smile again, turning me into a puddle. "I don't think we've met, Michael Walker."

It was sweet. Which annoyed me more. "Charlie. Bower." I broke the names up as I measured him up. "We've been in the same classes since the fifth grade." I shook his extended hand, pleased with the level of annoyance in my voice. The eye roll at the end, inspired. He scratched the back of his head trying to read me. You could tell he was thinking from the smell of burnt rubber. God. He. Looks. Amazing. He flashed that damned smile from the corner of his mouth again. "Seven years?"

Well, at least he can do basic math. I kept my snarky judgments about high school athletes to myself.

"You should let me take you to dinner. Make up for such a travesty."

Get it together Charlie. Speak. Now! He's waiting. "I'm good. Thanks." I picked my journal up, snatched my paint splattered canvas messenger bag and left the room as quickly as my feet would carry me.

I can only assume he sat there a moment bewildered and intrigued, because shortly thereafter a relentless campaign for my attention ensued.

CHAPTER 6
Charlie High School

It started slowly. First, with misspelled, grammatically incorrect notes stuffed in my locker. When those went ignored, he left flowers on Scout's windshield. The rumor mill quickly got hold of this information which only annoyed me, further digging my heels against his advances.

"You're so lucky Michael Walker is in to you. He is such a fox." some cheerleader unsolicitedly advised one day as she smacked her gum, "If you play your cards right, you could be his date to Homecoming."

Michael's sudden interest in me came with the interest of the entire student body. This was uncharted territory and I did not like it. I couldn't help but engage the future Stepford wife. "Shouldn't someone like another person for something other than what they look like?"

The busty blonde thought hard. I could tell, because her gaze stuck to the asbestos tiled ceiling. She smacked her lips again, "He has a really cool car."

Internal face palm. I should have known better.

A welcome distraction, the front office T.A. entered the class armed with call slip in hand. There was something about those little yellow pieces of paper that piqued everyone's interest.

"Charlotte Bower. You are needed in the principal's office." My Government teacher announced.

I found my way to the to the office as I clenched the small rectangle of carbon paper. What the fuck did I do?

As soon as I pulled the heavy, dark, glass door open, mortification set in. There Michael Walker stood, decked out in a tuxedo with a dramatically oversized bouquet draped over his long arm. He looked so fucking good, my teenage body melted. I mentally smacked myself out of it. You two have absolutely nothing in common. You are just a challenge for him. Is that the PA microphone in his free hand? Shit.

Before I could stop him, "Charlotte Bower, will you please let me take you to dinner Friday night?"

A collective "Awe." radiated through the campus.

I rolled my eyes with immediate discomfort. He put the microphone close to my mouth waiting for an answer. Embarrassment escalated to anger. "How many times do I have to tell you 'No'?", I countered storming off.

I stopped in my tracks when I heard his baritone voice behind me and echoing through the corridors, "I'm going to keep asking till it's a yes."

Another collective, "Awe."

I cringed with annoyance as I exited the building.

After the incident in the principal's office, any chance I had to finish out the year with anonymity was quickly erased. Now everyone knew who I was and somehow felt they knew me. Therefore giving them reason to comment on how I "was so lucky." and Michael "is a total catch." I was "silly to ignore him." My favorite was "and you'd be so pretty if-"

I was beyond annoyed. I was pissed. I never wanted to be under the glaring microscope of high school popularity, and Michael's attention forcefully slid my petri dish right across that stage. His daily advances hadn't ceased and now I was being bombarded by the entire student body. It was out of control. I begged my mom to let me home school the remainder of the year.

"Because a boy wants to take you out on a date? No." She never really understood me.

"Mo-m," I stretched it out in to two whiney syllables. "It's not that. He's not interested in me, like for real. He's only interested because I told him 'no'." I explained.

She looked at me with those mom eyes. You know the look; concern, love, disapproval all at the same time. "What's the harm in one date?" She pushed a loose curl too short to be pulled into my pony behind my ear. "You might have fun."

"Because we are from totally different planets." I answered. "We have nothing in common."

"So you immediately disregard him? You always say people look down on you because you're different. Aren't you doing the same thing?"

Damn you Mom! Throwing my hypocrisy in my face. "MOM! You're supposed to be on my side." I whined.

"Always. I'm just saying; just because he's different from you doesn't mean you can't enjoy his company."

I could feel my jaw drop in disbelief. Why does she always have to be so damn sensical?

I went to school the next day with the firm intension of avoiding all human interaction. It might be possible. The Homecoming rally was that afternoon and attendance was mandatory. You have to love small towns and forced school spirit.

The rally was most the way done and I had made it though fairly unnoticed. (Probably because I was hiding under the bleachers.) Then I heard his booming voice. "We're going to demolish the Spartans tonight." He paused for the cheers. "But I have this cloud hanging over my head." He paused for the collective awe. "I still don't have a date for the dance tonight. Again, collective awe. Shit. Please don't. "Now I have it on good authority, I've been voted Homecoming King." Cheers erupt, he continues. "I can't possibly show up without a gorgeous girl on my arm." A roar of girls offer themselves. "But there's only one girl I want to go with." He's really going to do this? Isn't he? "Charlotte Bower. Will you please come down here?"

Fuck. Fuck. Fuck.

Might as well get this over with. I shyly emerge from under the bleachers to a roar of cheers and applause. Every step in his direction gave me a sickening urge to run away.

When I reached him, he shot a smile that gleamed from his chocolate eyes. He leaned down and softly kissed my cheek. Another collective "awe." I flushed berry red.

He dropped to a knee. Even on a knee, his tall frame still reached passed my shoulders. "Charlotte Bower, will you please do me the honor of being your escort to the dance tonight?"

The crowd awed; I was on the spot. There was no escape. I thought of my mom and her calling me out on my hypocrisy. Fuck it. I shrugged my shoulders. "If I go, you have to call me Charlie. Only my Grandma calls me Charlotte."

The crowd erupted as if Michael scored another game winning touchdown.

Fuck my life.

CHAPTER 7
Charlie High School

MICHAEL'S BMW PULLED IN FRONT of my house a full twenty minutes before I heard my mom gleefully call, "Charlie, your date is here."

I touched up my lip gloss, primped my hair one last time and checked myself out in the full body mirror.

"Wish I were going." Dahlia pouted as she packed her hair and make up bags away.

I pulled a vintage lacy Hepburn-esque LBD from my closet. "I wish you were too." I stepped into the party dress. I didn't actually wear a lot of dresses, but I liked collecting all things vintage. The lines and artistry spoke to me the day I found it at the consignment shop. The fact it fit like a glove made it feel fated and now here I am. Weird, right? "I could really use a buffer. What do I talk to these people about?"

"Cosmo and body shots." She had been laughing at me since this whole escapade started. Balking as she zipped me up, "There is something romantic about it all though."

I was stuck between laughter and shock.

"What?" she shrugged as we giggled.

I pulled my cabernet peacoat from the closet and grabbed my matching clutch. "Nothing," my giggles subsided. "Just nervous. We haven't even done anything yet, and everyone at school already knows the ins and the outs of my life. They have even gone so far as to fabricate an entire parallel universe in which I am their leader. They hang on every word I say, because Michael Walker has deemed me intriguing." I took a breath. "Which; one — I'm not even sure he knows what that means. Two - well, I forgot where I was going with that, but it was a damn good argument."

"Got that out of your system?"

I shook the last of my nerves wildly from my limbs and slid my heels on. "Yeah. It's just, college guys are more, discreet."

"Or at the very least, you don't have to see them every day." Dahlia sympathized.

"Exactly."

"Well, you got their alpha. The bitches will fall in line, at least until you break up, then you will be the source of their wrath and entertainment."

Her matter of factness forced an explosion of laughter.

"Thanks for the encouragement." I hugged her on our way out of my room.

As I made my way down the hall, Michael's eyes grew large. "You look-" He paused trying to find a word. "Amazing." He grabbed both my hands and lurched his neck down kissing me on the cheek.

"Really?" I thought I looked like me, just in a dress. "Thank you."

He nervously fumbled. "I got you this." He picked up a blood red dahlia corsage that kind of matched my dress perfectly. He opened the box and slid the flowers over my wrist.

I couldn't help but smile at the gesture. "Thank you." I examined the flowers. "You know, my best friend's name is Dahlia?" Nodding in her direction.

"Yeah, so?"

Mental face palm. Be nice. I held my wrist up. "The flowers?"

"Oh, yeah." He nervously scratched the back of his head. "I didn't know the name of 'em. Just picked the most unique of the bunch. Kinda like you."

I knew it was a horrible line, but I melted. I couldn't help myself, I pushed myself up to his lips. "That's very sweet." I cooed as I set my heels back to the ground.

He opened the passenger door, gently guiding me in before getting in himself. God, please don't let my mom be right?

"Can I be honest?", He nervously blew air from his mouth before turning over the ignition.

"I wouldn't expect anything less." I answered as the car began to hum. Maybe it was his nerves, or his sweet gestures, or the moon, but I was swoony and hating myself.

"I'm really nervous. Like more nervous than I have ever been before. I can't get my hands to stop sweating."

He was endearing. "I make you nervous?" I flirted.

"Incredibly. Partly, because there's this anticipation, because of how I pursued you, and partly because you're you. You're not like other girls Charlie." I was lost in his voice. And those eyes. And those biceps. Geez. Those things are firm. "You're special, aren't you?"

My teenage hormones took control as I lunged in to his mouth. By the time my mind caught up to my body, I had unbuckled his belt and my hand had slid in to the waistband of his boxers. His hand had ran past the hem of my dress and up my inner thigh. (As long as it's safe, sex doesn't necessarily have to mean anything. But I was not going to be another tic on his didn't mean anything list.) I pulled the emergency brake. "We should get going." I said between kisses. "Don't you have a plastic crown to win?"

He searched my eyes, seeking permission that wasn't coming. "Yeah. I suppose you're right." He tried to mask his frustration as put the car in gear.

We arrived back at school. The gym was dark with the exception of the disco ball and strobe lights. Streamers and balloons had vomited all over the building.

The night went pretty much as anticipated. We danced, he won his crown. We laughed, found some common ground, and realized how different we were. He stepped away for a bit to hang out with his football buddies. A parade of girls bombarded me; telling how great I looked, how cute Michael and I were together, and "who knew there was a serious bod underneath all that flannel." All in all, a decent night.

When we pulled in front of my house, Michael turned off the car. He slid his hand behind my neck, pulling my lips to his his. He pulled away, keeping his hand at the nape of my neck, his dark eyes held my gaze hostage, "I really like you Charlie."

Automatically the words fell from my mouth, colder than intended. "You don't know me well enough, to know if you like me." I inadvertently crushed him. Quickly I kissed him to soothe the burn. "But I wouldn't be opposed to letting you get to know me." I flashed him my best rendition of his half smile.

And that's how we started. We dated pretty steady thereafter. Had a lot of fun in the beginning, but there was always a barrier between us. Two painfully different people. I figured I'd make it work. It was senior year. Why not end it as the envy of every girl in my class? And having such a good looking guy feeling on all your bits and pieces was a pretty fantastic consolation prize.

We were both going to Stanford. He on a football scholarship. I took out student loans to pursue journalism. We decided to see where this thing took us.

We were young and hopeful. Deep down I knew we weren't meant to be. We were too different. I never really saw myself with that Johnny and June type love. That all consuming, no matter what, always and forever, two hearts one dream type of love. I had a good enough guy. And in all honesty, I was really scared to take the world on by myself. I made the decision. I was in it for the long haul.

Two months before graduation, Michael blew out his knee in a third base collision. His athletic career was over. With no scholarship, Stanford was off the table.

I'm not sure what it was; pity, some convoluted idea of loyalty, actual love; but I had this pit in the bottom of my stomach, this waive of dread that Stanford wasn't in my cards either. It wasn't time for our paths to part; I dutifully deferred to help take care of him. It was only supposed to be a year, yet somehow, here we are, seventeen years later.

Over those seventeen years we had slowly but surely built our way up to Napa County Upper Middle Class. The big house, huge lot, meticulous landscaping, a long driveway lined with grape vines, the status cars.

Michael made a full recovery two surgeries and three years later. Shortly there after he slowly start grooming me for trophy wife life. His expectations of me slowly grew. He wanted to look, act, talk, be a certain way. Keep his home, not work. It happened slowly, incrementally, till one day I woke up feeling the furthest thing from myself. But on paper it was a good life. My family and friends would have me committed if they heard the turmoil in my head.

BONE PIERCING COLD JAR MY body awake. My eyes come to focus, I was still in the car. I glanced at the rose gold cocktail watch ten years of servitude gifted me, two thirty seven am. Shit. Michael was going to have something to say, I'd bet money on it. I was half tempted to stay in the car. I could dig my heels in quite deep if the occasion called. The G Wagon told me it was a balmy sixty three, which made me question how I got so cold. But questions, I'd pin till the morning, otherwise I'll have myself so worked up I won't sleep.

I tip toed in to the house, feeling like a high school kid, caught sneaking in after a night of God knows what. Michael's quiet anger burned a hole in me as I slinked between the sheets. Couldn't he just fight with me now. It was obviously weighing on both of us and nether of us were getting any sleep tonight anyway.

Nope. The air would sit fifteen feet thick. All. Night. Long. I could say something, "Michael." Frozen out. Nothing. Alright. "Goodnight."

My eyes grew heavy and dreams of yesteryear flowed through my veins. The depth of my sleep paralyzed my body but could not ease the burden of my restless soul.

CHAPTER 8
Charlie Modern Day

I WOKE THE NEXT MORNING, no longer in the concrete monstrosity I live. Is this a dream? I scan the room, trying to find something, anything familiar. Nothing but oddly, everything.

Mechanically, I made the bed, dressed in a white shirt paired with riding pants and boots and flawlessly navigate to a kitchen I have never seen. I pull a french press from one cabinet, grounds from another and a mug from the last as if I had done so a thousand times before.

I followed my body's lead as we walked out the front door and onto the porch. She sat us down in a wooden rocker, wrapping a shawl around our shoulders.

She softly rocked us and we sipped our coffee, watching as the sun began to peak over the hills. The sky faded from blacks to blues and purples then oranges and pinks, acres upon acres of rolling green hills uncovered in front of our eyes. I felt my heart warm as she clutched our chest. I was her, or she was me. Either way, we were one.

IT'S THIS MOMENT, RIGHT HERE; the still in the dawn, the quiet and calm. The homey aroma of hay and dirt mixed with morning dew dancing on the soft morning breeze. Watching the sky unveil my eight hundred acres of sprawling Kentucky country side. I have to breathe this moment in every morning. Savor it. Hold on to it as my reminder that I really do cherish this place when the stress and responsibility weigh on me.

The property had been in my mother's family since the Civil War, but it wasn't until 1895 when my Grandfather made the land profitable. He won himself a set of horses, a green broke Painted and an unbroken Rocky Mountain with two aces in the hole and a third in the river. Inspiration struck a few days later as he saddle broke the Rocky. Breeding, Board, and Training of Show and Race Horses.

It didn't take long for my grandfather to turn the majority of our orchards into roaming lands. Soon there after; new stables were built, the barn was refurbished, and two outdoor and an indoor training arena were added to the estate. He built an extravagant plantation style farm house with wrap around patios both up and downstairs to match his recent updates. His final project was a white split rail fence that encompassed all eight hundred acres of Ananke Farms.

When I was twelve, my mother and grandfather passed within days of each other. She from consumption; he from a broken heart and a shotgun blast through the chin.

I clenched the heirloom locket draped across my neckline as the pang of their loss flooded my memory.

At the of the reading of the my grandfather's will, we were all shocked to learn I had been listed as proprietor and my father listed as executor of the Ananke Farms Estate until my twenty first birthday.

Grandfather had made it very clear many years ago that "No O'Donnell" would take over his property. When Grandfather found out my mother was pregnant, he insisted I be given his last name or he would exile us from Ananke Farms, leaving my mother with a new born and no home or means. My poor father must have felt incredibly emasculated, but seeing I am Charlotte Sinclair and not O'Donnell, options must have been limited.

Father worked his way through the ranks, earning some sort of respect from my grandfather. He at least trusted my father enough to manage the stables and keep the books.

"Sorry Henry. I really have grown fond of you, and I trust you'll guide Charlotte through this difficult time with a loving hand, but you didn't really think I'd leave my life's work in the hands of the dirty Irishman who soiled my beloved Miriam?"

Henry erupted as the lawyer finished reading aloud. "A miserable bastard till the very end."

As I watched my father storm through the tempered glass doors with "*The Law Offices of Elliott Harper Esquire*" in gold leaf etched across and flip a nearby chair, I couldn't help but feel his loss and anger as intently as I felt my own. In that moment of empathy I realized there would be no time for childhood foolishness. There was land to tend, a staff to manage, the house to run. Bills to pay, the stables; it was overwhelming for a twelve year old to take take in. In all fairness, it was still a lot to take in.

After the reading, it was assumed I would take over the house and kitchen garden. Something about housework and womanly duty. I was lost in a haze, paying no mind. I had only seen my mother bustle through the house with Olivia at her side between my daily tutors and riding lessons. I had no idea what she did. All I knew was my mother was here and now she's not, and in some sort of cataclysmic joke, I have to to find a way to fill her shoes. The hurricane of thought swelled in the corners of my eye.

My only saving grace is Olivia. She is nineteen and one of the most beautiful women I have ever seen. Her eyes are shaped like almonds. She is exotic and mysterious with olive skin and dark wavy hair. Her full bosom makes me feel, well, inadequate.

Olivia was shocked in my line of questioning. How exactly does one answer, 'what were my mother's responsibilities?' Her honest answer eased my plea for help. "Well sweetheart," Her creole accent tickled my ears. "It may not have looked it, but a little bit of everything."

"What exactly does everything mean?" My puzzled pre-teen face pleaded.

"Don't worry about today." She offered. "Take the day to think good and hard, write down as many questions as you can think of. We'll meet tomorrow morning, cook breakfast and after, we'll tour the property. I'll point out everything I have seen your mother do, or the best that I know anyway. And if you have any more questions, you just ask along the way. I'm sure there will be bits I miss or don't know of. Her role was far larger than she ever let on and her presence is deeply missed." She paused to thumb away the tear forming in the corner of her eye and I was quickly reminded I was not the only one who lost or mourned Miriam Sinclair, with an audible breath, she chirped. "We'll figure it out as we go."

Appreciation washed away the sad puzzled look from my face as I hugged her tightly. "See you tomorrow then?" She nodded in reply. I turned and walked away; four steps in, I was halted in my tracks, my mother's voice rang in my ears. I turned and smiled, "Thank you."

I went straight to my room, pulled out a stack of paper and vigorously went to work. My young hand furiously scribbled every question I could think of. When I glanced at the nightstand, the clock read two thirty seven in the morning.

My back ached from sitting in the chair so long. I walked around the room and stretched before sliding between the sheets. My eyes are closed as my head hit the pillow, but sleep evaded me. The wheels in my mind wouldn't slow down. The darkness only speed them up. For the next hour and a half, I lay there, the minutes feeling eternal. The closest thing I can compare it to, is being a small child, waiting for Santa Claus to come, but the exact opposite. Tomorrow my life was changing and I was in no way prepared for it. All I wanted was for my mom to hold me and tell me it would be alright. But her not being here was the whole reason I was in this mess. I missed her and hated her all at the same time.

Breakfast and clean up were easy enough. My mother coached me through meal service enough times over the years. Under normal circumstances, from here I would bid my adieu and spend the next several hours with my tutor. After lunch, I would visit father at the stables and spend the rest of the afternoon on a long ride or brushing out one of the mares or in a stall cuddled up with one of the horses, reading a book. Knots twisted in my stomach. I knew today was the first of a very different type of day at Ananke Farms. At least I would no longer have to bear twice weekly finishing school classes.

First stop was a house staff meeting in the kitchen. My Grandfather's sister; eighty year old Great Aunt Vera, Olivia, and the twenty seven year old handyman Phillip and now for the first time, me. The meeting mostly consisted of each person rattling off what needed to be done that day and how the chores were going to be split up. Vera griped that most of the day's chores had landed on her plate since Olivia was taking me to tour the property. "She bloody well lives here. I think she'll find her way just fine!"

"All that is being asked of you is to wash and press linens, which you do anyway. You're just not happy unless your belly aching about something."

Vera shook her fist at Olivia, "So what if I am. I'm old. I've earned the right." She scoffed a laugh at herself.

Olivia rolled her eyes, "She says that every day."

Phillip diverted the conversation to a rant about rabbits. If he saw one more rabbit in his garden we were having rabbit soup for supper.

Olivia nudged me and whispered with a wink, "And he says that everyday."

I muffled my laugh and wink, quickly blushing. "Sorry, I hope that wasn't too informal." My mother's propriety echoed in the back of my mind.

"Mind you not. I find work is most pleasurable when you can find some fun in it and enjoy your company, well at least most days anyway." Olivia banished the thought with a flick of her wrist. "We should be on our way. There is much to see."

"WHATCHA DOING OUT HERE SWEETHEART?" My father asked as he took a seat in the empty rocker next to me. The shards of broken memory faded away, bringing me back to the blackened hillside and fiery pink sky.

"Just watching the sunrise, thinking." I replied as I sipped my now cold coffee.

"About?" Father pressed.

"Just how much has changed in nine years." I replied rocking my chair and sipping frigid coffee. I made it, I was damn well going to drink it.

"Yes my sweet girl. Birthdays have a tendency to do that to a person." My father reached out, trying to console me as he patted the top of my hand.

"Especially this birthday father." A sad half smile sat in the corner of my mouth. Although I had shouldered more responsibility than all of the girls I knew combined, there was something about turning twenty one tomorrow that terrified me. Even after all these years, I still could not wrap my head around the idea how drastically a life can change in one day.

I'd been mostly responsible for the property for a long while now. So the fact that it was going to be official tomorrow shouldn't be, but felt especially daunting. I know I'm ready for it, but did I want it?

I wish Olivia were still around. I could write her out in California, but it's not the same. This whole place hadn't been the same since she left with Phillip two years ago. It made sense. I was finally the age she was when she guided me through what my inheritance entailed. It only seemed fair that my teacher be able to leave when I became the same age. She was entitled to live her life after all. A tear formed in the corner of my eye. Before it fell, I take a deep breath, forcing it back to whence it came.

"Something the matter my dear?" My sniffles pulled Henry back from the abyss of his own memories.

"Nothing Pop." I kissed his forehead and walked in to the house.

CHAPTER 9
Charlotte Kentucky 1935

I WOKE THE NEXT MORNING feeling thirty five instead of twenty one. Today I am meant to take on the books, but money was a business I never really much cared for. Unfortunately for me there was no room in our budget to hire an accountant.

Faithfully and without complaint, my father continued about his duties as executor while maintaining his role as stable manager. But as I was growing up, he grew old. The physical stress of the horses, the mental stress of money management aged him faster than running the house had aged me.

"My wish for you was a happy life. I hope you see that." He said as we hunched over the ledgers.

"Very funny father?" My words fell harsher than intended. Softly I add, "I'm not trying to be disrespectful, but how can you say such things? Here? Now?"

"Well if you found yourself a nice businessman to marry, he can take care of this for you." He snapped.

I immediately fired back, "Yes, because I am quiet and meek and soft like women of my station are meant to be, right father?!" I paused, waiting for his reply. We have had this same worn out argument many a time before. He sat back as the storm raged. "And what makes you think I want that kind of life? I don't need to be taken care of. I need help! Grandfather ran the stable with a staff of ten. Just the stable. There are maybe ten of us now. To run the house, the stable, tend the orchards and livestock, the garden, all of it."

"What would you have me do? We have to sell a few horses and have our boarders full before we can hire anyone on. How are we supposed to do that when people are losing everything out there?"

The well prepared line served its purpose, calming me, at least in that moment. Henry had a spectacular way of making me feel as spoilt as milk left in the sun. It was a little difficult to complain about being spread too thin, whilst being reminded of a very real Depression spreading across our country.

"I understand that you live a very different life than girls your age. You own land, run a business, they are married with bellies bloated with child."

Why? Why you foolish old man? Why could you not leave well enough alone? Years of repressed anger bubble to the surface. (I have a tendency of unleashing it in disproportionate outbursts, especially on my father.) "Is that what it boils down to? How you are deprived of grandchildren?" Rage shook my body as my empty coffee cup flew across the room.

Desensitized to my outbursts, he didn't even bother to duck as the ceramic mug exploded overhead.

I watched as it was happening, like a spectator at a horse race, but I could not control it. The best way I can explain it is; I feel like I have this pot, weighing on my chest, always at a simmer, all someone has to do is brush the stove's knob with their hip as they walk past, and before I know it, I'm at a roiling boil, spilling over the top.

My father's warm eyes shimmered. She was too young to take on what she did.

"Sorry father." I take the seat beside him. "I didn't mean to erupt like that. I know you just want to see me happy. And for the most part I am. I just grow frustrated with this whole marriage thing. I want to be loved, have a partner who cherishes this place as I do. No title chasing, no ladder climbing."

"I understand your caution dear. But you have to be open to love to find it."

"It's hard when everyone you care for leaves. I have never known a true friend."

"Olivia was your friend."

"Yes, and she left." The flame was stoked. "How I am supposed to marry, if I can't even make a friend. Everyone who comes here eventually leaves. Lord knows I can't go away, abroad for a few months or college, New York, California, anywhere but here. But I bear the burden of duty."

CHAPTER 10
Charlotte Kentucky 1936

A YEAR HAD CAME AND gone since my twenty first birthday, marking the last time I fought with father about marriage. It also marked four months since his last attempt at match making.

Begrudgingly, I agreed at his attempts of finding me a husband. If for any reason, because I was tired. Tired of relentless gossip. Tired of harboring the weight of this place alone. Tired of fighting. I haven't the energy to waste on my father's foolhardy errand.

I wasn't any help to the cause; brash, stubborn and self reliant, all qualities deemed "unladylike".

My grandfather once explained, "Men only care about two things when it comes to taking a wife; training and bloodstock. Most men won't exude the effort to break a feral horse and they all want the polished, refined, blue-ribbon show mare, who's lineage could be traced back to the civil war and when confronted with the slightest bit of disobedience will unleash their crop across your hide without second thought."

The spoiled playboys, ivy league scholars and Wall Street brokers from reputable families that proved suitable companions based on my station wanted meek, mouse-like, wives. I had offended all of them in one way, shape or form within an hour of their arrival.

The suitor pool was rapidly shrinking and my father feared his meddling had done nothing but add to my already ridged reputation. Months of silence on the topic had me certain of one of two things; the blasted old man had either learned his lesson or was plotting something.

I slept in till seven in the morning. My birthday was the only day I ever took for myself. Even on Christmas I worked, at the very least feeding and exercising the horses. In all fairness, it's much easier to ask someone to work on a sunny March day than a snowy holiday.

A mild mannered rap at my bedroom door interrupted my internal rant. "Ms. Charlie, your breakfast is getting cold." Dahlia, our newest housemaid bellowed through the door.

I hired her on a few months after Olivia's departure. She was close to my age, but motherly. Her dark features were eerily familiar, it was only after she noted she hailed from Arkansas, a territory to which I'd never been, I gave up on my attempts to recall where I had known her from. Shortly upon her arrival, she decided to make herself the biggest thorn in my side, and there has remained comfortably steady ever sense, wriggling her way in to my heart and becoming a dear friend.

I flung the door open ruffled, "If I've told you once I've told you a thousand times, my name is Charlotte."

Dahlia matched every ounce of irritation in my voice, "Yes, Ma'am. That must mean I've told you a thousand and one times, there's a soft, sweet, funny girl buried underneath all that responsibility and horse shit, and her name is Charlie." Dahlia paused, "Now get to movin'.Your father wants to speak with you."

"Great. He must have invited another suitor to come stay." My stomach grumbled. Normally I would have eaten hours ago. "You said you made breakfast?" I smiled the toothiest smile I could muster without a cup of coffee in hand.

She pursed her lips, resting her hands on her hips, "MmmHmmm." Her irritated breath pushed me out the door.

"French toast with powdered sugar?" A hopeful twinkle shimmered across my eye.

"You'll never know unless you get your skinny ass down those stairs! Otherwise I'm going to feed it to the pigs."

I squeezed her as I passed the threshold. "Thank you."

"You're welcome Ms. Charlie. And Happy Birthday."

Dahlia slid a plate of beautifully golden brown pan toasted loaf slices, slathered in butter and dusted with powder sugar in front of me as I took a seat at the small square kitchen table. "So Ms. Charlie, what do you have planned for today?" She queried taking the empty seat across from me.

"You can drop the Ms., but please call me Charlotte." I answered smiling as I stuffed a bit of buttery toast in my mouth, "Ride into town, buy myself a dress I'll never have cause to wear again, stuff myself into said dress, then tea with my cousin and her snobby friend's. You know those overprivileged, lazy women do nothing but play cards, gossip, primp and complain of their children and husbands. Unless I'm around, then, they all gang up on me and preach how I should do the same." I paused for breath, offset by my bitter tone. "Happy Birthday Charlotte" I snarked.

"Sounds like a lovely day to me." Dahlia replied as she rotated a wash cloth round a plate.

My mother would have scolded me for bragging. I blushed as her words rang in my ears. While this wasn't specifically bragging, my mother would have quickly pointed out how petty I was being; complaining of playing cards and shopping. I retreated, "Sorry, I don't mean to..."

She shooed away my apology and interrupted, "It's okay Charlie."

"You're not giving up on that are you." The discontent in my voice couldn't hide the laughter behind my eyes.

"Never." Her directness left an awkward lull sending us both into hysterics.

"Do you want to come with me?" I offered as soon as the idea popped into my head. "We can get you and Mrs. Pierce a new dress as well." Dahlia scanned the kitchen taking a mental inventory. I crossed the room, grabbing both of her hands, pleading. "Please Dahlia. Please, please, please, please; shop and play cards and have tea with me." Dramatically shaking her to emphasize my plea. "Your company will actually make this excursion bearable."

"Only if I get to call you Charlie." She countered with a wink.

The day went exactly as predicted. Though Dahlia had no idea how vicious these women truly were. I introduced her as my friend and travel companion, but Cousin Rose (who was societal perfection with her tightly pinned hair, porcelain complexion and ruby lips) was quick to point out; Dahlia attended to her while she spent the whole of July at Ananke Farms last year. The murder of crows were obliged to treat her as such.

After a long day of "You cook everyday and launder?" or "What's it like to work for Charlie...that's what you call her right? I like that, I think I shall call you Charlie as well my dear." and my personal favorite, "If your ambition is to clean house, why don't you just marry, so the house you clean could be your own?" I had reached my breaking point. I scrapped my cast iron chair across the moss covered cobbles, intentionally making the feet screech over the shrills of the women and excused myself and Dahlia from the table.

"I thank you for a wonderful birthday excursion dear Cousin. However, Dahlia and I really must be headed back to Ananke Farms. I fear the place might have fallen to shambles without my very presence." The words were right for a proper exit, but fell from my mouth like poison daggers.

Before Rose could reply we were already four steps away and gaining pace. The main house drew closer and the voices from the tea garden faded, Dahlia broke the angry silence, "You must show me how to say piss off so eloquently."

We walked the halls of the familiar home, nothing had changed since the days when Rose and I would roam the halls, terrorizing the staff. My father was exactly where I knew he'd be; in the parlor, uncharacteristically smoking cigars and sipping brandy to appease his brother.

Uncle James had married up as well, but his bride's father approved of their union. I imagine it makes for quite a different experience. He was the one who ruined Rose; teaching her nothing but snobbery and elitism. Which made absolutely no sense to me, because that was the furthest from his roots. He grew up in the same poor Irish village as my father. Both our mother's had status and wealth, but we were raised to be vastly different people. It baffles me still; how people bound by blood can be so incredibly different from one another.

I walked in as Uncle James was babbling on about liquidating something. His business dealings always had a grimy taste about them, I found it an opportune moment for interruption. "Father, I have had ample birthday celebration. I am ready to return home."

"We planned to stay the night and stop at the feed store in the morning." He protested.

"Dahlia and I can ride home this afternoon with Gypsy and Persephone, you can drive the wagon home, just as we arrived." I crossed my arms, discrediting my father's excuse. He grew weary and I grew suspicious. "You're lying. You've always been a terrible liar." I dropped my arms in disbelief. "Tells left and right." I found no reassurances as I read the secrets behind his eyes. "What are you plotting old man?"

"Enough of this little girl! You will do as your told!!" Uncle James boisterously interrupted, flinging his heft in an attempt to assert his dominance.

My head snapped his direction. I felt ice run through my veins as I rolled my eyes and laughed with disbelief. It was cute he thought he had any clout.

The air thickened, "There was someone I wanted you to meet. He'll be here by morning." My father blurted.

I bit my lip in disbelief, "Un-Fucking-Believable." Shaking away the disgust.

Before I could begin to tear into my father, his brother chimed in "It's time for you to grow up little girl. Marry. Let a man tend that property, the way it should be." The toxic words gave me no sway. If anything my revulsion intensified.

"Those are not my reasons for her to marry." Father scolded. The slight puff in his chest made me gleam with pride. He reached for my hand, softening. "I am getting older and I want to make sure you are taken care of before I leave this world."

"I can take care of myself and Ananke Farms." I shot in the direction of my uncle.

"Yes, dear, but are you happy?" He questioned.

"As happy as I'm going to be. Can we just go home? I promise, whoever he is, it will most definitely not be a match. Especially if he," I scathed in my uncle's direction, "had any part in this."

My father hung his head in defeat, I was my mother's daughter and that meant stubborn as a mule and most likely right.

We gathered our things and started toward home.

CHAPTER 11
Charlotte Kentucky 1936

EIGHT MONTHS HAD PASSED. THANKSGIVING was a few days out and the property was vibrating with anticipation as preparations for the annual arrival of extended family were being methodically ticked away. I dreaded this time of year. Relations from all up and down the eastern seaboard, whose only commonality we share is our gene pool, were set to trickle in.

My home would soon become an all inclusive resort that due to shared ancestry, made it socially unacceptable to expect payment for their food, accommodations or entertainment. They hadn't even arrived yet and I was already counting the seconds until they grew bored with my quiet country life and hurried home to their cesspool cities to brag to their elitist friends how they spent their holiday horseback riding at Ananke Farms, where the only way in is a familial name or a high priced boarder fee, which were becoming fewer and farther between these days.

Which was gossip fodder, "Did you notice the stalls weren't full?"

"Oh yes, and they aren't running a full staff either."

"The house or the stables?"

"Appears to be both, and did you know they sold off some parcels of land, to tenants no less. Her Grandfather must be rolling over in his grave."

I could already hear the snickers. Once those women start blabber mouthing, they can't seem to stop. Naturally the conversation turns to me not being married and how "It's not right for a lady of her age or station to be unwed." and "Doesn't she know people talk?" Yes, I know you; you sad, boring, useless women, you talk. Incessantly. To one another. About the same useless shit day in and day out. I can not wait until this is over.

"Charlotte, can you come here a moment?" Father's call was a welcome distraction from the dizzying anxiety building within.

"Yes father."

Ledgers were sprawled haphazardly across his his walnut stained grand Palais executive desk. "I've been reviewing the books. Even though we are in the middle of a depression, we seem to be doing okay, well better than most anyway, even after losing a couple of boarders and having to sell those seventy five acres." He wiped a bead of sweat from his glasses, unsure why his nerves were rattled.

Impatiently I pushed. "Is there a point to this father? I am dreadfully busy."

"I was thinking after the first of the year, maybe we should hire a couple of hands, if we're lucky a groom." He paused, cautiously, "You would choose of course." adding under his breath, "you just run off the ones you don't like anyway."

"Sounds good." I motioned toward the door, "Was that all? There's a lot to be done before Uncle James and Rose arrive." Of course they will be first to arrive, and most likely last to leave. Most likely a pain in my ass the entire time. I had not spoken to my cousin nor uncle since my birthday and I had been content to keep it this way. But a can of worms I dare not open. I hadn't the time for an hours long lecture from my father on familial duty.

CHAPTER 12
Charlotte Kentucky 1937

THANKSGIVING CAME AND WENT, CHRISTMAS was a not so distant memory. Dahlia and I were cleaning up the last of the empty champagne bottles opened to ring in 1937.

Dahlia snarked as she examined the bottle's label, "Not only did she throw herself a party, but she went and drank up all the french stuff too."

"Sounds about right." I tossed another bottle into the growing pile of green glass. "Always the best for dear entitled Rose, especially when it's on someone else's dime."

"Did I hear my name?" Rose palmed her headachy forehead, grabbing a mug and pouring herself a cup of coffee, leaving Dahlia and I stunned. She fancied herself the Queen of Hearts and had terrorized my staff with her frequent demands, unable to serve herself a single thing since her arrival. "Well lovelies, I think it is time I return home."

"Just in time to clean up your mess." Dahlia snapped under her breath.

"What was that?" Rose scolded as she smirked from her cup.

"She said, when would you be leaving?" I stepped between them. "Don't worry yourself about cleaning up, so long as it doesn't interfere with your packing."

Rose sat her cup on the counter, "Well I can see I've worn out my welcome."

"Obviously." I fired back.

"Send for my carriage, and I'll pack my things?" Rose retreated.

"Already have."

As soon as I was able, I stuffed Rose into her carriage. She poked her head out for one last goodbye, "We really are different creatures aren't we. Not good or bad, just different." Her eyes were apologetic, but it would have been nicer to actually hear the words.

"Yes Rose, we are clearly two very different people." I coldly offered before closing the door on my cousin's pleading face.

CHAPTER 13
Charlotte Kentucky 1937

FATHER AND I PREPARED FOR our weeklong trip to Louisville. We hadn't planned for such an extended absence, but we were overwhelmed by the response to our ad, thirty applicants in total.

We intended to sell off two thoroughbred foals while in town. Unfortunately, The Depression had hit Louisville hard and no one was in the market for ribbon quality stock. Aside from selling off some corners of property and noticing that the monthly dues had been on the light side; I hadn't really seen the affect of the Depression. An eerie quiet radiated off the street as we passed scores of boarded up businesses.

It was up to me to ensure father brought home strong, experienced workers, not suitors. I hoped he'd know better by now, but sometimes, bless his heart, he couldn't help himself.

The last three applicants came and went without Henry realizing. He was lost in his thoughts. It was only when he heard me ask a thirty-two year old Texan who had spent his whole life on a farm in one capacity or another, if he could tend to livestock, that father came back to us.

Henry eyed the cowboy, hearty enough chap. "So, Michael, would you be able to return to Ananke Farms with my father and I?"

"Yes'm." Michael nodded, tipping his chocolate stetson.

"When do you plan to depart?" His words tickled my ears as his baritone voice vibrated through the room.

"We are set to depart Thursday." Father clumsily inserted himself into the conversation.

Michael glanced at my father, acknowledging him for the first time since our twenty minute interview began and quickly returned his attention toward me, shooting me a knowing smirk that sent a shudder down my spine. "That'll be fine sir." He answered from the side of his mouth, his eyes locked on me, determined to see how far he could see through me before I squirmed. He was a charming, handsome man, but something about him unnerved me. "It'll give me all tomorrow to get a telegram over to my momma, get some affairs in order." He shook my father's hand and kissed the top of mine. "Ms. Charlotte, would you please write the address down for me? So I can let my momma know where to send my things."

"Please, call me Charlie and of course." I answered scribbling the address on a scarp of paper.

"I thank you, Charlie." He replied with a tip of his hat. "See you Thursday morning then."

"For breakfast at the Inn first." I invited.

Father chimed, "Yes, breakfast would be nice."

There was a voice deep within me that wanted me to run as far and fast from Michael as possible, but he was an incredibly talented and qualified ranch hand. I stalled my doubt as Michael tilted his hat; letting his subtle smirk settle in the corner of his mouth. "Breakfast then." he offered exiting the makeshift office.

"What a strapping young man!" I rolled my eyes at my father's excitement as he continued. "Well younger than I." His wheels churn aloud, "You know you two-"

I throw my hands in the air interrupting, "No."

"But, you were so flirty."

"Friendly is not flirty." My hands dropped to my hips, hunkering down for the chiding. "Friendly does not mean marriage. It means friendly. As in, he is highly qualified, he knows what he's doing, if all goes well, he can take over the stables. You think he'd come on if I'd acted like the stubborn, hard-headed wench we both know I can be?"

Henry wrapped his arm around my shoulder, holding me in the crook of his chest, "I wouldn't go as far as to say wench." He smiled, "So what was this 'Call me Charlie' business then?"

I forced an awkward laugh. "Just following Dahlia's advice. Charlie sounds softer, I guess, that's what she insists upon anyway."

A tap on the open door's frame interrupts. "Excuse me, are you with Ananke Farms? I heard they were looking for help and was hoping to get on."

It was such a rare a moment to be playful and soft with my father, not burdened by business. The intrusion exposed a softness normally protected under an un-penetrable shell.

"Yes I am the proprietor of Ananke Farms." I answered with abrupt precision. I bit the inside of my cheek and circled the blonde, twenty-something year old boy as a lioness would her prey. He had innocent eyes and a goofy toothy grin that matched his spindly frame. "And you are?"

"Thomas, Ma'am." He excitedly shook my hand. "Beggin' your pardon Miss, I didn't catch your name."

"I didn't offer it." I fire back. "You were trying to get on?" My nose turnt up as I continued with such snobbery even Rose would have been embarrassed. "Tell me, what credentials do you have? Do you even know what we do there?" I didn't pause for reply, knowing full well he had no idea who we were. "We breed and train some of the finest horses in the country."

Beads of sweat gathered on his lip as he stumbled over his words; "Sorry Ma'am. I didn't realize such a young girl would-"

"Would what?" I interrupted.

"Have such a large task assigned her, Ma'am."

His carefully placed words unexpectedly softened me. My walls had receded, at least momentarily. "Stop it with that Ma'am shit, call me Charlotte."

Father offered Thomas some reprieve, "So Son, tell us what kind of experience you have."

"Well sir, to be honest, not a whole lot when it comes to showing or racing. I can ride. I'm a quick learn and work hard. I can do anything you put in front of me." Thomas' dopey grin was endearing and irksome.

I rub my temples, staring blankly at the vastness in front of me. "You saw the ad right?" Thomas opens his mouth to answer, but I didn't give him opportunity to interrupt, "Now correct me if I'm wrong; but that ad said 'experienced stable hands wanted', correct?"

"Yes Ma'-"

I throw my hand up, forcing his silence, "I'm not trying to bust your balls, but do you know how many people we interviewed for two positions." I paused for effect, "Thirty. You know how many were qualified? One. What is so special about you, that I should hire you and tell all those other people, 'sorry, no'."

"I'll work for room and board, no wages for twelve months. Then we'll renegotiate terms." Thomas answered without second thought.

"Deal." I extended my hand to seal just as quick. "I really must be going." I released Thomas' hand before he could feel how sweaty mine was becoming. I asked my father to, "Please get him sorted out."

"Interesting lass ain't she." Thomas' muffled voice queried my father as I left the room.

My father patted Thomas' shoulder, "You have no idea."

CHAPTER 14
Charlotte Kentucky 1937

My father, Michael and Thomas met for breakfast while I took toast and tea in my room and finished packing. Nerves settled in my stomach and I was far from ready to be 'on'.

After an hour, I was together as the day would allow. I met my father at our truck as an attendant hauled my trunk to the curb. He dropped the large leather box next to Thomas' feet as Thomas flung his canvas bag into the truck's bed. I gave the attendant a quarter and effortlessly picked up the trunk hurling it in to the bed, reveling in the look of shock and emasculation in Thomas and the attendant's face.

"I'da gotten that for you," Thomas offered.

I rubbed the weight from my hands, "No worse than flinging hay. Thanks though," rolled off my lips sounding more like a 'piss off' than intended, but I didn't care. I hadn't the time for hurt feelings and had already forgotten the exchange by the time I reached the passenger door.

"Allow me." Thomas politely offered as he reached for the door's handle. Our hands grazed and a violent bolt vibrated through me, forcing my hand away as if I had grabbed a hot pan. He smiled at my surrender and opened my door with a flirtatious wink. I hadn't noticed his coke bottle green eyes till then. They were warm and obnoxiously familiar, which irritated me beyond all reason. He demonstrated his gentlemanly manners as he guided me in to the truck and closed the door once I was seated in the cab. He pressed his arm against the top and leaned through the open window, "Thank you for bringing me on." A smile formed in the corner of his mouth. "You won't regret it."

Henry fired up the engine. The Ford V8's monstrous roar muted the crackling and shattering of iceberg walls as I snarked, "We'll just have to see about that."

Thomas squinted a smile through his wretched warm eyes as I fought the urge to squirm under his gaze. He folded, "Alright then."

As I SHUFFLED AND KNEADED against the bales of hay, Michael let out a bothered sigh. I picked a piece of straw, put it in my mouth, and leaned against a grassy brick, mimicking his posture. "Something special to that one."

"You can say so." Michael fired back. A twinge of jealously spiked in me as I looked over at the long legged cowboy. His face was covered by his chocolate stetson and I was unable to tell if he was politely entertaining conversation or fancied her.

A question I would pin for another day. There were more pressing things at hand. "Can I ask you something?" I buzzed.

"I reckon." Michael replied unmoved, not shy of showing I was a bother.

"Great." I eagerly smiled, "What exactly does a stable hand do?"

"I will break, train, and exercise the animals. Maybe get to ride in a show, if I play my cards right." He answered bored. He tilted his head, measuring me up with his one uncovered eye. "You'll shovel shit, wash the stalls, feed and water. Something you can't fuck up too bad." He added matter of factly.

"Thanks," I retorted watching the town behind us start to shrink. "Great talk."

The highway roads became dirt and soon after miles of white wood split rail fencing. Horses of all breeds and color scattered across the hillside. We passed a large white stable with two outdoor training circles, a dirt corral, two larger grassed corrals and what looked to be an indoor arena.

The seemingly infinite split rail led us past a barn and garden, finally stopping at the largest plantation style house I have ever seen.

THE TRUCK GROANED TO A stop. I hopped from the cab, making my way around back. I watched as Michael flicked his hat up, giving the grounds a gander, stretching his long limbs and breathing in the air. "More beautiful than I imagined." He offered of the property as I opened the tail gate hoping he had alluded to me as well. He tipped his hat, "Charlie."

A EXCRUCIATING PANG ROCKED ME as I witnessed the exchange. In that moment, I knew I hated Michael. I nodded my hatless head, "Charlie."

"IT'S CHARLOTTE." I SNAPPED. HIS congeniality vexed me for reasons not known "Best you not forget it." The words were sharp and precise. "Now put yourself to some use. Get these foals unloaded and clean out this trailer. Once you're done, come up to the house. We'll get you sorted out with a room."

"Charlie." Michael tipped his hat as I walked up to the house. I noticed a smirk settle in the corner of his mouth, a silent approval of Thomas' abuse. He walked toward the end of the trailer and began to untie two thoroughbred foals, "Hey Greenhorn." Michael jubilantly hollered for Thomas. "Looks like one of them ponies left you a gift. Best finds yourself a shovel and broom."

CHAPTER 15
Charlotte Kentucky 1937

THE DAYS TICKED OFF THE calendar. Weeks, months passed and spring bled in to summer. My evening rides grew longer with the late sunsets and warm nights. Night after night, dutiful Thomas waited till I returned.

The sting of aggravation radiated from him, snatching Gypsy's reins from me when I'd returned with Michael. While I enjoyed poking at Thomas, feeling him cross, even in the slightest, tugged at my heartstrings.

But there was no denying the effect Michael had on me; I found myself gentler, friendlier. I let him escort me to a barn dance a couple weeks back per my father's advisement and to my surprise, had grown fond of him. He made me feel carefree and delicate, something I hadn't felt in ages. I liked the way his hand felt on the small of my back when we danced, or when he would delicately tuck a piece of hair behind my ear, the way my face sat cupped in his large hand. The way his hat would shield the sun from my face when he bent down to kiss me. There were all these wonderful moments. Perfect moments.

That didn't stop the nagging thoughts though. He's a good man. Smart match. I'd constantly remind myself. He cares for me. Can help me tend this property. We have a lot in common.

He makes me laugh. I caught my unconvinced reflection in the hall mirror. So why don't I love him?

"Good morning Charlotte." Thomas intruded on my self berating as he spilled into the hall.

"Jesus Christ!" I jump six inches from my skin. "You can't sneak up on a girl like that Thomas!"

Immune to my chiding, Thomas began to retort, "I di-." The past few months had conditioned him to backtrack.

"Sorry Charlotte." It was first dawn and I didn't want to start the day in a dust up, even if it's sole cause was morning pleasantries.

Do you know how damned frustrating it is to watch the woman you know you are meant to love build a relationship with someone else?

Her and I are hard wired, heart to heart, even if she doesn't know it, I do. Since the moment I met her, I knew. Every argument, every salty exchange. It was part of something larger. She challenges me, forces me to be better; worthy of her. And one day, I will be, mark my words, her and I are destined. It's the strongest truth I know.

"See you downstairs for breakfast then." I intrude on his thoughts.

"Yes'm." Thomas shook away his intrusive thoughts, nodding his now stetson-ed head.

I had learned a great many things in my time at Ananke Farms but the first; a good hat and a hearty pair of boots are necessity. The memory of a sunburned head, soiled shoes and her laughing at my expense ran continuously through my mind.

I knew in that moment, with the slightest crumble of her walls, I would do anything to see that girl smile.

One thing we excelled at, was getting under the other's skin, or maybe just he with me. He challenged me. Which no one had done my entire adult life. I didn't know how to feel about it, so most of the time I felt angry.

We'd have a dust up, he'd think he have me cornered, ready to back down, then I'd send him off to unload the feed truck or check on the mustangs or some other errand to push back. He had kicked more buckets and knocked over more stacks of shovels than he cared to count. I had fired him at least four times that I could remember. But he would just go about his way till we crossed paths later in the day. I would say, "Thought I fired you?"

To which his reply would be "But then who would care for your horses?" Which always softened me, especially in the days after Gypsy's attack. He had spent a fortnight sleeping in her stall, tending to the wounds left by the bobcat that had been terrorizing our livestock all of that spring. It was then, I knew these animals meant to him as much as they meant to me and I felt the walls around my heart start to recede.

I could never decide if I was enamored or annoyed. More like annoyed I was enamored. Months of farm work had toned his back and torso and arms in a way I couldn't help but notice. His icy green gaze caught me staring as he heaved bales of hay. I flushed and froze before snapping an order, "Isn't there some shit somewhere for you to shovel."

My eyes gravitated to a small brown freckle in the sea of green. The disappointment in his face ached my heart. We have had hundreds of exchanges of the like but never did it yank at my soul like this moment now. He squinted reading my face, a momentary olive branch, allowing for backtrack. I probably should have, but did not waiver. His icy eyes, scanned me one last time. I'm not sure what he was looking for, but I felt his disappointment of it's absence.

Thomas fumed away, thrashing about the stable. Kicking over anything and everything within sight. Angrily stabbing at manure and hay from the vacant stall. "Anything else ya need done Miss?"

The daggers thrown from across the stable left me paralyzed, stabbing me in the heart, my stomach in knots, dizzy and voiceless. "There you are!" An arm wraps around my waist from behind as baritone vibrations tickle my ear. "I've been looking all over for you." Michael excitedly pulls my mouth to his. He kissed me like he hadn't seen me in a week. It was sweet, but there was this nagging anchor that refused to let me kiss him the same. Sometimes I wondered if he could tell. He dropped to his knee, "Charlotte."

I was looking down at Michael for the first time ever, "What are you doing?" I demanded. This can not be happening right now. Breathe. "And don't call me Charlotte."

"Charlotte," He nervously paused, "Will you marry me?" He bluntly proposed, pulling a rectangular ruby encircled with diamonds in a silver setting from his pocket.

The room was spinning. "You want to what?" I questioned overwhelmed. "Get up." I demanded pulling him to his feet. I ran my hands over my head, massaging the anxiety. After a few breaths, I dropped my hands. It was easy to catch his eye when his head was defeatedly dropped, all I had to do was look up. He smiled as I grabbed his attention, "You're serious? You want to marry me?" I questioned with a soft smile, trying to swallow the frog bouncing on my tonsils.

"Nothing would make me happier." He answered staring deep into my eyes, his plea settling in his brow.

I thought of my father and the future. I didn't know if I was in love with Michael, but I knew he loved me and maybe that was enough. "Then yes." I accepted, with what I was mostly sure was smile and a kiss. He wrapped his arms around me, hugging me so tight he lifted me from the ground. When my feet touched the earth below me, my gaze caught Thomas', watching the painfully intimate moment. The color in his face went from ghost white to berry red the second we caught each other's eye. He was wrecked. I felt sick. Michael kissed me again, gently sliding the ring onto my left ring finger.

I raised my hand to look at the promise I had just made, looking past Michael to Thomas in the distance as both our hearts rip in two.

CHAPTER 16
Charlotte Kentucky 1937

THE THREE WEEK HONEYMOON MICHAEL and I spent in Myrtle Beach were perfectly romantic on paper. The sand, the sun, but there was a nag I couldn't shake. The feeling of this not being my life. I was not meant for Michael and every moment spent with him made it painfully clear. I became increasingly detached. Feeling less and less myself, hazily floating from day to day.

The first sights of white split rail invigorated me with each passing post. We pulled up to the main house after the eternal drive up the private road.

The Model A barely come to a stop before I hurriedly spilled out, rushing in to my father's arms. "I've missed you."

An anchor pulled me in to my skin, feeling whole for the first time in weeks. "Hello Thomas." I greeted more formally than anticipated as a sense of home settled in my bones.

"Mrs. Morgan," he tipped his hat, his pace unfazed in his hurried stride toward the stable.

I let the callous reception go with an audible exhale. I could feel the electricity throb between us. I felt it in my dreams in Florida. I feel it more intensely now. Now, more than ever, I knew I had made a terrible mistake. All Thomas had to do was say hose two words, 'Mrs. Morgan' to ache my heart, and make me feel more alive than I had in weeks.

CHAPTER 17
Charlotte Kentucky 1938

RACE SEASON HAD MADE IT'S way back around and with the start of the new year, 1938 had proven no one was immune from The Depression. The only people left at Ananke Farm were Michael, Thomas and my two bratty cousins Theodore and Frederick (who go by Theo and Freddie) Sinclair, twice removed on my mother's side, the letter from their mother reminded me as she pleaded for their exile as penance for getting expelled from boarding school. She was at her wits end with the notorious seventeen and eighteen year old trouble makers. "The labor will do them good." she tried to reassure herself in the tear streaked page.

Michael and I had been married a little over six months and with each passing day I became increasingly removed. I had become a spectator, watching my life ticker away.

Every night as my eyes would flutter to find the backs of their lids, the same blasted dream would haunt night after night. A dark eyed maiden with a wild mane, from a land and time long ago, me I suppose, covered in soot and blood, howling at the top of my lungs amidst the chaos of invasion. My voice painfully muted. The harder I scream, the more the vastness fills my chest. The sounds of the battle deafen as my vision starts to haze. Dizziness and panic build and just as I feel the breath stollen from me, I jar awake.

Unable to sleep, unable to live. I'm lost; floating between two worlds.

The most alive I've felt in weeks was the throb in my toe after my foot found the side of a feed bag as I spew profanities fuming away from Michael and my father after the announcement of their decision to jump Artemis in competition, despite my opinion to the contrary.

Who knows how long Thomas had been standing behind the barn doors holding Ares, or how much of the argument he overheard. What was for certain was; I exited in such a huff, I did not see him until I ran full steam in to him, knocking myself to the ground, while he stood unfazed, offering his hand with that damned toothy grin splattered across his face.

I less than graciously grab hold; annoyed inaudible mumbles fall from my lips. A jolt of lighting explodes from my heart exiting through my finger tips as his hand wraps around mine. I dropped his hand like a hot pan, lost my balance and crashed back in to the ground.

"Sorry, Mrs. Morgan, thought I had you." He used both his hands pulling me up by the waist. When I found my feet I was buried in his chest inches from his parted mouth. I found myself lost in his shamrock green eyes. The urge to latch onto his pouted bottom lip pulsed through my body. He stepped away first, leaving a vacuum of space that suffocated my heart.

I brushed the dust and hay from my bottom, using the space to gather my wits, "I wish you'd call me Charlie. At the very least Charlotte."

"Sorry Ma'am, I just can't do that." He paused. "Something about propriety and what not."

"Propriety? Really? You never had a problem calling me Charlotte or Charlie before."

"You weren't married before." The words cut us both. He quickly changed the topic. "So, Michael is going to jump Artemis?"

"Not if I have my way." I softly returned still trying to shake the exchange.

"So he won't be riding Artemis?" He questioned.

"No, more than likely he will. Michael and my father have this tendency to gang up on me. Brow beat me from both angles." I thought back to the marriage proposal. "He'll probably get tossed and break his neck." A weird calm washed over me as the words fell from my lips. By the time they hit my ears, guilt instantaneously set in. "But what do I know? I only broke and trained her." I shrugged.

"If she's not ready -"

"What do you think I've been arguing?!" I interrupted. "Sorry, I didn't mean to snap. I'm a little hot about it all. And it really isn't your problem. You're sweet to listen." I thought about reaching for his hand but decided against it.

The day of the competition came and I pled my final case. "Please don't ride her. There's a difference between jumping fallen logs or training in the area, than with all these sounds and people. She's not used to the distractions." I begged as we trotted to the arena entrance.

Michael sat what seemed to be twelve feet tall atop her. "We're going to do great. You needn't worry." He leaned down and patronizingly kissed the top of my head before entering the arena.

Michael and Artemis were jumping beautifully. On track for an event record. They circled round to the final ten beam approach, she started her jump, and the explosion of a backfire in the distance spooked her. She shrieked, wide eyed, throwing her large body in to the air, tossing Michael from her back. When her front feet fell to the ground, she crashed all her weight on to

"MICH-AEL!!!!!" I shrieked the two syllables jolting awake and out of my plush bed.

Groggily, "What is it babe?" He clicked the TV on for light, half consoling his heavily breathing, sweaty, terrified wife. Half watching Sports Center.

"You're yo-" I trailed off as I frantically touched his face and neck. My surroundings came to focus. I realized it had to have been a dream; no matter how real it felt.

"Of course I'm me. Who else would I be?" He was irritated.

"I had this dream." I staggered between rapid breaths. "We

had a ranch." I paused for another breath and looked him in the eyes. "You di-" I couldn't finish the word.

"Kind of passive aggressive don't you think?" I was confused by his tone. "We have a fight and you start dreaming of killing me off, come the fuck on."

I couldn't believe this was happening. Were we seriously going to fight about the context of my dreams? At four something in the morning?

Annoyed I tried to smooth, "It wasn't that. This felt real, like I, we lived it."

"Okay." I felt his eyes roll as he turned off the TV and went back to sleep completely dismissing me.

CHAPTER 18
Charlie Modern Day

THERE WAS NO WAY I was going to sleep now, that dream rocked me to my core. I stumbled down the dark hall to my studio, found my way to my desk and started scribbling away in my journal.

The memories of this town haunt me. I feel generations of history in houses whose occupants I do not know. Sometimes I think it's the scars of my childhood.

It's the same in every town. The walls speak to me of good times and bad. It's not my memories that haunt me. But life itself.

The sky is a funny thing. She can be bright and full of the sun's warmth. With no warning at all, soft playful clouds darken, threatening a storm. But the soft kiss of the wind can blow those troublesome woes away.

The love of a man should be the same way.

Someone who sees all my light, my darkness, and fears it not.

There's something about the moon.

I follow her through the night.
Listening for the secret she wants to tell
Sworn to secrecy
Staring back at me, large and bright
Filling me with promise, calling me away

It hurts too much to feel her in my heart
Stuck here
Anchored
Unable to follow her pull.

If I follow her, the world will change
Nothing can go back to the same.

So I watch her cross the night sky
And let her tug my heartstrings
I know she has great plans for me
It is terrifying and exhilarating
To be so close to the dream
So I lay here caught in-between

This lull

This inbetween
Not the start
But not the destiny.

Drives me crazy
And mad
And frustrated
And all those things I don't want to be.

But it's the struggle and strife,
That keep the wheels churning in this lost little mind.

I woke, hunched over my desk with ink stained hands. Reading some of the things I pen is a feeling I will never get used to. These words never quite feel my own. Half the time I don't even remember writing them. Often surprised in the content. How unadulterated, how dark I can be.

CHAPTER 19
Charlie Modern Day

"THIS CAN'T BE IT? CAN it? This is as good as it gets? Seriously?" I demanded of Kennedy as we lie by her pool.

The centerfold worthy beauty untied her bikini top, dropping it on the stamped concrete exposing her perfectly engineered tits, blaming her exhibitionism on unsightly tan lines. An oversized pair of sunglasses and black floppy beach hat shielded her face as she pouted. "Being an adult is overrated."

"It's not that though," I rebutdtaled. "I look around, I see my life, family, friends, and I'm happy." Pausing to sip frothy margarita from a heavy fishbowl glass. "Then I turn to my left and see Michael-" My body tenses and disgust sinks into my face.

"Oh honey." She slapped my knee, cutting me off before I said something I couldn't take back. "We all have dry spells."

That's why I love Kennedy. I could mostly tell her what was going on with Michael and she would chalk it up to normal marital disputes. No judgement, no being made to feel crazy, just an empathetic supportive ear.

"You wanna talk about a fight? You should of seen the one when Greyson saw the AmEx bill after I spent a week in Paris."

"You mean last month?" I teased.

Her eyes widened and pitch heightened. "Oh no! That was

just a little exertion of masculinity after I 'went over budget'. No. No. No. This was the great blow out of 2012." She almost seemed nostalgic. "It was spring. It was Paris."

"And you had no limit." I understand Greyson's frustration, but deep down, I think he likes that she's obsessed with clothes and hair and makeup and ridiculously overpriced handbags. As far as trophy wives go, Kennedy is the ~~gold~~ I mean platinum (she would never let me hear the end of it if I made such a travesty of a comparison) standard for stay at home wives.

"And the food. And wine. And spas. And shopping. So much shopping." She was glowing, like a kid at Christmas. "I had to buy a trunk to fly everything home."

My thoughts immediately went to 'Louie', the Louis Vuitton trunk that had never gone anywhere but straight to the attic, and was now where trashy Halloween costumes went to die. "Wow Kennedy."

"Yeah." She sipped from her salt rimmed glass. "Not a good day at the Pierce House." Her obstinance was vomit educing.

Between the tequila and Kennedy's gross displays of consumerism my thoughts cycled back to my husband and how he wanted me the same from me. I was so close, almost there, and life would be so much easier if I could subscribe to a life less aware, but I just can't. There was always a shred of me that gripped tightly to who I was and over the years, I have fed that flame, and the girl of once was, grew and showed me who I was destined to become as I traveled down a road not meant for me.

Michael and I were twenty-five when we got married. It was more about celebrating the purchase of his second gas station than it was actually about us. The proposal was of the things all little girls dream of. How does one contain their excitement when presented with, "Well, we've stuck it out this long. Whatdaya say we make it official?"

I was already having doubts, but like he said, 'we've stuck it out this long.' What was I going to do? Where was I going to go? I had built the foundation of a life with this guy. It was too late. Too many wheels already in motion.

I remember staring at the made up clown in the mirror's

reflection, she dawned a ridiculous, sweetheart-cut, princess dress with fifty pounds of tulle. *This isn't right. This isn't what marriage, what love is.* Ran through my mind, but at that point it was a too late. Three hundred of our nearest and dearest had gathered to celebrate. Whether I was sure or not, I had to walk down that aisle.

"Do you, Charlotte, take this man?" I heard the pastor, but got lost in the question. Do I, Charlotte, take this man? "Charlotte?"

I shook myself back to the moment, "Sorry, yes. Of course I do." The crowd giggled, chalking it to wedding nerves.

And just like the proposal, the tenure together was equally romantic. There were exactly three days a year where Michael put the illusion of effort into our relationship. Valentines' Day, our dating anniversary and our wedding anniversary. The standard grocery store card and flowers, feels more like an inconvenience to him than any effort to make me feel the slightest bit special.

Today we had been married ten years. He sat across the dimly lit table and flashed me that half smile that melted me all those years ago. It seemed so long ago, like a fairy tale. I tried, unsuccessfully, to fain a smile. All I saw across the table was a man who wished to posses me. He didn't appreciate me for who I was. Even all those years ago. I was a prize to be won, a trophy to show off.

He didn't appreciate my art, writing, photography, music or film choices. He didn't understand my love of reading, the fact that I was a gigantic nerd, and one hundred percent okay with it. He didn't see me, he only saw his idealized version of me.

He didn't pursue me so vigorously all those years ago because he was actually interested in anything about me. Merely the fact that I told him no; I was a challenge and he always had to win.

"Charlie."

That fucking obnoxious snapping. This was becoming a habit. I made a note to discuss it's inappropriateness next time. No need to ruin a perfectly good evening.

"Hellllooooo."

I look down to find a plate of tomatoes and mozzarella in front of me. Shit. The waitress came and went and I hadn't even noticed, how embarrassing.

"I wish I knew where you went in that head of yours." Michael harped as he stuffed a piece of filet mignon into his mouth.

Even the way he ate irked me these days. "Trust me you don't. It's a mess up there." I diplomatically responded while I carefully cut my tomato and cheese into bite size pieces. "Scrambled ideas for a million different projects." It was a half truth.

We ate in silence as Michael hurried through his meal. He was ordering desert while I was only half way through my entree. He paid the bill as I took my final bites.

The ride home was equally rushed and painfully quite. I turned the radio on to break the deafening silence. But no matter the station, every song was a break up song. I caught myself realizing the sadness in Misery's lyrics as I sang and bopped along to the pop-y beat in the passenger seat.

As I sang along with Adam Levine, I cringed truly hearing his words for the first time. A weird thickness filled the car, I turned the radio off and we sat in awkward silence the rest of the way home.

CHAPTER 20
Charlie Modern Day

"Is this the life you really dreamed!" I shrieked as sheets of salty tear coat my hot red cheeks.

Michael reached to shake or hug me; neither of us were sure. His long fingers coil and constrict around my biceps. "You're all I ever wanted. That's good enough for me! Why can't it be good enough for you!?" He roared shaking me.

His six foot five frame towered me, but I had found my voice and felt seven feet tall. "Maybe that's the difference between you and me!" I shoved him off of me. "This-" I showcased the living room we were squabbling in like Vanna White, "is what you wanted. But I had plans. Dreams. And I settled for you!" The spite that rolled off my tongue rocked Michael and even surprised myself. "I let myself believe that this was the best it was ever going to get." The flood gates had opened, the release of truth was overwhelming. "I die a little more every day, because I know this is not the life I am destined for. I wake up every morning in a life not my own, and it makes me sick." I clenched my stomach feeling the nausea roll in my gut.

His eyes grew glossy. "I love you. Why isn't that enough?"

Without missing I beat, I fired. "I'm sorry, it's not. I've always cared about you, but I was never in love with you and that matters to me. I've just gotten to a point where I would rather be alone than live a lie. It's not only unfair to me, but to you as well." My words were killing him. "We've always been from different worlds. I was selfish. Too scared to give up stability for uncertainty. I'm sorry. I can't do this anymore." As the words left my lips, I felt free for the first time in a long time.

Michael opened his mouth to reply. I saw the rebuttal roil in his eyes. He must have seen something churning in me that even I wasn't even aware of. Defeat washed over him and settled in his heart as he dropped his head, turned around, and walked out the door.

Hours passed. I wore a spot in the hall as I paced the ambivalence off. Eleven thirty and still no Michael. He wasn't answering his phone or responding to texts. Fuck him. I bolted the door, turned out the lights and went to bed.

I washed my face, and brushed my teeth as a quiet relief settled over me. "Well Gypsy," I picked up the calico duchess who ruled my home, "Just you and me tonight."

The cat leapt from my arms, landing on the bed and circled and kneaded Michael's pillow with imperious delight. As she settled, I rubbed the orange spot on her cheek. "I think you like it better that way, anyway, Miss."

I pulled all the blankets to the foot of the bed, sliding under a lone sheet. It was hot and muggy, even with all the fans on and windows open, but there was no way I was tainting the new moon with refrigerated, recycled air. There weren't many nights like this in the valley, but they always seemed to bring the worst out in me and Michael.

This was one of those nights. I didn't even know what we were fighting over, what started it, or how it got heated so quickly. I didn't know what we were fighting over most the time anymore. We woke up one day, and found ourselves on opposite sides of the fence.

My blood boiled. Too many thoughts raging through my mind. A gentle breeze danced on the curtains and in the chimes and as the valley air cooled, my thoughts begin to slow and drift off to sleep. The blackness behind my eyelids glowed bright white before morphing into a thick fog.

THE DENSE GREY CLOUDS THIN, revealing a familiar lush landscape. I find myself in a large open field; un-penetrable, dark forest line the western border. To the north, a large stone manor and bustling village lay. My heart races and my eyes widen as inexplicable bursts of panic and fear pulse through my veins. A menacing breath on my neck pushes me toward the village.

I cradled my stomach to self soothe before realizing the tank top and plaid linen shorts I went to bed in had been replaced with a heavy green gown with delicate gold flowers stitched along the hem and up the bodice. The kirtle underneath cinch my waist taut as my bosom heaved over its top.

With each step toward the large stone manor, the panic waivers and I realize I am home as safety and warmth wash over me. The square was empty and quiet as I stroll the familiar, still, hut-lined artery. I drag my fingers across a shop's wall and snippets of fruit and fabric vendors bargaining with a local fisherman burst like rapid fire across my minds's eye as children's laughter drown out the salesmen's words.

Just as fast as the flood of memory came it was gone and I was returned to the empty village in front of me.

I reached the stone drinking well that sat in the town's core. The cool, crisp water tickled my nose as I sipped from it's ladle. My reflection in the clear shadowed water revealed, a flowered headband holding wild espresso curls in place as my locks draped well past my shoulder blades.

My moment of vanity shattered as the faintest sound of voices pull my attention and body toward the magnificent stone home. Whispers in my ear tug me toward the main hall where everyone in town had gathered, yet their collective voices were a dull hum.

I effortlessly wove through the crowded room, the laughter and jubilations aplenty, but still, only a soft hum buzzed. I must be seeing this time and place on a plane unnoticed to the naked eye. I can go unseen and heard, but there is a barrier between the two sides. There is bound to be some distortion on my end as well.

My thoughts and body both stop in their tracks and I trip over my own feet. My eyes glued to my mirror image at the head table, seated between a king and him. He was dressed in the garments of a bridegroom, but it was him. The man who had haunted my dreams. The soulful green eyes, heavy brow. I'd know him anywhere.

The King gushes with a chalice full of mead, "What a blessed union, the merging of our two families."

"Whoa whoa whoa!!!" I shouted, but no one heard. "I was married to him!? This is so confus-" I trailed off, dizzy. Disbelief pushed me in to the cool stone wall.

The King proudly boasted, "My daughter has chosen a brave, worthy man. He will keep us safe and strong long after I am gone." He paused, ensuring my twin caught his loving gaze, "May your reign be long," He raised his glass to toast, "and may you have any years of health, joy and prosperity, cheers."

The crowd raised their cups offering in unison. "CHEERS!" The sounds mugs clinking as the man who haunts my dreams looked dotingly at my doppelgänger. His strong brow scrunched until she caught his eye, he leaned in, whispering private tidings as he gently laced his fingers through hers, "I love you. With all that I am, and all that I have. I love you Charlotte." His words tickled my ear and etched my heart.

Enviously I gawked as he leant to kiss his wife. As their lips touched, I closed my eyes anticipating. A wave washed over me as his lips pressed in to mine and a dizzying vacuum snatched all the breath from my lungs.

My face flushed as my eyes opened and our lips parted. A sheepish smile fell in to the corner of my mouth as his scrunched brow and piercing gaze burned through me and tugged at my soul. "I love you Thomas. Always and forev-" I promised hungrily pulling his pouted lips in to mine before I could finish my pledge.

"Look at these kids!" The king proudly boasts. "At this rate, I'll have an heir in no time."

Immediately I was painfully aware of the hundred or so sets of eyes on me, I reluctantly pull my lips from Thomas; scanning the room of spectators, all familiar faces, but none I could tell I knew for certain.

Wait? I'm here now? They can see me? Rapid fire thoughts push my gaze to the end of the hall where I had been an unnoticed observer. This is so confu- I stopped, feeling the breath pulled from me. I nervously fidgeted and tugged at the waist of my kirtle, my breath becoming quick and shallow. My face grew hot and red as my gaze darted sporadically around the room and a whomping noise echoed in my ears forcing my head between my knees.

"Are you alright my love?" Thomas tried to soothe.

His ever changing green eyes darkened from icy to grey and filled with concern as he searched me for an answer. His worry gave me an uncontrollable sense of peace, a grounding that forced me to smile as I cupped his face. "Yes darling I'm fine, a tad dizzy is all."

"It's been a long day." Thomas decided as he warmheartedly guided my hand from his cheek to his lips. The delicate kiss atop my hand fired through my body and exited my toes. "I shall excuse us then."

CHAPTER 21
Charlotte England 1400

Thomas dutifully escorted his bride to our suite and paused at the entry, pulled my hand to his lips and brushed the tenderest of kisses against my tingling skin.

The tiniest of gestures forced my to heart skip and me to blurt, “I love you.”

He crooked his neck and smiled from his playful chartreuse eyes. “and I you.” He leaned in to kiss me, I lifted to my toes, meeting him half way. Our lips and tongues melted into the other’s, he pressed my body into the heavy wooden door, making a light thud. His strong hands roam freely, running up my neck and down my back, firmly working their way down as they find their way to my hips, wrapping around and clenching my buttocks as my legs contort around his waist.

He unlatches the door and we clumsily fall through the threshold. With urgency Thomas unlaces the bodice of my gown and kicks the door closed while his teeth scrape against the space between my neck and shoulder.

Deep passionate kisses and uninhibited hands explore the curves of the other’s bodies. He releases me from my dress and kirtle, exposing a sheer linen shift.

Every curve of my body becomes etched in his memory. “You are a remarkable woman.” Thomas stuttered through his gravelly voice, his stormy stare pulling me in.

I slid the shift from my shoulders, letting it drop to the floor, exposing my naked body, playfully arguing, "Compliments are hardly needed beloved."

"Doesn't make it any less true." He responded matter of factly as he slid his hand to the back of my neck and pulled me in for a hard deep kiss that caused our bodies to entwine and gently fall in to the soft bed of feathers.

WE LIE SLEEPILY CUDDLED, HER head nestled in my bare chest, and my arm draped protectively around her as my fingers combed through her dark unruly mane. "Charlotte," I paused till her eyes locked with mine. "I need you to know." Her interest piqued, "This is not a marriage for title or duty to me." I delicately ran my forefinger along her jaw line, lost deep in abyss of her eyes. "I am bound to you. Ever since the day we met, I knew I was meant to love you."

"That's preposterous!" She shrugged off. "We met when I was all of three days old." The intensity was far too intimate, making her uncomfortable and she was happy to break the moment with her snark. "And you were what, a toddler, still sucking at your wet nurse's tit?"

"It's true!" A silly, dopey, beautiful, uncontrollable smile sprawled across her face as I unabashedly defended my love. "And I will love you till my last breath and every day after that, for all of time." I pledged before pulling her lips to mine then pouting, "Wait, are you saying it wasn't the same for you?"

"That's exactly what I mean to say." She giggled and playfully nudged me with her shoulder, "I couldn't stand the site of you till I was at least twenty."

"Twenty?!" I knew in my bones she said it in jest, but for some unknowing reason, it rubbed me raw. I made my best attempt to keep the playful tone, "You mean to tell me that you've only been able to stomach my existence for the past two years?" I audibly exhaled my disappointment, "I think you lie."

I stared through her until she broke, "Alright, alright, I'll give you fourteen." she squirmed.

I WAS FEROCIOUSLY ROLLED ON my back, my hands pinned overhead, those roiling mossy eyes stabbing my soul. His words brushed my lips, as my bare breasts heaved in to his chest, "You know full well, the moment, that first moment, when we were wee babes, our eyes locked. And every time our eyes have met since, you feel it straight in your heart. I know it's true, because I feel it too. Every single time, our entire life. And when I kissed you that first time, it felt like everything I have ever thought for you, felt for you, being cemented in time. It's the strongest truth I know. More than the sky is blue or the grass is green. And that's how I know you feel it too."

"Every single day, since the moment our eyes met, till my last breath and every day after that, for all of time." I repeated his promise. As I finished the last word his lips enraptured mine stealing my breath, yet filling me with life.

Our lips parted and my eyes opened to a sterile, cold, modern, streamlined room lying in a empty California King with Gypsy licking my face. "You won't believe the dream I just had." I yawned, picking up the dainty calico and scratching her cheeks.

CHAPTER 22
Charlie Modern Day

Two days had passed and Michael had not returned home. I called his mother to ensure he was okay. It seemed the polite thing to do. She told me he had been staying with his cousin Freddie, "taking some time to breathe."

It was a relief if I'm being honest. I enjoyed the time apart, I felt more like myself when he wasn't around and I needed time to process this new dream, it had really turned me upside down.

There was more to the story, I needed to know what happened to them. I obsessively fixated on every detail I could remember, forcing memories as flashes and bits would cross my mind's eye, but mostly all I did was give myself a headache.

I used my journal to capture as many fragments of my dreams with Thomas as I could, trying to find common ground. Names, places, events, anything. How does this all tie together? Was a common question scribbled in my journal. Am I crazy? This feels crazy. But crazy people don't know they're crazy, so I'm not crazy, right? Was repeated many times over. Some days manic and messy, others neat and collected, making it difficult to decide which were true.

Ordinary
just always felt so

extraordinarily
boring.

I fear:
A life with no meaning
no dreams
no passion
or drive

I fear being a step-ford wife
walking the path that I am told
Because it is safe
and comfortable

Instead of going astray
down the road less traveled
to fulfill a destiny
a dream from long ago
a wish in the deepest pits of my restless soul.

It's wrong
All wrong
I say this with no
malice
or disgust

It's just over.

With each passing day I stay,
a bit of me goes dying along the way.

And when I pull the shattered pieces
from the abyss in which they were lost,

you disappear
further into a pit of despair.

Sometimes.
I get this paralyzing fear
I belong, nowhere.

"Maybe writing this all down wasn't the best idea." I conceded to Gypsy as I skimmed the newest entries.

I sprawled out onto my favorite patio chaise, plopped my journal and pen on the table next to and started puffing on an herbal cigarette as I sparked my Bic. Half a joint later, my head fell heavy against the pillowed rest and I watched the clouds roll in the clear blue sky. My eyes heavy with exhaustion but my mind wide awake. I sink deeper into the seat, my skin tingled as I felt myself falling through time.

I found myself returned to the same English village I had been obsessing over for days. Elation flooded me as Thomas lead his horse to me. I grabbed the rein, softly stroking the horses nose. "Be safe husband."

He dropped his rein and pulled me close by my hip as I playfully resisted. He put his hand on my five month bloated belly, encouraging the baby inside to summersault. I cupped his hand cradling my stomach, as a smile radiated across my face. He leaned to kiss my cheek, "We shan't be gone long. Just long enough to catch a stag or boar. I won't be leaving you," He promised, while his protective hand lightheartedly shook my belly, "or our little prince behind long."

He kissed me goodbye and as he pulled away, I found myself back in the patio chaise. Joint pasted to my lip with resin and saliva. An unexpected sadness washed over me as I ran my finger along the abdominal lines of my toned stomach revealing no baby.

I had never wanted children with Michael, but I had never loved or felt love from Michael the way my visions show Thomas and I loved one another. The prospect of creating life with someone who loves you so intensely sparked something within me.

Michael returned home a week later, but it was too late. I was forever changed by the latest vision. Snippets of the pregnancy and Thomas from long ago played on loop in my mind. It was all I thought of when I was awake and flooded my dreams as I slept.

I knew what I wanted, needed, and unfortunately Michael could not provide that. I was whole heartedly in love with someone I had never met. Someone I wasn't even sure existed, but if there were the slightest chance Thomas were real, I would never find him being tethered to Michael.

CHAPTER 23
Charlie Modern Day

"YOU DON'T SUPPORT ME! YOU tolerate me, you 'allow' me, but you do not support me." I couldn't tell if this was a new fight or the continuation of the previous one.

He raged, slamming his whiskey filled lowball against the wall. Shards of glass explode across the floor. "What do you mean I don't support you? I built a whole fucking wing for your hobbies!"

The fact that he said 'hobbies' proved my point. I threw my hands in the air and walked away. He didn't get that my soul lived and breathed art. I needed to be creative. Otherwise, I felt like I was choking.

More and more, the four carat cushion cut on my left hand felt like a shackle. This concrete monstrosity, my prison. I was serving penance for the sins of lifetimes past.

We were so painfully different, we sucked the life from one another, it was exhausting. He wanted the American Dream; the house, the cars, the trophy wife. He coveted unnecessarily expensive trinkets and cars, money and status. And he wanted me to want those things so desperately.

I just didn't.

There is nothing wrong if that is what makes you happy. It's just not what I want or need. I couldn't be bothered to give two fucks about keeping up with the Joneses.

Honestly, I would be a million times happier in a secluded mountain cabin or on a farm, a hippie commune. Somewhere where I can feel connected to the earth beneath my feet.

I needed the kind of love I had been seeing in my dreams. I needed to feel alive with someone, even if I were dying. With Michael, I felt like I was drowning. He loved me the best way he could, it just wasn't enough.

We had finally reached the point where there was no denying how different we truly were. I wasn't settling for someone who didn't see or appreciate the real me any longer. *Be fucking brave.* I raged inside as I violently thrashed paint across the canvas.

"I like it. Can I hang it in the den?" Michael waived a white flag as he leaned against the door frame, "I knocked. I don't think you heard me."

"It's not done yet." I barely acknowledged him. My brush-strokes still furious.

He passed through the threshold, his defeat casting a dark cloud in my workspace. "Look, I'm sorry. I know this stuff is important to you." Bless his heart, he really did try to understand me at times. "It just kinda hurts, it means more to you than I do."

He had earned my attention as I laid my brush down. "Michael, the last thing I want to do is hurt you. I think we're both tired of this incessant back and forth." A hopeful smile gleamed in his espresso eyes, "I have spent so much of my life trying to fit this image of who you want me to be." I couldn't help but use my hands to enunciate my words. Michael tried to interrupt, but I left no opening. I was cool, calm, collected, and needed to get this off my chest. "For years I've been told how lucky I am thee Michael Walker wants me." I used my best valley girl voice, "But not once have you ever stopped to think how lucky you are to have Charlotte Bower."

"Walker." He annoyingly corrected. "I don't get where this is coming from. You always seemed happy." he added aggravated.

He is never going to understand. "Seemed happy? Don't you think it would be fairly obvious if I were actually happy?" I goaded ready to fight.

I pushed the right button, an explosion. "Sorry for always explaining away 'Charlie tendencies' to our friends. Because showing up the French Laundry with paint splattered all over your body and in your hair is okay. Or getting lost in that fucking head of yours when people are talking to you. Or when you are locked down at your desk for weeks on end typing away at some nonsense you'll never let anyone read."

"No!" There was no backing down. This argument was happening from beginning to end. "Your friends! My friends accept my quirks. It's part of who I am!" I paused for reply. Nothing. "And I'm not embarrassed when I have a pen in my hair, or paint on my skin or get lost in my work. Why are you? Because you love the idea of who you think I should be. You don't accept me for who I am."

His face went white. My truth was stinging him like a swarm of bees. "It's not intentional." Michael managed to spit out as he wrapped his arms around the tops of my shoulders pulling me into his chest.

As his thoughts raced I could feel his sadness. *If I truly love her, I should let her go, right? Let her be happy. But what about my happiness? I am happy. Am I? Maybe we can get therapy? I should start 'dating' her again.*

His thoughts were dizzying and manic. I could feel a headache build behind my eyes. I had to put him out of his misery, "I want a divorce."

CHAPTER 24
Charlie Modern Day

Forty eight hours later I was vacantly staring at the no longer glowing, glow-in-the-dark stars glued to the ceiling of my childhood room. Life and visions and dreams and the voices of those long past keep my eyes wide.

I did the only thing I knew would silence the unwelcome guests whose talebearing held me captive. I pulled out my journal, my favorite Mont Blanc pen and opened my veins across the page. No thought went in to the free bleeding words scribing themselves across the empty pages.

Dawn's early light peered through my window as songbirds fluttered in the garden gnome birdbath that center-pieced my mother's cute but somewhat creepy collection. I needed coffee immediately. I had barely slept and when I did it was tortuous. It was entirely too early to enjoy the *Snow White*-ness of the backyard scene.

Seeing as my hair matched the Medusa covering of my hardbound journal, I'da probably scared all the critters off like the Wicked Witch of the West anyway. I giggled at my musings as I flipped through freshly penned pages. I counted a total of (fourteen) eight-inch by five-inch pages. The unfamiliar scribblings bled secrets that history forgot.

Children, playing as children do. Carefree kids of noble birth, tormenting each other with name-calling and pokes and prods and all the other abuses we call love as they ride ponies, chase fireflies and explore ruins the Romans left behind. The memory of their fifteenth century life, a casualty of time.

A quick snippet of a teenage Thomas teaching a twelve or thirteen year old version of myself how to wield a sword and shoot a bow as I gain strength and proficiency day after day.

Dizzying forces push me to the corner of a room while my father, The King, announced Thomas and his older brother Phillip were to be my personal guard.

"What need have I a guard? Much less two!" The unwaveringly stubborn ten year old made me laugh as she stomped toward the King's breakfast table, "I don't-"

"It has been decided." My father finalized.

With a humpf and frigid turn of the heel, I storm out of my father's chambers. Out of ear shot, I mock and rant, "It has been decided. How incredibly infuriating. He never listens-" I had been so lost in a dizzying rage I didn't see Thomas or Phillip as I plowed full steam in to Thomas, bouncing off his unfazed body and knocking myself to the floor, further adding to my foul mood.

He politely offered his hand; I slap away his succor and pair the brushoff with an indignant spew of profane insults. His patience dwindled as he snatched my upper arm and yanked me to my feet as I squirmed in protest. "Allow me highness." He forcefully aided.

"I can manage just fine Thomas, thank you." I declare as I collected myself. "Just like I can manage just fine without you or your brother's constant hovering." I quibbled.

Annoyingly diplomatic Phillip intervened, "The King has ordered it, so shall it be done."

"Well you shan't be needed long. I'm not going to sit in this stuffy old castle and hide. I will be a warrior; fight to protect my title, my land. Without a wet nurse, thank you." I stated as matter of fact.

"My Lady, you still have a bit of time before you even have the strength to hold a sword, much less wield it." Phillip argued. "And have a tendency of late to get yourself into trouble." I couldn't help but reveal my ten-year-old maturity, "Ugh. You are a bore. I can't believe Dahlia has been promised to such a lemon."

Picking on him was the only way I could mask my new found crush. I knew nothing would ever come of it. First, he was promised to my older sister. Second he was seventeen, a full fledged man. I was still a little girl, just starting to blossom into womanhood. And lastly, no matter who happened to catch my awakened eyes, my heart always turned to Thomas.

Several weeks had passed and the only use I had for either of my protectors, was when Thomas carried the heavy spool of emerald fabric I purchased from the market.

"What use do you have of this?" Phillip poked Thomas in his ribs, almost making him drop his load.

"What else?" I looked at the glistening teenager, realizing a sack of rocks had more sense than him. "To make a dress. Take some yellow thread, stitch some pretty flowers."

Phillip unfolded the fabric draped over Thomas' shoulder as we climbed the castle steps. "What, three dresses? You have enough fabric here-"

I cut him off. "Never you mind." unsure why his questioning unnerved me so.

"Sounds like a wedding dress to me." Thomas added.

"Shut it." I demanded.

Phillip poked. "Who would marry you?"

Thomas' mossy green gaze caught hold of me as Phillip's antagonization cut my heart. Swallowing my tears, I ran down the corridor, slamming my chamber door.

"Nice." Thomas scolded.

Phillip was unapologetic. "Toss off. She'll be right back to being a pain in my ass by supper."

Three days later The King announced Phillip and Dahlia were to be wed by the next full moon. Phillip was removed from my guard and traveled with Dahlia's to our mother's family's manor where they would reside.

It had sat empty for a dozen or so years now, but with the marriage of his daughter, my father found it opportune time to recolonize his once sprawling territory.

Phillip was lead to believe that he was being rewarded with land and title while securing our King's borders. He felt he was being exiled and meant to be forgotten, though I had never uttered a word of the exchange. The far off western lands were a treacherous three day ride through the dark forest and another two days through the moors that lead to the coast on which the house sat. His eyes burned with rage as he glared at me while our king proclaimed. I knew in my bones it would be many years before I was forgiven for a sin I hadn't committed.

Now it was just Thomas and I. I found his company pleasing, yet annoying and completely unfounded. That was, until the day some years later when he was actually of some use and saved my life. A horse had spooked, barreling loose and wild down the market street. Not paying any mind to my surroundings, for which Thomas had scolded me relentlessly, 'How do you expect to be a warrior if you are constantly running into things and people?' played through my mind as his arms wrapped round me from across the road forcing us both into the ground.

As the horse blazed by, I realized what had happened. Thomas quickly removed the sacrificial body shield that safeguarded his charge and pulled me to my feet. I brushed the scuffle from my dress, "Thank you Thomas."

He pulled my hand to his mouth and gently kissed the top, "You are most welcome My Lady."

I was unprepared for the wave of emotion that flooded me as his lips tingled against my skin. "Can we not tell my father about this?" I pleaded as I fumbled and yanked my arm away. I knew I would never going to hear the end of it. Careless this. Head in the clouds that.

"Apologies Princess." He denied, "Tis my duty."

"Ugh!" I threw my hands in the air and stomped toward the castle. "I hate you!" I screamed over my shoulder.

"You're welcome!" He playfully egged.

A soft giggle escaped my lips as I read the last words of the page. I was falling more and more in love with this story. Every bit made me feel closer to the person I am meant to be. It gives me hope that there is someone out there who could see all my flaws, quirks, the unpredictable moods, all of it and fear them not. Someone who fuels my drive and fire, someone refuses to let me be anything less than better than the person I was yesterday. Someone that swears I do the same for. He's out there. He has to be.

CHAPTER 25
Thomas Modern Day

I QUICKLY FELL TO THE torment of my dreams. Quick, short bursts of forgotten memory plague my sleep. People I had never met, places I've never been avalanched through my suffocated mind, burying me in a panic. Choking on a hard swallowed breath was the only way I could be jerked awake.

The phantasm halted in a sepia toned land; a small wooden apartment with a tattered 1853 World' Fair poster covered the wall. A bustling French Quarter and jazz tunes dance through the second story window but are drowned out by a haunting music box lullaby.

I leap six feet from my skin as my doppelgänger and the wavy haired brunette who has haunted me for eons push through the door, wildly entwined in one another. He pushes the skirt of her dress up, caressing her milky thighs as she wraps her legs around his waist, falling in to the bed. Between body exploring kisses, I see the brown toned Thomas mouth something, but I can't make out the words. All I hear is that blasted tune repeating for the third time.

My thumb tugged at my bottom lip, feeling hers linger. The taste of her soft tongue as it rolled against mine, the curves of her body tingle in my fingertips.

The room angrily spins. As I recover from the dizzying push

through time, the wild haired brunette swollen with pregnancy is revealed. She quietly waits radiating a peaceful joy her as she knits in her handcrafted rocking chair. A memory of carving and chiseling flash across as my eyes as she leaps from her seat.

She excitedly greets her husband with a kiss on the cheek as he walks through the door coated in grime and sweat. His hands black and blistered from the long days work. I look down at my own; clean, calloused and swollen, but from countless hours of instrument play, not years of grueling labor.

The room spins violently yet again, this time knocking me to my knees. When I pick myself up, I find the wavy haired beauty still ballooned with baby as if no time had passed until my Doppelgänger enters with his year old son riding on his back, the toddler's arms wrapped tightly around his father's neck. My twin leans down, tenderly kissing his wife, cooking at the stove. The unruly maned child's hair matched his mother's, with a set of glassy green eyes that reminded me of my own. He leaned, mimicking his father's dotting cheek kiss and squealed with childhood delight when his dad playfully warned, "You can't kiss her, she's my wife."

The happiness and love vibrates off the walls of this room and rings in my ears. Deep in my bones, I know with every ounce of my being, this is what I want. She is what is missing from me.

The room blurs and I brace myself for the spin. When everything comes to focus, two small children play in the corner. A little boy and a little girl. The little boy has the same strong brow as his father and the girl, an untamable mop of curls like her mother. She watches her father wash the grime from his shirt. His hard, callused hands run the soap and linen over the rungs of the wash board. Mother bursts through the door boasting her gleeful news as that same hauntingly happy tune repeats again as I read the excitement on her lips. "With child."

My look alike drops his wash, rushing to his bride, lifts her from her feet, joyfully kissing in celebration, as he swings her around, sweeping the hair from her face, looked deep into her eyes and said something I could not make out, but I hear that blasted warble for the umpteenth time as their love creeps in to the darkest corners of my heart.

I was lost in someone else's moment, I didn't see the warning signs when the spin hit, it's force flung me to the ground. The sepia tones of the scene felt cold, darker than the others as the joyful tune sobered. A thick in the air weighted heavy on my chest as a woman that looked like his wife, clung to the children.

The midwife exited the bedroom, blood covered her hands and apron. She looked at the girl, sadly shaking her head no. The woman unclenched the babies as she jumped from her seat, darting in to the room.

My twin sat in the corner; blood soaked, sweat covered, unconsolably weeping with a little bundle in his arms. His long hair mopped the wave of salty tears as his wife lie lifeless in bed. I was gutted, my heart had been ripped from my chest, each shard of shrapnel maiming as my heart shattered in to a million pieces.

The children's caretaker approached her brother, knelt down and hugged him. Brushing his damp locks back, exposing the baby's pink face. The newborn twitched his nose and she sighed with barbed relief, delicately taking the bundle from her devastated brother's arms, grabbing the other two children and leaving him to grieve.

Tears stream uncontrollably down my face. I felt the devastating loss as if it were my own. How horrible. I thought, wiping tears from my face. To be that in love, that happy and to have it all ripped away.

The room spun again. I braced myself. Instead of the home that housed an epic love, I found myself in a dank and gloomy bar. The brunette's husband appeared to have aged fifteen years as he sat alone; sad and bitter, guzzling glass after glass of scotch.

His sister burst in, three small children in tow. The baby, six months or so, held himself upright against her hip; the two older walked with hands linked and tethered to their aunt.

The adult siblings argue, but still, I hear nothing. Just the same bittersweet tune that has relentlessly followed me through this dream. The heartbroken man dismissed his sister, callously returning to his drinking.

She mouthed, "You're a lousy drunk." storming out, children in tow.

I watch as he sits on his stool for hours. Drink after drink after drink. No matter how much he drinks, he can never drown out his pain or the memory of her. The hole in his chest felt similar to the hole mine, though I couldn't decide which was worse; having lost her, or having never known her.

CHAPTER 26
Thomas Modern Day

'TWAS THE WEE HOURS, WHEN the sky softens from black to indigo when I jolted awake in my patio's chaise; parched, headache-y and mist covered. No matter how lovely the evening the fog always rolls in at some point; a true San Franciscan cliche.

I found my way to my notebook and charcoal pencils scattered across the espresso stained, wood coffee table and plopped into the sofa. Those eyes. Those large, dark, feral, expressive eyes. I smudged my thumb across the brow, softening her. Who are you?

The blankets piled atop my bed started to shuffle and grumble. When it settled, I found Phillip. Asshole, left me on the porch and stole my bed. The events of last night replayed in my mind. "Fuck." I scolded aloud. Can't say I don't deserve it.

A blessing and a curse, the torment of those eyes. What would I do if she didn't haunt me so? I drew another sultry set. This time wild ringlets flowed, framing those unforgettable eyes. I could see her so clearly in my dreams. But, when I woke, all that remained was her soulful eyes and untamable ringlet hair.

Before I realize, I scribble a song's worth of lyrics. Forgetting Phillip was, well there, much less asleep, I started plucking away at my guitar.

I had completed the bridge when he hopped from bed.

"Well at least something productive came out of that disaster of a night." Phillip snarked as he got himself a glass of water.

My back was to him as I hunched over my guitar, I threw my arm up in the air, acknowledging him. "Good morning to you too, Cousin." I shifted my body toward the kitchen and winced as I spoke across the flat. I hugged my guitar for protection, "There's coffee." All apologies must start with coffee.

Phillip had already poured himself a cup and was taking a seat in the oversized, leather, chesterfield chair and kicked his feet up on it's ottoman. "You know, I know you better than anyone. I understand there's a darkness about you. It's kind of what makes you great, but you have this tendency to unleash this horrendous venom on those closest to you." I knew where this was going, I clutched the acoustic tight to my chest, trying to shield my heart from the words that had to be said. "Don't push the few who actually get you away." He broke the tension by adding with a wink, "There are only so many of us who know you're a trying asshole and don't seem to mind."

Phillip was making me feel too many feelings for first thing in the morning, so I heaved the couch pillow at him.

He laughed and changed the subject as he sipped from his mug. "New song?"

"Beginnings of." I answered, scribbling the arrangement pulsing trough my mind into my notebook before it was lost forever.

CHAPTER 27
Charlie Modern Day

I SAT MY CORK LEATHER handbag on the vacant chair next to my stylist's station and checked my phone one last time before we started. "The judge signed off. It's done." Shone across the home screen as I gleamed at the confirmation of my emancipation.

I had walked away with the contents of my closet and studio, Scout, and five hundred thousand dollars. I could have fought for more, but I didn't want to feel reliant on Michael. I wanted to truly be free. All I wanted from him was fair compensation for taking care of him for seventeen years, just enough to comfortably set myself up in this new life. He put up no fight and the judge was happy to sign off without listening to the lengthy, drawn out, spiteful battle he was accustom.

Elation washed over me, or maybe that was the shampooing? How does she do that? It feels amazing, maybe it's my newfound liberation. I don't know, but great news combined with some form of pampering is something I hope every woman falls into at least once in her life.

"So what are we doing? Rose asked as she wrapped a towel around my wet head, guiding me back to her chair.

I stared at the divorcee in the mirror as Rose combed her thick chocolatey tresses. The question rang in my ears. It felt like life or death, but it was just hair. It was the oddest feeling, then a sudden clarity, "Chop it."

I had had longer hair, no shorter than the tops my shoulders for as long as I'd been with Michael. Every once in a while I would get ballsy and go about chin length. But I'd come home and he'd make some dick comment and make me feel like shit about it.

By the time she was done, the long heavy waves that somehow found it's way the bottoms of my shoulder blades, was now a sleek aline bob. The shortest part cupped the base of my skull and the longest tickled my chin.

"The second this gets wet-" Rose started to explain as she coated me with hairspray.

"Poof." My hands made an exploding gesture. I couldn't help but smile at the girl in the mirror. There you are, I've missed you. "Crazy, isn't it? How you can come in feeling like one person, and leave feeling like someone completely new." I asked Rose as I primped. I felt like a hypocrite; always giving Kennedy a hard time for her extended hours in front of a mirror, but today I couldn't help it.

The honkey tonk drinking tunes of Confederate Railroad blared from Scout's speakers as we sat at a red light. I noted it an odd transition when Allison Krauss began to sing the romantic classic 'When You Say Nothing At All.' Knots began to tighten in my stomach. The smell of burn and char tingled in my nose so potently I could taste it in the back of my throat.

In the background a soft horn grew aggressively louder, but I couldn't tell where it was coming from. The louder it grew the angrier it became. "Green means go! Dumb bitch!" buzzed past me waiving the bird. I shook the feeling and turned into the parking lot as the light turned yellow.

"My bad." I apologetically shrugged. So far the most obnoxious thing about leaving Michael, was the exponential increase of having to drive. Firstly, I hate driving. Secondly, and now fairly obvious, my distractions are far more than just a cell phone. It's a small town, I should take more cabs.

CHAPTER 28
Charlie Modern Day

THE DIVORCE HAD BEEN FINAL for months. I had grown lazy and let my bob grow unruly and now it rested somewhere between my shoulders and chin and I could mostly pull it back in to a pony. I had been settled in the new house for about two weeks, purposefully ignoring my friends and enjoying the solitude. I only answered Kennedy's text because she had threatened if I didn't she was showing up on my doorstep. Buzz. Fuck.

Too late bitch. Open the fucking door.

This was a full on wellness check. I hadn't been ignoring my friends because I was unconsolably depressed. To the contrary, I was enjoying having the time and space to just be. Was it bad two weeks had gone by? Well, that depends on who you ask. At least my ~~meddling~~ concerned friends brought coffee. "I've never been good with dates and times." I offered nonchalantly as Dahlia scrolled through the evidence of ignored methods of contact.

"Two Weeks Charlotte!" she roared. "You got lost in that head of yours for two weeks! How long would you have been stuck in there had we not intervened?"

"I don't see what the big fucking deal is." I antagonized.

"You act as if alone is the worst thing a person can be. More often than not, it's my favorite place in the world." I shrugged sipping from my cup of heaven, my complacence visibly settling under her skin.

"I kinda think that's her point." Kennedy chimed in. "Seriously, when was the last time you went outside-" She raised her hand cutting me off before I could interrupt. "Outside meaning off property, amongst people, not smoking a joint on the back patio." I was trumped. "Don't be a fucking hermit. What's the point of gaining your freedom, if you never do anything with it?"

"For fuck sake; I spent two weeks painting, smoking pot and getting settled in my new place. Had I been on a beach with a daiquiri you'd call it a vacation. What's the fucking difference?" I snapped back.

"A shower schedule for one. And random, never going to see this guy again, fuck he's hot, vacation sex." She answered with out skipping a beat.

"Kennedy!" Dahlia protested. I found it funny anyway.

She and Kennedy were on opposite sides of the fence with the whole divorce thing. Kennedy was of the opinion that, 'if you even think of the big ol' D you might as well pull the trigger, because deep down, something ain't right. And once that thought crosses your mind, it's just a matter of time. Why drag it out?'

Dahlia was convinced I was throwing away a perfectly good marriage, a perfectly good guy. Maybe it was a 'midlife crisis', like she so eloquently put in one of the many ignored texts.

It was kind of sweet that she thought we were worth fighting for. I just didn't have any more fight in me.

"Why don't you go freshen up, put some real clothes on and we'll take you to lunch." Kennedy offered. It was hard, but I was trying to not be offended. Kennedy's natural tone was a little insulting. So of course her nose would be a turnt up whilst dealing with her crazy shut in of a friend. She didn't mean anything by it. I know her heart and that's all that really matters.

CHAPTER 29
Charlie Modern Day

Lunch with Dahlia and Kennedy somehow escalated to several vodka cranberries later. From what I remember, three, maybe four? Which mostly likely meant five or six. How did I even get home?

Now I lie clenching to the edges of my bed, watching the ceiling spin. The room slowly came to focus. This isn't m- I dart up panicked, trying to negotiate my surroundings.

Debilitating dizziness threw me to my back. Deep breath in through the nose. Hold it. Now, slowly exhale through the mouth. Repeat. I cautiously popped one eye open at a time, this time more aware of my inebriation. I glanced around my new bedroom. Ok, cool. My eyes grew heavy. I was home, I was safe, I was passing the fuck out.

Hours later I was awaken by a soft howl on the night's breeze and the moon's call. Hanging brilliant and large in the clear night sky, her rays shone bright on my face. I rolled toward the night stand, searching for the clock. One in the morning; and still eighty degrees in the valley. When the clouds began to roll in, I thought the air would cool, but they weren't dense enough. Just heavy enough to cast a thick mugginess between the hills. Unable to stand the stickiness of my sheets, I fumble frustrated from bed.

I stumbled down the hall in my tank top and boy short panties till I fell into the light switch. I made my way to the living room, pulled a small wooden box from the book case, plopped into the couch, rolled myself a joint and let myself out on to the patio.

I sat on the porch step and found the moon as I lit my prescription sleep aide. Venus hovered close to the well lit rock. I inhaled the night air as the moon stared back. There was no sleeping; tonight I would be lost in paint and moon light. I hit the herbal cigarette one last time before extinguishing it into the concrete.

My new studio was a surprisingly nice Tuff Shed. It was small and quaint and looked like a country cottage. Finn had ran electricity and plumbed water for me, making it a truly functional workspace. I loved that Dahlia had Do-It-Yourselfer husband. Michael would have hired a contractor. As I assisted Finn through the project, a sense of pride I had never felt before washed over me. This new me was to be more reliant on self than money and I was enamored with the thought.

When we ordered the sixteen by twenty foot structure, we had sliding windows put in for ventilation. Because, you know, turpentine, ventilation is never a bad idea. I squealed with excitement when I saw the skylight option and it instantly became necessity. What artist doesn't want as much natural light as possible?

Nights like tonight, working under the moon, gave me a primal feeling. It was moments like this, where I felt most alive. Most free. Most at peace. I find appreciation in these moments, and guilt; because I couldn't feel like this with Michael, but if I had to let him go to feel like this, I'm okay with it. If being happy, more importantly, happy with myself, happy in my skin, makes me a selfish asshole, then so be it.

I had gotten lost exercising my thoughts and in the tug and pull of the moon. Splashes of oily rainbow covered my body. I pushed a loose piece of hair from my eyes with the one spot of my wrist not covered in paint. I step back from the canvas to see what I had blindly created.

A dark waterfront and flickering candle lit street lamps came to life from the mounds of oil splattered across in the canvas.

What the- I gently stroked the scene in disbelief. As the delicate lines of my fingerprints graze the paint; flashes of blood and the smell of death overburden my senses. Hands wrap around my throat. I can't breathe. I can't scream. My eyes flutter and roll to the back of my head.

The morning sun kissed the roof lines of my sleepy little neighborhood when I woke on the studio floor. My head throbbed as the room spun. "That was new." I said aloud, rubbing the back of my head, as I lifted myself to my feet.

The painting stood unmoved on its easel. Scanning the canvas for clues, my fingers hovered the globs of wet oily paint. Before the thought could fully form my hand fearfully snapped away from the painting, like one would pull their hand from a hot pan. I shook the thought and forced my hole palm in to the canvas, ruining a perfectly good painting. I felt like an idiot.

The visions had never been that sensory before. I see and hear shit all the time, but this was different. The fear, the panic of not being able to breathe, scream, was very real. I felt the crush of a man's weight against my throat. Nails dug deep under my ear, I felt my life slip away and it terrified me.

I collapsed into my grandmother's rocking chair, my head fell between my knees. Breathe. Breathe. That's right. Big inhale. Hold it. Slowly exhale. When the room stopped spinning I sat up, massaging my forehead. This vision was especially hard to swallow. It was too real. I didn't see it like a past life or a forgotten memory. This was a scar on my heart. Something dark, buried deep with in me.

CHAPTER 30
Thomas Kentucky

IT HAD BEEN MONTHS SINCE the accident. Charlotte seemed fine (well, as fine as could be expected) to everyone else. I was the only one who saw the torturous cloud of guilt that hovered her. She couldn't shake her haunting prophetic words. 'He'll probably get tossed and break his neck.' Sometimes I could hear her thoughts so loud it was like she stood next to me screaming.

"You can not possibly be serious? You are not going to jump Artemis!", No that's actual yelling. I heard Charlotte's voice echo down the entire corridor. "Michael died jumping that horse. I don't know how to prove to you she's not reliable. We can show her as a companion, that's it!" Charlotte literally put her foot down.

"We can fetch a higher purse if she ribbons." Henry argued.

"No. As the sole proprietor of Ananke Farms, I am saying no! A couple hundred dollars is not worth your life. Or Michael's." She paused as the ghostly reminder of that tragic days flashed across her downhearted eyes. "Maybe he'd still be alive had I stood firm the last time." She hated using her position to get her way, but it was far from beneath her.

"Sorry to interrupt Charlotte." I cleared my throat and a soft smile formed in the corner of her mouth as her name fell from my lips. "I just wanted to get Hera back to her stall. She's been run pretty hard today."

She welcomed my intrusion. "Hera." Her soft smile turned to smug pleasure as the name fell from her mouth. The black maned, eight-year-old Blue Dun was reliable and seasoned. "You want to jump father? Jump with Hera." She shifted her attention to me, closing the door on the previous conversation. "Thank you Thomas. Since you are here, a personal request?"

"Anything Ma'am."

"Would you be so kind as to escort me to the ball Friday night?" A hesitant tug held me back but I was quickly melting as her eyes begged, "I'm sure father has something you can wear." She paused, one overing Henry, clothes designed for his five foot eight fuller body were clearly not going to fit my six foot, thin, defined frame. "On second thought; head into town, put a tuxedo on our account at Winston's."

"You're too kind Ma'am. I ju-"

Before I could begrudgingly decline, she interrupted. "Please don't make me go alone. It's hardly going to be bearable as it is. Rose will want to gussy me up; my dress, hair, everything, I do will be wrong. I don't think I can bear being the subject of everyone's gossip without a buffer. 'Poor widow this. She didn't want him to ride that horse that. Her father -"

I couldn't allow her misery to continue, "I would be pleased to accompany you. If you don't mind the gossip that might cause."

"In case you haven't noticed, there isn't a whole lot I don't do that doesn't beget some sort of scandal." She smirked. "It's what happens when a woman chooses a life other than what society deems normal, and anything is better than the current headline." She smiled grabbing Hera's reigns. "Why don't you take the truck in to town. I'll put Hera to bed."

She gently stroked the mare's nose, I instantly became lost in her. She had a gentleness about her that few ever get to see. She was extraordinary. "It's nice to see you smile," fell from my mouth without thought. "I think that's the first time I've seen you smile since -"

Her gloomy cloud returned, "the accident."

"I wasn't going to say that." I defended.

"Well, what then?" she pushed.

"Actually, I was going to stop in my tracks before I stepped in it."

Her curiosity piqued, "Come with it now." She pulled at my shirt playfully. I got lost in her chocolatey eyes. Kiss her, flooded my thoughts as she poked, "You have to tell me."

I rubbed the back of my head, bummed I had missed my moment. Might as well get it out of the way. Against my better judgement, I begrudgingly answer, "Since you got engaged."

"Oh." She dropped the hem of my shirt and stepped back.

The vacuum of space ached my heart. A single step might as well have been a nautical league, the damage was done, she was lost to me. Might as well get it all out there now. "Sorry, I just mean for the 'happiest time in a girl's life', you kind of seemed to go through the motions."

"So kind of you to notice," her polished societal politeness forcing her to reign in her melancholy. "It's unfortunate you were the only one. None of that matters now I suppose." She blotted the tear forming in the corner of her eye before it could fall.

I reached for her hand, delicately lacing my fingers between hers, as her doe-y eyes met mine I felt her soul wrap around my heart. I slowly leaned in, my lips brushed hers she momentarily melted in, and just as quickly returned to ice as she shoved Hera's reigns into my chest before running away, "I have to go."

"Charlotte!" I hollered as I started to chase her. I made it to the barn's door before I abandoned the mission. "Damn it!!" I scolded, kicking over a bucket of feed. As the grain sprawled across the ground my anger boiled. "FUCK!" I kicked a stall door, stubbing my toe.

She avoided the stables, meaning me, the remainder of the week. There was an awkward dance through the kitchen door on Wednesday and on Thursday morning Gypsy, her favorite Buckskin, was gone before dawn.

It was well past mid-day when they returned to the stable, I was working barrels with Artemis. Gypsy galloped into the arena as Charlotte chastised, "You can't possibly be getting Artemis ready for Saturday's event?!" She demanded. "I was clear, she is not to compete."

I was still mounted atop the Azteca as Charlotte snatched the reigns, while dotingly stroking the horse's nose and mumbling half serious insults about dense stable hands. "You were ma'am. Just working her out a bit." I defended patting Artemis' muscular shoulder.

"Oh." She would never acknowledge her embarrassment over the unfounded scolding. "Well, then, go about your business." She said dropping the reign as she about faced cooly walking away.

I hopped from Artemis' back, grabbing for Charlotte's hand before she could escape. Fire pulsed through her finger tips. She turned on her heel as she growled trying to cover her flustered nerves, "Just what do you think you are doing?"

"Apologies." I inched in closer, forcing her walls to recede. Her large brown eyes were wide and wet with fear and hope and anticipation as the tip of my hat lightly brushed against her forehead, I softly offered, "Still need an escort for tomorrow?"

She took a deep nervous breath and her eyes seared my soul. Lost in her was the most naked I have ever felt. As my lips hovered inches from hers, it took every bit of restraint I had not to kiss her. "I went to Winston's. Rented a tux, tails and all." I smiled, mostly because I was proud at the fact I hadn't acted on the deafening urge to kiss her.

A soft laugh escaped my throat, the idea of me in a tuxedo was as goofy a thought as her in a ball gown. Both were foreign uncomfortable roles, far from who either of us truly were, but the requirements of circumstance, (her's by birth, mine through unyielding devotion) that we had to fulfill.

She shook her head as if she heard the question on delay, hurriedly she answered, "Yes. Thank you Thomas." Grabbing Gypsy's reigns she guided the Buckskin toward her stall and hollered over her should, "Meet you in the parlor, 8 o'clock?"

"Yes'm." I tipped my hat. As soon as I did, I regretted it. The motion didn't feel my own, it reeked of Michael.

That simple, stupid gesture, cast a wave of sadness through me. Before Thomas could see the flood of tears break their dam, I had mounted Gypsy and we were galloping off.

Tears coated my face as Gypsy guided me through the property. I released all the emotion I had been holding so tightly for the past ten years. She had taken us to our favorite Oak four miles from the main house, near the duckpond while a decade of pent up grief and anger spilled down my cheeks.

Gypsy grazed nearby as I thrashed my thoughts aloud. "I may not of been in love with Michael, but I did care for him. He was good to me. Even if it were only a short while. I know what people will if I start up with Thomas. I've already thought of a million foul things to say about myself."

I went on like that for hours. Gypsy grazed and napped in the sun until it began to sink over the emerald hills. I mounted the Buckskin and we made our way home.

She tried to slink in unnoticed. Unlucky for her, I could never, not notice her presence. I leaned against Gypsy's stall door and before I could let out a word she coldly snapped, "I'm fine." unmoved as she brushed the Buckskin's golden body. "Just needed some time to sort things out."

"It's not like you to just take off Charlotte. Did I-"

She cut me off before I could worsen the weirdness between us with whatever fell from my mouth next. "I'm just having a hard time is all." She opened up, "I never thought this would be my life. Who plans on being widowed by twenty four, much less responsible for all of this?" She showcased the rolling hills with her opened arm. "And then there's you." She returned to aggressively brushing her mare.

"Me." I piqued. "What about me?"

Realizing she had left more on the table intended, she shoved the brush into my chest and stormed off.

There was something there, but I knew enough about Charlotte to know that if you chase her, all you do is chase her off. An encouraged smile spread across my face as I took over brushing Gypsy out.

Moments later, the faintest squeak of a voice moused behind me, "You make me feel something I didn't know was possible." Her words branded my heart. "And it scares me, because if it hurt this much to lose someone I wasn't in love with, it would bury me to lose you."

I turned to answer but she had disappeared and managed to remain hidden the entirety of Friday. I hadn't seen her all day and was a solid ninety percent sure she'd bail on tonight. I knew her well enough to know; she did not want to deal with me nor Rose and the gaggle of gossip mongers she brought in tow. Regardless, I dressed to meet her in the parlor at eight o'clock. I had made her a promise, and I was going to ensure she knew, no matter what, I would always be there for her.

I waited. And waited. And waited. Till nine forty five I waited. I was about to give up, when she shyly emerged from the staircase. As she descended, I noticed how polished and taught her normally short messy hair was. Her ruby column dress made her look like the society girl she was, but never embodied. "Stunning." I managed to choke as she took my arm.

Uncomfortable in her gown and with the compliment she rambled. "Rose did it. And she made me wear these blasted heels too." She lifted her hem to expose matching red shoes. "She said she burned the one I hung out." Letting her skirt loose, "I bet she did too."

"May I?" I spun her around.

She nervously obliged. The deep plunging V exposed the dimples of her lower back as a gold tassel necklace swept across her bare skin. I was undone. The innocent smile she didn't want me to notice faded as our eyes met and my jaw was still on the ground. "What?" She grumbled, shielding her satin covered erect nipples with crossed arms and painful self-awareness. "Is it too much?"

"No." I stumbled over his words. "I've just never seen you so-"

"So what?" She defended.

"Exquisite." I answered frazzled. "Charlotte, you've always been the most beautiful girl in the room. Even in riding pants with manure on your face. "But this-. Wow." I gathered my rambling self and offered my arm, "Shall we?"

She blushed as she clenched my arm and wobbled in her heels. "You don't look so bad yourself," she complimented from the side of her mouth.

My eyes were glued to her as the moonlight shimmered from her cheeks. The string lights glimmered round the mulberry trunks, lining the path from the main house to the freshly erected party tent and danced on the curves of her wavy pinned locks. She was nervous and silent as she strategically placed each heeled step before abruptly breaking the quiet, cricket backed, jazz sounds coming from the tent in the distance with her brusque request. "I need you to do something for me."

"Anything." I was lost in her, she had no idea how serious a pledge I had made. If it meant seeing her smile; I had no idea what I was capable of.

Her pleading eyes looked like sparkling obsidian in the night's light. "Call me Charlie."

"What?" I wasn't prepared for such a simple request.

"I need to not feel like Charlotte Sinclair. I detest who that person is meant to be. And I need to know you see who I am past all that bullshit. The pomp, the parade. That, that's not me at my heart's core. I need you to know that, and if you are continually calling me Charlotte-"

My mouth crashed against hers as the tear cracked in her throat. Her tongue rolled against mine, leaving me intoxicated as I foolishly pull away. "Charlie, I have known exactly who and what you are since the moment I met you. Past the facade. Past the Sinclair name and the responsibility of this place. I see who you show the world, but I also see the bits you try so desperately to hide. I see you exactly as you are. Flawed but kind hearted." My smile hovered her lips.

She ran her fingers through my hair as she pulled my mouth in to hers. My hand found the small concave of her bare dimpled back, guiding her hips into mine. She pulled away first, giggling between much more innocent pecks, "We really ought to be going. I've made us tremendously late."

We strolled the last bits of the string lit path, as my mind raced through a million and five thoughts. The band's horn section was on fire as we traipsed up to tent's entrance. The fear and anxiety in her eyes begged me to flee with her, "I can't do this."

"Yes, you can." I patted the top of her hand in support and gently kissed her temple.

We walked through the doorway and I led her past the parade of gossiping trolls straight to the dance floor. No wonder she was dreading this so. Even over the upbeat swing of the band I heard the crows snicker; "Looking dis-shelved"

"That's not an appropriate dress for a grieving widow."

"Moved on quickly don't ya think?"

"Well, if my stable boy looked like that."

Gently I wrapped my hand around her waist, taking her right hand with my left and guided her across the floor as the tune slowed down.

"Don't worry about them." Her eyes glued to the floor as she nervously counted steps, my words forced her gaze up, "They only wish to see you fall."

A nervous smile formed in the corner of her mouth as I cheered her on. Her grace and beauty masqueraded her trembling nerves. The world would never how her heart raced as heavy as Gypsy's pounding hooves. Charlie lifted herself to her tippy toes and slammed her lips to mine, grazing my bottom lip with her teeth and my tongue softly rolled against hers. An explosion erupted in my chest as she pulled me in tighter, harder and shoving me away just as quick. She panted, "I'm sorry. I can't -" as she darted from the tent.

I chased after her I passed the gossip fodder;

"Another stable boy's tramp, just like her mother."

"Wonder what Michael would think?"

"You don't think they started up while he was alive? Do you?"

"What do you think her father thinks of all this?"

She hadn't even left the room and the assault against her

had begun. She was right, it didn't matter what she did, she was always going to be their source of ridicule and entertainment.

I was able to catch up her, thanks to the heels. "Charlie-" I hollered. "Charlie, wait!" I reached for her wrist, drawing her in to my chest.

She wriggled free as tears stream down her face, exploding, "What do you want from me!"

I held her by her shoulders, staring so deep in her eyes I could feel her soul, "You Charlie. All of you. Since the day we met."

"I'm sorry, but I can't." I barely make out the words between the sobs and her muffled words. I wrap my arms around her and softly kiss her forehead trying my best to be of comfort.

Gently I tilt her gaze up to mine. Her eyes swollen and wet, her face red hot, "You're not ready." I paused with a thin breath. "That's okay." I delicately kissed her lips, "I'm not going anywhere."

She palms both her cheeks wiping away the flood of tears. She grumbled laughing, removing the ruby heels from her feet. "There's no way I'm going back in there. Walk me to the house?" Her half smile told me she would be okay.

"If you wish."

We moseyed the string lit path back to home and as she cooly, out-of-nowhere offered a ray of hope. "I know I'm not the easiest of people. Thank you for your infinite patience." Before I could add anything she quickly changed the subject, "This dress is killing me."

"Will you be needing help removing it?" I winked. She nudged me with her shoulder and we laughed. I was only half serious anyway.

CHAPTER 31
Thomas Kentucky 1938

THOUSANDS OF LINGERING STARES, HUNDREDS of almost kisses, and twelve eternal weeks passed while Charlie and I remained in limbo. I was dying, while she was hidden in plan site buried in her work.

Our main focus was preparing for the Oldham County Expo. Charlie planned to jump Gypsy, Henry would run barrels with Hera, and in a strange turn of events, Charlie entrusted me to jump with Artemis. (Well, it was either trust or she was trying to kill me. I jest. I jest. A joke in poor taste that I'd never dare utter aloud.)

Training Sweet Lady Grace and Jumpin' Jehoshaphat for their upcoming races consumed Charlie for months. She doted on those horses as if she had birthed them herself. Many a night boundary and devotion forced my slumber to the stable's office while she cuddled with her children. She was playful for the first time in a millennia, calling me ridiculous and often rolling her eyes with her almost nightly scoldings of; 'laboring all day and not taking advantage of a hot shower or comfortable bed.' The comfort we had developed with each other led me to flirt, "...and what of your ridiculousness."

After a much heated debate, she headed my counsel and decided I was to bring on a jockey as she could not bear to do so herself. There was no way I could race those horses and win. Too tall, too heavy. Charlotte was a woman, and such as her curse, automatically dismissed. Under much noted duress, she caved. Her point was valid; she was easily fifteen pounds lighter than Alister and a solid inch shorter. Not to mention she doesn't take a salary or a bonus if they place. But our hands were tied.

The newly hired jockey mounted our chocolate thoroughbred and trotted to the start line of the practice track. A piece of straw hung from my mouth as I leaned against the track's fence and excitedly assess, "I bet JoJo shaves any easy ten seconds off his time." I towered Charlie as I stood on the split rail's bottom rung. "He's loosing about eight inches of drag and an easy forty pounds. He's going to fly." I floated my hand through the air annunciating my premonition.

Charlie's soft "humpf" and eye roll told me exactly what she thought of the revered Alister Buchanan as she joined me on the fence rung. "Don't reckon it'll make much a difference for Lady Grace though."

A few days later, the trailers were loaded and the caravan followed the river south to the Expo.

The horses were unloaded and stabled, camp was set, while trailers and trucks protectively encircled us. Charlie anxiously fidgeted as she fixed us a lunch. I wish she'd talk to me about more than the health of the animals. I could only image what dizzying thoughts ran through her mind. First hiring a jockey, now Henry falling ill. It was a lot all at once, but I didn't prod, I figured it easier to pry my hand from a bear trap than to get her to open up.

The announcer called the race overhead. "And Jumpin Jehoshaphat takes the lead. JUMPIN JEHOSHAPHAT WINS!! Jumpin Jehoshaphat sets a new track record!"

Pride and elation instantaneously exploded through my veins as uncontrollable celebration forces my fist in to the air, "Yes!! Told ya he was going to fly!" I was blinded with excited ecstasy, before I knew what I was doing I had pulled her body taught to mine and was kissing her. Surprised by my intrusion, she allowed herself to melt as my fingers lace through the short bobbed hair tickling the nape of her neck. My sense returned and I pull away embarrassed, "Didn't mean to do that, just got caught up in the moment." I nervously rub the back of my head.

Shock fumbles her words, "Nothing to be sorry 'bout-" Before she could finish, Alister an JoJo trotted down the row draped in ribbon and flower. Her attention distracted, she runs up to her horse and kisses his nose and cheers, "Congratulations Boy!" as the jockey dismounts.

I couldn't escape the pang of jealousy as Charlie's arms wrapped around his shoulders and she pulled her body in to his.

"You too! It's not too often, I'm happy to eat my words. Couldn't be prouder!" The seconds dragged as if eons before she finally unclenched her embrace.

"Thank you Ma'am. Have to say, he's a pretty remarkable animal." Alister patted the muscular front shoulder of her beloved JJ.

We wash our Monte Christos down with celebratory champagne as we anxiously wait for the seven races between JoJo and Lady Grace to pass.

Charlie kissed Grace's cheek for luck as she lovingly scratched behind the mare's ear. As Alister led the horse to the start line, Charlie took a seat and nervously awaited the start. Giddy by the first win and the bubbly, we eagerly listen to our Sweet Lady's race.

"Sweet Lady Grace is in the lead. The Morning Star is coming from behind. He's close, too close." A sudden collective gasp sucked all the sound from the stadium. The eery quiet shattered by blood curdling, ear piercing, gut wrenching sounds of anguish I was unaware any animal could make.

Charlie's heart split in two as the color fell from her face and the champagne glass fell from her hand, shattering on to the hard ground beneath us as her maternal instinct pushed her to the track as fast as her feet could carry her. We were greeted at the gate by the vet shaking his head, the somber nod confirmed our worst fears true. I squeezed her tight into my chest as the sound of a gun exploded, echoing through the stunned stadium.

CHAPTER 32
Thomas Kentucky 1938

THICK CLOUDS OF DEVASTATION FILLED the air as the rain followed us home. Buckets slammed against the windshield as I drove Charlie in stunned silence. I wanted to say something, anything that could be of comfort, but the words sat stuck in my throat choking me into silent submission.

The familiar white rails marked our path to the house and with each passing post, Charlie's eyes swelled until sheets uncontrollably coated her cheeks. She sniffled, wiping salty tears from her face. Before I could come to a complete stop, she had flung the truck's door open, racing in to the house and blowing past her father.

I heard her wail with the storm as I unloaded the trailers. My heart broke for her. I wanted to wrap my arms around her, squeeze her in tight and tell her it was okay to fall apart, I'd be there to help her put the pieces back together. I was not so foolish as to think I could shield her from the heartaches of this world, nor would I dare to assume that she'd let me, but there was nothing in this world I wouldn't do to lessen her burden if she'd let me. I pray with every inch of my being that she knows this truth, because for whatever reason, she could not bare to hear it aloud.

The clouds thinned as the wind pushed the heart of the storm north. My clothes were heavy with rain as I tapped on her door.

No answer. I try again, "Charlie." Still no answer. "Alright then. You know where to where I am if you need me."

As I pulled up a pair of dry of boxers I heard the V8 engine whine and turn over. Gravel bounced off my second story window as I watched Charlie speed down the drive.

She was gone all evening and well into the night. Henry's concern grew as I told him of our day at the track. Before he could respond to the briefing, the telephone rang.

"Thanks Finn, I'm on my way." I let out a sigh, hanging up the receiver. "She's safe. Passed out in a booth at Finnegan's, but not before smashing up a few glasses and breaking a stool." I informed.

"Oh thank goodness." Her father grabbed his chest with relief. "Would you please be so kind as to retrieve my daughter?" He handed me a few bills from his breast pocket. "To cover her damages."

I was already sliding my second arm through the wool lined sleeve of my denim jacket, "Yes sir." I grabbed the Model A's keys from the hook as the screen door slammed behind me.

The clouds pushed north, exposing the full moon, illuminating the night's sky. The slick muddy roads forced the Ford to fishtail most of the forty mile drive.

By the time I arrived to our local watering hole, Charlie had been snoozing for well over an hour. "Look at you. You're a mess." I brushed the messy locks the hair swept across her sticky, tear stained, face behind her ear. I slide my arms under her legs, wrap her arms around my neck and carry her out.

I unload her into the truck and her drunk eyes groggily flutter as she gains bearing on her surroundings, "Thomas?"

"Yes." I answered tucking her legs into the passenger side.

"I need a sandwich." She informed before falling in to a heavy slumber.

The whole way home she mumbled in heartbroken bits. Her pain radiated though me as I squeezed her hand in sad silence. She loves these animals more so than some women love their actual children. I couldn't even begin to image her devastation.

When the hum of the engine cut out, Charlie instantly woke. The loud, clumsy, belligerent mess is insistent upon on putting herself to bed. I bite my tongue and she tests my patience while I dutifully guide her from truck to house. Inebriation amplifies her already exhausting stubbornness as shoves me away and knocks herself to the ground.

Displeased by her own clumsiness, she unleashes her rage on me; screaming in my face, kicking me. Her palm cracked against my cheek as she slurs obscenities.

My frustration finally boiled over; I threw her over my shoulder as she screamed bloody murder the mile long trek up the single flight of stairs. I drop her on to her bed a little harder than I should have, taking a small pleasure in watching it sting, to which I was thanked with a fresh slur of half asleep slander.

I went downstairs, made a sandwich, and poured a glass of water. When I returned she was deep in a whiskey fueled slumber. I left the sandwich, water and two aspirin on her nightstand, pulled the blanket to her shoulder and leaned down to kiss her forehead.

Charlie tipped her chin, tricking my lips in to hers. I pulled back, looking in to her eyes. She consumed my mouth again, running her fingers through my hair, hungrily pulling my body in to hers. One of my hands ran up the back of her shirt while the other groped the soft supple flesh of her breast.

I had wanted this moment for so long, as she sucked my bottom lip clarity set in. "No." I pulled away, wanting to shoot myself for being 'nobel'. "I can't. Not like this."

Charlie flushed apple red, "Fine." as she angrily shoved me off her bed. "Get out!"

"I don't want -"

She shrieks, "Get out!!", and hurled the bedside glass at the wall. She missed me by a solid three feet which angered her more.

I stood there tightlipped. I was either going to shake the life from her or laugh and I hadn't decided which. Either would have dire consequences. I took a deep breath, turned around and walked away.

CHAPTER 33
Charlie Kentucky 1938

It had been months since Grace's accident and I hadn't been to the stables, much less ridden, since. It was far too painful, all I could see was the life I had tendered since birth and her demise at my hand. Grief had forced me to cancel the rest of the season, "I'm not sure if there'll be a next season!" I commanded in what my father called a fit of hysterics.

"Sweetheart, you need to calm down and quite honestly, get over it. At the end of the day, this is our business and sometimes that's the cost of doing business." Henry tried his best to be comforting and realistic at the same time.

All he did was infuriate. "The cost of doing business." I snarled. Rings of fire stoked in my eyes. "I'll remember that when your time comes Old Man." I immediately recoiled, "I'm sorry. These animals are so much more to me than business. Aside from you, they're the only constant in my life."

"Unfortunately my dear, that is just something you are going to have to get over." He pulled me in for a comforting hug. "I don't mean to be crass. It's just what it is. There is no changing that."

I broke away from my father's embrace and with a sniffle, solicited, "Does it ever get any easier?"

"I wish I could say yes dear, but for people with hearts like yours, no, it never gets easier."

"Hearts like mine?" The smile I forced could not mask the insult raging through my veins.

"Charlotte, my dear. You are very much like a turtle. Hard, almost impenetrable shell, but tender underneath the protective walls." My father responded with a loving hand.

For the first time in a long time and I felt like my father understood me. The tears began to well up again, I rip my hand a way proclaiming, "Bollocks!" darting up the stairs to my room and slamming the door.

I sat at my vanity aggressively brushing my short bobbed hair, muttering inaudibly. Only every few words fell fully formed from my lips. Insufferable. Incorrigible. Turtle. The nerve. An obnoxious tap at the door distracts me from my dizzying rant.

SHE FLINGS THE DOOR OPEN and I, some would say foolishly, am on the other side. We hadn't spoken more than three words at a time since the night of Lady Grace's accident, but as crazy as it sounds, something told me this was the moment to try and make it right. I could feel her boiling anger scathed as she opened the door. Her slow eye roll cut as she coldly questioned "What?"

"Is everyth-"

"You know Thomas. I really don't have time for this." She erupted, slamming the door in my face.

MY HEART SINKS AS I fall against the bedroom door, recalling that night. The night I ruined everything; the night I killed Grace, got so drunk he had to pick me up, take care of me, put me to bed. Him gently rejecting my drunken advancements. The embarrassment, the anger. All of it replayed as I cried in to my knees.

THE TENSION IN THE AIR was thicker than the humid summer afternoon that promised a lighting show later on. Her weasel of a father managed to snag a supply run, getting himself off property while I was left to wait out the hurricane.

"You'll be alright." Henry offered through the drivers side window. "I'll only be a week."

"You know she hates me, right?" I answered as sprinkles start to collect in my hair.

With an empathetic smile, he returned, "You and me both my boy." He patted the top of my hand with encouragement, and with that started down the split rail lined drive.

I turned toward the porch where Charlie leaned against the post with her arms crossed. With an irritated squint; drizzle turned to sheets, water dripped down my face and my shirt turned sheer, clinging to my torso.

Her chocolatey gaze caught mine, thickening the air as she let out a jilted, "Humpf," turned on her heel and disappeared into the house, slamming the door behind her.

The rain continued and the storm strengthened. The clouds grew heavier and darker with each passing day. Three silent days and nights passed between Charlie and I. It killed me, but I could not crack first. This ice had to be broken by her.

There was no sleeping tonight. The storm had reached it's apex, the air was hot and thick with a tangible restlessness. Rain angrily pelted the roof and windows as blinding flashes of fire explode outside the windows and the thunderous clap of the atmosphere slamming overhead while shrills of startled horses add to the chaotic orchestra.

I barely heard the tap at my door over the deafening storm. At first I thought it may be rain slapping the roof, but then I heard it again, this time paired with the faintest, "Thomas?" I open the door surprised to see white flag wielding Charlie on the other side; bottle of whiskey in one hand and two glasses in the other. "Have a drink with me." The plea in her eyes trumped the demand in her tone.

A warm smile cracked as I nodded and followed her to the kitchen. She poured two doubles over ice and slid the drink across the table. As the glass fell into my hand, an odd familiarity of the moment gummed me up as I searched the glass for the memory I disappointedly could not find.

Charlie poured her first drink down her throat and served herself a second, before spitting, "What kind of fool sticks around for such punishment?" I felt her brokenness as she finally mustered the courage to ask, "Why do you stay?"

"Because I know what life is like without you." Fell from my mouth without thought. "Even at your worst. Even if you hate me every day for the rest of you life. Getting to see you every morning makes it all worth it." I reached across the table, gently brushing my thumb along her jaw, lost in the abyss of her eyes. Before I knew what was happening, she lunged across the table and crashed her mouth against mine. It took every ounce of strength I had to pull her from me. I had been wanting this moment so long, but I had to finish. I gained the power to resist her pull long enough for my words brush her lips. "From the moment we met, I knew I was meant to love you."

A thunderous clap rattled the house as she dove in to my mouth. I pushed the table out of the way, pulling her body into mine. The room floods with blinding white light as my calloused and cut farm hand runs up her silky back, pulling her shirt overhead as she feverishly unbuckles my belt, desperate to satisfy the hunger between us.

"THOMAS? THOMAS," A BUXOM BLONDE rudely snaps in my face. "Thomas, wake Up."

I jerk up, finding myself on the patio chair; jeans unbuttoned, shoe and shirtless, with a non lit cigarette hanging from my lip, a watered down glass of scotch in hand and a vaguely familiar woman looking down at me.

"I lost my phone. Call me a car?"

"Yeah." I escorted the top heavy woman back into my flat.

The engineered blonde in my bed (Jennifer? Jessica? Blimey what was her name?) couldn't compete with the brown eyed girl that haunts me.

Flashes of untamed curls and large espresso eyes call to me. I spend hours lost in charcoal and paper. As the sky bursts into shades of oranges and pinks of sunrise, I feel a bare chest against my back, a blanket wrap around me and a kiss on my neck. "Whatcha working on?"

Feeling like granny caught me in the biscuit jar, I quickly flip my notebook over. "Jenn-" daggers fire from her eyes, "essica?" I had no control over the puzzled look that crossed my face.

"Lexy, my name is Lexy, Asshole!" She slapped the back of my head, grabbed her clothes, as she raged out the door and shimmied her denim shorts over her hips all in one motion.

I was unfazed. It didn't matter what her name was. She wasn't her. I flipped through my notebook. None of them were.

Those eyes, the untamable curls. They ruled my world, fueled me. Funny what power someone can have over you. Especially, someone you aren't even sure exists. At least I hope she exists. She has to exist. Why else would I feel her so deep in my soul if she weren't? And why do I find it impossible to make a real connection with any-, well one really.

Granted, I will not find the truest of loves with some bimbo groupie I pick up at a show. But there have been a handful of good girls I couldn't make it work with. All I seemed to do was irreparably damage them for the next chap that comes along.

I know I am a difficult bloke to be with. I am a slave to my art; if I hear her call at two in the morning, I answer. I can be swept away at any given moment and most women don't take kindly to being made a mistress, being left in the middle of the night for something, someone, their lover loves more than her.

CHAPTER 34
Charlie Modern Day

SEVERAL WEEKS HAD PASSED SINCE my last vision, even the other side was unusually quiet. Which was a nice change of pace. I was, dare I say, feeling normal. The intrusions, the lack of privacy, my eyes playing tricks on me, the nonstop chatter in my head; I didn't miss it one bit. Unless I actually stopped and thought about it, then the pang of loss filled the crevasse in my heart I hadn't known was there until the pool of hurt spilled over its brim.

Okay, maybe I did miss it. Like being able to help someone on the other side send a discreet message to a loved one. Like last fall, when Kennedy's grandmother whispered a cake recipe into my ear. I woke that morning with an insatiable urge to bake.

Dahlia was preparing another five star, three course meal for our tiny group. When I called that morning to let her know I had made desert, she aborted her plan for baked Alaskas.

I laughed at the relief in her voice. Even at nine thirty in the morning she was stressed about how much she had to get done. I would have offered more help, but A) she wouldn't accept it and B) I think she uses the stress as a driving force. Food is her art, and the stress is her process.

When Kennedy cut in the cake exposing a moist, chocolatey sponge and layer of cherry filling, she lost her mind. The blood fell from her face and she started hysterically crying. I was barely able to decipher between sobs, as she flung her arms around me, clumsily squeezing my neck. "I haven't had this cake since my Grammy died."

I smiled at the sweetness of the moment. And, since I'm an asshole, the first thing to cross my mind thereafter was, I hope she doesn't get snot in my shoulder.

The memory cleared and I found myself standing outside Kennedy's dressing room, hammering my fist against the flimsy door. "Are you going to be done anytime soon?!" I paused so she could answer. I saw shadows moving across the ceiling as she silently pulled another maxi dress overhead. "Come on! I want to get in a quick hike before it gets too dark."

Kennedy cracked the door, poking her head through. "Will you quit being such a baby! I'm almost done." The door slammed before I could rebut.

Somewhere over the years we had developed a sisterly dynamic. We poked and played at each other like we were squabbling little girls. "Next time we do this, I'm bringing my own car." I shouted through the door.

"No, you won't" she countered. "You refuse to drive on any roads with more than two lanes. It takes four highways just to get here." She playfully shamed as she jumped and shimmied into her skinny jeans. "That requires merging."

I shrugged, "True story." Kennedy opened the door, arms loaded with designer garments. "What's Greyson going to say about all that?" I waved my finger, encircling her heap.

"He'll complain about the credit card bill when it comes, but then he'll see how hot is wife is and get over it. Hashtag winning. Hashtag Fly as shit. Hashtag trophy wife."

"Ew." Barely able to contain my laughter, I scold. "I fucking hate you."

I help Kennedy carry a dozen bags to the gunmetal and chrome Range Rover. She had purchased more than she could tote, while I had my lone bag. Pretty much par for the course.

I had found myself snappy after our excursion. Kennedy blamed it on low blood sugar, prolonged exposure to fluorescent lights and unflattering mirrors, so we stopped for tapas before heading back up valley. My ~~ex~~ best friend was hell bent on pushing me on one of the two beautiful men that sat a few tables over. I argued, I had been out of the game for so long, there was no way I was going to shamelessly flirt with men, I felt, were completely out of my league.

"Quit being ridiculous Charlie." Kennedy poked. "You're one of the most gorgeous women I know. Even if you bury it under all that lesbian couture you insist upon wearing."

The gruff sounding blonde perked when he heard my name. His chin length hair was pulled in to a nub at the base of his neck and a few stray locks fell in to his hauntingly familiar hazel green eyes. He caught me staring and embarrassed guilt forced me to return a smile as a familiar pulse fired through my body once he exposed his toothy grin.

"That's your vagina waking up." Kennedy diagnosed after I told her of the exchange.

I disputed with an antsy giggle at her half right assessment, "No, it's more than that. I think I may kn-"

"You ready Thomas?" His counterpart's (had to have been his brother, maybe a cousin? They were too similar in appearance and stature to have not been related) British voice queried. The stranger's name momentarily rang in my ear, but was gone before I could fully form the thought that buzz and stung like a swarm of bees.

With a full belly, exhaustion from our excursion, the handsome blonde's flirty smile dancing through my mind, paired with Kennedy's sketchy at best driving skills, I found the backs of my eyelids quickly.

It only took a few moments before the green hills and small village I had never been to but have seen time and time again line the horizon. It wasn't till I had returned home, that I realized how terribly I had missed it.

Sounds of steel clashing and groans of distress grab at my attention. A flurry of familiar wild curls spinning and lunging and countering her attacker. I watch awestruck as Charlotte wielded her longsword with the grace and precision of a ballet.

Clanging of metal crashing against metal brought me back to focus. Charlotte thrusted her elbow across his face, with all the force of her tiny frame behind it. He stumbled as she pushed her heel in to his stomach. He lands on his hindquarters, splashing in the shallows of the crystal lake. She guides her sword's tip to his throat. A droplet of blood trickle over his heaving Adam's apple as her hand shook under the weight of the weapon.

A vacuum pulled at my heart as I saw I had injured my dearest love. I ran to his aid as fast as I could and with two steps was already there. The sword slipped from my fingers and crashed into the grass, "Sorry, I was a bit rough." uncontrollably fell from my mouth. I offered my hand, pulling Thomas to his feet, delicately thumbing the swollen bruise forming on his upper lip.

He cradled my hand in his as I cupped his face. "I can take it." He leant in, softly kissing me. "You did well today." He encouraged pulling away as he sheathed his sword. "You didn't hesitate," he coached. "I pity the man who finds himself on the other end of your blade." He grabbed my hand, guiding me to the blanket laid underneath a shady Oak.

I pull bread, cheese, apples, and brandy wine from my horse's sack. The equines graze and sip from the lake as we enjoy a meal well earned.

Thomas stretched himself across the shroud, propping himself up on his forearm. He bit into an apple and advised, "That gown is the only reason you didn't get the better of me early on. You're bloody brilliant." He continued to praise as I gingerly ground myself, sweeping my legs to one side as the skirt of my dress encircled me.

"Thank you. I would like to wear something a little more conducive to battle, not station, but I am sure if the occasion were to ever call, it will be in this blasted dress and kirtle. Best to train as such."

My answer impressed him, "A strategist as well." he squinted through his glassy green eyes as he took another bite of his apple, "Combined with your kindness, the love you show your people, and that unbridled ferocity of yours, you have all the makings to be a spectacular queen, My Lady."

I always had a hard time with compliments. Especially when they came from him. I hated standing out in any way, shape, or form. I grounded me eyes and blushed. "Thank you Thomas." Desperate to change the subject; I feverishly dig through my bag, finding my codex, "Ready?" I shook the leather bound pages of 'The Symposium', nervously bitting the corner of my bottom lip.

We lazed under the cloud of shade our favorite tree provided while I read from the pages aloud. I read all the way through to the end of Aristophanes' speech and reached a stopping point. I snapped the book shut and looked down at Thomas as his head lie in my lap. I staggered a breath; the power of the words in this moment, marked my heart. I innocently brushed a loose strand from his eyes, leaned down and touched his lips to mine.

He rose to his knees, straightening our kiss. He slid his hand to the nape of my neck, pulling my mouth deep and hard in to his. As our lips parted, he firmly groped my breasts. Guiding his lips across my cheek, behind my ear and down my neck. I let out a soft sigh as the graze of his teeth ran across my bottom lip and his calloused hand ran up the inside of my bare thigh.

Thomas broke away, his eyes lust filled and breath rushed, he gently pressed his forehead to mine and tickled my lips as he spoke. "I have something to tell you."

"What is it?" The air was thick, I couldn't bare the void between us longer. I eagerly delved into his mouth.

Between kisses and bits of blissful laughter, he spat, "We are-to be- wed."

The mood was abruptly chilled with disapproval as I shoved him off of me, "What do you mean we are to be wed?"

Confused by my animosity, Thomas nervous but happily continued, "When the moon is new and the stars shine bright, a celebration feast will mark your twenty second birthday. The King has decided." Fury and disbelief pulse thought my veins. I rage as I snatch up my belongings and saddle my horse. "You mean to tell me, I am to be married in less that a month, and it 'has been decided' without even the thought of asking my opinion? Not only did it not cross my father's mind but your's neither!"

Poor Thomas was lost in my reaction. He stutters, "I- I though- I thought this is what you wanted."

I scolded as I mounted my horse. "But if you had thought to ask, then you'd have been sure!" Before Thomas could reply, I dug my heels into my horse and we were in full gallop toward the village.

Thomas hopped on his horse, chasing his betrothed. Had his target been anyone else, he had easily caught up. But I had always been a better equestrian. Every gain he thought he'd made racing through the countryside; I'd advance as well. He chased me to the steps of the castle, where I abandoned my horse at the gate and stormed through the manor's cool stone corridors.

His long legged stride helped him catch up in the foot race. I was shoving the heavy wooden doors of the King's private chamber open when Thomas reached my hand. The king and several advisors were surprised by the intrusion. "Get Out!" I ordered. "All of you, I require a moment with my father."

The high priest leaned toward General Frederick Belcher's ear. "She must have heard the news."

"Defiant at every turn. Thomas will have his hands full once he is king." My future father-in-law smirked settling his hands atop his belt. "But hardheaded women birth boys who turn into strong fighting men. This pairing is sure to leave us a hearty heir and a general or two to lead our armies."

The king gave a weary smile that without word, vacated the room.

The men cleared as the attendant struggled to pull the heavy wooden doors closed behind him. I couldn't help but notice, how much heavier they seemed to the servant. Anger can make you do some pretty remarkable things I noted as I looked down at my tiny arms, impressed with what I had done.

"I am guessing this visit has to do with the news of your betrothal?" My father greeted with an unreciprocated hug and kiss on the cheek.

"How could you just decide something so very important about my life, and I not even be privy to the conversation?"

I tried to mask my hurt with anger, but my king saw straight through me.

"My dear." He took my arm as I guide his aging body to a chair in the corner. "This was something that was decided long ago. When you were first born, and the midwife said, 'It's a girl,' again." He paused trying to not sound disappointed. God had blessed him with four, healthy, beautiful daughters, but no sons to succeed his throne. "In that moment I had to secure our future, our lineage." He consoled, "Frederick was my childhood friend, my most trusted advisor, it was time his service and allegiance be rewarded. Your sisters had all had marriages arranged to secure alliances and territory. Your marriage was meant to secure our legacy. It was what needed to be done. That is why I ensured you grew up together. The reason I assigned Thomas as your guard all those years ago, so you would have plenty of time to open your heart to him."

"I do love him Your Grace." I answered staring at the floor. A little lost in the readiness of his reasoning, irritated by his ability to calm my rage.

"Then why the discord?" He tipped my chin up with his index finger.

I shook away the limpidness and challenged, "Because Father, you didn't even ask my opinion. You gathered in a room. Probably this room with a bunch of men and decided my life! Without a second thought as to what I may think of it." Proud of my tongue lashing, I continued. "How am I to rul-"

The frail grey man roared, reminding me he was still very much my king. "Let me be clear. You will be crowned queen, but you will not rule." As the words rolled off his tongue, he realized the lashing as I recoiled. His tone softened. "I am sorry my daughter. You are very much a leader to your people. I am proud of how you've developed your skill with blade and bow. You have a kindness about you that is lost on no man or beast, but at the end of the day, you are a woman; the kings of the other realms will not respect you. I could not bear to leave you in such a vulnerable position; men will not follow a leader they perceive as weak, strikes will be made against you."

"And that will be their undoing." I countered. "This is my land, my people. I will defend her to the death if needed."

"I haven't any doubt, my dear, but you will do so with Thomas as your King." The finality of his words pierced my heart. My argument carried no weight.

"Father -" I reached for one last plea.

"It is the will and order of your king!" he finalized.

"And so it shall be done." I bowed in defeat. I turned to exit. Thomas was standing in front of the doors, quietly observing. I was lost in such a rage I hadn't even noticed him. "What are you doing here?" I snarled, as he opened the door.

"I was hoping to explain." he softly answered.

No words he could say would be right. My blood boiled as I snarled, "Explain what? How everyone has a say how I am to live, except for me. How it's 'decided', and I have to stomach it."

Thomas grew agitated as I stomped the halls. He hastened his step to keep my pace. He snatched me by the upper arm, pushing me into the corridor wall. The cold stone bit at my shoulder blades as it pushed through my layers of dress. "You are acting like a spoiled brat! That 'I'm the princess, do as I say' monster who makes everyone miserable if she doesn't have her way!" He dropped his hand holding my waist. I found myself lost in his sea of green as his lips inched closer. Gravitating to the freckle of brown, anchoring my gaze to his. His lips brush against mine as he whispers, "This is what you want. What we want. Why can't you, just for once -"

I couldn't resist him any longer. I dove in to his lips, sliding my hand around the back his neck, pulling his mouth tightly in to mine. A clumsy mess of tongues and teeth crashing about, Thomas leaned against me, sandwiching me between his firm body and the stone, I could feel his bulge tremor as he pressed against my leg.

"You were always exemplary at breaking nags dear brother." Phillip smirked as he intruded.

An embarrassed caught feeling washed over me as I pushed Thomas off. I anxiously brushed the skirt of my dress flat in an attempt to repair a dis-shelved feeling.

It was hard to tell if Thomas was defending his betrothed or annoyed by the intrusion as he jumped his brother. "She is your future Queen and I your King, you shall address us as such."

Phillip playfully dismissed. "I highly doubt it."

Before Thomas could explode, I defended to my own surprise. "His honesty is refreshing Thomas. Just like you with I. Someone to be both loving, yet bold enough to tell us -"

"When your a down right pain in the ass." Phillip chimed in.

I shot daggers. "Thank you Phillip." I acknowledge through clenched teeth. "To put it simply, yes." Adding, "But someone, who knows your heart. Has seen you at your best. Your worst. Someone who keeps you grounded, in all the chaos and stress that title and duty provide."

Phillip playfully smiled adding, "Someone with years of experience navigating through your complete and total ability to be a pain in the ass."

Thomas puffed his chest, "Do not speak to her like that."

"Just a joke little brother." Phillip mimicked the movement.

I stepped between them. "I haven't the time to witness the next in an endless list of Belcher brother fights. That aren't really fights at all. More just like rolling around on the ground until Phillip pins you forcing you to yield, because neither of you is really going to hit, much less kill the other." I rolled my eyes. "Just let it go." I slid under Thomas' arm, falling into the crook of his chest and kissed his cheek.

"As you wish beloved." He pulled my hand to his lips leaving a tender kiss that radiated thought my veins.

Phillip rolled his eyes, "Quite the diplomat," sighing with disgust. "I beg your pardon My Lady, I must take my leave." He poked Thomas in the ribs as he walked past adding, "Before I wretch." Thomas angrily swatted his brother's hand away.

I couldn't help but smile. Even after all these years, they were still the same silly boys from what seemed like an eternity ago. It was comforting to know that steadfast Thomas and his dutiful Phillip would be by my side through and through.

Thomas laced his fingers through mine as he led me through the manor, back to our unattended horses. The world and time fell away, where he led, I floated. All I could see was him; there was never any choice about it, my heart had belonged to him for as long as I could remember. In actuality, betrothal to Thomas was not only anticipated but desired. Desperately. I had only protested to the marriage on principal.

My three older sisters had all had their marriages 'decided' for them. All three of them honored their father, and served their king's will without hesitation. All three of them have also had the life sucked from them.

My oldest sister, Rose, reminded me, "A woman's happiness is of no consequence for such arrangements of our station. We are regarded slightly above cattle; nothing more than a bargaining chip amongst men to secure title and land. The notion of true love is a thing of naivety dear sister." when I asked if she were excited as she dressed for her impending nuptials. I could feel the etch her jadedness left on my heart as the memory played.

The closest thing to happy any of my sister's had, was Dahlia with Phillip. She had always been infatuated with him, and he was more than happy to marry for land and title and to appease his king. They seemed happy for a little while, but it had been ten years and still no heir.

My sister's pain radiated off the pages of her tear streaked letters. She rarely came home anymore. Citing her duty in Phillip's absence, but I knew it was because she couldn't bare to face our father. Our king was never one to contain his disappointment.

I had never paid much attention to the idle talk that seemed to buzz the manor like locust. Mainly because it was always untrue and primarily about me; but when I heard Phillip's name paired with Olivia, a servant girl, my interest piqued.

Aside from drinking heavier than I was used to seeing, Phillip seemed his normal self at the feast. Olivia lingered a little longer than needed as she filled his plate. I watched him, watch her as he found the bottom of his glass time after time. When she disappeared behind the tapestry and down the corridor, I noticed as Phillip discreetly followed.

I tailed him, though I'm not sure why. I knew what I'd find. Phillip with his pecker buried deep under her dress. I had already made the decision, no matter what I found, I would not to tell Dahlia. Not because of Phillip's caught plea. Not because he was my promised's brother. Or the fact he was one of my truest friends, a trusted advisor, a relationship I couldn't afford to strain. None of that mattered. I chose not to tell my sister for the news would only break her. Her knowing would change nothing and only cause her pain. It was pointless, and Phillip was a far better husband than either of my other sisters had. As disgusted as I was with him in that moment, I knew there were far worse men out there.

"HEY! MS. DAISY. WAKE THE fuck up!" Kennedy shoved me awake as my eyes fluttered open. The new garage door still threw me off, but I was in my driveway. I must have slept the whole ride home. "And what's with that goofy look on your face?"

I arched my back, stretching my shoulders and gathered my belongings. As I exited the car I shoved her back, "What's with the goofy look on your face. Oh wait, that's just your face." and spat my tongue out. I kissed her cheek goodnight.

Kennedy hollered out the window as I approached the door, "Call me."

I waved her off as I slid the key, turned the latch and fell heavy through the door. I pinball down the hall in a sleepy haze, floating between then and now. I was back in the dream before my head hit the pillow.

CHAPTER 35
Charlotte England 1400

DAWN'S LIGHT SPILLED THROUGH THE window as I filled my satchel with bread, apples and goat's cheese.

The wooden door creaked, "Is My Lady off for the day?" I was caught by my confidante Eve. We were close in age, friends even, but somewhere along the line title and station delegated she was forced to tend to the house while I was free to do as I please.

That was the thing I never quite grasped about station, how we could be born and raised in the same home, feed from the same wet nurse, yet she was the servant and I was the served. My father tried to explain it once in the terms of family. "We feed, house and protect and in trade they help where they are best suited." But he was trumped when I questioned the massive disparity between quarters and clothing. It was not by any means a fair trade, an injustice I would fixate on and would make priority once I was Queen.

I leaned against the butcher's block where she peeled potatoes, "Yes Eve, my daily ride and lessons." Trying to mask my perturbed tone by nibbling on a corner of bread. I was on high alert as house chatter had been unyielding since my marriage announcement.

Eve stared me down questioning while potato and knife still in hand, "With Thomas I presume?"

I blushed and straightened as I snapped. "Yes, with Thomas. He is my guard after all."

She smirked and turned her eyes to her potatoes.

I fumbled my bag, spilling its contents. "I really don't like being the topic of idle gossip, especially in regards to Thomas." I meant to sound more scolding as I re-bagged my lunch.

"Not sure what to tell you My Lady," She continued peeling, "that's what servants do." She looked up, "Gossip of those they serve." She smiled at my annoyance. "And your and Thomas'," she paused searching for the appropriate word, "misadventures; are a favorite topic of discussion. You two are far more entertaining than all of your sisters combined."

"And what exactly do you mean by 'misadventures'?" I playfully disapprove, throwing a potato skin at her.

She fired me a look that screamed, 'Where to start?'

"Never mind." I broke the silence with a soft giggle as a laundry list tickered through my mind. "No need to start rattling off a list." I picked up my bag and kissed her cheek. "I'll be on my way then. Have a good day."

"You too My Lady." She returned to her infinite basket of potatoes.

I beamed with excitement as I raced up the hillside path, making my way to the stables. The ride was by far the peak of my day. Or was it besting one of the best swordsmen of the land, though no one would believe a woman could do such a thing. Or to just be away from the watchful eyes of the castle, away from the pressures of duty, the time and space to just be. Maybe it was a culmination of it all.

"You look like you have a million thoughts racing through your mind." Thomas greeted with a peck on the cheek, taking the satchel from my shoulder.

I smiled shaking my racing thoughts. "Just a little winded. Blasted kirtle squeezes the breath from me." I fidgeted and tugged at the binding cloth that heaved my bosom high and cinched my waist taught.

Thomas politely offered his hand as I mounted the chestnut horse without his aide. He smile expecting no less as he mounted and we started our trot through the country side. The emerald hills rolled to the north until they butted up against the dense forest of the west.

We rode toward the hills till we reached the ruins of an old stone cottage a few hours ride from the village. The once straw roof was long gone, one of the walls had eroded over the years and the three remaining had crumbled to different heights.

Rumor was it belonged to the hermit midwife who helped birth me. She had fallen ill and passed away when I was a young girl. With no one to take over, the cottage deteriorated but even in it's current state, it felt more like home to me than the suffocating manor walls.

Thomas pulled water from the well and filled the trough he had built a while back, the horses grazed, and I unpacked my satchel, spreading a blanket under the large Oak.

"So Highness, what shall we practice today?" He proposed.

I laid on the blanket savoring the sun's warmth. "Can we just take a moment? Enjoy a bit of this beautiful day first?"

"As you wish." He laid under the warm sun next to me.

We watched the soft white clouds roll past, cuddled on the blanket. I turned my head to my betrothed, lost in him; those emerald eyes and strong brow, reached right through me, wrapping round my heart. The freckle of brown in the pool of green pulled me in. I tenderly ran my thumb along his strong jaw.

He broke first, shamelessly plunging in to my mouth. His strong hand placed at the small of my back held me in tight, guiding us up to our knees. My soft bosom heaved over the top of my gown, pressed in to his chiseled chest as he stole the breath from me. He ran his fingers through my hair, I exhaled a soft moan as he firmly tugged my head back exposing my throat to the world and mapped the length of my neck with soft nibbles and firm kisses, gently guiding me back to the ground. He tastes my neck and shoulders, his hand finds its way up my thigh and under my dress, his kiss glided to my mouth. A gravely groan of desire rumbled from his throat as his calloused hand firmly groped my bare buttock. My eyes fluttered apart, noticing the fluffy white clouds starting to grey.

I darted up concerned, our premarital rendezvous screeching to a halt. "Do you smell smoke?"

Not to be distracted, Thomas continued nibbling at my neck. "No." sliding his hand further up my inner thigh.

I pushed him off me and stood up as I pointed. "Seriously, look at the clouds."

Irritated he stood to appease his princess. He rolled his eyes up to toward the clouds. The clouds to the west were soft and white like sheep's wool. The clouds from the east grew blacker by the second. Disbelief roared from his lungs as he pieced it together. "The village!"

We raced home, leaving behind the remnants of our perfect day. Our fears realized the nearer we drew, the panic and screams of our people, smoke thick in the air, fires ablaze. We were under attack.

Pushing our horses as hard as we could, Thomas hollered over the thumping of eight hooves pounding the earth beneath them. "Stay close Charlotte." He ordered. "Have your sword ready. The blade strapped to your thigh, get it into your belt as soon as you can. And if you must fight, do not pull the blade from their body, till you see the life leave their eyes!"

The closer our racing horses drew, the further away I felt. Helpless seconds passed feeling eternal.

Our gallop seized at the first sight of people, shouting instruction and comforting those whose path I crossed. Flame and blood coated our normally serene landscape. Our people scattered and terrified. The Northmen breathed chaos as if it fed their soul. Wide eyed they feverishly swung sword and ax, some used bow and arrow to mow down those who fled.

Everything around me blurred; the sight of a toddler covered in blood and soot stole my focus. His tear stained face pained as he tried to shake his mother's lifeless body awake.

Blood pumped heavy through my veins as I watch the scene around me. My vision went red and everything except my enemy faded from sight. The sounds of havoc deafen. Hot copper and dirt filled my breath, all Thomas had taught me flowed effortlessly through my body.

Time slowed to a snail's pace but my body moved at a inhuman speed, like the fabled jungle cats from exotic lands far away. I plunged my sword through three Northmen and their woman archer before any thought crossed my mind. A splash of hot coppery blood sprays across my face as I pull the long steel blade from the archer's belly, crimson ribbons trickle down my arm. The motions of my training paired with an indescribable ferocious instinct was more freeing than I had anticipated.

For the first time ever, I felt at home in my own skin. I felt alive, a glimpse of who I am meant to be. I summon the beast from the depths of my belly, unleashing a righteous roar, claiming my place amongst my men.

A tiny terrorized shriek pulls my attention to a line of unburnt shacks. Two guardsmen keep my pace as we kick in doors, manically searching for the plea. With each empty dwelling precious seconds are lost and visions of what could be shatter my soul and hasten my pace.

One last scream begging for help and tugging the strings of my heart confirms her location; I slam the whole of my body against the door and pry the disgusting brute off the eight year old. His lifetime of sin played across my mind's eye as I shoved my sword through his side, feeling his ribs splinter under the force of the blade and piercing his heart.

As the monster fell limp to the ground, the tear stained eight year old, tightly gripped my waist and I wrapped my arms around her, protectively pulling in; her panic melted in to relief as she sobbed into the waist of my blood stained gown. I could only focus on the rip at the shoulder of her dress, images of what could have been violently loop through my mind, rattling me to my core. I drop to her eye level, hugging her tight. "You're safe now." Her sobs start to soothe. I tuck her loose hair behind her ear and lock onto her hot, red, pale blue eyes. "Stay here, out of sight." I turned to exit, but in her fear, she refused to let me go. "I will not let anything happen to you." I promised as I cupped her soot and tear streaked face. "Now, out of sight."

I carefully exit the straw house as Thomas and Phillip lead the charge, chasing the last of our attackers off. It was over. The demons of the North were dead or fleeing and our home was safe, for now.

Covered head to toe in blood and soot, I collapsed on the step, my corseted bosom heaved as I gasped for breath. My sword fell from my hand, the clang of the steel jangled on the stone path echoing through the eery silence. No matter how frequently I trained there was no preparing for the heat of battle, or the crash when it was over. I was no where near as prepared as I had thought. Something I hadn't the time to worry on. My eyes scanned the village, assessing the chaos. I rise to my feet and order, "We need buckets. Water. Get the fires out!"

CHAPTER 36
Charlotte England 1400

THE SMOKE PLUMED THROUGH OUR devastated home as we aide the injured and collect our dead. Thomas was jarred while Phillip impressed by my order to spike and line our village's edge with the heads of our fallen foe. I needn't my advisors to know that the blood of one's enemy was the best marker of territory.

Street by street, home by home, Thomas, Phillip and I assess the damage of the day. I returned to the castle steps and crash in to the cold cobbles, defeated by exhaustion.

The blood of our attackers coat my skin and clothes, though I hadn't noticed, I was numb. Thomas helped me to my feet, coaxing me to the grand hall.

Phillip praised, "You did well today Princess. I am proud to serve you."

I was unable to speak or even acknowledge the compliment. The grief of the day weighed too heavy. The men guided me to my chambers, and sent for Eve.

She washed the stains of battle from my skin and dressed me in fresh garments.

A hot bath and clean clothes returned my senses as I stomped down the hall with righteous urgency. A wave of unbridled clarity vibrated through me as I burst through the heavy wooden doors of the throne room where my father and his advisers were fully immersed in strategy and combat plans.

"She is terrifying with a blade. The fact that she is a woman, does not negate the fact that she is a better warrior than most our men." Phillip passionately defended. "She has proven a worthy ruler and it is only where she lead that I will follow."

"Thank you, Phillip." I graciously accepted making my presence known. All the men fell to their knee in acknowledgment. I approached Phillip and Thomas, having them rise and smiled. "I had excellent tutors."

The rest of the men returned to their feet. General Belcher returned to business at hand, "I beg your pardon My Lady, but a woman, the princess no less, has no business on the battle field. I understand needing to protect yourself-"

"You are absolutely right." I interrupted. "A spoiled princess has no cause for battle but a queen, leads by example. Protecting her land, her people, side-by-side with the men who risk their lives for her. The Northmen had women warriors, I know, I shoved my blade through one of their archer's kidney. What is between my legs does not determine for what I am suited and it'd be foolish to dismiss me due to some silly notion of a woman's duty. Our enemy does not see any difference between man or woman, whether it be who wields a weapon or who parishes from it. We should be preparing our people as such. It is crippling and stupid and dangerous that half of our community is unable to protect themselves. It's bad math, and while I am no strategist, I know enough to know more is better than less. Starting tomorrow, I want those women who wish to learn, taught the skills of weaponry." My tone sharp and unyielding.

"I apologize My Lady. I do not think it proper for you to be in battle. Thomas should have never let -"

I interrupted the General again. "Forgive me Sir, but I am the Princess. Thomas does not let me do anything and it does not matter what you find proper. The opinion of my king is the only one I mind."

"Your Grace." He addressed my father. "You can not possibly believe that -"

The king raised his hand. "My daughter has always professed her desire to serve; that she would defend her land, her title, and her people with her last breath. She leads with strength and kindness. Admirable traits many other nobles lack themselves."

There was no veil to the disgust that washed over the General.

"And she is adored by the people for it." My father finalized. "She has proven herself. At the request of your sons, she will rule as Queen."

I tried to ease the situation. "Our dear Frederick, I am not wanting to lead armies or coordinate battles. I fully plan to leave that in your capable hands. But if someone knocks on my door looking for a fight, they leave will leave in shambles if they are fortunate enough to walk away at all." I reached for his hand.

"Apologies Highness." The withered old man offered. "I have a hard time seeing you as more than the little girl who I was sworn to protect."

"I understand my friend," I kissed his cheek, "and I know I make it a difficult task." I gently cradled his face looking into his battle worn eyes. "Please trust in the lessons you and my father," my tone kind and gentle as I took a step back, "and your sons, have instilled in me." I turned, pleading yet firm. "I understand there is a very real, very violent world of war out there. I have no intent to seek it out, but I also have a firm understanding of the severity of our situation. An aging king, the next in line by marriage not birth, a land without an undisputed male heir. Anyone can march into these lands and try to take what has been my family's for a century. That is something I simply will not allow."

My father beamed with pride. His thoughts almost audible; *Graceful, compassionate. Nurturing. Firm, unwavering. She listens to her advisors, takes the information for what it is and forms her own decision. She is a far better leader than I could have ever hoped to have been.* He couldn't contain his smile as he watched the future fall in to place.

CHAPTER 37
Charlie Modern Day

BROKEN FRAGMENTS OF LAST NIGHT'S dream disappeared as the disapproving sun shone bright on my face forcing me from my bed by seven thirty in the morning. I examined my hands for blood unconsciously ensuring it had only been a dream for my body ached as if I had actually been to war.

The Charlotte of Medieval England was younger than I now, but knew the strength of her voice and was willing to fight for the people she loved; while I was just discovering mine and learning how to fight for myself. It was inspiring and upsetting. The regret of should have been, could have been started to churn in my soul as the painful realization that I had never become the fully formed woman I was meant to be settled in my heart.

Gypsy pounced on my uterus from her window sill perch unapologetically interrupting my self reflection. The calico screamed in my face. I heard "Feed Me Bitch!" between bellowing meows.

She arched her back as I scratched her hind end. "Hungry?"

Before I could finish the question, she darted down the hall to her bowl in the kitchen. I pulled a sweatshirt over my camisole and threw my hair up in a sloppy bun. Gypsy's howls grew louder and more frequent. "Hurry you useless human."

"Shut up!" I hollered down the hall. "I'm coming."

Gypsy purred and cooed as she gobbled her overly priced, all natural, nutritionally balance, sensitive stomach, hairball control, blah, blah, blah. "Spoiled rotten." I scolded, knowing full well it was my own doing. It was obvious who was in charge around here as she wiggled with snotty pleasure cleaning her plate.

I rolled my eyes walking past the orange and black brat as I pulled my wooden stash box from the cabinet, plopped on to my couch and hunch over my coffee table. Gypsy head butted my ankles while I rolled a joint. She followed me through the sliding glass door, escorting me to the patio. I kicked my feet up in my chaise and lit the herbal cigarette and she stalked gnats.

"What do you suppose we do with ourselves today Gyps?" I asked puffing on my hand rolled cigarette. She had turned her attention to a gnarly spider in the apple tree that had petrified me for a good week now. "Have fun with that." I coached. Lord knows I wasn't going anywhere near that eight legged monster and heaven forbid it actually make its in the house, or my studio. The thought sent a shudder down my spine.

Working myself into a fit of hysterics, I was convinced thwarts of spiders had taken residency in my studio over the last ten hours. I cautiously turned the knob of my tiny cottage, pushing the door open with one foot, armed with broom in hand, swatting the air feverishly. I flipped the light switch and opened the curtains. No spiders. Not even a cob web. "It exhausting being crazy." I told Gypsy as she perched herself in the window's sill.

I had spun myself into a sizable anxiety attack, which weirdly enough produced some of my best work. As spiders engulfing my workspace flooded my thoughts, paint spread across the canvas effortlessly. My thoughts drifted to a far away land as shapes took form across the canvas.

CHAPTER 38
Charlotte England 1400

My belly had swollen with the moon through seven cycles. I begrudgingly gave up my daily rides some weeks ago after a heated, drawn out debate with my father and husband. The thought of mounting a horse now seemed like an awful joke as I waddled through the rows of straw booths, fetching fabrics and eggs and chatting with the villagers. Sewing and cooking were a refreshing change of pace, but I quickly grew bored harbored within these castle walls.

The summer day came and went while the heat and mugginess held it's way well into the night. I tossed and turned trying to find comfort. With the ever growing baby adding to the already uncomfortable heat, I gave up on any idea of sleep. I pulled a linen shift over my naked body and leaned out the window, wafting the sheer sheet of fabric, a last stitch effort to create the illusion of a breeze.

The oversized moon grabbed hold of me. I had never seen the her in such a way. The largest she'd ever been. I reached out, thinking I may touch her. Shades of blood and amber, she was on fire hanging in the night's sky. It was beautiful and terrifying. Enchanted by her pull, I watched as she crossed the night sky, till she sank below the western hills. Her lover, the sun, rose in the east, chasing away the darkness in which she shines. His radiant rays fed her soul and she mirrored his devotion. Such as their curse, a love of beautiful ruin. For only brief moments in time, may they share the same sky.

Thomas wrapped his arms around my embarrassingly large waist, cradling his son through my belly and kissed my exposed shoulder. "Did you sleep?"

"No." I dreamily replied, my gaze glued to the horizon. "I watched the moon."

Thomas interrupted. "All night?"

"She was beautiful." I softly continued. "and frightening." I turned to my husband.

He smiled playfully offering, "Like you beloved," as he dotingly kissed my temple.

I shook away my dazed state. Playfully pushing my husband away. "Sod off." I smiled from the corner of my mouth. With the next breath, a wave of paralyzing fear flooded my body.

Thomas felt my body tense. "What is it my love?"

He sits next to me, rubbing the small of my back trying to be of comfort. I stare through him as the barrier between yesterday and tomorrow blur and I feel heartache and destruction unfold. My eyes well with tears. "I don't know." My voice trembled with panic, "Everything is black, I taste smoke, smell death. and the pain, so much pain." I sob between labored breaths grasping my chest. Thomas protectively cups my face as tears stream down my cheeks. His stormy concerned eyes bring me back to today. "What's happening?"

He searched my fearful eyes, trying to find the answer. Something, anything, that would make me feel better. "I don't know," fell from his lips. He squeezed me tight and stroked my hair as I uncontrollably sob. In his attempt at comfort, he blurted the first thing that came to mind. "A warning maybe?"

I sniffled in his chest. "Some warning."

Thomas broke the embrace and tilted my head up forcing me to be lost in his calming sea of green. With one look, he could tell me everything I needed to hear. Whatever life threw our way, as long as I could find my way back to those eyes, everything would be alright.

CHAPTER 39
Charlotte England 1400

I WADDLED TO THE END of the hall and Thomas guided me down the stone steps. In the last week or so my belly had grown so large I had lost sight of my feet. I laid in bed sobbing for hours the day I noticed. I felt ridiculous, weak, uncomfortable, and foreign in my own skin. I hated every minute of it. So much so, I begged the midwife to "Cut this thing out of me."

Her calm was infuriating as she cooly replied, "He'll come when he's ready."

I had been pouting for days. The thought of being left behind while Thomas and Phillip hunted boar flared up the stir crazy that months of being trapped within these manor's impermeable walls had brewed. I missed my bow terribly and couldn't even remember the last time I had picked up a sword, but I bit my tongue and made the trek to the stables to dutifully see my husband off and prove a moderate distraction while he readied his horse.

Everything was familiar, but not, as I accompanied Thomas and Phillip to the village's edge. Words that were spoken. The way the wind danced through the trees and horse's mane. The smells. All of it was unsettling. I kissed Phillip's cheek for luck as I had a hundred times before, but today, as soon as my lips grazed his skin, my heart flipped upside down and my stomach twisted in knots. Thomas leaned in to kiss me one last time before mounting his horse. When our lips touched fear and panic washed over my body, paralyzing me.

Tears streamed down my cheeks as I choked. "Something isn't right, please don't go."

Thomas thumbed my tears away. "All will be fine beloved. I shan't be gone long." He tried to comfort, kissing my forehead.

"Please, don't go." I pleaded with hot, red, wet eyes.

Miriam, the mid-wife, wrapped her arm around my shoulder. "Fret not Your Grace. I felt the same when I carried my children. Uncontrollable worry is part of it and once you birth that babe, it'll never truly go away."

Thomas appreciatively nodded to the old woman and mounted his horse. She cradled me as she guided me back to the manor. I looked over her shoulder back to my husband and mouthed, "I love you." His strong green eyes caught mine as he smiled, dug his heels into his horse's ribs and was gone.

Miriam's kind warmth soothed me as she steered me back to the castle. She sat with me for several hours, but I never could shake the feeling of panic. "Maybe some fresh air then? she suggested. "A stroll through the market will do you some good."

"Maybe." I answered between sniffles. The sadness and panic and fear were dizzying and driving me mad.

Her diagnosis was correct, the fresh air did me good. Calm found me as I strolled the village pathways. A small boy presented me with a bracelet of twine and yellow dandelion. I graciously accepted his gift, letting him slide it over my hand. He blushed when I complimented, "The King will be jealous, this trinket's beauty rivals all of our gemstone baubles."

I caught a glimpse of a man whom I had never seen before lurking in the trees. Blood streaked his face and his eyes were wild. I had seen men like this before. "Miriam, quickly, get the everyone to the manor! Call the guard! Hurry! Go!" I shooed.

"But My Lady-" she tried to question.

I roared. "Do as I say!" The first man I came across was a fisherman I had spoken to moments earlier. Manically I explain, "I just saw one of the Northmen scouts. We need to prepare for an attack. Who knows how far out or how many there are?" I briefed as we purposefully walked to his booth. "Do you have a spare sword or blade?" I asked.

"This is the best I have Your Grace." Offering his filet blade.

"It'll do," I accepted.

THE CALM, WARM, SKY WAS still and blue. The hunting party had stopped to break under My Queen's favorite tree near the crumbling cottage we lazed and trained for countless hours. I propped myself against the tree's trunk as I had done hundreds of times before and rested my eyes.

One of the riders commented on the grey clouds rolling in. "Maybe a summer shower." A second disagreed, stating it was too late in the season for a downpour.

I hadn't paid them any mind, until the winds shifted; I inhaled immediately identifying, "Smoke!" Phillip yelled before I could form the words. "Coming from the village!"

I was mounted and gone in one sweeping motion. My horse raced his hardest home sensing my urgency. My brother and a stampede of hooves pounded the earth behind me.

We arrived to the village engulfed in flame. Smoke filled the dizzying scene. The men left behind vehemently holding the line between the savages and the stone walls that protected those who could not fight.

"Charlotte." I scanned the scene, hoping she would not be so foolish, but knew her all too well to think she would be cowering behind our fortress' walls. When it came to her realm and those who fell under it's protective cloak, she had a blind, fearless, reckless regard for her safety or the baby she carried.

A wave of red washed over me. My heart felt her pull as my sword mechanically moved back and forth, side to side, plunging, stabbing, circling round, mowing down eight men who stood in my way. I shoved the heel of my boot into an invader's chest, freeing his corpse of my the blade as ribbons of crimson run down the hilt.

I paused for breath, scouring the havoc filled scene for any sign of my beloved. The wind pushed plumes of smoke through the street exposing Charlotte in the distance; swirling long blade over head. Her pregnant belly exposed, covered in filth and blood and soot. She plunged her blade in the stomach of her opponent, not pulling the blade from him to she saw the life leave his eyes. *That's my girl.* I shake the sentiment from my mind, racing to her aide as she wildly stabs and slashes at any Northman that stand in her path.

"Charlotte!" I hollered as loudly as my lungs would allow.

I KNEW HIS VOICE ANYWHERE, manically I searched till I caught his storming eyes and rush in to his arms. Thomas placed his hand on my belly, kissing me with in a blissful sign of relief. I could feel his fury. I had fought with child, so close to term no less, but he knew there was no use arguing, especially now. He grabbed my hand, dragging me to a hut that hadn't caught fire. "Stay here." He urged.

"But Thom-" I tried to rebut.

"Damn it Charlotte, do not argue with me, just stay here. Please." He forcefully ordered as his eyes begged. He pulled me in to his chest and tenderly pushed my chin up till my eyes met his, "I can not return to this battle and protect our home if I am distracted with worry for you and our son. Please, for once in your life, please don't fight me on this, please, just stay here."

I begrudgingly wavered. Had I not been with child I would have undoubtedly continued my campaign, but I knew it was far too dangerous. I was slower, less agile and extremely vulnerable. "Please be safe." I kissed his cheek.

I CAREFULLY EXIT THE DWELLING, ensuring my presence unnoticed, securing my Queen's position. The men battled on, an eternal flood of Northmen finally start to thin. My lungs filled with smoke and the coppery stench of death. The sounds of metal clashing and wood shields splintering masked the roars and cries of the battlefield.

In the distance I hear her shriek, "THOM-AS!" in two clear pained syllables.

"Charlotte." I fret, racing to the hut where I had left her. I burst through the door, finding a large brutish man with fresh claw marks streaming blood down his cheek, hovering atop my wife, pulling at her clothes as she rabidly slapped and punched and kicked her attacker away.

I FELT THE HEFT OF the man lift from me as Thomas grabbed the brute by the shoulder and plunged his sword through my attacker. The point of the blood soaked blade came clean through the man, making a small slit in my gown. Thomas pushed the dead Northman's body to the side. Lifting me to my feet, squeezing me tight as I melt in to his chest.

He unburied my chin forcing my gaze into his. Those eyes, those ever changing, stormy eyes that carried away my worst fears even in the middle of a war field. I knew it true, but he needed reassuring. "I'm fine," breaks the silence with a smile and kiss.

Thomas' lips crashed into my mouth as his tongue rolled against mine, I felt him violently ripped away. Three northmen burst through the hut's straw wall. I snatched up the dead attacker's sword, screaming wildly and swing the blade round. A severed head drops to ground and shortly behind, the body to go with as Thomas fights the other two off.

"Charlotte! Run!" He orders as he fends off the invaders.

Tears of paralyzed panic stream my face. "No, I can't -"

"Just go!" He pleaded.

He mustered a burst of strength with deep nasal breath, gaining advantage over one, coming from behind and using his sword's edge to slit the enemy's throat, releasing a spray of hot red blood into the air. The final brute's attention turned to me, his long ink and blood stained arms grabbing at me. I pulled the filet blade from my belt and sliced my attacker's hand. Thomas kicked his opponents body to the floor and advanced toward the man threatening his wife and child.

The two men battled vigorously as I watched, frozen in shock. They fought and ducked and dodged and evaded one another for what felt like hours, though mere minutes passed. Finally Thomas, maneuvered round the brute, plunging his sword between the man's shoulders forcing the northman to his knees before collapsing to the ground.

I rushed to my husband, squeezing him tight as I possibly could. He brushed the hair from my eyes and feverishly pressed his lips to mine. As we parted, I was lost in those eyes. "I love -"

Thomas was unable to finish. The warm stormy eyes I had loved all my life had lost their glisten and gone cold. I knew that look. Before I could finish my thought, I felt a warm sticky fluid running down my belly. Blood. I looked down at my hands. Hot, sticky, coppery blood covered me as Thomas fell to his knees.

His limp body crashed to the floor, I found the bleeding weakened northman had used the last of his energy to lodge a knife into Thomas' kidney.

A roar brews in my belly escaping my throat "NOOOOO!!!!!" Fury and shock hit me first, as an animalistic urge to protect rages through my veins. I pulled the knife from my husband's side and plunged it hilt deep in to the skull of his murderer.

Rushing to my husband's aide, I cradle him in my arms as he drew his last few breaths. His blood soaked hand reached up for my face, staining my cheek,. "Do not cry my love." He coughed blood, "I will see you again. I promise.", using his last breath to comfort me.

"Please, no. Stay with me." I begged, cradling his limp body into me.

I WAS SHOOK BACK IN to the present drenched in sweat and screaming. I swallowed air trying to catch my breath but the devastated feeling of loss crushed my heart. The canvas in front of me depicted the violent loss that played in my mind. Paint splattered across my clothes and skin reminded me of the blood and soot that covered me in the vision.

Rattled by the detail of the painting, I packed a fresh bowl of herb and puffed from my glass pipe as I closely examined the work. The leafy filigree on the hilt protruding from the Northman's head, gripped my stunned attention tightest.

CHAPTER 40
Charlie Modern Day

"WHY NOT? WE'RE ALREADY HERE." I caved to Kennedy's brow beating. We had already had mani/pedis and facials. Why not get a massage and hit the pampering trifecta? I know that's four things, but according to Kennedy, the nail combo counts as one and there was no arguing with that amazon, especially when she felt her logic sound.

I had a shitty night. I couldn't shake my latest vision and found a fresh painting in my studio that I had no memory of working. The image was haunting but the memory it was tied to ate at me.

On one hand I had seen all the potential, all the love I am capable of; capable of giving, capable of receiving. And on the other, I had to watch it all be destroyed. So here I am, ready to get the tension rubbed out. Compliments of Greyson Pierce, be known to him or not.

Kennedy jumped and clapped with glee. "Yay!" her dramatic excitement for everything makes her appear much younger than her forty-three years.

"Excuse me ladies." A tall, chiseled blonde, whom I could only assume was named Heidi or Hilda interrupted. "Your rooms are ready?"

"Our rooms? Are ready?" I questioned Kennedy with a sour look.

"Well yeah." She shrugged as she sipped her mimosa. "I made the reservation last night. Duh."

I scoffed rolling my eyes. "I should have known."

Kennedy drops her empty glass at the end table, grabs her Birkin, and heads toward the rooms. Blocking my path, she playfully whispered, "Yes, you should have." and kissed my cheek as if she were a mafia boss signing a death warrant.

She skips down the hall, bubbly as her champagne. Catching up to the attendant, "Is your name Heidi?" The thought to mouth ratio on Kennedy was dumbfounding. Any thought that pops into her meticulously blown out head flops from her lips before it's fully formed. Granted I found it humorous, but that's because I'm kind of an asshole. Those of a feather and what not.

"Actually it's Hilda." The leggy blonde corrected.

"Yeah. I figured something like that." Kennedy's long stride held the annoyed attendants pace.

I laughed watching the comedy in front of me unfold.

"My grandmother's name was Heidi." Hilda replied.

I stopped in my tracks while Kennedy twirled down the hall. I shook the coincidence away, following Hilda's path. Manic thoughts race through my mind. *Did I-? There's no way. I firmly brushed the thought away. I was just being a jackass. Swedish massage, Swedish names. Cliche, painfully obvious. I'm not psychic! Well, not in the hand reader for hire sense. Am I? God, I feel crazy. This is crazy making. You're not crazy. You have seen too many things to know it as anything but truth. It's just infrequently enough to make you feel crazy. Jesus, I sound fucking crazy.*

"We're here ladies." Hilda stopped and pointed. "Mrs. Pierce you're in this room. Mrs. Walker, you're two doors down."

"Ms. Bower." I corrected. I flushed not meaning to sound so harsh. I quickly backtracked, "I'm sorry. I didn't mean to-"

"No need." Hilda politely raised her hand, cutting me off. "Situations change."

Moments later the masseuse entered. After a short introductory and discussion on type of massage, noting any problem areas, "I hold a lot of stress in my shoulders." I informed as I disrobed and slid my naked body under the sheet.

The lights dimmed, and wind chimes and whales sounds filled the air. The masseuse started kneading. "Let it go. Let it melt away." She soothed as she buried her elbow under my shoulder blade.

With the soothing sounds of raindrops and wind chimes and knots being kneaded, I found myself slipping into fast heavy sleep. I opened my eyes and found myself on the dark cobble streets of sixteenth century Dublin. I walked the street I had never seen before with a sense of familiarity. For reason unknown, the candle lit street lamps rattled me straight to the bone.

I explored the quiet streets, trying to see or feel something familiar. Nothing, but I knew in my soul I had been here before. Why was this so familiar? Street lamps, cold cobbles. I felt my pupils widen, "The painting."

A sharp pinch at the back of my arm made me jump from my skin as I pulled the pieces together. "Allow me to escort you home miss." I looked into a familiar face. The heavy brown. The dark eyes. His deep voice vibrated in my ears long after the words were spoken, "There are ruffians about."

Something deep within me wanted to flea. I reluctantly accepted his arm as I struggled with the pit in my stomach and strolled the streets of what looked like Ireland some time during the Tudor King's reign.

We strolled and laughed our way through the empty corridors. I sip from his flask as I tell the Englishman tales of old Irish lore, the constellations and moon. The moment feels perfect, fated.

Maybe it was the moon, or the whiskey, but I couldn't help myself, I thew my arm around his neck and pulled his lips in to mine. I sighed a lustful smile as I shoved my tongue in his mouth, running my fingers through his long dark tangled locks.

He slammed my body into the stone wall, making my head bounce. I rubbed where it hit and smiled as I bit his bottom lip.

My eyes met his large dark gaze. My lust turned to fear as strong his hand pressed from my breast up my chest and wrapped around my throat.

"You little cunt." His fingers tightening around my thin neck.

"You think you can steal from me?" His nails dig behind my ear, breaking the skin. "You think I wouldn't notice!"

"Mrs. Walker. Time to wake up." I heard a female voice and light tapping on my shoulder. "Mrs. Walker -"

"Thank you very much." I sat up. "That was amazing." I was more tense now than an hour ago.

The masseuse exited the room and I wrapped the oversized cotton robe around me. What, the fuck, was that? I slid my feet into the hideous spa shoes. Dreams and visions were nothing new. But this, this was different. This left an awful pit in the bottom of my stomach. I knew this story did not end well.

As the hot water overhead rinsed the massage oils down my body, I obsessed over the remnants of my dream. Trying to pull together as many details as I could remember. I was tangled in a web of thought as I dressed and brushed my hair.

It can't be a new dream? A different life? Can it? Geez, how many are there?

"How was your massage?"

I heard someone ask something, but I was was stuck on a train that had no brakes. How does this tie to the painting?

"Charlie?"

Some sort of warning?

"Charlotte!" I heard Kennedy that time.

I shook myself to life in front of me. "Sorry, it was great, really relaxed." I lied.

Kennedy read my face, and didn't buy it. "You okay? You've been out of it lately."

I see ghosts. Have visions. There's this guy, with these amazing eyes. And he totally haunts my dreams. Most days I feel certifiably crazy. On top of that I just got divorced. Not that it's not what I wanted, but doesn't make it any less devastating or heartbreaking. Yeah, I'm fucking aces.

I smiled at her concern. "I'm fine. Just need some B12."

I knew she knew I lied by the way she crossed her arms and turned the corner of her mouth. She was taking a mental note. "Mmm Kay." I would bet money she was filing this encounter away for her and Dahlia's next intervention.

I fixated on that blasted dream the whole way home. The visions had me thinking. Mainly because they were all I could think about, to an unhealthy degree. But I was taking away lessons of the past. Nothing in this life is random. Some way, some how, we always find our way back to each other. Fate has a way of changing your circumstance so all the right people cross your path, in the moment they are meant to, guide you to the person you are meant to be. It all has to mean something, right? If not, that means that the opposite is true; and I really am sick, in desperate need of anti psychotic meds and psychiatric help. So it has to be real, it has to mean something.

I was dizzy.

"Don't scrunch your forehead like that." Kennedy mothered while singing off key with the radio. "You'll get wrinkles."

CHAPTER 41
Charlie Modern Day

HAZY SNIPPETS OF FOREIGN LANDS and times long past flowed from one into the other as I tossed and turned. Scattered scenes and lives, but always the same familiar green eyes. I never feared my darkness, because the light in him chased my demons away. We were both irreparably damaged, but the shattered pieces of my heart wove a beautiful mosaic with his brokenness.

The dreamy fog faded, exposing cobble streets of Tudor controlled Dublin bustling under the morning sun. It was a stark contrast to the nighttime alleyways of my vision, where the candles glowed gently atop their posts illuminating the dark stone road. A thick slime coats the dark damp air, only the unsavory were about at that hour.

AS A YOUNG GIRL I learned how cruel and uncaring men can be. My father sold me into servitude at the age of nine, just days after my mother passed. The tavern owner showed pity on a terrified little girl and feeling a kindred soul, took me in as his own.

While all his girls were spared the violence that comes with the prostitution, I didn't have to sell myself. He grew to become more of a father than the one who sired me. While one fed me to the wolves, the other shielded me from the dangers of this world. I spent the next six years bussing dishes and fighting off the advances of the drunken patrons. Being raised in a whore house; I understood sex and commerce better than I could read. I knew a woman's worth was directly dependent on what she demanded. Most men thought a woman's body her only contribution, but if used properly, they are our best asset. Sex can be empty and meaningless yet still enjoyable and most definitely profitable. I just didn't see the point unless you intended to wrap your soul around the other person.

"So when is Thomas going to come take you out proper?" A crimson haired beauty asked as she hoisted her porcelain freckled bosom up and cinched her corset.

"Oh Eve, I doubt he ever will." I swooned, rolling my eyes as I flung hopelessly across her bed and buried my face in the pillow.

"Why? It's not like your a whore." She giggled. "Not that it matters, much, I've had more marriage proposals than I care to count."

I propped myself up to my elbows. "So why are you still here?"

Eve was quick and matter-of-fact in her response. "Because, if I am to give up my life, my freedom, and trade that for a life of subserviency," She waived her hairbrush punctuating her point, "You best believe it won't be for any Doyle, Duff or Shamus that walks through that door. I reckon more like the type of bloke you're holding on to that virginity for."

I shrugged in agreement.

Eve gave herself one last gander in the mirror. "Well, we best be headed downstairs before Phillip starts hollerin'."

Skipping down the stairs, I stomp the last step, catching Phillip's disapproving eye. I could hear him now, 'Could you at least act like a grown woman?' I couldn't, not tonight, playful innocence danced through me, the air tingled with the full moon. Pixie blood must run through my veins.

It seemed a lifetime ago, being shoved through those doors on that freezing night. The night my life was forever changed, but nights like tonight, the memory ran fresh as yesterday.

The lean, scraggly blonde boy was slightly older than I when he eagerly introduced, "Hi! I'm Thomas, this is my sister Dahlia." Even then, I could see the chiseled jaw that lie under his round cheeks. "Who are you?" He questioned as his glassy green eyes seared my heart the moment I laid eyes on him. I knew right then that he would to play a huge part in my life.

I had been with Phillip less than a year before I realized Dahlia was a wind, breezing in and out of our lives. He didn't seem to mind his wife disappearing for months on end having had the time to know her soul. My heart was ripped from my chest and the breath stolen from me the first time she left, grievous injuries I never quite recovered from.

She couldn't bare the stink of the air or the incessant noise of the city. "I can't feel the earth beneath my feet or hear the leaves dance on the wind." I recalled her saying when I caught her slipping in to the night. "I can't live with all this cold hard stone. I need to be amongst the moss and tress where only in deafening silence can the voices of prophecy be heard."

When I repeated the message to Thomas and Phillip I was shocked by their non-surprise. "She was never meant for the crowdedness of village life, she craves the solitude that only nature can provide." Phillip offered.

"One of the faire folk." Thomas added.

I sat wide mouthed to their non reaction. Phillip comforted, "No need to worry, this is not the last we'll see of her."

And he was right, she always found her way home. She'd stay a few weeks at a time and appeared as if by magic mere hours before the first time I bled. She stayed with me the entire spring educating me on life and womanhood. "I can't imagine what you've been told by those girls." she berated.

It broke my heart every time she left. Each time more so than the last. More than it broke my heart when my mother died. More than when my father dumped me at the tavern to fend for myself. The void of her presence pained me.

"Chin up, our tale has many years of entwining." She foreshadowed, "You and Thomas have a destiny about ya and when it plays out, I will be there." She kissed my cheek, one last motherly comfort before disappearing into the night.

CHAPTER 42
Charlotte Ireland 1530

THOMAS' BODY GREW, FILLING OUT to an impressive degree. His arms bulged as he swung the long blade over head. His interest in sword play started from a laughable to an embarrassing degree hobby to something he was fairly proficient in. When the blacksmith offered lessons in exchange for labor, he found it a smart trade and shortly thereafter, his education began.

I would sneak away from the tavern and spy as he trained. My eyes glued to the movement of his chiseled torso. His strong jaw looked much more protruding with sweat, ash and dirt smudged across it. His muscles would flex and gleam as he hammered the red hot metal and when he used his wrist to push his wayward locks from his glistening brow, I lost all my sense and was left a trembling pile of mush.

"Whiskey please." He ordered as he swung his leg over a wooden stool. I poured the drink and set it in front of him, he grasped my hand before I could release the glass. His molten gaze caught mine forcing a begrudged smile to form in the corner of my mouth. "One of these days I'm going to have enough money saved to take us away from here."

"Is that so?" I played, "And exactly what would we do?"

"Farm goats." He answered as if he has spent countless nights thinking of it.

"Farm goats?" I grilled. "Because you know so much of goats or farming, all those hours spent behind the fire and hammer."

"We could get on a ship, go to England, France, anywhere." He argued, "Doesn't have to be goats." he added, pouting into his glass. "Better than here, with you working the room. Nothin' but trouble if you ask me. Running your hands all over them drunk fools, pulling from their pockets whatever ya come across." He warned for the umpteenth time. "You're going to get yourself in a heap and have no bloody idea how to get out of it."

"And what would you have me do?" I demanded. "Whoring, healer, mother, midwife." I counted on my fingers. "That's about all the choice I got. And what of Phillip? After all he's done for us, just up and leave?"

"Dahlia blows through every few months, he'd be fine."

Dahlia! I thought. 'You and Thomas have a touch of destiny about ya.' The words rang in my ears like church bells. I hadn't thought about it since the night Dahlia said it all those years ago. Now, without warning, the thought stopped me in my tracks. I grew dizzy, grabbing hold of the counter. The words echoing over and over.

CHAPTER 43
Charlotte Ireland 1530

WEEKS HAD PASSED AND NOTHING changed. Life went on with it's self as it has a tendency of doing. I was serving patrons evening drinks when a familiar silhouette crossed the threshold. Even covered in layers of sweater and shall, I knew it was her. "Dahlia!" I shouted, hopping over the counter and pummeling her to the ground with uncontainable excitement. I squeezed her tight, breathing her in. The disbelief was more than I could bare, relieved tears streamed down my face as I illegibly spat. "I've missed you."

She rocked me as a mother would to soothe her fussy baby. "I know." She tucked a wayward curl behind my ear and cupped my face, "We must talk, tis urgent."

"What's going on?" Her visible concern worried me.

She lead me to the room she shared with Phillip and motioned for me to sit on their bed. Before I could question, she snatched my hands in hers, closed her eyes, and started mumbling in old tongues.

Fear started to simmer in the pit of my stomach. "Dahlia-" I tried to interrupt, but with a sharp flick of her wrist, I lost my words. A heaviness churned in my heart, the trouble boiling became too much to bear, I ripped my hands from her grasp and the weight immediately lightened, "What's going on?" I demanded.

"I had a vision." Dahlia answered, her eyes still closed, grabbing my hands again.

I snapped away my hands and rested them on my hips using annoyance to veneer my anxiety. "A vision? Come on Dahlia, what's going on?"

She yanked my hands back in to hers. "All I know is you are on a dark path. Mayhem is brewing something wicked and has you in his sight. Now sit down, shut up and let me see if I can make some sense of it."

Ten eternal minutes passed before my fingers started tingling under Dahlia's crushing grip as she mumbled in a barely audible mess of tongues. "Enough already! What's going on?" I broke, forcing my way to my feet and rubbing Dahlia's clench from my palms.

"I don't know," defeat coated her weary voice. "I can no longer see it. A raven visited my dreams." She stared through me, searching her memory. "Whispered, 'Both bless'ed and cured. Two hearts, one destiny. Powerful love, bound together for eternity.' Her hands tremor-ed as she repeated the message from her midnight visit, "There's darkness headed your way."

"A bird?" My trepidation unleashed in frustration. "You hauled your hind quarters all the way out here because you had a dream? About a bird?" The disdain scathed harder than intended.

"Not a dream. A vision." She scolded, "A warning."

CHAPTER 44
Charlotte Ireland 1530

THE MOON HAD GROWN FULL twice and was well in to it's waning decent since Dahlia's visit. For all the times she had left us behind, this time was the first time it hadn't ruined my world. All she did was stir up trouble, getting Phillip and Thomas riled up over nothing.

"A warning from Dahlia, no matter how cryptic, is something to be taken seriously." Phillip scolded some weeks back. "She's tapped into something up in those hills. And I'm not sure she even understands to what extent."

"What do you suggest I do then?" I questioned embroiled with defiance and annoyance. "First you say go. Then Thomas argues that whatever might happen, might happen on the road. And you counter with, 'It can happen here.' Then it turns in to me locked away in a bell keep for all eternity. For what? Too hide? From fate? If Dahlia is right, then my story is written. There's no outrunning that. I won't hide away or fear living today because of might happen tomorrow." I look at the man who raised me, releasing a delicate sigh. "You shouldn't either."

"Take a few of days. See if you can track down Dahlia up in those hills of hers." Phillip negotiated. "It'll make me feel better. If you're safe anywhere, it's with her."

I crossed my arms, rolled my eyes and let out a jilted hmph, soaking in his offer. Finally I caved, "As you wish."

"And Thomas will accompany you."

"Yes sir." I accepted begrudgingly.

Thomas and I started our journey the next day. The three drawn out days of walking wasn't the hard part. The hard part was the eternal silence. We knew the other's mind was racing, neither one of us brave enough to reach out first.

I just wish he'd tell me he loved me. He talks of a future but he's never kissed me. I mean really kiss me, like a lover, not a friend, not even close, not once. Does he only include me in his plans because he feels like he will inherit me from Phillip? Another burden to bare, like he will eventually inherit the tavern. Why is he so bloody frustrating! And why I am more concerned about him than this supposed perilously doom hovering? And now we're headed in to the hills to find Dahlia, as if she would be able to change any of it.

My thoughts were rudely disturbed as my foot caught hold of a lifted root, throwing me to my hands and knees. Thomas rushed to my aide, "You alright?" He interrogated, grabbing my elbow and guiding me to my feet.

I snatched my arm away annoyed but more so embarrassed, "Just fine!" I huffed stomping ahead.

IF THE FATES DON'T KILL her, I just might. Why does she have to be so damned stubborn? Defiant, hostile. Charming, witty. Beautiful. Stop! You will not get lost in her. Not now, you mustn't let her your muddy your mind.

"THAT'S HER CABIN, IN THE distance." I announced, as I trudge ahead determined.

CHAPTER 45
Charlotte Ireland 1530

THE DANK DWELLING SAT COLD and empty as Thomas examined the fireplaces' ashes. "Doesn't look like anyone's been here for a few days, maybe a week?"

I plopped myself onto the wooden bench letting out a bothered hmph. "Some seer, couldn't she see we were coming?" Thomas fired the look that always had a way of telling me exactly how much of a spoiled twat I was being without ever saying a word. "I guess we wait." I offered immediately changing my tone.

By night's light and the glow of the fireplace we shared our meal and laughs and the darkest corners of our hearts. He was different, I was different. Whatever imaginary force held us back there, was absent here. The way the flames danced in his eyes haunted me as they wrapped around my soul. For the first time, I felt home.

To pass the day, he worked the land while I buzzed around Dahlia's cottage, tending to her herbs and neatly filing her scattered books. The quiet simplicity of country life gave me a sense of peace I never knew possible. Maybe it was the open hills, or the air fresh from the stink of the city. Maybe it was wishful thinking. Maybe I was just being a swoon-y fifteen year old girl; but this life we were playing at, I wanted it more than anything.

Two full weeks had passed since our arrival with no sign of Dahlia. I had grown concerned, till the first night of the harvest moon. A calm wave washed over me. The tingling in my lungs tickled as I drew in the night air, silent words danced through the wind and sang in my ear. I knew in my heart, she was fine.

"I don't think we're going to see Dahlia anytime soon." My stomach knotted as the words fell from my lips. "We should probably head back." The thought of giving up our pretender's life was devastating but it was unfair to leave Phillip worried. There was no way to send word. Not until I learned how to send birds with messages or have words dance on the wind, like Dahlia did.

"I agree. We'll head out first light." Thomas acknowledged, shaking his hypnotic trance as the flames danced with his freckled iris.

I woke the next morning as drips of water stung my nose. At first I hadn't noticed, but by the fifth or sixth it had grown to a nuisance. I jumped from bed, opening the shutters, exposing an angry, swirling black sky as heavy sheets of rain slammed against the straw roof. I hastily opened my bedroom door, headed outside to examine the storm but was delayed. Thomas appeared on the other side, fist up, preparing to knock.

"Guess we won't be leaving today." He stammered at the sight of me in my shift.

I felt his embarrassment and grew self-conscious, awkwardly slinking behind the door. "Looks like." I answered, slamming the portal in his face.

Three days the storm brewed, gaining strength with each passing night. "You'd think Dahlia sent the storm to keep us here." Thomas said one night as we shared a stew.

"You and Phillip really think she's that powerful?" I questioned, dipping my bread in the gravy.

"All women are, they just don't know it." He paused. "I think the spread of Christianity is nothing more than a device for weak men to suppress a woman's true power."

"Careful there, might get tried for witchcraft." I played.

"Exactly my point." Thomas fired back. "And you grew up with the pagan ways same as I; you know this to be true. You can't tell me you've never heard words unspoken or seen glimpses of what has been or what is yet to come. You forget Charlotte, I see you, all of you, even the bits you try to hide."

The storm raged as I read from one of Dahlia's texts and Thomas ran the sharpening stone across his knives and sword. It gained in strength till all it's force hovered overhead. Lighting ripped the night sky open. The thunderous boom of the sky mending itself rattled the cottage, Mother Nature reminding us of her sovereignty. She pulsed in my fingers and toes, my skin tingled and I could no longer fight her primal pull.

"Thomas." Lightning struck, making the whole house glow white. Circling him slowly, closing in, as a lioness would her prey. The room grew dim again and I found myself in his arms, his lips crashed in to mine as the sky slammed on itself exploding over head.

He gently pulled away, reading my soul. He began to say "I love-"

I banged my teeth into his as I clumsily forced my lips to his. I didn't need him to say it. Everything I ever needed to know was stored behind his eyes. I ran my fingers through his hair, stopping at the base of his neck, pulling him close to me.

He mirrored my motion. Our inexperienced bodies press tightly against one another. Untapped desire fuels us as we stumble around the living room, knocking over a chair, until we fall against a wall. He presses my back into the wooden beam. I wrap my legs around his waist as he firmly grabs my rear, pressing me deeper into the wood. I exhale a soft groan with his forcefulness. He glides his lips along my neck, nibbling his way to my ear. I blissfully exhale as the room filled with blinding white light. Rain slammed the cabin and thunder hammered overhead as he guides me to the floor.

His thick callused fingers delicately untie the laces of my bodice releasing my heaving breasts. His teeth dragged across my chest and into my neck as his fingers slid up my thigh, making my insides tremor.

His mouth hovered mine as his lust ladened eyes sought approval. "Are you su-"

I had never wanted anything more than him in that moment. Before he could finish, I slammed my mouth against his.

CHAPTER 46
Charlotte Ireland 1530

THE MEMORY OF OUR COULD have been life faded from my mind as I swirled a towel over the bar that increasingly felt like a death sentence. Everything had changed since that trip. Thomas was different, I was different, we were different. Our life in the hills was drastically different than it was here. Here we quarreled all the time. He wanted me to quit the pick pocketing 'before it gets you in a mess a trouble.'

I knew in the pits of me I should quit. I didn't need to do it. The extra money was nice and it's not like I stole from anyone who hadn't stolen something from someone in one way or another. More importantly, I had an uncontrollable urge to be defiant at every turn. I couldn't give in so easily, could I? The dizzying, conflicted, annoying voice of my guilty conscience mercilessly circled my thoughts.

"You look like you're having an intense conversation up in that pretty little head of yours." The baritone voice broke my internal rant, "Don't suppose you'd like some real company?"

I turned my attention to the man in front of me; dark eyes, strong slopping brow, and tall, much taller than I. I smiled politely, trying to hide my frazzled nerves. "Why yes, a good distraction would be a welcome relief." I extended my hand, "Charlotte. Something to drink?"

The dark eyed man accepted my hand, politely kissing it. "Michael, and a whiskey please."

The moment his lips grazed the top of my hand, slime wormed across my body. "Is that an English accent I hear?" I queried as I poured his drink.

"Tis, that a problem?"

He was an attractive man, seemingly respectable, but something about him felt off. I couldn't put my finger on it. "English or Irish; your money spends the same here." I diplomatically answered, sliding the glass across the bar, unintentionally thickening my Irish draw.

He sipped from the glass as he complimented. "Who knew such a pretty girl laid beneath such a befuddled look." The depth of his voice accentuated his condescendence, something I loathed. "What vexes you so?" And patronizing, he took another sip.

"You see, I just had this huge spat with my, well, I'm not quite sure what he is-" I continued to tell the story of the fight I had with Thomas and pour drinks. All marks were the same. Love a good heartbroken, damsel in distress. Someone they perceive as weak. Easier to manipulate, take advantage of. Little did they know their patronization called to my demons like a moth to a flame.

"Would you care to join me for a breath of fresh air?" I asked as I wiped the dramatized tears from my eyes. I grabbed a fresh bottle of whiskey, rattling it by it's neck, dressed with a mischievous smile I giggled, "So we don't get parched."

Michael offered his arm, guiding me through the tavern. We strolled the cobbled streets as he mostly led the conversation. He was all too eager to boast tales of his earldom and wealth. He was in exile while legions fought to restore his family to their rightful place upon the throne. I hadn't paid any mind to a word he said as I was bored the moment he opened his mouth. It seemed every Englishman I met was some relation to King Richard III and Michael was all too eager to be more of the same.

The only time I cared two bits of what he had to say was when we passed the blacksmith's shop. Thomas was outside sweating and hammering steel as we sauntered past. I laughed at what

Michael said like it was the funniest thing ever to be heard while touching his arm and chest. Which confused him because he had just told me his father was murdered by usurpers as he protected his cousin, the rightful king, when Michael was a small boy. His cold, dark glare of disapproval sent a shiver down my spine.

I realized whatever he had been rambling on about, laughter was not the appropriate response. "Sorry." I apologized, embarrassed. "I do that sometimes, laugh when I shouldn't. Nervous tick I suppose."

Menace glimmered across his dark eyes. He pulled me close to him. His hand firmly placed at the small of my back. There was no pulling away. "I make you nervous?" He smiled, forcefully pressing his lips into mine.

He parted our mouths, slithering his tongue against mine. My stomach clenched. "More than I care to admit." I elfishly pushed him away, though his kiss really did give a vomit inducing feeling.

We wandered the narrow stone streets for hours till the sun began to sink. "Want some supper?" I offered.

"I would," he hiccuped. The whiskey had been long gone, but poor Michael was still feeling the effects. His delicate English stomach couldn't seem to handle Irish whiskey.

Michael made a crutch of my small frame as I guided him back to the tavern. Thomas was firmly perched upon his favorite stool. His eyes lifted from his glass to my general direction. He was relieved to see me home and safe; I could feel his heart, even through the disgusted look on his face. He rolled his irritated eyes and turned his attention back to the bottom of his glass. I returned the gesture with a look just as nasty as I guided oblivious Michael in to an empty booth.

I REFUSE TO LET MY worry eclipse my fury as I spied on her from over my shoulder and glared down the barrel of my glass. I knew her move, it was only a matter of time before she got what she wanted. Once she did, she would leave him to pass out in the booth, while I pray to the gods that this bloke, was drunk enough to forget her face and company. I emptied my glass, slamming it atop the bar. No danger hovered her tonight and I would not give her the satisfaction of my concern.

An hour later I came to bed. I pulled a small leather pouch from my bosom. The coins within made a heavy jangle. I couldn't help but smile with a twisted sense of accomplishment.

I slinked into bed, wrapping my arm around Thomas' chest, trying to nestle up. He rolled away, refusing my olive branch. The pain of his rejection superseded any need I had for defiance. I made a silent promise to be better; for him, for us, better for myself. I apologetically kissed the nape of his neck before closing my eyes to a sleepless night.

CHAPTER 47
Charlotte Ireland 1530

I WOKE THE NEXT MORNING and Thomas was gone. I shrugged it off, Thomas in a snuff with me was nothing new. He would not budge and I, unlike his steel, refused to bend. "I'll track him down in a bit." I promised my reflection as I pulled the laces of my bodice taught. I already knew where he was. One of only two places he ever is; better he hammer on that steel, than hammer on me.

I DIDN'T EVEN BOTHER TO look up when she arrived at my shop. I felt her coming three buildings away, our hearts were connected. The closer we were, the more intensely we felt the other. At least that's what I thought anyway. Lord knows what runs through that thick skull a hers.

"THOMAS." I PAUSED WAITING FOR him to look up. He continued hammering away on the red hot steel. "Thomas." I tapped my foot annoyed by his non-response. Finally, I yell "Thomas!"

He looked up, briefly acknowledging me, sniffed, pushed the sweat away from his brow with his wrist, coldly answered, "Yeah," and returned to hammering.

We quarreled, frequently, but this was worse, this was a non-fight. He wouldn't even look at me. He was not giving in on this one and he was right. I picked from that man specifically because he had asked me to not to and I made a point to rub his nose in it. "What the hell is wrong with me?" I finished my thought aloud.

"Buggered if I know." He coldly answered, his attention dedicated to his task.

"I don't know why I did it." I paused, sorting through my thoughts. "You fought me so hard. Like all of a sudden I was doing something wrong, even though I've done it for years."

THEY WERE THE SAME EMPTY words I'd heard over and over again. Ever since the first time I'd asked her to stop. And again when Dahlia came with her warning. I continued hammering my frustrations, ignoring her tired speech. I wasn't caving.

"I'm sorry!" she blurted, knotted between annoyance and guilt. "You happy now?"

The half apology only angered me further. I slammed my hammer and sword into the fire, stoking the hot flame as an explosion of hot amber waterfalled to the ground. "Sorry for what exactly?" I raged.

I WAS TAKEN ABACK BY his scathing, I was trying to apologize. "For the pick." I bit my bottom lip nervously. "Because, you know, you asked me not to."

Thomas stormed at me; instinctively I jumped back. The only thing separating us was the log patrician that framed his shop. "You think that's why I'm so bloody pissed?" His anger faded to disappointment. "Thieving from men like that, doesn't do anything but put you in unnecessary danger. You have this looming warning of peril that you don't take seriously." He hadn't stopped to breathe. "And why wouldn't I want you to stop. After our time in the hills. You think I like watching you flirt and fawn over other men, regardless of if it's a scam? It churns my fucking stomach inside out." The power of his words made him clench as he grabbed his well defined abdomen, shoving a violent heave back from whence it came.

It was the same argument he always presented, but today, the words sank in. I finally heard his concern and love. It had always been there. I was just too damned stubborn to hear it.

With every word, I edged closer to the wooden barrier until my hips pressed into it. "I'm in love with you." Thomas' voice cracked, exposing how I had broken him. He tenderly brushed my cheek. "I always have been. Since the day you were pushed through those tavern doors."

I pushed myself up to my tippy toes, clumsily falling against his lips. He laughed when our teeth banged into each others, knocking him off balance. I looked into his warm green eyes, finding my grounding rod of a freckle. I whispered in his ear, "Let's just leave. You said what? England? France? Anywhere."

He pushed me back by the shoulders with excitement. "You're serious?" Pack up and leave?" I smiled, nodding yes as his excited toothy smile infected me. He scooped me up and over the barrier and kissed me as he spun me cradled in his arms.

I giggled as we spun. A sense of ease pulsed through my veins, this was the right thing to do. Thomas gently returned my feet to the ground. Still entangled in his arms, he kissed me once more. "Than it shall be done." He kissed my temple, and returned to his hammer.

CHAPTER 48
Charlotte Ireland 1530

I FOLLOWED THE COBBLE STONES back to the tavern, watching the lamp lighter methodically light each candle. The air nipped at my nose as a searing pinch at the back of my arm made me jump from my skin. "Allow me to escort you home Miss." I looked up to a familiar face. The heavy brown. The dark menacing gaze towered over me, "There are ruffians about."

A knot twisted in my stomach as his long fingers wrapped firmly around my arm, tightening his grip with each hurried step.

He dragged me down a dark alley. My head bounced off the cold brick when he slammed me into the wall. "You little cunt." His spindly fingers tightened around my thin neck. "You think you can steal from me?" His fingernails dug in under my ear. "You think I wouldn't notice!"

Boiling rage festered in his eyes, the weight of his heavy body funneled through his palm, crushing my throat as my toes manically dangled from the ground desperately searching for the earth inches yet leagues beneath me. I swat at his hands, trying to free myself. He laughs at my feeble attempt as tears stream uncontrollably down my checks. I try to scream, but only release the faintest mouse squeak. His grip is tight and he is amused with my struggle to break free as his fingernails dig deeper behind my ears. I feel the skin break and droplets of blood sort to trickle down my neck. A wave of darkness washed over me and my eyes flutter, rolling to the back of my head.

A flash of bright white light pushes the darkness away. The tightness around my throat loosened as I choke on the balloon of air filling my lungs.

The fiery rage in Michael's eyes turned cold as the stone I was pinned against. A cough of blood explodes across my face. Thick, sticky, warmth soaks through my dress. Michael's knees buckle as he collapses to the ground, Thomas is thankfully revealed as he pulls the blade from Michael's ribs.

My feet hit the ground as I fell into Thomas' arms. Still choking on air I feel the searing pain of a lingering hand around my throat. Hysterical, I stammer painful broken sentences of fear and disbelief and appreciation. Thomas can't make heads or tails of the actual words, but he knows my heart. He hugs me tight as I unconsolably sob into his chest. He gave me a tic or two, then a firm shake. The resolve in his grey green eyes calmed me. Pulling me back to here and now. I was already getting lost in a web of manic thought. He coached my breathing. "We. Have. To. Go. Now." He enunciated every word as he stared into my semi vacant eyes. I could feel myself disappearing. He grabbed my hand and we vanished into the dark fog.

I was able to shake off enough of the shock to register Thomas' message and blinked in acknowledgement. He grabbed my hand, guiding me through the narrow cobble allies. We slid in to the tavern unnoticed, except by Phillip; who's eyes followed Thomas as he dragged my catatonic shell to our room.

Thomas delicately sat me in the bedroom's chair, kissed my forehead and wiped Micheal's blood and spit from my face before feverishly tossing our clothes into sacks. Phillip burst into a hurricane of garments strewn around the room. "What the bloody hell is going on?" He exploded as he knelt down examining me.

"She's fine." Thomas continued shoving items into bags. "That Michael guy was chokin' the life from her. I stuck him just in time."

Phillip circled the room once to digest Thomas', albeit brief, but detailed account. He stroked his nonexistent mustache, trying to absorb what had just happened. Reality set in and in that moment so did panic. "You have to get out of here, before someone starts looking for him."

Thomas holds a wad of clothes up in his hand and dramatically shoves it into the bag, emphasizing his plan already in execution.

"The passage to France is still some weeks out." Phillip wasn't helping. "You have to get off this rock."

"I know. Doesn't help us tonight." Thomas focused on packing. He wished Phillip would go away. He couldn't have this conversation right now.

Phillip's wheels spun. He paced the room, matching the manic pace of his thoughts.

"You're wearing a trench in the god damned floor." Thomas snapped.

Phillip stopped in his tracks. "You going up to Dahlia's cottage? At least for a bit."

"That's the immediate plan, yes." Thomas stuffed the last few items into the sack. With his task complete, he had lost his distraction. He placed his hands atop his head as he worry set in, "It's going to look off. Everyone saw her with him last night. And we just happen to disappear after this bloke shows up dead?"

Phillip heard the concern in Thomas' voice. It was the same fear he had. This was Dahlia's warning coming to fruition. "Not if I tell anyone who asks, that you're on holiday, celebrating your recent nuptials."

"Like we up and got married?" Thomas clarified his alibi.

"Like you up and got married." Phillip confirmed. "Not like it's that far fetched of a story." He punctuated with am ill timed wink.

Thomas nodded in agreement. "Yeah, that could work." He let out a minute sigh of relief.

"And what of her?" Phillip pointed to my shell in the corner.

"She'll be fine." Thomas picked up the bags. "Just have to get her safe." He helped me to my feet. "Come check on us in a couple of weeks? So we can figure our next move." Thomas hugged his brother goodbye, grabbed my hand, and we slunk out the back door, disappearing into the night.

I CARED FOR HER AT Dahlia's cottage for six weeks with no sign of of my sister. The house sat empty with no trace of her since our last stay, those few perfect days a lifetime ago.

Phillip had visited twice. His advisement both times was to stay put. Michael's death was still gossip fodder amongst the town's folk and Charlotte had barely said two words since the whole ordeal. She never slept, barely ate, only if I coached her bite by bite and some days that didn't even work. She was thin and grey and worrying me to the bone.

"She seems better." Phillip lied. "The bruising on her neck is mostly gone."

My thin smile didn't hide my concern. "She's in there, somewhere." I gently guide a loose curl behind her ear and cupped her face, staring into vacant eyes. "We'll get her back." I turned my attention back to Phillip. "I'm more concerned about Dahlia. Where is she?"

Phillip answered without a second thought. "Where she is needed." That's the answer she had always given him when he asked where she was going or had been. Seemed appropriate now.

"She's needed here! Can't she see that?!" I unintentionally exploded. I was far more stressed than my notorious calm showed.

"I don't know what to tell you." Phillip sighed unable to help. "I still feel her touching my heart, I know she's okay. Where ever she is, I have to believe it's more important than her being here. That's what she always asked me to trust before, that's all I can do now."

"Have faith?" I blurted. "That's your solution; to fix Charlotte and avoiding the gallows?"

Phillip let the harshness of my outburst roll off his shoulders. We were in dire straights, tensions were high. He calmly answered, "Yes. That's all we can do." He pulled his cape over his head and exited the straw and wood house.

I WAS TRAPPED IN MY mind. That night looped over and over all throughout the day and haunted my dreams at night. The way his eyes were roiling with anger one moment and empty the next. The hot copper smell lingered, the feeling of warm blood on my cold hand. I could still feel his fingers clenched around my throat. Every now and again I gently rubbed where his fingers had dug deep underneath my ears. The gouges had mostly healed, only a small bit of scabbing remained.

"Was it real? It feels like a dream." Phillip and Thomas broke their conversation, staring at me in amazement. "What? What is it? Why are you staring at me like a god damn turkey leg?" I questioned puzzled by their reaction.

Thomas picked his jaw up first. "You realize you haven't said more than two words in over a month?"

"Really?" I grew cautious. "It felt like-" I tried to quantify time. I couldn't believe how much had passed, but where I was time felt infinite yet nonexistent. Maybe it had been a month. "Michael's really dead?" I had seen the life leave his eyes so many times, I already knew it true. I grabbed my stomach with one hand, to steady myself from the heave of nausea. "And-" I delicately ran my forefinger down the space between ear and jaw feeling those spindly fingers clenched around my throat.

"Yes." Thomas softly answered as he pulled me into his chest while I unconsolably wailed as the night replayed in my mind.

CHAPTER 49
Charlotte Ireland 1530

"WE ARE GOING TO HAVE to go back." Thomas filled me in on the events since that fateful night, our honeymoon alibi, everything. "We can only travel for so long." His tone grew weary. "And there are people waiting to talk to us."

"So everyone thinks we're married?" I asked, confused by all the details.

"Yes." He was more scalding than he meant, "Is it such an unimaginable thing?"

I flushed having hurt his feelings. "I didn't mean-" Stumbling over my words. "It's not-"

"I'm sorry. I meant it to be playful." I buried my face in his protective chest, squeezing my arms around his waist as he apologized.

"I'm a bit more snappy as of late."

The thought crossed my mind and a smile wrapped across my face. I searched deep into those steady jade eyes. Gravitating toward my favorite fleck of brown. "Let's do it."

Thomas laughed, pulling his neck back to read my face. "Do what?"

"Get married."

My resolve rattled him. "You can't possibly be serious?"

"Is it such an unimaginable thing?" I smiled, throwing his words back at him.

HER WISH WAS MY COMMAND from the moment we met. I'd trudge through the bowels of hell if it meant to secure her safety or happiness. I had no control over the lengths or depths I would travel for her. It was something cemented in time long ago. "Alright," I smiled as I leaned in to kiss her. "We'll head south. There is a string of villages there. I'm sure we can find a priest to marry us."

CHAPTER 50
Charlotte Ireland 1530

It seemed as if each village we passed through was just like the last. I found a Dahlia, a Phillip, Thomas, even myself at every stop. No matter where our travels led, we always managed to find a tavern were we could find a room for a night or two. It's patrons more of the same as back home. Our circumstance could have fallen on to any of these people. *But it happened to us* echoed in my barbed thoughts.

The further south we traveled, rumors of a seer gained in strength. Thomas and I agreed, that we should follow the story's trail. It was the only half credible lead we had to Dahlia. I'm pretty sure if Dahlia wanted to be found, she'd a turned up already. My pessimism wasn't worth expressing aloud. No sense in pissing all over the closest thing to a plan we had.

In our latest stop, we heard news that relations of Michael had been scouring the country side. Looking for a "thieving whore" who had turned up missing after Michael's death.

"Well at least they got the thieving part right." I tried to joke as we settled into their room for the night.

"It's nothing to laugh at." Thomas cut me off. "You can, we both can swing for what we did." I absorbed the seriousness of his tone. He slid in to bed and pulled the blanket over his head. "Goodnight."

The finality of the conversation struck me. I reached for him. My finger tips hovered inches from his shoulder. The thickness in the air filled the void between. "I didn't -" I whispered softly, the words barely leave my lips. He rolled, pulling himself as far away from me as the small straw bed allowed.

Ever since that night, I had been a jumpy jumble of nerves. I shook away the remnants of my tormentor and reminded my self Thomas would never hurt me as I curled up behind him and hugged him tight. Softly kissing the back of his neck, his cold rigidness started to melt. "I'm sorry."

He rolled over, stared deep into my eyes, burning a hole into my heart. I am forever lost in that sea of green. My gaze finds the anchoring brown flecks. Those little freckles, that always seem to tell me everything is going to be alright. "I don't mean to make light of it. I have to laugh, otherwise, I feel as if I may do nothing but cry. Or even worse, get locked back up in my mind. Thomas, I am so sorry. For everything. Ruining your life-"

Thomas sat up quickly, "You didn't ruin my life." He thumbs away a stray tear as he tenderly pulls my lips in to his. "You are my life." We lose ourselves in the other. The release of salty tears run down my face as he eases my heart.

Morning's light flooded the room as I pushed the shutters open. The crisp air grazed my skin, sending my body abuzz. I stare blankly out the window dizzy with thought. Something was different.

Thomas kissed my bare shoulder as he wrapped his arms around my waist, pulling me close. I turned over my shoulder and my gaze caught his eyes. "Do you feel that?" I asked.

He smirked, as he gently bit the back of my neck, "I got something that you can feel?"

I laughed, playfully pushing him away. "No, seriously."

He held my shoulders tight, reading my large concerned eyes, his body shifted from playful to protective within a second. Growing up with Dahlia he learned a long time ago to never question a woman's intuition. Women have a great power that men try to stiffen, mostly succeeding. The spread of Christianity throughout Ireland, the loss of the pagan ways, the connection to the earth had reinforced this belief in Thomas.

"What is it?"

I hugged myself. Either brushing away the cold or self comforting. Thomas was unsure the reasoning. "The air, it's just," I paused, trying to find the words. "different."

Thomas heard enough. He feverishly shoved clothes into our sack as he spoke, "That's our cue to move on." Any warning was warning enough to spook him into haste.

"What do you mean?"

"We best be on our way." He shoved my dress in the bag. "A shift in the air is nothing to be tested."

"What?" I questioned overwhelmed.

"Now don't be so stupid Charlotte! Whatever story plays out between you and I-" I snapped harsher than intended as I halted our packing, "It was destined. Since the day you walked in the door of that tavern all those years ago. Who knows, maybe before then!" Why am I yelling? She looks like she's about to cry. "Don't take no god damn seer to see that!" Why are you still yelling? Is that a tear? Stop being such an asshole. I threw my hands up, "Sorry." I inadvertently shout. Taking a breath, "I don't mean to make you cry, but I believe, I believe in it all and if you tell me there's a shift in the air, I bloody well believe it." I inch closer to her and lift her chastised chin up. Her sad eyes were wet and reddened. Knowing I had caused her pain broke me. "I take it to mean, it's time to go." I apologized as I gently kissed her lips and shoved a sack into her hand.

Our expedited departure was validated the moment our feet hit the bottom step of the stairwell. The tavern was buzzing with rumors of a witch who had been crucified. No one knew for sure. Some said north. Others said south. East. West.

A flash of the Dahlia's cottage flashed across my eyes, rattling me so hard I lost my balance, tripping over my feet.

Thomas caught me by the arm as I shook the lost stare away. "What is it?"

"I. Need. To. Get. Out of here." I staggered between quick shallow breaths as the walls began to close in on me. We exited as quickly as our feet would carry us without causing too much attention.

Heading north, the village to our backs, the openness of the emerald country side ahead. I knew our words were finally safe.

I vomited, "It's Dahlia. At the cottage." Choking on every word. "I saw the whole thing." Tears streamed down my face. "They killed her. Cuz of us, cuz of me. It was never about her being a seer. They just used that as an excuse when they couldn't pry the information they wanted from her." I wept, falling to my knees.

Thomas dropped to me. "Are you alright?"

"I. Just. Need-" Each word was interrupted by a struggled attempt for breath.

Thomas guided me to my feet. "Take all the time you need." He rubbed the space between my shoulders comforting. "Just not in the middle of the road." He led me to the side and we sat beneath a shady tree. "Damsel in distress, crying in the middle of the road, might cause some unwanted attention." He was making fun of me. "Low profile and what not."

His playful wink made me laugh. Which caused snot to explode from my nose, forcing us both to erupt with laughter. I flushed with embarrassment and wiped my upper lip. With one look, I could feel his heart in mine. No matter our plight, as long as we had each other, we were going to be alright.

CHAPTER 51
Charlotte Ireland 1530

EACH HEART WRENCHING LABORED STEP toward Dahlia's cottage filled my heart heavy with dread. The putrid odor of her charred flesh soured my stomach as her murder play on loop in my mind.

The heft of a man on top of me and the smell of whiskey stung my nostrils as I feel him breathe on her neck. His hardened hands roam her body as he forced himself into her. When his violations didn't break her he took her piece by piece. First fingers, then toes, eyes, then ears. His blade was dull when he shaved her skin away. And through it all, she refused to bend. She knew she was dead, she was just waiting to die.

There was no stopping the steam of tears. I howled, collapsing to the ground as the spikes went through her hands the first time I saw it. Feeling her pain as my own. Blood gushed from the cavity appearing in my hands. My chest tightened, I couldn't breathe.

"Charlotte?"

I hear Thomas faintly in the static. Everything around me is hazy. I feel the pull of death.

"Charlotte!"

His voice is louder. I feel him rattling me, begging for an answer.

He's panicking, "Charlotte-" Eyes welling with fear. "Please come back to me."

Cradled in his arms, the defending static ring starts to fade. The fog begins to clear. I feel my eyes flutter open, "Thom-"

Before I could finish his name his lips exhaled a sigh of relief in to mine. "You gave me a scare there Love." His forest green eyes locked with mine as he gently tucked a sweat covered lock behind my ear. "What did you go?"

"I watched your sister die." I softly answered.

CHAPTER 52
Thomas Ireland 1530

WE DREDGED ALONG FOR DAYS. She seemed to have lost all sense of time; a prisoner to her thoughts. Most days she didn't see the country side or hear half of what I had said. At night, she tossed and turned, crying out for Dahlia. The guilt of what we were sure to find eroded her to a sad, broken girl I could not recognize.

Dahlia was just as Charlotte described. My poor, sweet sister. Her scorched body, hung limp for weeks outside her cottage. I cut her down and buried her beneath her favorite cherry tree, making a silent vow I would avenge her.

Drained, in every sense of the word we entered our, at one time, happily ever after. The house felt heavier, darker. It could have been Dahlia's light was no longer here to warm it, but there was an off charge in the air.

"Phillip!" Charlotte cried as the glimmers of candlelight filled the room exposing his bruised, swollen, limp body, bound and gaged to a chair. Sweat and blood streaked his battered body. She rushed to his side, frightened to tears, maniacally fussing at his binds. He let out a soft groan. "Thomas! He's alive."

I pushed through the dark, cutting my brother in law free from his binds. Phillip's eyes gleamed relief as they rolled to the back of his head, falling into my arms.

"What the f-" Everything went dark.

CHAPTER 53
Thomas Ireland 1530

I GROGGILY FLUTTER MY EYES as the warmth of the fireplace against my face pokes me awake. Trying to recall what happened, I reach to the back of my head, examining the source of an excoriating throb, gingerly prodding a candlestick sized welt. I roll over to see Phillip rebound to his chair. Charlotte motionless, bound and gagged on the floor next to him. Panic pulses through my veins. "Charlotte." I gently thumb her bruised cheek.

A cold steel point slices across the room landing precisely at my throat. My eyes snap shut in anticipation of certain death. A moment passes before I realize I am still very much alive. My eyes slowly pop open one at a time as I scan my surroundings. With the blade still pressed against my neck, a drop of blood runs over my Adam's apple as my breath deepened. "Wouldn't do that if I were you."

English accent. Fuck. I exhaled cautiously, painfully aware of the blade. I couldn't make out the face of the man. He was seated in the shadows. He flicked his wrist, moving the long blade effortlessly from my neck, pressing my chin up. "Stand." He moved the sword, directing my head. "Take a seat, we are meant to have a little chat."

I cautiously move to the chair I was assigned. Scrunching my brow, I search the shadows; the build recognizable, the English accent, a dead give away. Some relation of Michael's, come to claim their justice.

A soft wind breezes past as the blade quickly pulled away from my throat. The tip moved to Charlotte. Rage stirred in my seated collectedness. "I know her part in to all this." The blade was back to my chin as the intruder measured me up. "But how do you fit in all of this?" The question was rhetorical. "I'm still trying to figure out if it were you that did my brother in, or if it were that thieving cunt." He pulled the blade toward the ground, leaning against it's hilt, seated on the edge of his chair. "Ya see, she only sort of looks the murderin' whore type." A gleam of twisted admiration smirked across his dark eyes, squinting through his heavy brow. "But you." He waved his index finger softening his booming voice. "You are most definitely a savior of damsels in distress."

He made a thunderous clap as he pops up to his feet. "At all costs, am I right?" He kneels down to Charlotte's unconscious body, pulling her limp torso into into his lap. "And for tits like these -" Watching his spindly fingers run over her bosom ignited me as I lunged from the chair. With his free hand Michael's kin pulled the sword to my throat. "Just as I thought, the incessant hero." He snarked, shaking his head. Using the blade to guide me to my chair. "You just wait till that little bitch comes to." He spat the words in my face as he bound me to the chair.

I stared into the fire for hours. Hoping, praying, devising any way to get us out of here until I heard Phillip groan his last breath.

"Well that was a little-" The menacing brother spoke, "underwhelming." he shrugged disappointed as he kicked the chair over with Phillip's shell still bound to it.

I closed my eyes, taking a breath, and swallowed hard as my blood boiled. We were jammed up and there was nothing I could do.

"I grow board." Michael's avenger nonchalantly announced as he examined his finger nails. "Wake the fuck up!" His voice boomed as he kicked Charlotte in the ribs.

Charlotte coughed awake. Her eyes fluttered as she rolled and groaned in pain. She came to a confused focus on me, bound to my seat. I mouthed to her "It's alright." Not sure if I was trying to reassure her or myself. It was apparent neither of us were walking away from this.

"You're awake. Good." Confused, she didn't recognize the baritone voice. He ran behind me, pulled my head back by my long dirty blonde locks. My throat wide and exposed. A quick flash of silver, and I could feel the same vacant in Michael's eyes that had haunted her, settle in my eyes as a hot ribbon of red streamed down my neck.

"Noooo!" My shriek muffled and disoriented, as I watch my beloved murdered in front of me. I fight my binds, trying to reach him, but can not move. As Thomas lay there, drowning in his own blood, choking on his last breaths, I felt the best bits of me dying as well. Without him, there was nothing worth fighting for. I accepted my fate as the man who killed my husband hovered. He plunged his sword in to my chest, I felt the steel slide between my ribs and pierce my lung as I drown, coughing the blood that fills my lungs in my final breaths.

The man squats down next to me, leaning into his blood stained sword. "You know, I had planned to make him watch while I fucked you in every hole till you bled, but your little nap took a great deal longer than planned and I have a boat to catch." He spits in my face as I choke on my last ragged breath. I feel life slip away, my eyes go cold as he walks away, shutting the door behind him.

CHAPTER 54
Charlie's Journal - Modern Day

I have always felt connected to the earth and other side. I hear tongues dance on the wind and blowing through the trees. Some days I feel like I communicate with animals better than people.

I understand that dark that follows the light. Over the years I had managed to keep the dark at bay while still letting the lost and light speak.

After many obsessive Google searches, I have determined I have what they call "retro-cognition". It is impossible to touch, pretty much anything without seeing flashes of history surrounding the item. I feel people's emotions as if they were my own. I sometimes think I feel other people's emotions more intensely then they feel themselves. And most importantly the dreams. The same handful of dreams night after night. The dreams that managed to sneak in from the darkest corners of my mind into the nooks and crannies of my heart, until they festered over the entirety of my life. Those soulful haunting eyes that lead me through the most tumultuous time in my life. The emeralds that kept my course true.

This was different. I had never experienced anything like this before. It had been building beneath my shoulder blades for days. When the pain became unbearable, it shifted, settling into my shoulders, wrapping around the base of my neck. The weight of a kettle bell crushing my chest, engulfing my heart.

My breath, shallow and staggered. Panic set in, my heart rate increased. Jitters violently shook the whole of me. My skin goose-fleshed.

I had an uncontrollable urge to lie with my palms up, my wrists were exposed as my veins bulged. Pins and needles tingled through me. Anxiety, anticipation, but oddly no dread. I would welcome the release of vomiting, but the knots only tighten in my stomach.

Not a panic attack. That's much more of a tailspin feeling.

A blinding white light washes a calm over me. I hear scratching, a white noise. I can't tell what it's saying. But somehow understand. Tears flow uncontrollably from my eyes. Not tears of sadness. But of release. The weight on my chest starts to alleviate, but the tingling feeling lingers in my wrist.

It felt like my track was being ripped from the path its on and moved another direction. All the hurt, the struggle, the strife that has happened, has lead me to where I am meant to be.

When the wave passed, I stepped outside and take a seat on the patio. The sky is clear blue, butting against the golden hills of summer and green vine sprawled through the valley. A soft breeze whispers in my ear. I clear my mind, letting the wind speak. As it changes direction and dances through the chimes, I breathe in deeply, exhaling slowly. I am at peace.

I shake the last lingering bits of tingling through my body. But the mark on my heart will never fade.

Hours, days pass. The mark on my heart pulses strong. A hopeful ache. I can't help but smile. Like the universe revealed a secret. A glimpse in to the future. Stay your course, everything is about to change. Stay strong. Be brave.

When you experience something so profound, you are forever changed. It leaves it's mark. I couldn't help but see the world differently. I was blissful, at peace. I know there is no reason to worry. Whatever happens, is meant to happen. Just another step along the road of fate.

A hopeful haze radiates from me. I feel the future pulsing through my veins. This dreamlike state made me feel the falseness of this life. Those green eyes cross my mind's eye. The tingle in my wrists flare. The smile in my heart floods my face. He is real. Keep your faith.

CHAPTER 55
Charlie Modern Day

Wanna go dig through som vinyl, get Blondie's and let college guys hit on us?

I HADN'T REALLY EXPECTED DAHLIA to reply seeing I had been ignoring her calls and texts for a few weeks now. I had been in a mood and felt it best to hunker down and weather the storm in solitude Buzz.

17 or 36, there is no growing out of hot college guys hitting on you ;)

Consistently a better friend than I deserve or than she ever got in return, she added before I could reply.

Yes vinyl. No Pizza, fucks with my acid reflux. Crepes?

Did you call me old & mention acid reflux in the

So, Berkeley? Day? Time?

I double bubbled.

Saturday?
Pick you up around noon?

Deal. xoxoxo

The city's heartbeat was music to my ears as I boxed up my leftovers and handed them to the first stranger I saw crouched against a wall dying to be seen. The calm, sunny, warm day was perfect to stroll. The homey scent of pizza, patchouli, and exhaust lingered on the mural lined streets as we perused the mix of boutiques, head shops and street vendors we frequented as teenagers. I bought a new mala bracelet and slowly we found our way home; Amoeba Records.

Dahlia looked nostalgically upon the faded sign, "Lots of memories." She cooed as we stepped through the threshold.

"Kinda like going home." I matched her sentiment.

"No matter what is going on in our lives, we'll always have this place." She was getting sucked into the magic and memories music makes. We spent countless hours of our youth here, music junkies in the worst of ways. Every cent we ever earned went in to adding to our collection or going to shows.

I smiled as I wrapped my arm around her shoulder, "Awww. I love when you get all sappy."

We sauntered past a dirty blonde rocker guy with his dark wayfarers shielding his eyes from the harsh fluorescents overhead. His pheromones and cologne cast a three foot radius, as I breathed in his familiar musk, an electric pulse fired from my fingers and toes. My eyes where immediately glued to him, which is why I bashed my hip into the table's corner and shouted, "Fuck!" as I gracelessly bounced off the wooden abuser, rattling the milk crates filled with precious black gold.

I watched his shoulder rise when he half laughed at the thud of expletives behind him. He was tallish. Taller than me, which was no difficult task. His tone, defined back wore through his black linen shirt. The top two buttons undone exposed part of a tattoo that I was dying to see the rest of. His dark jeans were fitted, but not skinny (Thankfully, can we all agree camel tail is not a good look?) and his black combat boots untied.

I blindly flipped through records, trying unsuccessfully to hide my staring. "Dahlia." An exuberant blurt escaped my mouth rather than the moderate whisper I had asked tech control for. The school girl giddy spread across my face was blatant as I motioned her my way. She smirked as she sashayed to me. "Remember forever ago when you said something about a tattooed musician type?"

"Vaguely."

I nodded in the direction of the strong backed form a few rows in front of us.

Her schoolgirl playfulness was bubbling over the brim as she indiscreetly tip toed to the end of our row. "Nice." When you have been friends with someone for so long, you kind of regress to teenagers no matter how old you are. "I have to get a better look."

My face grew hot as she drew closer. She plopped herself in front of a box of records that put him directly in front of her, the mischief in her eyes said it all, she was going to embarrass me.

She flipped through the stack in front of her, while sizing him up. "Charlotte!" His ear perked as my name rolled off my now ex-best friend's lips. He turned my direction, peeking over the top of his glasses. I caught of sliver of grayish green as a flirty half smile fell in to the corner of his mouth and I instantly turned to mush.

Oh my god, this is not happening.

"Pretty pristine 'Pearl'. You want?" She waived Janis at me with an obnoxious smile across her face.

I wanted to crawl under the table and hide forever. "Yeah."

She skipped back, record in hand. I had the insatiable urge to run away, choke her, or cry. Maybe all three. We may be thirty-six, but in that moment, we were about fourteen.

"He is fucking gorgeous." She said loud enough for him to hear while she poked me in the ribs. "The thin simple silver nose ring is the tits. Not too much, just a little 'I'm rock n roll baby' vibe."

"Can you stop?" I whined, crossing the threshold from embarrassed to mortified. I knew he could hear, I just hoped he wasn't paying any mind to the two stupid girls causing a scene in the middle of the Classic Rock section.

"And he smelled delicious."

"Seriously, I beg you, please stop." My mortification pushed every ounce of blood in my body to my face as I watched him cross the store and asked the counter clerk about Stevie Ray Vaughn.

As the words fell from his mouth, Dahlia lost it. "An accent?" she moaned, "Fuck me." (Vulgar Dahlia rarely ever made an appearance anymore. Something about 'growing up and being too old for inappropriateness', but when she did, she was absolutely hilarious. Except in this case in which I was mortified. Nevertheless, It was refreshing to see her unadulterated. It was too far and few between. It's a precious moment when people let you see who they are behind the walls in which they hide.) I couldn't contain my laughter as she begged, "Please, please, please, bang the shit out of him so you can tell me all the sordid details."

"I love sordid details." We both instantly flushed berry red when we heard the gravelly British words behind us. We begrudgingly about-faced, and there stood the sexy rocker man. Another button had managed to undo itself, exposing two thirds of the family crest on his chest. Flashes of English country side burst like rapid fire as I imagined his lineage.

I was frozen. Dahlia choked on her words, "How much of that did you hear?"

The tempting devil pushed his thumb and forefinger together for measure, putting us out of our misery, "Just an eency bit." "And just how much is an eency bit?" I somehow managed to pull my jaw from the floor.

"All of it." He smiled as he pushed his sunglasses atop his head, holding his long locks perfectly in place. "Accent, fuck me, something about 'bang the shit out of him', that tends to grab a bloke's attention." He smiled, exposing all his teeth. His eyes gleamed, obnoxiously familiar green eyes. "I'm Thomas by the way." He extended his hand. "and you are?"

"Thoroughly embarrassed." I smiled, shaking his offered hand, searching his eyes. My gaze gravitated toward a brown flake, my heart skipped. Those eyes. The pins and needles feeling I had felt in my wrists so many times before, radiated through my body. I was lost in him.

"Nothing wrong with a healthy sexual appetite". He winked, I melted.

"You going to tell me you name?" He teased, "I think it only fair seeing as you and your friend there already violated me six ways from Sunday with your filthy little minds." It was amusing seeing Dahlia squirm. You could tell it was the first time in her life she actually thought she may die of embarrassment.

"Charlie." I unconsciously bit my lower lip, instantly hating myself for so quickly reverting into a horrible cliche.

He and I spent the next two hours, flipping through records and talking, not like strangers getting to know each other, but old friends catching up. It was weird, there was something about him that felt like home.

"Music is engrained on my soul. I can't pick a favorite song or record. There are so many pieces that I connect to on different levels, that guided me through different parts of my life, make me feel different parts of myself, or just flat out make me happy. How do you pick a favorite when each piece is sewn into your fabric? It's the same for art or books. I can't choose a favorite piece, because if done right, you should feel something. That moment of finding something within you, it's like religion to me. It makes me see parts of the world, parts of humanity I didn't know existed." My nerd button had had been pushed and I was rambling. "Sorry, I-"

"No. Don't be. It's endearing to see someone passionate about something. We tend to barely scratch the surface with people these days, terrified to let anyone see our true selves." I felt understood for the first time in a long time. "I get it, I'm the same way. It's the curse of an artist; desperate to be seen, but pushes everyone away. I crave solitude, and it's hard to find someone you can be alone together with, if that makes sense."

"Artist?" I questioned.

"Yeah, I draw some, but I'm a musician by trade. Being creative feeds my soul, the space between pencil and paper feels more like home than any roof I've had overhead." Two hours with this guy and I already felt more understood by him than seventeen years with Michael. I know I sound like an asshole, but it was one of those 'you either get it or you don't' type things, and Michael just never got it.

"Where did you go just now?" Thomas lurched his neck, forcing my eyes to his.

I smiled nervously, shrugging away my distractions, "Sorry, I do this thing, where I disappear in to my thoughts and the world kind of fades away." I was cringing inside, why was I being so open?

"Why are you sorry? Because you're introspective?" He was laughing at me. "When is that ever a problem?" Maybe Johnny and June isn't the stuff of fairytales after all.

Dahlia's 'time to go' glare pushed me to the register. She started her way towards the car while I lingered, exchanging numbers with Thomas before giving him an friendly peck on the cheek goodbye. Before I could get two steps away, he grabbed my wrist, pulled me in to his chest and I fell effortlessly under his protective arm. A flash of the same motion ran through my mind's eye. I couldn't tell when or where but I knew I had felt this moment before.

I finally found what had been missing from me, I couldn't bare to see her go so quick. I begged as my fingers playfully danced with hers and I became lost in her mesmerizing espresso eyes, "Have dinner with me."

"I'd love to," I nodded to an ever shrinking Dahlia, now a full two blocks ahead. "but she's my ride."

I could tell he didn't hear 'no' a lot by the frustration settling in his brow. "What if I take you home?"

"I don't know how things work in the UK, but here, you don't let people you just met know where you live. Crazies and what not." The sass rolled off my tongue as the words tangoed with my hips.

She was a snake charmer and I was stumped. A glint smile settled in my eye and I accepted her challenge. "Okay then, a proper date. I'm playing a set at a coffee shop in The City Wednesday night."

He laced his fingers between mine and leaned in. I gravitated toward a brown fleck in the sea of green. "Come hear me play. We'll grab a bite after?"

"Deal." I smiled and his lips dove into mine. Electrified copper pulsed through my veins. His intense gaze seared through me as I stumbled over my feet and words. "I have to go. She'll leave me." I pointed up the street as I tried to collect my shattered nerves.

I gathered the shards of my cool exterior and darted up the street attempting to catch up with Dahlia's quick pace. Flashes of a satin red dress and slow dancing under the moon, a violent storm hovering a straw roofed cottage, the muscle memory of ballet like swordsmanship, all raced through my mind.

CHAPTER 56
Charlie's Journal–Modern Day

Was it he,
    who haunted me
    who vexed my dreams
    and made it impossible to breath

Was it he,
    who forced to see the falsehoods and lies
    and I had been living a life not mine

Was it he,
    who I destroyed homes and broke hearts for

Was it he,
    who gave me hope in fate and destiny?

The demons and battles you fought,
prepared you for this.

So what's it all mean? How do we move toward tomorrow, when so much of us is rooted in history? Do you think he's seen the visions too? Should I even ask? That sounds fucking nuts, right? 'Hey we just met, but I think we've loved each other for eons.'

How do you fall in love with someone, you've already loved an eternity? Is there a fall at all?

CHAPTER 57
Charlie Modern Day

"For fuck sake." Kennedy pouted into the bottom of her wine glass as her mile long legs dangled from the kitchen counter. "I miss everything."

Dahlia interjected, "Embarrassed beyond all comprehension, yeah, you missed out." She rolled her eyes and flushed at the the memory as she popped a piece of gruyere into her mouth and sipped her pinot. "The only thing that would have been worse, would be if I had shat myself. For a second I thought I did."

Focused on the innocent peck of a kiss running on loop in my mind, I was unable to hear the white noise my friends produced.

"So you're going, right? Why would you not go? He sounds scrumptious." Kennedy grilled from the bottom of her glass.

Kennedy is talking to you. Answer her. I shook the voice from my head. "Yes." fell from my mouth more concise than planned. Nervously I softened, "I'm going. It's just so weird to even think about, I haven't been on a date in like eighteen years?"

Kennedy's eyes lit up like a six year old at Christmas, "Shopping?"

The next day she was dragging me from store to store. No creature in this world was more in their element than Kennedy in a mall. It was my worst nightmare and she gleamed with delight as she forced me into dresses and skirts and prints I would never wear in a million years.

Several hours and a hangry outburst later, I had called an end to our excursion. I was done being her barbie doll. I needed food, jammies, a joint and my bed.

"I can't believe we shopped all day and that's what you came up with." Kennedy wore her emotions on her sleeve, especially her disdain for my wardrobe.

I snapped back, "I'm meeting him at a coffee shop. What am I supposed to wear, a ball gown and gloves?" I was proud of my purchases. I bought a new pair of dark jeans, a simple long sleeve black top, a soft pink silk scarf with delicate black lace overlay, a killer pair of crochet wedges, and a large pair of gold Tiffany hoops that Kennedy demanded I buy.

"I just thought after all these years, I'd have had a positive influence on your wardrobe choices." She snubbed her nose in the air.

"Thanks, I guess." I answered rolling my eyes, playfully offended.

CHAPTER 58
Charlie Modern Day

By the time Wednesday rolled around I was crawling out of my skin. I had never been so nervous in my life. I had called Dahlia three times already. She had known me for far too long to even begin to process how to handle this giddy beyond all control version of her oldest friend. I must have been annoying, I was annoying myself. I was never that kind of girl. By my fourth phone call I could hear her frustration, "Come on Charlie, I have to get some work done."

Oh yeah, people do that. In the divorce I received a lump sum pay out that paid for my new (downsized and much warmer) ranch style house. I sold my paintings and photographs to cover the monthly expenses. Which blew my mind, I never thought I would actually be able to live off my art.

"And isn't Kennedy a better source for which shade lipstick to wear?"

The lightbulb shone overhead. Ding. Ding. Ding. I should be using my best reference in all matters girl. "Duh, sorry, love you, bye." I hurriedly hung up and dialed my favorite fashionista.

Over the years Kennedy and I had grown really close, never minding the fact she was seven years older than I and we were vastly different women. She was full hair, full face, full dress, all day, everyday, while I was not. I think what I appreciated about her the most was, she was who she was, she embraced it. I think she found the same sense in me, even though we were at different ends of the spectrum.

She was at my house within the hour; armed with two Dutch Brothers lattes, hair blown out to perfection and eyes perfectly winged. She even made yoga pants look glamorous. I always admired her way with accessories, but when you have a long giraffe neck, to match mile long legs, you have room to play with big and bold. She kissed my cheek and handed me the keys to her Range Rover. "There's a bag in the trunk. Can you fetch it for me Butch?"

I smiled, kissed her cheek, accepted the coffee, and greeted, "Good morning to you too." I opened the trunk to find her twenty-seven inch roller suitcase. When it plopped to the ground, I roughly gauged the weight at twenty pounds. As I dragged the bag through the threshold, I had to ask, "What the fuck is in here?"

"Essentials." She cooly stated as she sipped from her paper cup.

A wave of caution washed over me. "Essentials?"

"Hair, makeup, I'll give you a quick polish change to match your clothes. I brought some shoes, a couple of outfits. Hopefully convince you to wear something, anything else."

I sipped from my cup, "Ah. Essentials." After hours of primping, arguing, and Kennedy torturing me with flat irons and eye lash curlers, I was ready. I let her switch my long sleeve black top to a lacy black camisole. She layered me up with several gold necklaces and wrapped my curly messy ponytail with the pink and black lace scarf I had bought. We topped it all off with those gold hoops I swore I'd never wear. Admittedly, Kennedy did a better job on my make up than anticipated. It was clean and simple. Very little face. Perfectly winged, smokey eyes and a soft lip. A stark contract from her fully contoured face. I gushed at my reflection in the mirror, "Wow."

"I wish you would wear a different pair of shoes. I hate those wedges." That was a forty five minute argument I refused to budge on. She was trying to push her Jimmy Choo pumps and I countered with Dr. Martens. She shot me a look of disgust and the discussion was dead.

She shrugged in defeat, "Well, you look mostly doable."

CHAPTER 59
Charlie Modern Day

As I DROVE INTO THE city, anxiety started to flood my body. My palms were sweaty, I couldn't believe how nervous I was. The only time I had ever really experienced an out of control feeling was in my dreams and the occasional panic attack. In my day to day life, even when I speak to the other side, I felt in control but as I crossed the Bay Bridge, the tailspin feeling of my dreams hovered.

I found a parking garage a few blocks from the coffee shop. The brisk air of a summer evening in San Francisco stabbed like pins and needles on my already tingling skin. Thank God I didn't let Kennedy talk me out of wearing a bra. My nipples already felt like they could cut glass.

I don't really remember walking into the coffee shop. I was lost in a typhoon of nervous thought and I walked right past Thomas. He grabbed my by my upper arm stopping me as I blindly breezed by, "Sorry. I didn't see-"

He thankfully interrupted my nervous embarrassment. "You look beautiful."

"Really? You think" I nervously twirled a loose curl at the base of my neck. "Not too 'I'm with the band'." Did I just use air quotes? I'm the worst. I have never been so nervous. Or awkward. Ever. He's talking. Pay attention!

"No band. Just me and her." He points to his acoustic Les Paul posing center stage under the glow of a spot light.

I felt a flirty smile sit in the corner of my mouth, "Her? What's her name?"

"Charlotte." When the name fell from his lips, a half squint fell into his brow, like he was watching puzzle pieces pull together.

A voice came over head. '...and now Thomas Black." The roar of applause for such a small coffee shop took me aback. He obviously had a following. I made a mental note to Google him later.

I pressed my lips to his cheek and whispered in his ear, "For luck." He squeezed me hand and walked toward the stage. The small gesture pulsed straight to my heart. I felt the same bewildered look that Thomas had just a moment ago cross my face. No way.

He strummed a few original tunes as the gaggle of girls sang his songs back to him. Every time I looked up, his eyes caught mine. It was invigorating and way too intimate all at the same time. His hazel eyes seared through me, forcing my gaze nervously to the bottom of my coffee cup.

"So I don't normally do covers-" I have to admit I was turned on by the way he leaned into his guitar as he spoke into the microphone. "But I met this girl the other day and I haven't been able to get this blasted tune out of my head since." There was a collective aww. It took me back to the day of the PA debacle. Forty strangers in a coffee shop vs. the entire student body I had to see daily. Embarrassing, but nowhere near the scale, I might survive this. "She's here tonight." He pointed over in my direction. "So I'd like to sing it for her."

Forty sets of eyes turned their attention to me. Nope, still embarrassing. Is it possible to actually die from embarrassment?

The sound of a familiar tune pulled me from my thoughts. He began to sing the words of an old Allison Krauss song that I'd heard a million times before and always seemed to trigger glimmers of memories past.

The chords he played and words he sang flooded me. Flashes of all the lives that have haunted me; England, Ireland, Kentucky, all of them. The air thinned and the room began to spin. His chartreuse eyes, why did I gravitate to the brown fleck? My knees wobbled, I was going to pass out, or vomit, or both. I bolted for the door.

I heard the abrupt clang of a guitar crashing to the floor behind me. As the fresh air hit my skin, his fingers wrapped around my wrist. He pulled me to him, searching my eyes and reading my soul. In that moment, I felt my heart touch his. He pulled me in to him, feverishly crashing my lips in to his. I surrendered to his determined kiss. For the first time in this life, I felt alive.

He pulled away first. "I'll be right back." Our lips intertwined again "I have to get my guitar." He sweetly kissed my forehead before disappearing back into the shop.

As I waited I became lost in my dizzying thoughts. Is that? Can't be. Am I crazy? He had to have felt that too?

I opened Scout's tailgate and Thomas laid Charlotte's case gingerly down. I slid into the driver seat and anxiously gripped the steering wheel mustering my courage as he slid in on the passenger side.

He blurted before I could summon my strength, "I have to ask you something."

"Okay." I caught his ever changing green eyes abuzz with manic thought.

Nervously the words fell from his mouth as he stumbled to find a way to spit it out. "Have you ev-? Do you? The thing is-? Hmph. How do I say this without sounding crazy?"

I slid my hand to the back of his neck and he inched so close, that my words tickled against his lips as they fell from my mine, "I've dreamt of you too."

He softly smiled as our lips met in a tryst eons in the making. He pulled away, staring in to my heart as he ran his thumb across my jaw. In that moment I knew it was true. This was the man who time after time, one way or another, I always found my way to. The one my heart was promised to a millennia ago. A powerful pulse vibrated through me as I pounced him, stealing his breath and clumsily pulled him over the seats and in to the back of my SUV.

CHAPTER 60
Charlie Modern Day

"SLUT!" KENNEDY SANG AS I told the story.

Dahlia sipped from her wine glass. "In the back of Scout? Really?" She made no attempt to hide her judgement. "How old are you?"

Kennedy defended, "I think it's hot. It sounds hot. I mean, my panties are wet."

I let them hash it out as Dahlia scolded. "No one gives two fucks about your panties Kennedy." I couldn't hide any longer, she directed her chiding toward me as she waived her wine glass and chastised. "Some guy sings you half a song and you think 'what the fuck, I'll bang him out in the back of my truck.' She emphasized her disappointment with a shrug.

I felt like I was twelve, being chewed out by my mom. "Not exactly, but essentially, yes." I mimicked her bothered movement.

Kennedy laughed uncontrollably as she wiped a tear from her eye. "I fucking love it." She egged.

Dahlia's disapproval shifted to Kennedy. "You're not helping."

"For fuck sake D. She's thirty six years old. Who cares that she got turned out in the back of her car in some parking garage by an 'insanely hot', your words, not mine, British musician." Kennedy didn't stop for air. "Is that really the worst thing in life she could have ever done? Quit being such a judge-y buzz kill dude."

Dahlia was trumped.

I laughed. "BURN!"

"BOOM!" Kennedy made an exploding gesture with her hands and all three of us erupted in laughter.

I bit my lip as I reminisced. "It was hot. Like super hot. He knew every inch of my body and I his." the memory made my skin flush. "We were devouring and breathing life into one another. It was such a primal experience." I paused for reflection. "Like our bodies were made for each other. It's never been like that before. Never." My eyes widened with emphasis. I felt a buzz in my pocket. "My pants are vibrating." I joked.

"So are mine." Kennedy laughed.

"No. I'm serious." I pulled my phone from my back pocket.

I still owe you a proper date.
Dinner tomorrow?

Is it weird that I read his texts with an accent?" I asked after realizing I had.

Yes.

The new message buzz rattled loudly on the kitchen counter.

I'll send details in the morning.

I was trying to play it cool. My heart fluttered. A date I didn't have to plan or coordinate in anyway. This was uncharted territory.

"I'm so jealous!" Kennedy dramatically folded herself over the back of a dinning room chair. "That new, exciting feeling. You only get that once."

I understood what she meant but in a sense it wasn't new with Thomas. It was more like we found each other again. It was hard to explain. My phone lit up and rumbled across the marble. I swiped the screen and felt an obnoxiously large smile spread across my face. I heard a distant, "Must be him." I couldn't tell which one of my snarky friends it was.

k. ;-)

I couldn't help but hear his gravelly accent as I read and flashes of his teeth dragging along my neck and collar bone ran through my mind. A soft breath and a half smile escaped the corner of my mouth.

Dahlia chimed in, "You are not going to leave us hanging like that." Their playful melodramatics combined with this nauseating overwhelming urge to gush and squeal like a pre-teen girl had me hand the phone over without thought.

"I also request the company of my lady for the whole of Saturday as well." Kennedy read aloud in her best British accent. "Well, that's hot." she added sans accent. "What should we reply?"

I snatched the phone from her as soon as I saw her thumbs assume the texting position. Just in time, I read her draft.

Send me a dick pi

"Kennedy! Seriously?"

I handed the phone to Dahlia. Unfortunately I had done so, right as she sipped from her glass of wine. An explosion of laughter sprayed Melbac all over my face and shirt. My friends burst into hysterics, Dahlia fell to the floor while I stood stunned and covered with wine. Assholes. I grabbed the towel from the counter and wiped my face while playfully scolding, "I hate you both."

Dahlia gained her composure first, wiping the tears from her eyes. "Love you too Boo."

Kennedy added between giggle bursts. "You. Should. Ask. Him. What kinda. Shoes to wear."

I rolled my eyes and my thumbs went to works.

The whole of Saturday huh? May I enquire as to what we will be doing?

The phone was vibrating with response as I showed the girls, weirdly seeking approval.

"Top Secret Love. Dress in layers. Comfortable shoes." Kennedy read aloud, her accent returning. "See, I told you shoes are important." She gleefully sang.

See you then.

Counting the hours

Le sigh. I hate being this swoon-y. "Ugh." Annoyed, I shook myself hard. "I am not this girl."

"What?" Kennedy continued with her increasingly bad accent. "Happy?Glowing? Vibrating with life?" I hate it when she's the one making sense. I couldn't tell if she was expecting an answer or was a rhetorical question. I stared at her blankly. She continued fighting annoyance. "There's nothing wrong with it you know."

"I feel like I'm tail spinning. Out of control. And I don't like that shit."

"You're not tail spinning or out of control. You're waking up. You are truly alive for the first time. You're scared because you know you can fall in love with this guy. Real love. Where you can share the darkest bits of you with him, giving him the power to destroy you, but trusting him not to." She reached for my hand. "Everything you have ever known is about yourself is about to change and that fucking terrifies you."

I was taken aback. Of all the years I had known Kennedy this was the most maternal I had ever seen her. The softness and sincerity in her voice brought a tear to my eye.

True to form, Kennedy could never stand for a moment to be too heavy too long, "Plus, you know, if it doesn't work out, talk about one hell of a notch for your lipstick case." She sipped her wine and winked. "And just because he said wear comfortable shoes does not mean you can wear those god awful jailhouse slippers you insist upon wearing everywhere."

"Firstly, they're Vans. Secondly, they are the definition of comfortable shoes." I counted on my hand for theatrics.

"Ew." Kennedy's disgust made both Dahlia and I laugh. "Please, for my sake. At the very least wear come cute ballet flats. Let me feel like I had some sort of an affect of fem-ing you up."

"So motorcycle boots and flannel it is."

My poke engulfed Kennedy in playful rage as she pinched the back of my arm, "One of these days I'm going to set fire to that closet of yours."

CHAPTER 61
Charlie Modern Day

I've been thinking about

THE LAST TIME I DATED, texting wasn't quite a thing yet. What the hell does that even mean? I hate texting. He could be talking about anything. Context is lost without cadence. I swallowed nervously and clicked send.

About

Three excruciating minutes later my butt pocket buzzes.

The thing is, I can't quite plan a proper date without being presumptuous.

I couldn't help the schoolgirl giggle that escaped me. Play it coy girl.

Presumptuous?

Two new texts arrive before I could finish the first. As I read an uncontrollable smile spread across my face. Maybe this texting this wasn't so bad after all.

If I plan a date down here, I presume you want to drive down here. And if I plan something up there, I don't want you to feel like there is a presumption I'd stay the night.

I mean I would enjoy it, but don't want you to feel as if it's expected.

I have to tell you, as I reread "enjoy it", the urge to fling myself off the roof crossed my mind. I'm a rambling idiot, even via text.

I put him out of his misery.

"Hi." His green eyes gleamed as he leaned against his apartment door. "Come on in."

The small corner studio had floor to wall windows with the partially obstructed city view that only a third floor apartment could offer. I hate that sounded kind of snobby. I enjoyed it, it was a front row seat to the pulse of the city.

The windows were lined with white twinkle lights. Pressed into the L of the window were two leather chesterfield couches, a small coffee table nestled in-between, instruments scattered everywhere, four guitars from what I could see, (I imagine more carefully stowed away) a keyboard, bass, and electric drums, all still on their stands. I remember mouthing wow, realizing how serious of a musician he must be. I was kind of in awe and a glaring reminder I still needed to Google him.

I was used to having my art confined to a corner of the house, tucked away. The part of me that could easily be hidden. His was strewn about, proud and on display, sewn into the fabric of his being. That's how it should be.

My eyes began to well, so I directed my attention to array of framed black and white photographs. "These are great." I examined. "This one of the bridge from Fort Mason is stunning."

"Thank you." Thomas handed me a glass of red wine.

I was impressed offering, "Another one of the many talents of Mr. Black," and resumed my close inspection of a fog woven redwood canopy. A telltale sign draws my eye as "You shoot with film?" gushed from my mouth.

"Good eye." He answered as he tied his apron strings, "I hope you don't mind, but I thought I'd cook for you."

The gleam of the twinkle lights paired with his forest green eyes and that smile, if I had walked in an ice cube, I was surely a puddle now. I took a large nervous gulp of wine. "Culinary artist as well?"

He scoffed. "Hardly, just a Shepard's Pie. My mum's recipe." He winked. "Hopefully anyway."

As Thomas chopped and mixed and browned dinner, I leisurely strolled the studio. I couldn't help run my fingers up and down the brick walls, the same as you would run your fingers along your lover's body. She was an old building. Survived 1906, a testament to her strength and character. I stared down at the street. The bustle of the busy city street layered with generations past. It was astounding to see the history of this street unfold in front of my eyes. Horse drawn carriages, old cable cars, Model Ts all mixed with SUVs and Hybrids.

I felt hands wrap around my waist from behind and lips graze the back of my neck. "Decent enough view." Thomas' gravelly voice tickled my ear.

Shaken back into the moment, I turned to kiss him. "It really is." Our mouths melted into one another. A twinge caught my nose. "Do you smell-" I twitched my nose to identify, "smoke?"

"Blast!" Thomas darted to the kitchen, pulling a black heap from the oven. He slid the tray onto the stove's top defeated.

"Awww." I tried to comfort, but could not contain my laughter.

Thomas dropped his head in exaggerated shame. His loose locks of hair covered his eyes. "Reckon I know what the broiler does now." He apologetically offered as he pulled out his phone and scrolled for a number. Forty five minutes later, there's a knock on the door and Chinese food on the table.

I could tell he was stewing. "You know it's not that big of a deal right?" I asked as I bit into a pot sticker. "I've burnt like hundreds of meals." He looked at me with those big green eyes and I lost all verbal control. "Seriously, and I've caught fire to my kitchen, twice." He shook his head silently laughing, as he shoved mushu pork into his mouth. "Are you laughing at me?" I playfully demanded.

Thomas straightened up shaking off the notion. "I would

nev-" He burst into hysterics before he could finish.

"Well I'm glad I can amuse you." I threw a waded up napkin at his face.

"Come here." He reached for my face, pulling my lips to his. "Thank you."

I questioned puzzled. "For what?"

"Laughter and perspective." Confusion settle in my brow. To alleviate, he added, "Laughter to break the disappointment." His toothy smile spread ear to ear, "And perspective that it could always be worse. At least I didn't burn the place down."

"Hey!" I playfully protested. "I told you that to make you feel better. Not so you could make fun of me."

He pressed his lips into mine, pushing my mouth open as he ran his fingers through my hair, sliding his hand down the back of my head to the base of my neck. The motion instinctively made my body pull towards his. He pulled his lips away, but held his hand in place firm behind my ear. He looked deep into my eyes, piercing my soul. It was the most intimate, naked exposed feeling of my life. He was so close that when he spoke, I felt the words dance across my lips as they left his. "You make me feel better in a way I'm not even sure how to explain. You heal an ache I didn't know was there until I met you."

I navigated his sea of green, till I found my grounding rod fleck. I knew exactly what he meant. When I plunged my lips into his, flashes of fire and blood and the English country side pulsed through my veins and into my mind's eye.

"Are you alright?" Thomas' eyes grew concerned as I abruptly pushed away.

I wiped the stray tear running down my cheek away. "I'm alright. It was just a little too intense for a moment there."

He squinted trying to read me. "Can I ask you something?" I shrugged trying to shake off the weirdness I had created."Remember the other night at the coffee shop? When you said you dreamt of me, does that happen to you a lot?"

"All the time." I was staring at the ground and the words started to fall uncontrollably from my mouth. "Lives and deaths through the ages. Bits and flashes from different times and places.

And when you feel the most doubt in your heart, is when a dream will present itself, tightening it's grip on you." He slid his fingers between mine forcing my gaze from the floorboards into his eyes. "And no matter when or where, the dangers or struggles we face. One thing remains steadfast and true, that's me and you." He gently kissed the top of my hand. Flashes of Ireland filled my vision. My eyes gravitated to the floor as I watched the scenes cross my mind. "Do you ever see flashes of the past or visions?"

"Is that's what happening to you right now?"

The question pulled me back to the studio. I shook away the remnants. "Sorry," I flushed, "Yes, not just us though. I see all kinds of stuff, life as it was, the spirits that linger." I took a soft breath. "Sometimes just as clearly as I see you now." He looked kind of freaked out. "Are you okay? This is weird. I know. A lot to dig-"

Thomas finally found words. "I- I think it's quite- I mean- I'm actually kind of jealous."

My face could not hide the shock that roiled inside me.

He continued. "I think it would be less crazy making to see the world as you do. All I have had, is your face haunting my dreams.

He was soft and mindful, but for some reason 'haunting' sounded a little harsh. I understood what he meant, he had haunted mine. "It doesn't help. It just muddies the line between reality and delusion. Except now I know you're real, so it makes me question everything I've eve thought or seen or felt." His soulful green eyes grabbed my gaze. They were the eyes of home, and I knew it now more than ever. "So, you believe me?"

"In seers, psychics, fate. The Loch Ness Monster, aliens, the lot. I have a philosophy. 'Why not?' I'll believe until it's proven otherwise."

I have to admit, my heart swooned. It was refreshing to have someone I could be open and honest with and not be made to feel like an absolute lunatic. I knew that instant, I was home.

CHAPTER 62
Charlie Modern Day

I LAID NEXT TO THOMAS, my bare breasts tucked into his chest as he softly combed his fingers through my hair. I looked up into his eyes, he was lost in thought. A soft smile formed in the corner of his mouth. His accent, made the words sound exponentially more romantic as he twirled my curls around his fingers. "You Love, are quite literally the girl of my dreams." I couldn't bear to look in to his intense gaze any longer. The intimacy of the moment had already triggered my fight or flight reflex. "And that scares the bloody piss out of me." I sat up intrigued. "It's a lot to live up to." He looked at me, only a sliver of hazel remained, his pupils were wide with thought. "A lot has played out when it comes to you and I." He hugged me close as his ramble continued. "But what does that mean for us today? And we have this weird dynamic. Like, I know you, but no, I don't really. That's a lot of pressure to put on a new? New/old? Old/new? relationship."

For someone who wasn't psychic, he seemed to pinpoint exactly what I was feeling? Or was I feeling it because he was? This is the extra maddening. Empathy makes you question every feeling and every thought toward a feeling you'll ever have, because there is always the very real possibility it wasn't even yours to begin with. I couldn't find words. The only thing I could find were those eyes. We slinked back between the sheets. Our limbs entangled, I couldn't tell where he ended or I began.

I spent the entire night nestled in his chest. I fell into the space without thought, like going home. When his protective arm cradled me in, flashes of lives past; memories, kisses, deaths, everything flooded me. For the first time I didn't fear my memories, for the first time, all of it made sense.

I don't think Thomas slept one wink. Even in a heavy slumber I felt him tenderly stroke my hair, the rise and fall of his chest and every so often a breath un-rhythmically louder than the others.

I wanted to stay up with him. Talk till the sun crept through the blinds, but I couldn't. The safe, home feeling was euphoric, intoxicating even. I was in the deepest sleep I had been in many many years. I couldn't wake up, even if I tried.

When I sleepily fluttered my eyes awake to the sun filled studio, an uncontrollable smile spread across my face. I was energized, more so than I had been in a long while. I rolled over to an empty bed. The sleepy smile I couldn't control disappeared and reappeared just as quick when I found a daffodil and note laying on the empty pillow.

Inhaling the perfumes of the yellow flower as I read; *Went to get coffee. You were so peaceful, couldn't bear to wake you.*

I hate when Dahlia is right, and this was one of those moments. I have to remind myself not to tell her that my inadequate planning had forced me into a walk of shame moment. I had to try and find my clothes, if anything at the very least my panties before Thomas returned. I woke to find myself in a two sizes too big Sex Pistols shirts. The sleeves had been cut off deep into the side of the shirt. I caught a glimpse of myself in the mirror as I tied the back of the shirt in to a knot. Have to admit, for thirty-six your old tits, my side boob game was on point. Don't get distracted, find your panties. I quickly found a trail of clothes from the the kitchen table to the bed. Skivvies, check. Jeans, check. I finger brushed my teeth and checked myself out in the mirror. *Not bad Charlie.*

The door knob turned and Thomas fell through the threshold as he maneuvered three cups of coffee, a bag of groceries, keys, and his phone. "You're up, great."

I pulled my messy wild curls into a sloppy bun atop my head as I crossed the room bare foot. "One of those for me?"

"Ah, yes, it dawned on me when I got to the coffee shop, that we never actually had gotten to the coffee drinking part of our coffee date." Thomas unloaded his arms onto the kitchen counter. "So when I got to the counter and the barista asked for my order, I realized I had no bloody clue. So I ordered 2 lattes with add shots and something with Chai." My lip uncontrollably curled, "But as the word Chai rolls off my tongue, it dawns on me you are not the sort of girl that drinks chai." He hands me a paper cup. "I bet no on pumpkin spice is a safe bet too."

I smiled as I took a sip. "Yes, definitely a safe bet. Latte or dark roast drip with cream and raw sugar." I sipped from my little slice of heaven. "And always an add shot." I kissed his cheek as he unloaded the bag groceries. "What's this?"

"Breakfast." He digs to the bottom of the bag, "And a toothbrush."

The playful smile gleamed from his eyes. I snatched the toothbrush from his hand, "I'll be right back." I declared, disappearing into the bathroom.

After I had given my teeth a proper scrubbing, I walked back to the kitchen, wrapped my arms around Thomas waist, and wedged myself between him and the counter. I tippy toed up and reached for the back of his neck as I pulled his lips into mine. Relief washed over me as I finally kissed him the way I had been dying to since I woke. As our lips parted, I whispered, "Thanks for the toothbrush." I could feel my words touch his lips. I found that lonely fleck of brown in a sea of green and found myself lost in thought. I wonder if it tickled him as it did me.

Before I could finish the thought his lips were entwined with mine. He pressed my body into the counter. I could feel my body flush as my legs wrapped around his waist. Sense grabbed hold of me, "Wait. Wait. Wait." I stuttered between kisses. Finally I was able to peel him off me,"Active stove tops and the distraction of kissing do not mix." I let out a soft laugh. "We've learned that once already."

His eyes were locked into my soul; lips parted slightly and pouted. I melted. "You started it." He pushed my hips on top of the counter as he unbuttoned my jeans.

His lips moved seamlessly behind my ear and down my neck. "Well, at least make sure the stove is off." I managed to blurt out between sighs of pleasure.

CHAPTER 63
Charlie Modern Day

I PAIRED LEOPARD PRINT FLATS with dark blue skinny jeans, my favorite fitted Johnny Cash tank and a red and black plaid flannel. I took a picture and text the girls.

Kennedy immediately replied.

Why do you always have to look like you're about to crawl under a truck?

Dahlia chimed in.

Johnny Cash? Seriously?

They're both too easy. I had already changed in to the 'pre-approved' blue and black plaid shirt dress and leggings. According to Kennedy, so long as I cinched up the waist with a cute belt and paired it with booties, it suddenly goes from 'lumberjack to chic'. All I saw was added opportunity for me to trip over my own feet. I snapped another pic and sent it off as I examined myself in the mirror.

Toss on a couple of necklaces, slap on a watch. I've done all I can. ;-P

Dahlia buzzed in.

Always there cheerleader K.

Kennedy's face popped up on my screen as it buzzed across the dresser. I answered the FaceTime call, before I could say good morning she was barking, "Undo those top two buttons."

"Good morning." I greeted as I obliged. It wasn't worth the

argument, I would just button it up in the car.

"Lorelei had it all wrong. Diamonds aren't a girl's best friend, cleavage is." I imagined her grabbing her silicone filled set. Seeing as she still held her phone, she had not, as grabbing her boobs was a two hand minimum job. "The cleavage gets you the diamonds." She emphasized with an obnoxious wink.

I could not hide the look of disgust on my face. I swallowed my judgement and laughed. "There are so many things wrong with that statement. I don't even know where to begin. And really don't have the time. So on that note; I love you, have a good day, bye." I kissed the phone and tapped the end call button.

Dahlia had sent a string of texts during my what I can only assume was meant to be a motivational call.

I didn't have the heart (or balls depending on your perspective) to tell her I already had a toothbrush at his house. So my thumbs entered 'Love you too Boo!' instead and I clicked send.

At nine in the morning, the valley still had a blanket of fog nestled between the hills. Which meant it would be foggy all day in The City. I grabbed my chunky grey knit cardigan and matching slouchy hat. When I shoved my hands in the sweater's pockets, I found a pair of grey gloves that I had cut the finger tips off of, finishing my ensemble.

Whatever Thomas had coordinated, it was down on the waterfront which allowed me to take the ferry, a welcome relief. Driving in The Bay gives me the worst anxiety. Plus it eliminates that awkward do I stay or do I go. I'm either on the last boat or I'm not, and then it's kind of decided. I bit my bottom lip as a flash of skin crossed my mind's eye.

Thomas was waiting for me at the Ferry Building. It was obvious he had been waiting a bit. His cheeks were slightly pink from the crisp fog nipping his skin. You could tell he wished he had headed his own advice and layered up. Whatever was under his wool lined denim jacket wasn't nearly insulting enough. His fitted black jeans had holes dramatically worn through the knees. Only a few groupings of thread held the ends together. My eyes made their way to his shoes. Combat boots?! Those meddling bitches.

I smiled as I went in to kiss his cheek hello. Before I had turned my head he had already plunged his lips into mine. He firmly ran his hand up the small of my back, pulling my body tight into his. His spare landing at the base of my neck holding my mouth a willing hostage against his.

I have to admit when he finally released me, I was a bit unhinged. The exigency in which he kissed me was as if he hadn't kissed me in a thousand years. It was primal, tantric, lust laden. "Hello." He finally offered as he his lips parted mine.

"Hi." I breathed staring at his lips.

"God, I've missed you." He whispered as his forehead fell into mine. His hands firm between my shoulder blades, holding me as if the miles between us were torturous and he couldn't bare the inches parting us now.

I softly kissed him, whispering back. "I've missed you too."

When his hands fell from my back, I was left with an exposed feeling. In his arms I felt safe and shielded. It was such a natural feeling, that it wasn't until it was gone had I realized it missing. I laced my gloved fingers through his as we strolled down Market. The warmth of his touch pulsed through my veins. This is what home is meant to feel like.

"Coffee?" Thomas offered as we passed a cafe.

I smiled. "Always."

Thomas ordered two lattes as I waited at a small round table. I noticed his jacket unbuttoned as he carried our coffee to the table.

Johnny Cash, the sleeves had been cut deep down the side like the Sex Pistols shirt I had confiscated.

I have to admit, even for me, I found it odd I had wanted to wear something similar, but really I was more upset that I had let Kennedy and Dahlia talk me out of my comfy clothes.

"Nice shirt." The family crest peaking through the side of his shirt caught my eye as I sipped my coffee.

"You know. I had this really great Sex Pistols shirt. It was seriously like my favorite shirt." He playful accused as he stirred a raw sugar into his latte. "Then this chick stayed the night. She wore it around the flat the next day, haven't seen it since."

The wink as he sipped from his cup melted me. I tried to pull it together, "That is the oddest thing." I smiled big, changing the subject. "So what are we doing today?"

"Going to jail." Thomas gestured toward the bay, but the fog was so dense you couldn't even see the water thunking heavily against the pier's footing.

"Alcatraz?" I guessed.

I must have made a disapproving face. "What? You've been?"

"Actually, no." I was worried about the history of the place, this would be a long day. I tried to recover the best I could. "It should be fun." Not really. I never understood the appeal of paying to go to jail. Cement blocks. Steel bars. Pretty sure they all look the same, but I wasn't going to dump on his effort.

"What a tosser!" Thomas slapped his forehead. "Good one Black. I can't believe I was so bloody stupid!"

His outburst was confusing, "What are you going on about?"

"You're psychic or clairvoyant, something to that affect right?"

He was slightly loud, it made me self conscious. "Something like that. I don't know. Sometimes I see things. History will play in front of me like a movie. I feel things more than most."

"Yeah, so let me take you to a notoriously violent, reportedly haunted hotspot." It was cute how hard he was being on himself. "I'm such an ass!"

I slide my arms into his coat. The sleeveless holes in his shirt made it so I could wrap my arms around his bare torso. I looked up into his self hating eyes, "It's cool, let's go. It'll be fun."

Thoughts and anger stormed through his grayish green eyes. He looked down at me and kissed me forehead. "I have a better idea." He threw his arm up and flagged a taxi.

After a short cab ride, I found my self standing outside a brick building reading a weathered sign;

The Black Trumpet
Musical Supply

"What are we doing here?" I laughed off my confusion.

He grabbed my hand, guiding me through the door. "You've been?" He was pleased with himself.

"Can't say that I have." I smiled.

The door jingled, tapping a brass bell when Thomas pushed it open. An attractive looking older fellow stood hunched over the counter, flipping through the pages of The Chronicle. His club master framed glasses appeared over the top of the paper. "Thomas, see you brought a friend today."

"Yes, Uncle Henry, this is Charlotte." The stumble in his voice was cute. He was embarrassed, as if he had been scolded for forgetting his manners.

I offered my hand, "Call me Charlie."

He folded his paper neatly and laid it on the counter, taking my extended hand. Henry's hand was wrinkled and knuckles swollen with arthritis, but his grip still strong. "Nice to meet you Charlie." Highlights of his life flash before my eyes. I smile and a glossy twinkle glistens in my eye. "You must be something special. He never brings anyone here."

"Henry!" Thomas intruded embarrassed. "You're killing me."

"Oh, come on." I playfully tapped his chest. "It's nice change of pace. You see Henry, It is usually I, who is being embarrassed by loved ones."

"Well anytime you want a chuckle or two about him as a wee lad, you come on back and see me. I'll make us some tea."

"It's a date." I winked.

Thomas grew uncomfortable and slid between me and the counter. "Well thats enough with introductions." Grabbing my hand, he dragged me away. "We'll be around."

"I'll just follow my ears." Henry returned to his paper. Out of earshot I whisper with a sweet pout. "He's cute."

"Like you want to have his babies cute?" Thomas playfully questioned as he weaved me through the display of instruments.

"Totally, like five, at least." Banter had always been my strong suite.

Thomas pulled an old skeleton key from atop the door's frame and slid it into the slot. The old bronze lock whined as it tumbled over. With a dramatic thud, the door popped open. He shrugs an explanation as he flips a light switch. "Keepin' it locked is the only way to keep it closed. Just too cool a knob to replace with something new."

"I know what you mean." I ran my fingertips across the filigreed knob as I crossed the threshold, feeling it tumble over hundreds of thousands of times, "They just don't make stuff like this anymore." I cooed.

"So Phillip and I have this deal with my uncle." Thomas explained as he guided me through the huge storage room filled with just about every instrument imaginable, scattered, yet organized. A couch, coffee table, two lawn chairs, and a pink flamingo capped with a Santa hat and wrapped in white Christmas lights were the only non-musical items from what I could tell. "We get to practice here, rent free. Customers come in, look around, on the fence about buying a piece. They hear us playing, ask for lessons, Henry gets a cut to cover our expenses, and on a good day sells an instrument. It's a pretty sweet deal."

I only heard half of what he said. I was admiring not just the complete strings section, but horns too. "Yeah, pretty sweet." Was all I could spit out. "You guys are like serious musicians?" My tone more surprised than intended.

"Phillip spent five seasons with the London Symphony Orchestra and two with the San Francisco Symphony. He's actually the reason we came out here." Thomas shared as he took at seat a one of the two pianos.

"Chasing the dream you could say." He smiled, acknowledging the irony.

His fingers danced effortlessly across the keys. I took a seat next to him on the bench. He looked at me, fingers still dancing away. "You play?"

"No, I wish. My brothers do. Tried to teach me, it just never stuck. I can read music through. It's weird the way my brain works. I get theory, but application is a totally different story. Like, across the board. Science, Math, Sports, it's so weird."

"Wait. Wait. Wait." Thomas' fingers halted, immediately silencing the room. "You write? And you read music?" Shaking his head with excitement. "Sweetheart, you're a songstress."

"Ha." I scoffed. "The one fault in your hypothesis is that I do not sing."

"Yet." He replied with certainty. "I bet you have a journal in that big ol' bag of yours right now."

His evaluation was correct. "Maybe."

"Let me see it."

"No." My protest was playful and only half serious.

"Do you trust me?" The sea of green caught my heart.

The room fell away and only he and I sitting on that bench remained. "I do." I dug through my purse, pulling an eight by five spiral bound kraft brown notebook that said 'It's okay. Writer's are supposed to be weird." on the cover. The certainty in which I handed it over so blindly was dumbfounding. I didn't think twice about letting him read the pages of my bleeding soul. The thought of anyone else even knowing what the cover even looked like made me nauseated.

Thomas paced the room as he thumbed through the book. His facial expressions fluctuated with the pages. Sometimes his brow scrunched with sadness or concern, others his eyes lit up with laughter; then he found something. "This. Let's start here." He took a seat on the couch, picking an acoustic guitar from the rack of four.

"What?" I eagerly reached for the open book, to see what had chosen.

"Ew. That? No."

He had already started strumming.

"I'm sorry
I can't be what you ne-ed
I'm sorry
It hurts you
I need to spread my w-ings.

You call me,
Selfish.

Heartless.
Evil.
I know that you're angry
And that's okay.
But I can't stay

The light strumming ended with a heavy clap against the body of the guitar. He continued strumming his melody. "This is a great start. We can tweak it till it's right."

Thomas started marking up the scribbled poem, "Yes, this can most definitely be something."

He looked up at me staring bewildered as his left hand scribbled effortlessly in my notebook, embarrassed, he drops the pen. "Sorry. I should have asked."

"No, it's cool." I waved away his apology. "I'm actually surprised at how okay I am with it. I mean, once I got past the overwhelming urge to heave from embarrassment." I sat next to him on the couch. Our thighs grazed, as he strummed the guitar, a thick electricity filled the room. "But that has more to do with my own hang ups than you."

It was the most intimate, non-intimate experience of my entire life. Sharing a piece of my heart, my soul, with this man. Trusting him with my inner most thoughts. I had never felt as safe or free as I did in that moment.

The piercing clang of a symbol broke the protective barrier of our private session. "We interrupting?" A male voice asked as a girl giggled softly behind.

"Dad said you brought a girl back here but I wouldn't believe it unless I saw it with my own eyes."

Thomas was annoyed. "Charlie, this is my cousin Phillip and our bassist Liv."

I waved, "Hi. Nice to meet you."

"Well at least we know you won't be bothered by the fact he gets all knotted up with his work. You seem to have the same affliction." Phillip playfully poked.

I flushed. "You can say that."

"I'm famished." Liv interrupted. "Can we fawn at the new girl over a burger?"

CHAPTER 64
Charlie Modern Day

I HADN'T REALIZED HOW HUNGRY I was or that seven hours had passed until we took our seats on the wooden picnic bench next to the food truck.

Phillip sensed my fatigue and abruptly warned, "Being his muse can be excruciating. Better take care of yourself."

"So you're one of those dreamy types too?" Liv questioned as she shoved a fry into her mouth. Her mysterious green eyes and olive skin were almost too intense to look at without her dark locks to help break it up.

"I'm not sure I kn-"

She interrupted, answering her own question as she bit in to her burger. "You get lost in the work. In a constant haze. Teetering the line between the real world and the world in your head." She took another bite of her burger. "You have to be. It's the only type of person Thomas can stand to be around for more than eight solid minutes without becoming cross." She didn't have a British accent like the boys but spoke like them; the phases she used, her cadence and her mannerisms, she had been around a long while. "My only question for you is-"

I felt a wave of protectiveness coming.

"How can you even understand what the fuck he's saying

half the time? His words are a jumbled mess and half the time he sounds gurgled, like when you run a garbage disposal." Her poke at Thomas made us both laugh. "What's amazing is, there is zero trace of it when he sings."

"I know, weird right?" I chirped.

Thomas interrupted. "I don't like what's going on over here."

"Just turning your girlfriend against you is all." Liv smiled through her squint. "What are we doing tonight?"

"I want to get back to the shop and finish up that song I, we," Thomas quickly corrected, "were working on."

Phillip intervened. "Sorry Mate. You know the rule. One hour outside in the real world for every two you lock yourself up. So by my counts, you have a solid three hours to kill."

"Who came up with that blasted rule? What a waste of time." Thomas protested.

"You, a few months back, when you didn't leave your flat for four days because you were all twisted up in a dream and a song." Phillip sternly reminded.

A dream and a song? A few months back? I wondered if it was during the same time when I shut myself in for two weeks.

"And it seems your chick suffers the same affliction." Liv observed as I turned my attention back to the conversation I had become the topic of. A lightbulb burned so bright over Liv's head, I could feel it's radiance, "Lets go bowling!" she blurted just as quickly as the thought came.

Thomas groaned and rolled his eyes in protest.

"Oh, come on! It'll be fun. We can play teams now," she campaigned.

Thomas reluctantly agreed after some pushing from Phillip.

"Yay! I call Charlie!" she announced.

CHAPTER 65
Charlie Modern Day

Two rounds and six pitchers of beer later, we were in the eighth frame of our final game. This was the tie breaker in a battle of sexes for the ages. Glow bowl was well under way; dance tunes blared overhead, light dizzily spun as it bounced off the disco ball and the pins glowed bright under the blacklight.

I filled my lungs with vital breath and prepared my approach, Make it. Make it. Strike!! "YES!" I spun around in the slide-y bowling shoes and my feet almost fell out from underneath me as I gloated, "Take that!"

"You have an alarmingly strong competitive streak in ya." Thomas moped with his lanky limbs haphazardly sprawled with defeat across his chair.

The automated scorekeeper bellows, "Whomp. Whomp. Whomp." and an animated turkey dances across the screen. Phillip guttered, twice.

Liv held her own, earning a spare. And now it was Thomas' frame. We were ahead, but not enough to breath easy. I calculated the scoreboard, Thomas needed a spare plus six to win.

The go-go dancer of my early twenties refused to let that happen. 90's Hip Hop Classics (that made me throw up in my mouth a little bit. When did I get so fucking old?) dumped overhead, filling the room with a heavy bass line. My hips grab hold of the rhythm and my feet glide across the floor while West Coast legends spit verses that force my matured, awakened, feminist mind to cringe at the horribly offensive lyrics I used to mouth word for word twenty years ago.

"Whomp. Whomp. Whomp." The score keep hollers.

Yes! When all else fails, distract. I sank back in to my skin, painfully aware if the six eyes glued to me as if a twelve inch dick had magically sprouted from forehead.

"I've never seen anyone dance like that before." Liv picked her jaw up first.

My skin tingled and went ice cold, except for my cheeks which were feverish and felt six shades of red. I had been caught, I had lost myself in the music and time disappeared. And now I've gone and mucked up the first real place of belonging I had felt because of my incessant weirdness, gah, why can't you just be normal for one god damed da-

Phillip intruded on my self berating; "You don't just count time and find rhythm, you get lost in it. It consumes you."

I grew increasingly uncomfortable with how centered of the conversation I was becoming.

"And you write, yes? Liv puzzle pieced.

"Yeah?" I still hadn't the foggiest what she was yammering on about.

"Sweetheart, you're one of us." Liv's large Coke bottle eyes shimmered with encouragement. "You are meant to create, preform."

I scoffed reminding her, "Except for the fact that I do not sing or play an instrument."

"Yet." She answered matter of factly. "You'd be surprised what that Thomas can charm people in to." She rubbed the back of her stubble coated head emphasizing her point.

CHAPTER 66
Charlie Modern Day

My phone danced silently across the wooden coffee table before I flipped it over and the photo of sixteen year old versions of Dahlia and me squeezing the life from the other in post pierced tongue jubilation lit up the screen. The truth or dare shenanigans that lead us to the tattoo parlor's chair, the infection we both suffered and the scolding we both received from one another's mom fondly played through my mind as I hit decline call. The memory felt like yesterday and a million years ago all at the same time.

I shook the moment away and set the phone down, knowing the call was not important. She was reminding me for the umpteenth time that she was hosting dinner tonight. Thomas and I had been dating a few months now and it was due time we make our way over for a proper grilling.

"You need to take that Love?" He asked as his stormy green eyes met mine, burning a hole through my soul and panties simultaneously.

"No." I fired without hesitation. His elm-leaf eyes reached through me and wrapped around my heart fueling the urge to shove him in to the couch and straddle his lap. "Not at all." I panted softly against his lips as his hands glide up my back.

His firm gentle hands roamed up my spin and settled between my shoulders, setting my skin on fire. He pulled my shirt overhead, covering my eyes and binding my arms. He held the cotton garment firmly in place and his lips hovered mine. The blood ran hot through my veins as he lingered and teased. Every nerve ending exploded with anticipation when his barely cracked smile gazed my tingling flesh.

I DRAG MY FINGERTIPS ALONG the curves and divots of her back, intoxicated by the longing hunger that radiated from her until I am drunk off of her need and want. Her desire and grinding hips fill me with unstoppable urgency, as I drop her bind to the floor and plunge my mouth against her lace covered chest, mapping the way from my breasts to neck.

THE SCRAPING OF HIS TEETH against my skin made me dizzy with anticipation. The excruciating millimeters of agonizing ache was alleviated when his lips greedily crashed against mine with his hands firmly placed between my shoulder blades, pulling my soul as deep in to his as our shells would allow. He rose from the couch and I wrapped my legs around my waist. Our lips entangled and our attention only on one another, a tangled mess of limbs clumsily bouncing off the hallway walls till we fell into the guest room.

Thomas plopped me down on the bed harder than he meant, my head lightly bounced off the mattress.

SHE GIGGLED AT MY GRACELESSNESS as I quickly apologized and delicately prodded at her non existent injury. The abyss of her eyes took hold of me as she grabbed my hand and told me she was alright.

A smile gleamed through that sea of stormy green as he pulled his shirt over head and slunk into bed. His hand grazed up my back and behind my head, pulling me to his mouth.

As the warm water caressed my body, I could feel his lingering touch. I ran my fingers across my soft smile. This is what made the struggle and strife worth it. The divorce, and torment of the visions, I had to go through all that, to get here, to enjoy this small moment of unadulterated bliss.

I dressed, towel dried my curls while I brushed my teeth. I stared at the woman in the mirror, and she stared back. It's kinda fucking amazing to know I'm not crazy, shrugged then spit into the sink, It was a bit touch and go there for a bit. Trust in yourself. *Trust in him.* A voice in the back of my mind added. I shook her voice away. No matter how often it happens, it still feels weird. Violated, not always. Uninvited, yes, but comforting nonetheless. Which makes it sound more crazy right? That I find comfort in random voices floating around my head, more so than my real life friends and family. *You're talking in circles.* Maybe I am crazy.

The light beaming through the living room blinds was impossibly bright. The vibrations from the coffee grinder radiated from my hands all the way through to my toes. The euphoric aroma of the grounds only became more heavenly as the hot water gurgled through Mr. Coffee.

I felt a presence behind me as I pulled two mugs from the cabinet. A blissful smile creaked across my face as I turned around, "Goodmor- Shit!" The mugs shattered as they bounced off the tile floor.

Mrs. Jimenez, you startled me. I greeted in silence, trying to pull my heart back in to it's chest.

Mrs. Miriam Jimenez was the previous owner of the 1960's ranch house. Her and her husband bought it new in sixty-two, and here she resided till the day she died, and, well, thereafter. Normally I would only hear her, on occasion I'd see her sheer. But with my senses heightened, there she stood, like she was really here, in my? hers? our kitchen. I cautiously reached toward her and as my hand delicately brushed her cheek, she was gone.

"You okay," Concern echoed down the hall and Thomas appeared in the kitchen before his query finished. "Charlie?"

I shook Mrs. Jimenez from my mind and distractedly answered, "Yeah." He had picked up a few large pieces of broken mug before I shooed, "Oh Thomas, don't worry about that." while grabbing a broom and dust pan from the pantry.

He pulled two fresh mugs from the open cupboard and filled them with warm, chocolatey smelling, coffee as I swept up the shattered ceramic and discarded them in to the trash.

I could tell by the skeptical look painfully plastered across his face he wanted to probe further but had decided against it.

Thomas' wheels were spinning, trying to find the right words to ask the questions we were both painfully aware that he had been dying to ask. Questions we knew needed to be asked. Questions that required honest answers, and I would have to trust him not to fear those answers. And even if he did, he still had a right to know exactly what he was getting himself in to.

THE PANIC STARTED TO SHIMMER from her eyes and her breath sped as she worked herself up in to a dizzying roulette of manic thought. Before she could spin herself out of control, I threw my arms around her and tenderly kissed her forehead.

AND WITH THAT SIMPLE KINDNESS, all the voices in my head silenced. All that remained was the steady thump of our two hearts.

I TUCKED A LOOSE WAVY tress behind her ear, and made sure to hold her gaze as I softly whispered, "You don't have to hide from me Charlie. I see you, exactly as you are. Always remember that."

I FELT HIS LIPS PRESS against my temple and his words pierce my heart. He wrapped his arms around my waist and pulled my body to his, punctuating his pledge with an accepting comforting kiss. I knew in that moment he wanted me, all of me, and all that entailed.

"Mrs. Jimenez popped in for a visit. I thought she was you. She startled me. I dropped the mugs." I offered (non) nonchalantly between awkwardly spaced sips of coffee. "I woke up this morning and all my senses were heightened. I saw her more vividly than I normally do." I nervously sipped again shrugging off the event. "No biggie."

"Fascinating." Thomas answered over the top of his cup. "This heightened sense thing, that happen much?"

He hadn't dismissed me. I hadn't realized how starved for acceptance I was until I had it and "Voices usually. Sometimes a sheer, or a historic overlay running parallel to today, but never anything so vivid. She was as clear as you are in front of me now." fell eagerly from my lips as quickly as they formed in my brain.

"Yeah, I think I might drop a dish or two myself." Thomas offered.

It was odd talking so openly about my experiences. I had always been so guarded, and this was the bit of me I buried the deepest. Anxious, and needing to do something with my hands before I bit them down to bloody stubs, I whipped up a fruit plate with yogurt and honey.

"What? No granola?" Thomas quipped as he dipped an apple slice into into his yogurt honey mixture.

I opened the cabinet and pulled out a sealed canister marked, "Dahlia's Homemade Muesli".

"Touche."

The retro analog kitchen clock read ten twelve as the Golden Girls theme song interrupted. "Shit!" I gulped down the last of my coffee.

"She's going to kill me."

"What?"

I grimaced, "Dinner..." and pushed myself to the tips of my toes, my lips landing on his and playfully gritted through my teeth as I added, "With Dahlia...and Finn."

"Ambush, nice." He joked as he wrapped his arms around my waist and playfully kissed my cheek.

"I hadn't meant it to be. She's been asking and I finally caved. I meant to ask you last night," I bit my bottom lip. "But we were, um, busy." The way his eyes seared through me, made my clothes feel liquid. They could melt into a pile on the floor at given moment.

CHAPTER 67
Charlie Modern Day

I PULLED THE PARKING BRAKE on Scout as we sat curbside of the Morgan Family craftsman when I noticed an all too familiar Maybach in the driveway. "Full disclosure," I nervously blurted. "this may be an ambush."

"What makes you say that?" Thomas scoffed.

"See that obscenely expensive car in the driveway?" I pointed to the glossy black Mercedes. "That's Greyson's car. He doesn't live here. But you 'don't park a quarter million dollar car on the street.'"I mocked. "That means Kennedy's here, like I said, ambush." I nervously apologized, "We don't have to do this. Actually, if you want to leave-"

He stopped my hand as I turned over the ignition. Every manic thought that had been racing through my mind fell away and all I could hear was the husk in his voice as he settled my anxious nerves. "Dinner party, no big deal, something proper couples do all the time, right?"

"Couple?" I playfully nudged. We hadn't talked about it and I was fairly confident where I stood, I was just didn't want to assume.

"Now don't you go playing stupid Charlie, you are far too beautiful a soul for such an ugly look." He grabbed my jean covered thigh, and my eyes darted from his tattooed, ringed fingers to his grey-green eyes as he softly thumbed my jawline. He leaned over the shifter and kissed me with the perfect balance of firmness and reassurance. He stole my last bit of breath when pulled away, leaving me lingering for his burst of life. "But if it makes you feel better, will you be my girlfriend?" and batted his long eyelashes.

"Shut it." I playfully pushed him.

He laughed as he exited Scout. "Isn't that sweet, we're even starting to talk like one another."

"Nauseating." I answered as I opened the driver side door.

He held my hand as he lead me up the rocky walkway. A flash of a dim cobble alley crossed my eyes. For a moment I was lost in time, unsure which world I was anchored, until I heard Kennedy shrill, "It's about time bitches!" as she flung the front door open pulling me back in to my skin.

"This is Thomas." I introduced annoyed and embarrassed by Kennedy's overall Kennedy-ness, as she wrapped her arms around him pressed her body into his. "And this is Kennedy."

Unapologetic, she explained, "I'm a hugger."

Thomas seemed unfazed, "Pleasure to meet you."

He squeezed through the threshold that Kennedy blocked, preoccupied with her ogling. "You are a fucking beautiful specimen of man."

"Don't mind her," I grabbed Thomas' hand, guiding him toward the kitchen. "she's our local hyper sexual cougar and firmly believes in equal opportunity sexual harassment." I threw Kennedy a dirty look over my shoulder, "But she's a house cat. All meow, no bite."

"Those of a feather baby." Kennedy fired back as she kissed her middle finger and blew in my direction.

Thomas interjected, "Oh, she bites." His half crooked smile melted her.

"Imma just get this out of the way now so we can enjoy the evening, okay?" Kennedy closed in on Thomas, forcing his gaze captive in her wing lined and lash extension-ed eyes, "You're damaged and sultry and brooding and charming and mysterious." Thomas eyes gleamed, Thanks, I guess. "Just the right kind of fucked up that sings to Charlie's special blend of fucked up. I can see it, radiating off of both of you. She's goin' to get lost in you, if she hasn't already." She was nose to nose with Thomas, and her words brushed his lips as she ran her fingers through his hair. She always did have an issue with boundaries, she would never cross the line, but she would march straight up to it just to make you squirm, as if it were her favorite sport. "You break her heart..."

"Dually noted ma'am." Thomas answered with the same jest.

"Ew, don't ever call me that again." Kennedy ordered as she lead us through the parlor and into the kitchen where Dahlia was whisking and basting and stirring and scuttling away.

"So Thomas, did our Charlie at least give you a heads up of what to expect this evening?" Dahlia teased over her shoulder.

I cringed in to Thomas' protective chest. "Interrogation, sexual harassment paired with an amazing meal." He managed to successfully summarize how I anticipated the night to go regardless that I had forgotten to ask him to dinner much less take the time to debrief him on the shady cast of miscreants I align myself with.

Dahlia shoved a covered dish back into the oven before I could sneak a peak, "Sums it up."

"And I was promised copious amounts of wine." He winked and I watched Kennedy melt.

"Dinner without, blasphemy." Dahlia playfully winked back.

She had grown to enjoy his company and flirty banter since recovering from her epic embarrassment over a lunch date where he categorically refused her apology because "Every great love affair needs a grand beginning to tell the children." (Yeah, how do you not swoon when you hear something like that.)

"That accent, fuck me." I heard Kennedy's thoughts.

"Kennedy!" Dahlia scolded. Nope, she said it that out loud. "Sorry Thomas, filters and tact are something we tend to lack around here. Though we usually try to at appear as if we have basic manners whilst making new friends." She swatted Kennedy's leg to reiterate her message.

Thomas waived away her words.

"Well I'm glad Charlie here could get your dick out of her mouth long enough to bring you around for a proper introduction." Kennedy goaded as Dahlia fired a scathing glare. "I've been dying to see what the fuss is all about," she bit her bottom lip as she undressed him with her eyes, "and Darlin', unlike most things in life, you do not disappoint."

I couldn't pour my wine down my throat fast enough, Dahlia was mortified for me. Thomas giggled with bemusement, I knew he was a keeper.

An irritated throat clearing came from behind me, "I would apologize for my wife's behavior, but that would mean there was some sort of intent to correct said behavior." The clean cut, dark haired man who was equally as tall as his statuesque wife extended his hand. "Grayson Pierce."

"Thomas Black." he matched the hearty shake. "No need to apologize, I think it's hilarious."

"Yeah, it's cute and funny at first." Finn squeezed Thomas' shoulder.

"Until one night, you're at dinner, and they start to harassing the wait staff." Finn sipped from his crystal glass of scotch.

"Are you tellin' lies!?" Kennedy stomped.

Thomas smiled over his shoulder. "Tales of wait staff harassment?"

She sipped her Bloody Mary and shrugged. "You ask one waiter if you can see his abs and everyone gets in such a tizzy."

"It was more the you sliding your hand up his shirt and feeling them Sweetheart." Greyson cooly added.

"C'est le vie." she toasted.

Thomas bust into laughter, "See, hilarious."

Greyson playfully warned. "Please don't entertain," He motioned over to Kennedy's general direction. "this."

"Anyway," Kennedy blurted rolling her eyes trying to hide the fact that Greyson's thinly veiled disapproval crawled through her skin and rattle her bones.

Dahlia pulled a heavenly smelling dish from the oven and slid it's covered contents onto to stove top for rest. "So why don't you just change your voice mail to, 'Hi this is Charlie. I can't get to my phone right now because I'm too busy humping my sexy musician boyfriend. You can leave a message. But I won't call you back. Because I'm getting banged out by a ridiculously good looking tattooed guy.'"

"You know I hate you right?" I answered as I popped the garden fresh cherry tomato that I stole from the salad top into my mouth.

"Love you too." Dahlia cooly answered, then immediately shrilled, "But what the fuck?!"

"Like you said," The snark rolled off my tongue. "too busy humping my ridiculously good looking boyfriend, jealous?"

"Incredibly." Kennedy instantly replied. The three of us looked at each other, bursting into hysterics.

"Seems you are just as bad as they." I heard his gravelly voice behind me. I cringed, and turned around with flushed with embarrassment as he wrapped his arm around Kennedy's shoulder and plopped a big ol kiss her on the cheek lightly tussling her hairspray shielded mane.

She melted as she breathed in his neck, "You smell so good. Charlie," Kennedy called frazzled.

I took a weird pleasure in her rattled nerves, "Yes."

"I love the way he talks." She was still occupied the space between his chest and under his arm, the place where the gruff in his voice tickles your ears most, "Can we keep him?"

"That's the plan Doll." Thomas answered hugging her tighter. He was matching her tick for tack at her own game, she loved and hated every second of it.

CHAPTER 68
Charlie Modern Day

DINNER WENT WELL BEYOND EXPECTATION. My friends were their normal embarrassing selves and Thomas managed to keep up, which was a welcome relief. We're an acquired taste; like stinky cheese, we either go down smooth with a nutty finish or leave a funky taste in your mouth and there is no in-between.

As we exchanged hugs and thank yous Finn and Dahlia walked us to the door. I kissed Finn's cheek good night as the front door opened. Aside from Thomas the rest of us let out a gasp of surprise; Michael was on the other side. My eyes darted to Thomas, then to Michael and back again. I was immediately nauseated.

Dahlia stepped through the threshold, breaking the tension filled silence first, "Michael, what are you doing here?"

"Just swinging by, wanted to see if you'd let the husband off his leash long enough to grab a drink." He caught my nervous stare. His eyes then drifted to Thomas as he measured him up. At six-five, he looked down on everyone, but tonight he felt cold, mean. "Charlotte," he offered short and unmoved.

"Michael." I returned his tone. "This is Thomas." Thomas politely extended his hand and surprisingly, Michael took it. "So nice to see you, you look well, but we've got to be going. Tell your mom I said 'hi'." Nervously fell from my mouth as I dragged Thomas down the drive by the lapel of his jacket.

I felt Michael's scathing stare follow us to the car and as we loaded ourselves in. I threw my head into the rest and turned to Thomas. "Well, that went well as could be expected."

I needn't be a seer to read Thomas' face, he was seeing the puzzle pieces were falling together. "Was that Michael, like thee Michael?"

"My ex? Yep." I grabbed the steering wheel and turned Scout over.

He looks back to the front door, watching the tall form enter the house. "I was going to say Michael from the dreams." The befuddled look on his face was adorable. "Why does he seem so bloody tall? I don't remember him being that tall."

CHAPTER 69
Charlie Modern Day

"If I'm being honest, it started as a hormonal battle between intrigue and disgust." I answered Thomas' borderline invasive questions as I played with his long blonde locks while his head lie in my blanket covered lap. "Back then I hadn't seen many visions, but repulsion was a natural reaction. I chalked it up to him being the campus stud and I was, well, far from one of the crowd."

"Do you think the visions had anything to do with you pulling away?" Thomas asked looking up in to my eyes. This conversation was far more intimate than I was accustomed. Had Michael taken this much interest in our relationship, I would be telling a much different story.

"I can't say they didn't. But I was never really whole heartedly in it to begin with. It was weird. I knew he was always meant to play a part in my path but he was never meant to be in it the long haul. I always joked he'd be a great first husband, even before the past lives started presenting themselves." I slinked down next to him. "Can we not talk about this? It's weird; talking about him, the visions, with you." I pleaded.

He swept the curls from my furrowed brow, gently tucking them behind my ear and reaching the darkest corners of my being with his stormy green stare. He pressed his lips into mine, involuntarily I grabbed his hand, cupping my cheek and let out soft sigh.

I had longed for a feeling of wholeness, of completion. In his arms, lost in his eyes was where I found it. All those dreams made me feel like I was losing my mind. They were messages to hold out hope, he would find me, just like he promised all those lifetimes ago. I had found the home I had been searching for. A stray tear swelled in the corner of my eye and rolled down my cheek.

Thomas caught it mid way, thumbing it away. “What is it Love?”

I laughed and the swell of tears streamed down my face uncontrollably. “Nothing.” I swiped one side of my face. “Nothing at all.” I sniffled. “It’s just kind of crazy to think about what was, what is. All the steps to took to get to the this moment. I’m just really happy.” I wiped the other side of my wet face. “I never thought I would feel like this, like it wasn’t in my stars. That I would only ever be tormented with what was, I hadn’t seen the possibility of what could be.”

CHAPTER 70
Thomas Modern Day

THE TUTORIAL AND INSTRUCTIONAL SEMINAR I sat through just to get behind the wheel of Charlie's beloved Scout was, intense, to say the least. By the end of the class I had learned that the fully restored, 1969 International Scout 800 body was 1957 Chevy Teal. Not to be confused with any other shade of teal, as it is a very specific color. And though the color wasn't exactly period correct, it looked pretty and it was her car and she could paint it whatever the fuck she wanted. (Apparently this was a sore subject with someone at some point.) The hard, white leather top was removable. She used as many original parts she could, which included many trips to scrap yards and scouring the internet for new old stock.

I couldn't help but imagine her; wrench in hand, messy bun, her cover all arms tethered around her waste, a grease covered tank, exposing her toned biceps and carved shoulders. When I interrupted her spiel to inform her of my newly formed fantasy, she laughed, pulling a picture from the glove box. It was her, exactly as I imagined.

Scout was in much rougher shape. She was missing her hood and had about four shades of patina, a term I had recently learnt meant rust. In another photo, she was tipping over the driver side fender. Her toes dangled off the ground, her head looked to be where the engine should be and her arm lost deep inside.

I thought it odd that I had described her exactly as she had been. I shook it off. Maybe I was just really getting to know her. And honestly, me seeing her as she was years ago wasn't as bloody weird as me seeing her as she was several lifetimes ago.

She had continued with her crash course on Scout. The interior was the same white leather with teal piping. Aside from ascetics, everything was modern. There was something about torque and suspension and some other buzz words I was able to make out. I was especially thankful for the ABS brakes and power steering as we cruised the windy coastal road.

If I'm being quite honest, listening to her babble on about that car was incredibly sexy. It's nothing short of miraculous when you see glimpses of a person one hundred percent unadulterated. It's not too often that someone drops the veil and lets you see the real, messy, them. And watching her light up; it was impossible not to fall in hopelessly love with her.

But on the other hand it was incredibly emasculating to know absolutely nothing about vehicles in comparison to your girlfriend.

"City Mouse. Country Mouse. I suppose." she answered when I expressed my embarrassment.

"What?" I didn't understand.

She laughed at me and a loose curl dropped into her eyes. She tossed a handful of hair back without thought. Every stand fell perfectly into place. I was lost in her, with no possible hope of return. "Nothing, it just means you adapt to your surroundings. You lived somewhere where parking fees are atrocious and public transit is fairly efficient. I grew up in Calistoga. Where the only way out of town for the unlicensed was the hourly 10 bus up and down the valley. There was something about being stuck at such a young age and knowing it, that made me decide stuck was a place I never wanted to be." She kicked her head back into the passenger seat rest. I couldn't tell through her dark Ray-Bans if she was crying or contemplative. A quiet eternal ten second lull passed. Right as I opened my mouth to ask, she offered with a soft smile, "Sorry. That was an expedited trip to Awkward-town, wasn't it?"

And here we are now, cruising down the 101. The smell of salt on the crisp ocean air. Wind whipping through the windows, both our hair furiously flying around. *The Boys Of Summer* blared over the speakers. I was having a quintessential Californian moment. I felt like I was in the middle of a Jeep commercial or something. Normally feeling so cliche would have sent a violent wave of disgust through my veins. But when I looked over at her, the sun bouncing off her dark glasses, waves crashing against the sandy beach behind her, I was mush.

Pandora chose John Mellencamp's version of *Wild Night* next and I caught Charlie perk up from the corner of my eye. She danced and wiggled in her seat and as the second verse played she belted along with Me'Shell.

My eyes locked on her, though I should have been paying attention to the curves of the road.

"What?" The perplexed look on her face was adorable as she scolded. "Jesus Christ Thomas. Spit it out, do I have a booger in my nose or something?"

I reached across, grabbing her hand. I pulled it to my lips and kissed its silky top. I caught her gaze briefly, returning my attention to the coiling highway. "I had no idea you could sing like that." I caught her eye again, longer this time. "You're kind of spectacular."

Her cheeks flushed red as she turned the stereo down and rolled her window most the way up. "I was just playing around." she recoiled in insecurity.

"Charlotte, you are bloody brilliant." I squeezed her tiny hand. "You grossly underestimate yourself, we're going to have to do something about that."

She smiled when her name rolled off my lips. "I could never do what you do." She paused, carefully stringing her words together. "Up there on that stage. The naked exposed feeling would cripple me. Performing and creating are two entirely different monsters. I could never be so open and raw with the masses. Sharing my work is terrifying enough as it is."

"To be quite honest, it is completely unnerving." I paused for dramatics.

She was baited, “Thomas?!”

A playful smile fell in to my face as I continued, “But exhilarating and liberating all at the same time.”

She turned her whole body toward me, and with a soft smile, kissed my cheek. I could tell she was asking me to drop the subject.

“I’m totally getting you up on a stage.” I egged.

“Yeah, I don’t think so.” She smiled, her tone trying to close this topic.

I flirted with the line between playful and pushing. “Mmm Hmm. We’ll just have to see about that.”

“Are we fighting?” Charlie snapped, her joke coated with just the right amount of harshness to successfully shut the door.

I didn’t want to escalate to a full on argument by pushing too hard. I just see a greatness in her I’m not sure she is aware of. “Yes!” I answered laughing. “You are insufferable.” I pulled her hand back to my lips and smiled.

CHAPTER 71
Charlie's Journal–Modern Day

That damned Thomas can be so infuriating! He catches me singing in to the mop handle once, which he reminds me of almost daily and now this.

I adore that he's so supportive, and he really pushes me to surpass the bounds of what I thought possible. Writing music with him feeds a beast I had no idea was churning within me, but I am in no means a singer. I have no intention of being propped up on a stage to be exposed to the masses, no matter how hard he pushes.

I create to soothe my bleeding soul, not for accolades. I haven't eaten at my favorite restaurant in months solely because they show my work and have no problem asking top dollar from some tourist who 'must have this one off the wall'. It's impossible to enjoy a meal while you see people examining and commenting on your heart's work.

I was not meant for the glare of the spotlight.

I would rather be lost in the shadows.

But there is something enchanting at the thought.

Weaving one's words in to magical spells that etch in to memory.

CHAPTER 72
Thomas Modern Day

The sounds of Pandora switching from genera to genera, the monotonous sound of road and wind combined with the crisp, salty, air crept up on Charlie. She slipped into a nap, her seatbelt cradling her head as her journal lay open in her lap. I reached over, sweeping the hair from her face as she sweetly slumbered.

I was completely and totally enamored with this wonderfully paradoxical creature. Her vat of insecurity draped her exquisite beauty. She is talented beyond all measure, which is extraordinary and infuriating at the same time. She can hammer out two verses and a chorus in an hour while I spend days, weeks even, agonizing over a singular line.

When she is lost in her work, the world fades away and she unleashes all her love, hope, fear and dreams on to the page in an unabashed exorcism. It is only when she allows others to see, does her uncertainty show. Damn Michael for making her feel as if the best bits of her are wrong and weird. It's going to take me a lifetime to undo the damage he did.

CHAPTER 73
Thomas Nassau 1702

THREE WEEKS COME AND GONE in the blink of an eye and my time in Nassau was coming to an end. Phillip was chummy with the Quartermaster from Ananke's Revenge and secured me a position aboard. I was excited for the work, but conflicted. I hadn't expected to meet someone like Charlotte, and I was in no way prepared to leave her.

I had to go but in the deepest pits of my being I knew I had been drawn to Nassau to find her. My whole life had been one gigantic magnetic pull to this place, this moment in time, her.

I shook my thoughts away and gathered the last of my belongings. I'd be at sea for a solid month. By the time I return, I'll be a distant memory to her. I am here to make my a life, not hole up in some tavern on someone else's shilling, a woman's no less. What kind of man is that?

I stripped the bed and left the linens on the floor as she instructed and released a dreary sigh. The chore made my heart heavy, confirmation I was actually leaving.

I KNOCKED ON HIS OPEN door, leaning in to the frame and crossing my arms to hold myself together as the sadness settled in my heart. "Packed, ready to go?" I would never admit how unhinged I was seeing him leave.

"Pretty much." Thomas replied, shoving his last shirt in to his duffle.

Don't Go. Rang like church bells in my ears, vibrating through my body, hoping he would hear the words I hadn't the courage to say.

He dropped his bag to the ground, wrapped his arms around me, and squeezed me tight. I sink into his chest and breathe in the warmth of his neck. I knew this was goodbye. My heart shattered as he broke away first and held my shoulders firm. "I want to thank you for your kindness." Holding my gaze hostage with his haunting eyes, "I intend to return the favor."

His breath on my skin tickled my skin as his eyes penetrate my shields and worm into my heart. My body stiffens at the thought of goodbye. The nightmare of him grey and dying flashes across the back of my eyelids as I try to blink the horrid thought away. All I can muster is, "Safe travels."

I WAS DISAPPOINTED YET ODDLY relieved in her goodbye. Gently kissing her forehead, I begrudgingly offer, "I'll see you soon" to finalize our farewell as I grab my bag and exit the room.

EVERY STEP HE TAKES, BREAKS me a little more. Halfway down the hall I gather the slightest sliver of courage, "Thomas."

HER MOUSE OF A VOICE flings my hopeful body around, "Yes."

"YOU ARE ALWAYS WELCOME BACK." fell from my mouth while my heart begged, *Please don't go*.

Her large coffee colored eyes glistened with vulnerability. Walking away from her was the most difficult thing I have ever done. I half smiled trying to mask my reluctance, "And so I shall return." I promised before disappearing down the stair case.

SIX FULL WEEKS HAD PASSED before Ananke's Revenge returned to port.

As word made it's way to the tavern of it arrival. I refused myself any excitement. Thomas knew where to find me if he so desired. I was deflecting my fear, fear he may not return. It happened all the time. Nassau is a place you pass through as quickly as possible on your way to where you're going, not somewhere you stay and make a home. "Why do you think such things." I scold aloud shaking the thought from my mind.

"Dahlia, I need some air." I report, dropping a towel atop the bar and untying my apron strings.

"Are you alright? You don't look well Cousin." Dahlia's concerned query was sweet.

"Nothing a stroll on the beach and fresh air can't fix." I offered as I grab a bottle of rum and trudge toward the ocean.

CHAPTER 74
Phillip Nassau 1702

THE GULLS DEMANDED THE RETURN of fish heads and guts to the ocean, suppertime was on the horizon as the sun sank into the Caribbean and Charlotte had not returned.

"It's not like her to and disappear." Dahlia's worried voice cracked.

"She is in love with Thomas and too damn stubborn to admit to anyone, including herself." I sneered, "And now she's gone and worked herself up, I for one, am over it. She's been impossible for weeks." The fact that I mechanically and without fail continue to stock dishes behind her mahogany bar while she was off galavanting around picked at a scab.

Dahlia gave an understanding nod, "She has been a tad prickly as of late."

The tavern doors flung open in a mighty gust of anticipation. Dahlia and I perk, hoping to see our fearless leader had returned home but were equally relieved that our dear Thomas found his way back to us.

The scraggly sailor eagerly marches straight to the bar, drops his bag, cheerfully squeezing both Dahlia and me in. His leg swings over a stool as I pour us each a glass of rum. Thomas excitedly buzzed, "So all is well?"

"Just another day in paradise Mate." I report, chasing the update with a wink and my celebratory shot.

Charlotte stumbled through the doors and Thomas' attention immediately drew to her as if he had felt her coming from blocks away, tracked her steps and anticipated her arrival that very moment. The way he filled with life just catching of glimpse of her made it painfully obvious she had dominated his thoughts during his absence.

"Thomas?!" The hopeful gleam in her voice did not hide her mis-buttoned vest and sandy ratty hair. The booze had forced her to release more excitement than intended. I'm not sure if he caught the longing need in her bloodshot eyes, but I did. Normally she was better at keeping her emotions from flooding over their dam but want and whiskey have a funny way of tearing down the walls from which behind we hide. He rose from his stool and met her with a hug in the middle of the room. He breathed her in, relieved that she was in his arms. When they break, Charlotte's glossy-eyes can only focus on his lips as she drunkenly sways, "How've you been?"

"Good." He rubs the nape of his neck with nervousness. "It was rough, but we faired well."

I SNAP A MOTION FOR Phillip to pour a round of drinks, though I am entirely too intrigued by the motion of snapping itself. Thomas, gentleman he is, takes my arm and guides me as I wobble to a stool at the bar. We each take a seat and I pound my rum, slurring, "So tell me of your adventure." It took every ounce of self control I had not to run my fingers through his hair, I had forgotten how sexy he is.

"Absolutely." He offered, scratching the back of his head, before nervously asking, "Do you think I could get a room and a hot bath first? It's been a exhausting voyage."

Phillip was obnoxious with his eagerness to chime, "Your room is still free." as he stared me down, knowing full well why I had chose to lose money letting a boarder room remain empty for six weeks.

Before Thomas could catch the exchange, I blurt, "Yes, the

room you were in last is vacant, you know the way." I sloppily flung my arm in the direction of the stairs and in the same breath holler, "Dahlia!"

She had been seated on the other side of Thomas the entire time, popping her head around his back. "Yes Charlie."

She appeared is of by magic. "Oh, there you are. Will you set our friend up with bath please?"

Phillip rolled his eyes as I heard his barbed thoughts. *She has to be drunk. 'Please' is a word that is not in her vocabulary.*

Thomas picked up his bag, headed toward the staircase, and paused with one foot on the first step. "Thanks Charlotte. I can pay you this time." He finished with a wink.

"What a refressshing ssssentiment." I giggled at my inebriated slur.

Night had fallen before I returned downstairs. I felt human again after my first bath in weeks paired with a long nap in a decent bed. I was ready for a hot meal and to catch up with my long missed friends.

I had sobered and was in the foulest of moods. I tasked Lexy with tending to Thomas; making sure he got a meal and keep to his glass full. My orders were firm, I mustn't be bothered. I was already under my own skin and didn't want to unintentionally unleash on an innocent bystander. The fact I had acknowledged my brooding only solidified my fear of this evening's delicate balance.

When I first arrived, my pockets were empty. Except for Olivia, the other girls really paid me no mind, aside from the occasional vulgarity to make me blush for sport.

Now that I had returned from a profitable voyage, I held

their fancy. Girls draped themselves in my lap, pressed their bosom against my face, played with my hair, relentlessly flirted, and all the other tricks to steer a man towards their bed. Just as I rebuffed Olivia, I turned down every offer for pleasurable company I received. I knew my first night on island as she kicked fifty sailors out of her bar after an altercation that caused me a bruised lip and a nasty cut that Charlotte was meant for me. I'd be damned if I'd let anything sully my chances. From the second I saw her; I needed, wanted, had to have her. My time away only fueled my obsession.

I MUSTERED THE STRENGTH AND emerged from the kitchen for the first time all night, immediately wishing I hadn't. I caught Thomas' guilty eye as one of the girls sprawled across his lap. I felt my fires stoke, about faced and returned to seclusion of the kitchen.

The crashes and banging of slamming pots and pans I washed, slowly exhaust my temper. Lexy bust through the doors checking on the continual commotion and string of expletives that bleed in to the main room. "Everything alight?" She asked with caution.

"I'm fine. Damn things just got away from me." I lied.

"You know he pays those girls no mind. In fact, as long as I've known him, you are the only thing that draws his eye." Lexy offered meekly. She felt she may have crossed a line, but it was too late to retreat.

She was right. "Did I ask for counsel from a two bit whore? Go make some use of yourself and find a dick to put in your mouth!" I felt out of my skin as the words fell from my mouth and the metal mug flew across the room.

"CHARLOTTE!" The kitchen doors flung open and Lexy pushed past Dahlia as fast as her feet could carry her. "What has gotten into you?!"

"You're right, this is entirely my fault. If I treated them like the whores they are, they'd know their place in things." I coldly answer returning to the dishes, unmoved by my cousin's scolding.

"THIS IS NOT YOU CHARLIE, most of these girls are your friend, at the very least you show them a basic level of workplace respect. What the bloody hell is going on?" Dahlia dug.

My fingers wrap around the washbasin's rim, squeezing my agitation in to the metal instead of around my cousin's throat. Why could they not follow simple instruction and just leave me the fuck alone? I close my eyes and slowly exhale. I turn my head toward Dahlia, a snake ready to bite. Calm, collected, I slowly release my venom, "Nothing is wrong." Staring in my cousin's paralyzed face, she debated on running but was unsure if the predator would enjoy the thrill of a chase. "My patience for employees speaking out of turn has been lost. You all need to remember your place."

Offended, Dahlia flared, "You all? You forget Cousin, I have been by your side since we were children. There is no one in this world who cares about you more than I. I am your strongest ally, do not be so foolish as to push me away."

I strike to sting, "Do not speak to me of love nor loyalty. If it weren't for me, you would be selling yourself just like the lot of them somewhere down the road. I've done horrendous things; I've killed for you. I've cut and hid away the best pieces of me, turned myself in to a monster, all so you wouldn't be subject to the misery of this fucking island. If you think you can survive two days on this cursed rock then go on with ya, see how far you get with your big doe-y eyes and unbloodied hands."

Dahlia recoiled, shock crossed her face and rage glossed her eyes, yet she remained silent. Having taking enough of a beating she threw her hands up in the air and walked away.

I SNATCH DAHLIA BY THE arm as she darts by. "Everything alright?"

Tears well and her voice cracks, "No Phillip, everything is not alright. Now, if you'll excuse me, I am going to retire for the evening."

Seeing her hurt broke my heart. I let go of her arm and pull her in to my chest where her tears fall uncontrollably. I stroke her hair and soothe, "Everything will be fine by morning." I look into her tear streaked face, thumbing a salty sheet from her cheek. "Go, get some rest, I will take care of things here."

I watch her disappear up the stairs before I roar through the kitchen doors. "WHAT THE FUCK IS WRONG WITH YOU?! You have your cousin in tears, Lexy is a mess, you disappear half the day, came back piss drunk and useless, then you hide out in here all bloody night." Charlotte's brokenness cast a black shadow over the entire kitchen. Her eyes swollen with unreleased tears. I was taken aback, I had forgotten she was capable of feeling hurt, much less crying. "Aren't you going to put up a fight?" Her eyes filled to the brim forcing me to retreat, "Well, don't just stand there and take it."

"I just can't Phillip, not tonight." A tear rolls down her cheek. As she wipes it away another takes its place. She moused, "This place has worn me to the bone. I never wanted to be like this."

She lost control of the tears as they stream down her face. I had never been able to stomach a woman crying. I cross the room and pull her in to my chest. She releases years of pent up emotion in to my shirt. When her eyes have emptied, she pulls away wiping her hot face, "I am sorry. I never meant for you to see me like this."

"I think there are some other people you owe an apology." I return, "Can I be blunt?"

"No." She answers, then with a sniffled laugh let out a meek, "Yes."

"This is about Thomas. You've been impossible since he left. Now you've gotten yourself so worked up, you went and spiraled completely out of control."

She takes a seat at the small square table. She wanted to argue, deny that Thomas had any impact on her, but she was drained and we both knew it would be a lie. She just sat there, staring at me blankly as I spoke.

Finally, she stands up, "I think I may retire for the night. It's been a trying day." As she walks to the kitchen doors, she pauses. "Will you be alright for the evening?"

"I'll be fine, get some rest, make amends in the morning." I gently advise.

ON MY WAY TO THE stairs, I catch a different girl in Thomas' lap from the corner of her eye twirling her finger in one of his long blonde locks. I felt my blood boil and quickened my pace through the main room and up the stairs.

I found my room and washed the tears from my face. My mirror's reflection is hideous, her eyes puffy and red. I reminisce of the night's unfolding, what a bloody disaster. I slip into bed, and snuff out the lamp.

Sleep evades me. I lay there, tossing and turning. Hours pass and eventually the noises from downstairs fizzle and die as I count the ceiling planks repeatedly.

The sound of mens voices climbing the stairs wake me from the first bits of sleep I had managed. Lying in bed, I hear the gravelly whispers of Phillip and Thomas exchanging 'goodnights'. One of the bedroom doors open and close but the second had not. I sit up to see the light under my door has a shadowy blockage.

I hop from bed and investigate who could be lurking at such an hour. I open the door to find Thomas on the other side.

"SORRY. DIDN'T MEAN TO WAKE you." I offer. I had been staring at that door for what felt like an eternity mustering the courage to knock.

She steps away from the door, silently inviting me in. "Wasn't asleep. So, What do I owe the pleasure?" She offered as she lit the vanity's candle.

The defeat in her voice caught me off guard. I had practiced for weeks about what I'd say when given the opportunity. Tell her there wasn't a minute that passed where she hadn't consumed my thoughts. I was drawn to Nassau for her, it killed me to leave. I only did to earn a living, so we could build a life together. That I was empty till I met her. I ached for her while I was gone. Could feel home in her eyes. Thousands of different conversations and reactions had played out in my mind.

Some ended a with passionate tryst. Others with me chasing her in a continual battle of hot and cold. Some with a slap to the face or knee to the groin telling me to "Sod Off!". This was Charlotte after all. The possibility of the latter was more than realistic than her running away to the Americas with me, raising a family and living to a ripe old age watching the sun set each night from our rockers on the porch. Countless nights I stared at the hammock above me thinking of her. All those dizzying scenarios played though my mind now as I stood in front of her.

"Thomas it's late. I've been in a mood all day. Wha-" Before she could finish her berating, I pulled her in and kissed her hard. As my teeth crashed against hers, I ran one hand across her cheek to the back of her neck. The other firmly pulling her hips into mine and slowly running my rope callused hand up her spine from the small of her back up between her should blades.

Charlotte melts in my mouth. Wrapping her arms around my body. I kick the door behind me closed as our furious mess of limbs roam and grope and tug at the other's garments. My calloused hand runs up her silky thigh, across her stomach, and firmly gropes her soft breasts. She lets out a soft sigh as I rub my bulge over her night dress.

AS HIS SHIRT FALLS TO the floor, he scrapes his teeth across my collar bone and my brain catches up to my body. Reality of what is happening sets in. I jolt up, pushing him off with such force he falls from the bed and everything comes screeching to a halt.

"Is everything alright?" Thomas asked concerned as he picks himself up from the floor.

"No. No, it is not. I think you should go." I jump from my

bed, briskly walking across the room and open the door with such expediency that the task is complete before the thought.

Confused and frustrated, he snatches his shirt from the floor and stomps to the door. He stops at the threshold, looking down at me. He holds his confused stare till I look up and he could read my face. A coldness settled in my eyes; I was standing my ground, he had to go. "I guess that's goodnight then." He surrendered.

"Goodnight Thomas." I shut the door.

Behind the door, I cross to the vanity, splash cold water on my face and look at the sight in the mirror, releasing a sigh. "Solid day at the office old girl; got stinking drunk, successfully hurt just about everyone that cares about you and opened a flood gate with Thomas, bravo. Tomorrow ought to be fun." I silently sneer in the mirror.

MY ATTRACTION TO CHARLOTTE WAS painful and obvious as paced my room trying to walk off the frustration. Why did I kiss her? I went there to say 'Thank You'. Well partly. At least I know she likes me. *Don't be so foolish as to think that one fool hardy tryst with Charlotte constitutes her actually having feelings for you.* God, I'm never going to go to sleep.

CHAPTER 75
Charlotte Nassau 1702

I ANXIOUSLY ROSE BEFORE THE sun having never really slept. I dressed and made my way to the kitchen. I needed an ice breaker for my apology tour and breakfast for the house was the easiest way. Thankfully, Dahlia found her way was down first. I knew she deserved so much more than an olive branch, she required an actual apology.

"What's going on in here?" Dahlia asked, pouring herself a cup of coffee.

Flipping the bacon in my skillet, I answer with a smile. "Oh this, nothing, just my semi-annual 'I'm an insufferable troll, thanks for loving me anyway' breakfast."

"Ah, yes. That time of year already?" Dahlia smiled and sipped coffee.

I turned to my cousin. "Dahlia." I paused taking a deep breath, "I was wrong and out of control last night. I should of never said those things to you."

Dahlia probed, "And?"

"And what?" I snapped.

"You're sorry! Why is it so damned difficult for you to say you're sorry."

I was surprised by the hostility in my cousin's voice. I couldn't recall the details of what was said, but I'm sure it was mean spirited. Trying to lighten Dahlia, I playfully add, "I said I was wrong. That never happens. You don't get both." I nervously laugh filling the awkward lull, "Dahlia-"

She looked up, "Yes."

"I am sorry."

A tear rolls down her cheek and she reaches to hug me. With a laugh between sniffles she jokes. "You said you were sorry and wrong. I think hell might have actually have froze over."

Phillip entered the kitchen immediately gravitating to Dahlia's tears. He anxiously scans the room, the air was fairly light, deciding no intervention needed, he quipped, "Apology breakfast? Has it been six months already?"

"By my count four and a half. But yesterday was especially wretched." I matched Phillip's sarcastic tone with a wink.

And he winked back, acknowledgment was all the apology Phillip needed. I appreciated that about him. Aside from Dahlia, he knew me better than anyone. He knew me when I was young, before I inherited the tavern. He had seen the toll Nassau had taken on me. Helped me take the reins and keep the business afloat when my father died. He was by all rights one of the few bits of family I had.

"So what are you going to do about Thomas?" Phillip picked.

I laughed to myself. How quickly he can go from loving and understanding to utterly infuriating. Nonchalantly I shrug, "Something the matter with his room?"

Irritated Phillip scolds, "You know what I mean."

"I am most certain I do not" I fired back.

"Really?" he sniped.

I cross my arms, holding firm. Thomas enters forcing my eyes to move from Phillip to him.

Only Phillip could see me squirm though my solid stance. Not wanting to ruin the start of a good day, he waives his white flag. "We'll talk about this later."

I drop my arms, seemingly surrendering. "Very well then."

Thomas intrudes. "Good morning. Sorry, did I interrupt."

Finding myself thankful for the intrusion, I answer with a smile steering Thomas toward the stove and away from Phillip.

"No, we were just finishing up. Make you a plate?"

"We will pick this up later." Phillip reiterated.

"What was all that about?" Thomas asked puzzled.

I was caught, I didn't want to talk about how I was a drunken mess last night or how I managed fuck up just about every friendship I have and while I was very much attracted to Thomas, last night was not the time, place or circumstance to act on those feelings.

Uncomfortable, I let out a soft sigh and smile, quickly delivering an excuse. "That, nothing. Just need to sit down and talk bar stock and bills."

SHE WAS LYING. PHILLIP WAS far too intense for a conversation about money and rum. I shook it off and left well enough alone. I was tired, last night was awkward, the morning was shaping up to be about the same and I had my own Charlotte weirdness to deal with.

She handed me a plate filled with eggs, bacon and fried potatoes.

"Thank you." Our hands graze in the pass off and discomfort immediately stiffened us both.

"I have to go." Charlotte abruptly shatters the silence. "Check on the laundry."

I DARTED THROUGH THE DOORS leading to the main room silently cursing *dumb fucking twat,* before mortification set in at the realization of what I had done settled in. I about face, reentered the kitchen and exited through the back (correct) door, hastening my pace as I pass Thomas. Adding to the the tension filled room, I try my best to ignore his presence and my embarrassment but there is no hiding the blunder or that it had rattled my already shaken nerves.

As she disappeared out the back, I let out a relieved sigh, filed the encounter away and pushed through the kitchen's swinging doors.

I pull up a seat at the bar as Phillip furiously stacked dishes. His mood softened seeing his friend approach. "So what will you do with your day seeing you are officially a guest and not an employee of the house."

His thinly veiled query was received as the 'sod off' he intended. "Not sure exactly. Everyone I know works here." I shrug. "At first I thought I might be of some help here." I paused waiting for Phillip's approval. Sensing it wasn't coming I added, "But I have a feeling it's not the best day for that."

Phillip nodded in agreement.

"Can I ask you something?" I asked, "About Charlotte?"

"I would prefer you didn't, but if you must." Phillip replied bored.

Ignoring my friend's bluntness, I continue. "I just don't understand her."

Phillip interrupts while pouring himself a glass of rum, "I'll tell you this with years of experience under my belt; there is no understanding her. You can accept her. You can love her. But you will never understand her." Tossing back the drink he changes the subject. "Any idea when you head back out?"

"Four, five days." I answered. In the back of my mind I wasn't sure if I could bear to leave her yet again.

Dahlia and Charlotte push through the kitchen doors, pulling my attention their way. Charlotte is rattling a list of things as Dahlia followed, noting each task. They breeze by me and Phillip, list increasing in length. I watched as Charlotte passed, she coyly looked back, our eyes meet and she softly smiled before turning her attention ahead.

I smile as I pull the glass to my lips. "How can one tiny woman be so exquisite and terrifying all at the same time?"

"Necessity." Phillip grimaced as the burn of rum trickled down his throat.

Feeling a need to leave before I wore my welcome thin, I

proposed, "I'm headed to the docks, check in with the quartermaster. I'm sure he can find something to occupy my time."

Phillip looked at me with an appreciative smile. "See you for supper?"

"Of course." I answered.

CHAPTER 76
Phillip Nassau 1702

ANOTHER DAWN HAD TURNED TO dusk in Nassau as the sun sank into the ocean and relief washed over me. Normalcy had returned home as a nice Caribbean trade wind flushed the lingering thick from the air.

Not long after dinner service started, Thomas warily returned. I took the seat across my friend as I delivered his dinner plate. With a release of regret I offer, "I should apologize for being such an ass this morning. There was a lot going on and I released my frustration on you. And not that I'm making excuses, but living with a house full of women is enough to drive a bloke stark raving mad."

"No need. Its been a weird couple of days." Thomas answered with a toothy grin as he bit into a chicken leg.

A devious smirk crossed my face, "I said should. Doesn't necessarily mean I did." I gently punch him in the shoulder.

"Ass." he dramatically massaged his wounded arm. He leaned into the table, his demeanor changing from playful to weighted and inquisitive.

My good mood was quickly hampered as Thomas' tone changed. I braced myself.

As if on cue Thomas drops, "Charlotte?"

I cringe and give Thomas a pleading look. Please don't make me do this.

In return I read Thomas in dire need of counsel. With a defeated sigh I break first. "What about her?"

Thomas gave me an appreciative half smile before dropping, "Am I crazy to pursue her? You think she'd have me?"

"Yes you are crazy. She is stubborn, has an explosive temper and is down right nasty at times." I firmly reply, then soften, "But I think you would be good for her. She was a different before this place. I see glimpses of that girl when you are around. She's light and funny, she drops her armor. She wouldn't just have you. She'd love you."

Filled with excitement Thomas can longer hold his news. He blurts, "I kissed her!"

I am stunned into silence.

Words kept falling from Thomas' mouth. He couldn't control it. "Well more than kissed her. Last night. After you went to bed. I was standing outside her door thinking about her. All of a sudden the door opened and she was scolding me about-" He paused to find the memory. "Well, I don't know anymore. I didn't know what to do or say, so I kissed her."

I sink into a chair absorbing the information, massaging my temples, "Excuse me." I stand from my seat and walk to the bar before Thomas can protest.

The events of last night and this morning looped through my brain. The new information mixing in. I pour myself a shot of rum. As I swallow the first shot, I'm pouring the second before the first hit my belly. By the third, the liquor and information settle in.

I return to Thomas' table with the remainders of the bottle and glasses for the both of us. I wobbly pour a set of drinks. Wide eyed and soused, I shake the blurred images away. The rum had taken it's desired effect. With a sarcastic slur, "Sorry about that. There has been an increase of dramatics around here as of late. That was the last bit I could handle sober. As you were saying?" I sat, waiving him to continue as I kicked me feet up on the table and sip from my glass.

Thomas was confused by my drunken mockery. "I thought you just said I'd be good for her. So why is it wrong that I kissed her?"

"It's not you. It's her. She's a major pain in my ass. An

unpredictable, moody, persistent pain in my ass." I sulked into my chair.

Thomas was empathetic to my plight. A smirk crossed his face, relaxing into a playful grin. "How dare you say such slanderous things of my beloved."

The door swings open and a familiar looking brute pushed his was in. My drunken thoughts were detoured. He looks familiar? Who is that?

Thomas beat me to it, "My first night here- Isn't that the one of the guys from the fight?"

Thats right! I remember now, the fight! I search for the memory.

Before either of us could react, Charlotte vehemently strikes through the room, cutlass in hand. She said no words as she reached the brute, shoving the blade through his hefty belly, pulling it up into his chest, serrating every organ from intestine to heart. She slowly slides the blade out, hissing, "I told you to keep out of my bar or I'd kill ya." She digs her heel into the man's chest, leverage to pull the blade from his pungent body, "I keep true to my word."

The brute falls to his knees and slumped to the ground.

A calm and collected Charlotte turns around. She blows a loose strand out of her eyes, "Thomas, Phillip, perfect. Will you please get that", pointing to the body, a pool of blood leeched from the opening of his chest as intestine spilled from the cavity. "out of here?"

"Ha, you said please." was all that could fall from my drunken mouth.

Thomas was stunned, trying to put the pieces together. "What? You just? Are you alright?"

"A lot better than that bloke." Charlotte coldly chuckled, the bloody sword still in hand.

THE CALLUS IN CHARLOTTE'S VOICE caught me off guard. I knew she could be vicious but never imagined I'd witness such an act. Everything around me began to blur. The word necessity rang in my ears over and over again until it all came together. I finally understood; the tavern, Nassau, why she acted as she did, all of it, was necessity. Charlotte was not only a landlord or employer. She was a safe haven. She would protect her home and her friends, violently when needed. This place had hardened her. Made her numb to blood and violence. It was the cost of doing business in Nassau. Understanding theory was very different compared to seeing it happen with your own eyes mere steps from you.

"Snap to boys!" Charlotte ordered unnervingly playful. "He's soiling my floors."

I stared at her a moment, then shook away the disbelief, before helping Phillip pick the body from the floor and carry it out. We drag the man a few doors down the cobble alley.

"This is good." Phillip instructs as we drop the body. "Close enough to use as advertisement. Far enough so we don't get the stink."

"Not the first I take it." I queried.

Phillip looks at me as he wiped his hands with a towel tucked in his belt. "Far from Mate." I scrunched my brow, confused by Phillip's indifference. "It's just one of those things. She can't very well let some scalawag in here after a very public incident. Opens the floodgate on all sorts of trouble. Once in a while used to be all the time. We had to fight and kill and bleed to live in the peace we do today. Count your blessings you weren't around for those early days."

I scratched the back of my head, processing the information. "I get it- I guess it's just hard for me to see her as that person."

Phillip sternly interrupts as we walk back. "She's a business woman in a pirate's paradise. She has to be fearless, cold, unwavering. It's a huge part of who she is." He pokes me repeatedly in the chest, ensuring the words make their way to my brain. "I think you could be good for her. But you have to except all her, even the ugliest bits. She's not going to change. She can't; it'll be the death of us all. You better make sure she is what you want, that can you handle what that entails. That you won't tuck tail and run when things get ugly. I can see it, she loves you, wether she knows it or not. But she is who she is. If you can't handle that, leave now before this goes any further. It'll sting, but far less devastating than if you leave her on down the road anyway."

I swallowed my lashing hard. Phillip's warning raced through my mind as we walk back to the tavern. I was lost and dizzy with thoughts by the time we returned. Phillip said nothing I hadn't already known. I had just never stopped to think about what it all meant. What I wanted, what she wanted. I just knew she consumed me. I grab a bottle of rum, and slide into an empty booth. I search the bottle's bottom hoping to find some resolution.

"You look like you could use someone to talk to." A soft familiar voice offers. My legs were stretched, my back slouched against the booth's wall. I pull myself forward to see who it was. My inebriation makes it difficult to cover my indifference when I realize it's Olivia. "You don't get paid to talk." My drunken state made the quote come out more insulting than witty. As the words fall from my mouth I hear the harshness and quickly retract. "Sorry, I didn't mean that."

As my red glazed eyes caught hers, her gaze softened and a smile snuck through, she would take pity on this drunken fool tonight. "I know, care if I join you?"

"I'm not much for company right now." I replied. Olivia crossed her arms defiantly. I could tell she wasn't going anywhere anytime soon.

"But if you feel the need, please sit." I mumbled something inaudible about the stubborn women in my life under my breath.

I ENTERED THE MAIN ROOM, arms full with dinner plates. I looked up catching Thomas gaze and Olivia in his booth. I felt my face grow hot as I push through the room delivering the meals.

Better in his booth than in his lap I suppose. I try my best to suppress my fury, I refused to have a repeat of last night. I needn't let my jealousy get the best of me. Pleased with my self control, I breeze past Thomas and Olivia several times unfazed.

With each pass Thomas tries to grab my attention. Finally as I pass one last time he jumps from his seat, grabbing my forearm, stopping m in my tracks. Our eyes meet, fire explodes through our bodies. "Damn it Charlotte! Will you just listen to me! I'm not into all that." He motioned over to the balcony with girls draped over it.

"Those types of services aren't rendered at this facility." I fired back. "Try the place up the road. I hear they have the prettiest little man."

Thomas let out a jilted "Hmph" at my barely veiled innuendo. Running his fingers through his hair, he bites his lip, wide eyed at my accusation, quickly gathering his thoughts. He opens his mouth to begin his retort. Knowing it would only lead to a quarrel, he quickly changes his plan. In one sweeping motion, he grabs me by the shoulders, pulling me in to him, he slides one hand down between my shoulder blades to the small of my back, holding me firmly in place, I was unable to escape his clumsy, ferocious, teeth banging kiss.

I allow myself a moment to melt into the lingering kiss. As Thomas glides his other hand from my shoulder blade to the nape of my neck, I break the kiss and slap him across the face, leaving a sting in my palm.

"Welcome home!" Phillip joked as came from behind patting Thomas' shoulder. The audience had grown sizable; Dahlia, Eve, Lexy and Olivia all watched from the safety behind the bar.

CHAPTER 77
Charlotte Nassau 1702

THE HOURS PASS WHILE I hide in the kitchen. The never ending flow of dishes a welcome distraction as the kiss that flashes non-stop through my mind. *I can't believe he kissed me like that! The gaul!*

I didn't feel the soft smile creak through as I ranted. Phillip bursts trough the doors lifting me six inches from my skin as he catches my lingering grin. "Something funny?" He had his inclinations but dare not say them aloud.

"God damn it Phillip, you startled me?" I scold, as a stack of clean plates crashes and bangs into the floor.

His knowing smirk gave me a violent urge to stab him in the leg with a fork. "Just wanted to let you know I made last call."

"Thank you." His proactiveness proved, yet again, annoyingly useful. "Get 'em out, and shut it down." I replied exhausted. "I'll be out in a minute."

I pushed through the swinging doors, letting out a sigh of relief when I see Dahlia wiping the tables, then Eve flipping the chairs upside and placing them on the table tops. Lexy not far behind with a broom. "What a night!" I announce. Crossing the room, and locking the door. "Busiest we've been in a while."

Collectively the girls look up and smile then look at each other, their cue to head up stairs. Out of the corner of my eye, I catch Phillip tenderly squeeze Dahlia's hand as they exchange goodnights.

I wait for my cousin to disappear up the flight. "Why do you hide your affection for one another? Do you think I am blind?"

"Uh..." The surprise sticks to Phillip's throat.

"It's no secret, why treat it as such." I pressed further.

Searching for words Phillips finally answers, "Just always presumed it forebode I suppose. You and I run this place together, she's your cousin. Seems like it could be messy."

"Because lord knows I have no experience with messy." I blurt with laughter louder then I had meant and gently add, "Go to her, I can finish up here."

I WAS STUNNED, A SOFT understanding Charlotte. It had been so long since I'd seen that side of her I thought she was long dead. "Alright then, guess I will retire for the evening." I gently kissed her cheek, "See you in the morning."

AS PHILLIP WALKED AWAY I felt one last presence in the room, coming from the back booth. I made my way to the table. One more wrong to right. Before I could sit, Thomas stood to greet me. The air shifted, and I was left dizzy dancing between on guard and at ease. I picked up the almost empty rum bottle and poured two final glasses. "Night cap? Compliments of the house."

Thomas slowly closed in on me, our bodies inched closer, almost touching. His body vibrating through his linen shirt and as he looked down at me, his sea of green searing through me and his husky voice tickled my ear, "I have benefited enough from the compliments of the house."

I rolled my eyes and picked both glasses up, extending one to Thomas. "Don't be like that. Have a drink with me."

I TAKE THE GLASS FROM her extended hand and we both sit in my booth. "Charlotte", I paused till her dark warm eyes caught mine and reach for her hand, "I need you to know-"

HE WAS SAYING THINGS THAT I was not in a mind space to hear. Before he could grab my hand and steal my heart, I snatch my glass, slam my drink and interrupt, "Thomas don't. It's been a trying day."

AND SHE WAS GONE AND up the stairs before I could say anything further.

Obsessively I replay the moments over and over in my mind as I pace the main room, lost in rapid thought. She is so bloody frustrating! Hot one minute, cold the next. How can she be so dismissive?! There is no denying whatever this is between us.

Determined, I dart up the stairs two at a time. My frustration lead me to her door and propelled my fist to produce two loud thumps. "Charlotte" The knocking continues, "Charlotte, open the bloody door!"

I FLING THE DOOR OPEN, "Jesus Christ Thomas! What the fuck?!"

He grabs my waist, pulls my hips deep in to his as he guides my mouth to his. I melt in to the kiss, as his hand firmly runs up the back of my nightdress. "No!" Explodes from my lungs as I shove him a away.

"Charlotte don't be like that..." He reached for my hand.

I cross my arms, frigidly replying, "Get out."

He stared me down with no intentions of leaving until he

spoke his piece. "You are something to me and I am something to you. I know it, you know it. And we owe it to each other to see what that is."

"THOMAS, PLEASE JUST GO." SHE had a vulnerability in her voice I had never heard before. There was no hiding my surprise. "I can't be like this, with you." She continued. "You make me feel out of control…weak...I can never appear weak." Her voice trailed off as she the possibilities flashed across her eyes.

She closed the door behind me. I heard the latch click and an audible sigh on the other side.

"Not quite the ending to the evening you had imagined?" I heard the soft feminine voice down the dark hall.

From the shadows floated Olivia in her curve-hugging, off-the shoulder, veil-thin, night dress, "Not at all." I answer.

She reached for my hand, slowly pulling my body in to hers, "Want to talk about it?"

"No." I pressed my lips to hers as we bounced of the hall walls, falling into her room. I pushed her body into the door as my hands hurriedly roamed her curves.

CHAPTER 78
Thomas Nassau 1702

I WOKE THE NEXT MORNING headachy and alone in an unfamiliar room. I was pulling up my breeches and puzzle piecing the night together when Olivia burst through and I jumped "What are you doing? Why wouldn't you knock?"

She fired, "Why would I knock? This is my room!"

"That was you? Bugger Me! What a bloody disaster." I picked up the rest of his clothes and bolted out the door.

"Disaster? What an asshole!" she crossed her arms, put off, answering a now empty room.

As I exited Olivia's room, Charlotte entered the hall from the bathroom. She saw the panic settle in my face as our eyes meet. "You have got to be kidding me." She uttered with a disgusted snarl storming down the stairs.

"FUCK!" I holler, kicking the hall's wall.

"Whoa Whoa Whoa...What did that wall ever do to you?!" Phillip intervened.

I ran my fingers through my hair and took a ragged breath. "Shag Olivia."

Phillip followed up, "The wall shagged- Oh wait- NO!" He gasped, "You didn't?"

I bit the side of my lip, wide eyed with self hatred. All I could do was tilt my head and shrug, acknowledging my mistake.

Phillip stared me down, keeping the berating in his head to himself. The disappointment on my face said everything Phillip could have. There was no point in kicking me while I was down. "Fine mess you've made Mate." Phillip offered with a shoulder squeeze and headed down the stairs.

"UGH!!" I punch through the air in a hissy. "How can I be such an imbecile!" I grab the banister, rushing down the stairs for damage control.

I reached the bottom of the stairs to find Charlotte busy with breakfast service. Manically I try to explain, but every attempt is rebuffed. Cold, hard, silent stone, was all I received. I wished she would scream or curse at me. Hell, even stab me with a fork. Something, anything, she gave nothing.

After about an hour of trying, I realized there was nothing I could say or do to fix this, not now. She needed time, room to breathe. I dropped my head in defeat, and headed toward the docks.

DAHLIA GLEEFULLY HIT THE LAST step from the stair case and could feel the air in the room turn thick and eerily quiet. A drastic change from the jubilant mood of last night. She saw her cousin floating around but could tell from her stature she was to be left alone. She found me behind the bar, pulled up a seat and smiled, "What's going on?"

I tenderly laid my hand atop hers. "Go to the laundry. Keep your head down. I'll fill you in later." She stood up, leaned across the bar and kissed me on the cheek. I watched as she disappeared through the kitchen.

"Looks like you heeded my advice." Charlotte somberly approached the bar. "Don't know why you shooed her away so fast." she pulls up a seat, "I could use her out here today. I fear I am not well."

"Pardon my presumption. I was anticipating a much fouler mood. I just couldn't stand to see you unleash you fury on her." I answered.

"Fair enough." I was saddened by the defeat in her voice. She continued, "What exactly am I supposed to be mad at?" She paused. "He has no ties, no commitments to me. So why do I feel this sense of betrayal?" I opened my mouth to reply, but Charlotte continued. "I'm going to take a nap. Please send one of the girls up in an hour or so to prepare me a bath."

I looked at my friend with sad eyes and squeezed her shoulder. Any further comfort would force her to tears. "Aye."

As Charlotte sulked up the stairs, I mourned the girl I once knew, when she was young and bright and full of life. The woman before me was a shell of who she had used to be. This vile island had eaten away her delicateness, forging an impenetrable shell. For a moment I thought Thomas could be the one who freed her from the prison she built around herself, but now that hope was dead.

Lexy passed, interrupting my defeatist thoughts. I shake my head bringing myself back, "Lexy…"

She about-faces, "Yes."

"Do me a favor and send Dahlia this way."

"Of course." she answered as she changed course and walked through the kitchen doors.

Moments later Dahlia entered the main room. I told her of my early morning discoveries. "Oh poor Charlie." She empathized. "She must be heartbroken."

"If I didn't know her I would say you couldn't even tell, but she is devastated."

"And what of Thomas?" Dahlia poked.

"Took off to the docks. Turned tail and ran out of here as soon as he realized she wasn't interested in his excuses." I paused. "Can you go check on her? She asked I send someone up to prep her a bath. I think you're the only one she would care to see."

"Of course." She kissed my cheek and headed to the laundry to pick up fresh towels and heat water for the bath.

THERE WAS A GENTLE RAP at my door. "Charlie, you in there?" I didn't answer, she let herself in.

Dahlia found me against the far wall, knees buried in my chest. Tears turned to salt, pasted to my cheeks. A half empty bottle of rum sat next to me. I sip from my glass. The calmness in my voice can not hide my rage. "You know he came to me last night? He was going to tell me he loved me." I paused for another swig. "And what do I do? I sent him away!" The glass flies from my hand sailing across the room. "In a god damned whore house of all places!" When the glass exploded against the wall, my anger turned to heartbreak as I buried my face in my knees and quiet tears roll down my cheeks. "Why am I like this?"

Dahlia crossed the room, dropped to the floor, cradling me as I loose control, weeping unconsolably. My tears soak the chest of her dress as she sat silently stroking my hair.

Minutes of sobbing pass. I had cried myself out, and now it was time to pick myself up. I wipe my face dry with the palm of my and use my index finger to blot the last few drops from my eyes. "Sorry Cousin," I choked out a laugh. "I don't know what has got in to me."

"If you don't mind me saying," Dahlia paused for approval. I smiled and nodded her to continue. "That was more than just what happened this morning. Granted it started with Tomas-"

I cut her off, "It's this god forsaken island. It eats at you bit by bit, until one day you're gone, just a shell. Your soul is the price paid for paradise."

Dahlia brushed the salty damp locks behind my ear. She held her hand to my cheek a moment. The small gesture of affection raised my spirits. "You can only be strong so long before you break dear Cousin."

I swept the wrinkles from my dress as I stood. "That's just it Dahlia, I'm not sure I want this. I inherited this life. I didn't choose it, and now it's turned me into someone I don't even recognize."

"What are you saying?" Dahlia quizzed.

"I don't know. Probably nothing. I'm sure after a soak and the rest of this rum," I pick the bottle up and swish the remainder, "I'll be back to my charming self."

I pulled my cousin to her feet and we exit the room and headed toward the bathroom. Dahlia unties and helps remove my dress and corset. I pull my shift overhead, dropping it next to the tub. Stepping into the hot bath and gingerly sink in to the water.

"Will that be it then Cousin?" Dahlia queried.

"Yes dear." I answered as Dahlia headed to the door. Before she exited I abruptly add, "Dahlia-"

She stops at the door. "Yes Charlie."

For the first time in a long time, I spoke with a softness and vulnerability, "Thank you. I would be lost without you."

"And I you Cousin." Dahlia added with a gentle smile as she exited. The exchange warmed Dahlia's heart. It was the closest thing to I love you she had received from me in many years.

I picked up the bottle of rum by it's neck, took a gigantic gulp, and sunk deeper into the water.

"YOU'RE IN ALARMINGLY HIGH SPIRITS!" I cried out as Dahlia skipped down the steps. "I mean considering." I back step when she shot a scowl all too familiar to Charlotte's.

"Oh Phillip, you know, nothing holds our Charlotte down for long. She's like a hurricane. She comes blowing through ferociously, leaving a trail of damage in her wake. But if you make it through the night, you'll hear the song birds by morning." Dahlia eluded.

I smirked. "Poetic, not helpful, but poetic."

She gave me a flirty shove. "She's Charlotte. There is nothing a long hot soak and a bottle of rum can't fix."

Dahlia gave me a quick kiss while picking up an apron and tying it's strings round her back. "There is work to be done." As she began to clear the tables of their dishes. She bustled around the room, moving dirty dishes to the kitchen and returning with clean ones as I watched the conflicted battle rage inside her.

My cousin, my flesh and blood, my best friend, is upstairs right now drowning a broken heart. Confronting years of inner demons. Breaking down in every sense of the word. And here I am, smiling ear to ear like a blubbering idiot. Everything I had wished Phillip felt for me was real. I couldn't be more happy in this moment. Why am I such a selfish silly girl? Charlotte has given up the life she dreamt of so we can be safe. And happy...so happy. Damn it Dahlia! Get it together. This is all that Thomas' fault. If he coulda just kept his damn britches on none of this had happened.

Thomas pushed his way through the tavern doors and headed toward the stairs. "Oi! Where you going?" Dahlia hollered as he blew past.

"I have to grab my things." Thomas answered.

"She didn't say anything bout you having to leave." Dahlia chased him up the stairs.

As he shoved his clothes into his duffle he hurriedly briefed, "The ship is ready a few days early. We're shipping out tomorrow. I'll just sleep on the boat. Save everyone some grief."

"Thomas-"

"It's just what's best." He snapped as he walked past her and headed down the hall.

She poked her head out the door and pleaded as he reached the steps, "Are you going to at least tell her good bye?"

"No." He dropped his head in defeat, and was gone.

DAHLIA BURST INTO THE BATHROOM, I was mostly submerged with a washrag over my eyes and an empty bottle in hand dangling from the tub's side. "Charlie! Charlotte, it's Thomas, he's leaving! He's leaving right now!"

"Good riddance." I coldly replied and sank deeper in the tub.

CHAPTER 79
Thomas Modern Day

THE FILM IN MY MIND tickers away, bringing my attention back to the cliff side drops of the windy, single lane, coastal highway. I was gutted and infuriated at how the Thomas of Nassau was so stupid and careless with her heart. A grievous mistake I would not allow repeated.

To think I had the audacity to chastise Michael for his shortcomings, as it turns out, I am no better than he. The only difference between he and I, was which side we stood when the line of fate was drawn.

I looked over to Charlie, peacefully napping as the sun danced on her chocolatey curls and felt unworthy. I made a silent promise to never be the reason for her pain again.

CHAPTER 80
Charlotte Nassau 1702

IT HAD BEEN FOUR MONTHS since the series of squalls ripped through the island. The sea had claimed several ships and Ananke's Revenge was still unaccounted for.

Now that the letters had ceased, I regretted burning the ones that arrived shortly after Thomas' departure. I had received a handful of sealed envelopes, all written within a few days of each other, some written the same day as one or two others.

When the first set arrived with his familiar script my heart filled with joy. Knowing he was safe and near enough to write was all the solace I needed. I had no interest in his tales from the sea nor his pleads for forgiveness or professions of love. I coldly sipped whiskey as the wax seal melted and parchment caught flame from my bedside candle. The second set arrived with the storms, so now they sit sealed on my vanity. Unable to hear his words, but afraid to let his memory go.

You'd never know the incessant darkness that hovered in his absence by the warm sunny morning. The gentle breeze pushed Ocean's spray through the widow's wooden slats. Another perfect day in paradise. The gulls squawked, hovering the fish boats waiting for the heads and guts to be dumped into the sea. The market abuzz, busy with bargaining and trades.

I had taken to walking on the beach in the mornings. Breathing in the fresh air and feeling the pulse of the town. If Thomas taught me anything it was I could be at peace. There were parts of me that were horrible and ugly. The bowels of this cursed island were home, there was no getting around that and that required a less rigid moral code, but I didn't have to be stone all the time and if anything, letting the softer Charlotte shine though made my explosive anger that much more dramatic adding to my myth and volatile reputation.

My tortured conflicted thoughts break with the sounds of waves crashing against the sand. I had to let go. It was the only way to find peace. Peace with Nassau. Peace with the tavern and the life it forces me to live. Peace with Thomas. Peace with myself. I pepped as I strolled the cobble roads, finding my way home.

A fresh set of masts peek between the buildings from the dock side of town. Thomas?! The thought made my heart skip a beat and smile as I quicken my pace.

I returned to the tavern in the same fashion as I did every morning. No need to get the other's hope up for not. As the morning turned to noon then faded to evening my heart broke a little more with each passing hour. Shortly after sunset I excused myself for the night. I quietly snuck up stairs, buried my face in my pillow and cried until I fell asleep.

I did not wake till late the next morning when Dahlia forced me to rise. "What is it Cousin?" She queried, peeling the covers from me.

Before Dahlia could prod any further I shot up "Nothing. Just sour stomach." I finger combed my hair, pulling the long tresses over my shoulder, "Can you fetch me a glass of water?"

"Should I tell Phillip you won't be down today?" She offers the glass.

"Please."

She searched my face for some sort of tell, "I'll let you rest then." I settled back in my bed as Dahlia exited. Quickly falling asleep, a welcome relief. The night was restless; flashes of a primitive English country side, fires, death and pregnant bellies flooded my tormented dreams. I refused to maintain hope

I would see him again. It was destined to lead to heartbreak.

The subdued rustling from downstairs goes unnoticed while I nap for hours. As the sun began to sink the rumblings grew louder stirring me from my sleep. I groggily wash my face, dress and comb my wild mane and reign in my tailspin thoughts as I pull my tresses it into a tidy little bun atop my head.

I tied my apron round my waist as I made my way down the stairs. I catch Phillip's eyes as I hit the last step. Relief washes over his face, an extra set of hands just as supper service had started. I squeezed my way cross through the busy room to the bar. "Seems busier than usual?"

"Ananke's Revenge ported." Phillip answered as he pours drinks. "They've been trickling in all day."

The way he said it, so matter of fact, so cold, I couldn't bear to ask the follow up question, but found it falling from my mouth. "And Thomas?" Just saying his name aloud made me lose my barely there togetherness.

"Word is, he's down there, fell ill. It's not good. Some of the men who got sick-"

I cut him off before he can spit whatever horrible news he didn't want to choke out. I tugged at my apron strings, "I have to go-"

"Dahlia and Lexy already went to fetch him. Olivia has made up his room with rags and medicines." Phillip continued. "We'll get him straight upstairs. Dahlia and I will sleep in Lexy's room. Lexy will bunk with Eve. And we'll keep him quarantined to that hall."

"And I'm to take care of him." I finished his sentence.

I WAS SURPRISED IN THE delicateness in her voice. I partly expected a combative response seeing how they parted. But she was loving and worried. None of it mattered, he was at death's door and needed her. A light radiated in her that I hadn't seen in a long time. *God, please be with my friends. Please heal Thomas. For if you take him, you destroy Charlotte. She can not bear his*

loss. He ignited something inside her we all thought died long long ago. She has fought to stay strong for so long. She is too fragile now. You will irreparably shatter her, a fate I fear she would not survive. Please. Do. Not. Let. Him. Die.

Dahlia and Eve hurriedly push through the doors, holding them open for the two men dragging Thomas' limp body in. I rushed to the girls' aide. "How'd you manage to find help?" Swinging one of Thomas' limp arms over my shoulder, bearing most the ragged sailor's weight.

"We've already had the fever sir." I took a closer look at the chap. He couldn't of been more than sixteen. "My brother and I, two weeks before he." He took a breath as we topped the staircase.

"Well I thank you for your help." Charlotte chimed in. "And may I ask your name?"

"Michael ma'am, and this is my brother James." James appeared to be the older of the two. Nineteen or so by my guess.

"Pleasure to meet you Michael. Please enjoy your evening, compliments of the house." She smiled softly, dismissively adding, "We have him from here." She looked to Dahlia, instructing. "Will you make sure they have a room for the night." She looked over at two young men, "And girls too." she added winking at Michael making him flush as she led me and Thomas down the hall.

CHAPTER 81
Charlie Modern Day

I WOKE CRADLED IN THOMAS' arms, as he carried me through the threshold of a sleepy beach motel room. The scent of salt lingered in the air and on his skin or maybe that was the remnants of my dream, I couldn't tell. Heavy grogginess weighed on my body. I nestled my head into the soft spot between Thomas' shoulder and neck.

He delicately unloaded me onto the bed, tucked a strand of hair behind my ear, and kissed my forehead. "Were your dreams pleasant?"

What a loaded question. How odd it was to have dreamt of him and he actually be there when I wake. It kind of makes the good parts that much sweeter and the bad parts not so devastating. "Realistic." I answered honestly.

"Well, if you want to freshen up; looks like there is a fantastic little dive down the beach."

I couldn't help but pick on him. "Sunset dinner on the beach?" His jaw dropped when he heard the snark in my words.

"Oh that's terribly cliche." He pouted as dread washed over his face.

"It's sweet." I softly kissed his pushed out bottom lip. "Things are cliche for a reason. Everyone; even deep introspective artist types can enjoy them." I pouted the words, playfully pushing him away, and rolling my eyes. "Let's go. It'll be fun. I could totally go for fish tacos and a beer."

The Rip Tide was just as wondrously cliche as Thomas had feared. It wasn't an actual locals dive like Thomas had hoped. It was a touristy 'dive'. Growing up in wine country, I totally understood the difference and his disappointment.

The dance floor was packed with couples of all ages and people watching had always been my favorite sport.

I hear a faint whisper on the wind. "Charlie."

You can always find the couples working on their marriage. Or away on a sordid tryst.

"Charlie." I heard, only slightly louder.

Or the old couple in the middle of the floor, who have genuinely loved each other for the better part of four decades.

I feel calloused fingers wrapped around my shoulders. Lips pressed firmly to mine. His bottom lip pushing my mouth open to receive his tongue. The forceful kiss brought my attention back to Thomas in front of me. I shook away my thoughts.

"Where did ya go there Love?"

I squinted, smiling with my eyes, "Sorry. Just got sorta swept away in my head."

"You know I'm kind of jealous." His notorious half smile flooded me with self-consciousness. He softened to a full smile, pulling me into his chest, he softly kissed my forehead and it warmed my heart. "I could only imagine how the world looks through your eyes."

Something deep within me urged, "Show him."

"Do you trust me?" escaped my deep self soothing breath.

Green eyes pierced my heart as he tilted his head trying to read me, "Of course."

I grabbed his hand and dragged him toward the water. The pale blues were quickly darkening as the sun disappeared into the ocean. We walked to the water's edge. I kicked my sandals off, letting the mild waves wash over my toes.

"What are we doing?" he laughed nervously.

"I don't know. Shut up and close your eyes." I wasn't any

reassurance as as I delicately touched my right index and middle fingers to his left temple.

Flashes of the beach's history flooded my mind. Like flipping channels on a old tv. Memories etched on this place, forever frozen in time.

Thomas staggered back and his head fell between his knees as he tried to catch his breath. "Is that? Did you see? Have you ever?"

I smiled sympathetically. I remembered the first time I saw a vision. Afterwards my mom thought I was having an asthma attack. It quite literally takes your breath away. "Catch your breath." I rubbed the space between his should blades as he hunched over his knees. "Yes, that's how I see a lot of the time. Yes, I saw what you saw. No, I have never done that before. Yes, it was weird, but something inside me told me to." I answered his half spat questions in order.

"The fact that you understood my broken sentences and successfully answered them in sequential order no less, is the least weird part of that." Thomas regained his breath. "Makes all of this mind blowingly weird." He paused letting all the pieces settle. Full of questions he started with, "Did you read my mind? Is that how you knew what I was saying?"

The mild waves rolled against the sandy shore and the partial moon shone bright in the clear black sky as we walked away from the water to drier sand. "No, I can't read minds. I don't know, maybe I can? I just kinda knew what you were feeling, because I was feeling it too. It's kind of a nuisance more than anything. I feel crazy, constantly questioning what I just heard, saw, felt." I was saying way too much. "I don't really like talking about it." I stood up, brushed the sand off my butt and started back toward the restaurant.

Thomas quickly caught up. His long legs dredged through the sand much easier than mine. I felt his strong fingers wrap around my wrist. Before I knew it, my lips were entwined with his. One of his hands on my lower back, pressing my hips in to his. His fingers laced tightly through the hair at the nape of my neck. The swooping motion made my knees buckle, except his embrace held me upright.

Dizzy from thought and vision and Thomas stealing my breath with his intoxicating kisses, I pushed away. He tilted my chin up, forcing my gaze to his. "I never want you to feel like you can't tell me something. I believe you. Always."

CHAPTER 82
Charlie Modern Day

I HAD HAD THE MOST soul bearing, fully exposed, intimate/non intimate moment ever in my life. I had never been so free or honest. This was uncharted. My path led me to this love I had dreamt about. The fact that now it was in front of me rattled me to the core. Every nerve of my body, painfully aware. I was exhilarated and terrified.

The thing about the dreams, the visions, the lost bits of time was; good, bad, or ugly, they always came to an end. I had only just found Thomas, the coming to an end part scared the hell out of me.

"Your tacos any good?" Thomas asked as he assembled a fajita.

I hadn't even tried them yet. Wait. Half of one was gone. Okay, I had. I was eating whilst lost in thought. That can't be good. I'll have to look into that more. "Yes." I answered before the pause increased into an awkward length. "You want a taste?"

He squinted, measuring me up. He reinforced his accusation by pointing his fork at me, "You're lying."

"What?" I was shocked by his correct assessment.

"You have no idea how those tacos taste. You were lost up in that head of yours." He waived his fork around punctuating his sentences. "You can't hide from me Charlie. I see you exactly as you are."

The softness in his voice made a stray tear roll down my cheek. "Sorry. I just need to be anchored back every now and again." His candor warmed my heart. For the first time in this life, I didn't have to hide who I am. I was free.

CHAPTER 83
Charlie Modern Day

BLAME IT ON THE STARS, or the moon, or the waves crashing into the beach, the music floating on the salty night air, or the bottle of wine we shared over dinner but in that moment under the night sky, with him, dancing and laughing, I felt weightless and breezy.

He cupped my face, his green eyes looked grey under the moon's light. I searched for the brown fleck I had growingly become obsessed with. His wide toothy smile gleamed through his eyes.

"What?" I smiled as we swayed to Allison Krauss.

"Nothing." was unconvincing with the beam across his face. His lips plunged into mine and I felt his heart touch mine. He pulled away, "Just wondering how I made it through life before you." I was breathless. He continued, "From the moment I met you, I knew you were what had been missing from me my entire life."

I pushed myself onto my toes, kissed his bottom lip and nestled in to his shoulder. "Shut up and dance with me."

CHAPTER 84
Thomas Modern Day

CHARLIE IS DANGEROUS; THE KIND of woman who can keep you memorized for hours, never truly knowing how bewitching she is. Comfortable in her skin, yet painfully unaware of how exquisite she is. A natural beauty. Which is too far and few in-between these days. She's kind, smart and wicked funny.

She moves to the music as if she's invisible. The reggae dance hall sound takes hold and she becomes weaved into its fabric. Her body rolls effortlessly with the rhythm. Lost in her own world, she has no idea, all eyes are on her.

Her stormy brown eyes told a story as her hips rocked and swayed to the music. The salty night air was warm and familiar. Everything fell away and became hazy. Only Charlie and I remain.

Except we are different. A fire glows in the distance, masts lined the beach's skyline, palms sway as a hazy dream starts to form.

PHILLIP HURRIEDLY LAYS MY DRENCHED, grey form on the bed. "This is worse than I expected." I faintly heard under the deafening, swirling, whomp sound that rang in my ears as Charlotte sponged sweat from my face and neck.

"We have to get this fever down." Her mind races as she blots the beads pouring from my unconscious face. "A cold water bath!" The idea fell from her mouth as she thought it. "Go tell the girls to start filling the tub."

Lost in fever fueled delirium, I hear Phillip holler instructions. Within minutes the girls mule buckets of cold water as fast as their bodies allow.

PHILLIP EXTENDS A HAND TO help lug Thomas. "No, you've exposed yourself enough. Change your clothes and burn the ones you have on. Go!" I bark, shooing him out the door.

I throw one of Thomas' arms around my shoulder, propping him against my petite fame. I take those first labored steps down the hall, slowly dragging Thomas behind.

Eventually reaching the bathroom, I strip Thomas to his breeches. With some struggle, get him in the cold tub. I watch his unconscious body shiver at the sting of the cold. Still sleeping, Thomas finally relaxes into the cool water.

I kept hawk like watch as he sleeps. The minutes pass as if hours. Thomas flutters his eyes open, "Charlotte." The effort to raise his hand is excruciating, regardless he reaches for my check. I pull his hand in, cradling my face. "I've missed you." With his sweet message, he exhausted all his energy and immediately fell into a fever fueled slumber.

While he slept, I nursed, continually blotting his face and neck with a damp rap. A half hour had passed and Phillip poked his head through the door, "How is he?"

"Don't know yet." I exhaled heavily. "Still alive. I am going to need your help getting him out of this tub though." I paused. "Sorry, I hadn't thought that out very well."

Phillip opens the door and enters as he scans the room, finally landing on Thomas arms and head draped limp over the tub's edges. Trying to reassure both of us, he offers, "When have any of your plans ever been thought out?"

I gave the faintest half smile. I appreciated the attempt but we both knew the situation was too dire. "I put his clothes in a pillow case. Please burn the whole sack?"

"Of course." Phillip answered as he pulled Thomas from the water. I swung each of Thomas' loose legs over the tub walls. Phillip held Thomas up as I pulled a pair of linen britches up is legs and around his hips finally tying the drawstring.

"I've washed the sweat and muck from him. His fever is at bay," I paused, drying my hands on my apron. "for now." Using the top of my wrist to push away sweat and loose hair in one movement. "I need you to help me get him to his room now, then keep away unless I ask." I looked up at my oldest friend with worry filled eyes. "I couldn't afford for you or one of the girls to catch this nasty business."

"You worry too much." Phillip assured. "Except of yourself. What happens if you get sick?"

"Impossible." I smirked, "I'm much too sour a person for illness to claim me so young. I am meant to be a mean old lady who swats passers by with her cane."

He scoffed at my premonition. Partly because it held some truth and partly because it seemed absolutely absurd at the same time.

We reach Thomas' room, I push the door open as Phillip drags Thomas through the threshold. Phillip plops Thomas on the bed and Thomas grumbles an inaudible obscenity. "Good sign?" Phillip looked at me with a hopeful smile.

"I guess. At least we know he's alive." I cringed as the ill timed words fell from my mouth.

Phillip's disapproving scowl confirmed it in pour taste. I dragged the stool from the dresser over to the bedside and dipped my rag in the small water basin, blotting Thomas' forehead.

"Do you have everything you need?" Phillip replied.

I looked down at Thomas and pushed the sweat laced locks from his brow. "For now." I answered.

Phillip offered his company one last time as I shooed him away. He picked up the sack of sweaty clothes on his way out the room. "Straight to the furnace." I ordered as he shut the door.

I looked down at Thomas with immeasurable concern, "Fine

mess you've gotten yourself in." blotting away the sweat as it streamed down his face and guiding the rag behind his neck to try and pull the fever from his head, "Fine mess indeed."

A sudden snatch of my wrist makes me jump from my skin. "Charlotte-" Thomas softly spoke as his eyes fluttered open. "I was having the worst dr-" He is asleep before he could finish his sentence.

I watched for hours as he groaned and tossed while he slept. My heart ached for him, to watch his pain was unbearable.

Phillip brought soup and bread for two, while Thomas slept. "Mind if I take my meal with you Charlie? You could stand the company." He asked with the friendly nod and a tray in hand.

"You really shouldn't." I answered.

"Well the way I see it, I already got myself exposed, and you look like you need a break. You've been up here for most the day and are exhausted. Those boys said they were sick for days. There is no way you can do this on your own."

I absolutely hate when Phillip was being perfectly reasonable. He took too much joy in seeing me wriggle. You are right. Three words impossible for me to put together. "I could stand to wash off." I danced around his argument.

We ate our meal in silence. I was grateful for Phillip, someone who knew exactly what I needed. I didn't need to talk or express my worry. I just needed to know I was not alone, and he fit that bill perfectly.

Two days came and went the same way. On the third morning, Phillip suggested, "You've not fallen ill. Why don't you tend to the bar this morning?"

"You think that's a good idea?" Doubt and grog coated my voice.

"It looks like he's made it through the thick of it. All he's done is sleep the past few days. There is not a whole lot more you can do. But you can be of use downstairs. Maybe down in the laundry just in case, but out of this dank room."

Damn you Phillip with your intolerable common sense. "I guess you are right." I choked on my words. Phillip began to smirk, "Don't you dare say a word or I'll cut out your tongue!" I playfully ordered.

Phillip exited as I walked the room picking up soiled linens and towels. I shoved them into a sack before stopping at my room to change my clothes and freshen up. One last glimpse in the mirror and gently prodded my puffy eyes with my forefinger, silently acknowledging how awful I looked.

There will be no living with Phillip now that I've gone and told him he was right. I thought gleefully pulling dried linens from the line and folding them. The fresh salty air was serving me well. Hours had passed. Lexy and Olivia were washing their delicates gossiping of the men who came in the previous night. I was never one for idle chit chat, normally finding it boring and a waste of time, but today it was welcome, a sense of normalcy returned.

I made my way back to Thomas, immediately cursing myself for taking such an extended break. His fever had spiked and flattened, but not without leaving him in a soaked bed. His sweat drenched the linens clean through to the mattress. I pulled him from his bed, wrapping one of his arms round my shoulder and dragging him across the hall to my room. I rapidly strip his bed and flip the mattress, hauling the dirty linens down stairs and returning with fresh.

Phillip peaked in as I put the finishing touches on the freshly made bed. "Where is Thomas?" His tone, equal parts snooping and concern.

"His fever spiked. He sweated through the bed. I put him in my room so I could change the linens and flip the mattress." I explained between labored breaths.

"Not like you've been sleeping there much anyway." He snarked as we returned to my room to retrieve Thomas. "How do you manage to sleep in a stool hunched over night after night?" A wicked smile crossed his face, "And I really have no care for your ridiculous excuses as to why you have a man in your bed. Your affairs are none of my concern."

I let out an annoyed exhale as we crossed the hall to my room. "You know this isn't the most opportune time to be poking at me. Can't we just get through this," I motioned over Thomas' sleeping body.

"Hogwash. You know as well as I, he is going to be fine. His fever dwindles daily. He wakes here and there, nothing coherent yet. But he's with us!" Phillip had been obnoxiously right the past few days and it was driving me mad. "And when he comes to, you are going to have a lot to sort out. The sooner you come to grips with that-"

"Alright already. I get it." I interrupt. "Can you just not be so abrupt about it right now?! Or ever for that matter?" Taking a breath I add, "If I am being an insufferable cunt, fine, point it out. Other than that, keep your opinions to yourself."

"You're just yellow." Phillip smiled.

"And what of it? I asked you to shut it. Shut it." I asserted.

"Sorry mi lady." Phillip retorted with a sarcastic bow.

"Sod off." I harshly exchange. With a smile, I soften, jokingly adding "Make some use of yourself and go drag your friend back to his bed."

Phillip guided Thomas from my bed and back to the familiarity of his room. Phillip was pleased by Thomas' progress. This move was the most mobile Thomas had been. Still unconscious and incoherent, but his legs and feet aided just enough to make the short walk significantly quicker.

Wish he coulda done that for me, I thought as Phillip guided Thomas cross the threshold in record time. I couldn't help but think of how impossible a task it was just an hour ago. His entire body, heavy and limp. I ended up having to drag him by his under arms. I tried to sling one of his arms round her shoulder and prop him up as I dragged him, but his weight was too much for my petite frame and I dropped him and he let out a slight groan of pain but in his flu fueled slumber. "Sorry Thomas!" I whispered loudly, hoping the commotion could not heard from the first floor.

Phillip guided Thomas as he slid between the fresh sheets. Thomas mumbled something inaudible to Phillip while slipping back and forth between consciousness.

Phillip gave my shoulder a comforting squeeze and exited the room, I closed the door behind him and headed to the window. "A bit of light and fresh air will do you some good. I diagnosed as I opened with window slats.

Just as I had done a hundred times over the passed few days; I sat on the stool next to Thomas, dipped a rag into the basin and blotted the sweat from his face, watching over him till I until my eyes refused to remain open. I felt my upper half gently fold over the bed and I was asleep.

THE EVENING SUN CREPT THROUGH the slats of the window. Vibrant oranges and radiant reds dance across the walls. My groggy eyes flutter awake for the first in what feels like centuries. As I became more aware of the world, I hear gulls squawking in the distance. I looked around the room. The tavern? Gently raising my head, I scour my surroundings. Charlotte asleep hunched over my bed. Her palm barely grazing my thigh, I give it a gentle squeeze.

Startled, she jumps at the groggy realization, "Thomas! You're Awake!" She exclaimed jubilant.

"Not dead on account of you." I gratefully returned.

Relieved by my recovery, Charlotte pops up, excitedly gathering dirty linens and rags. "How are you feeling?"

"Weak. Like I've been to battle." I took a breath, "But I don't feel the death's breath on my neck as I did before." I saw the exhaustion wear on her face, but she was still more exquisite than I had remembered, "Was it bad?"

"Yes." She answered honestly. "You had a terrible fever, for days. It took constant attention just so you wouldn't burn up. Cold water baths, cooling rags. You had hallucinations. Tossed and groaned from fever pangs and awful dreams. It was dreadful."

"I am sorry to be such an inconvenience." I meant it playful but the words left my lips sour. I was not stupid or naive. I knew how we parted and I knew she had not forgiven me, I hadn't forgiven myself.

"Thomas, don't say that." She stood up and flattened her gown. "We were all worried about you." She heads toward the door. "Glad to see you on the mend."

"Where are you going?" I reach for her wrist. My dreams and hallucinations were about her. Lifetimes of love and loss. I begged God, or the devil, I'm not sure who answered my call, just to let me see her once more before I leave this world. Give me the opportunity to atone for my sins against her. My prayers had been answered, and I knew I could never leave her again.

"To freshen up. Get us something to eat, and tell everyone of your recovery." She smiled as she heads out.

"Don't be long!" I shout as she closes the door behind her.

CHAPTER 85
Thomas Nassau 1702

I SPEND TWO FULL WEEKS on my back before I grew frustrated with Charlotte and Phillip's constant fussing. "There is a bonfire tonight and I plan to see more than these four walls and your two's faces." I argued.

And I did; spending the night catching up with shipmates. Boasting tales of besting death, laughing and drinking with friends, but no matter what I was doing, who I was talking to or where I was, my eyes gravitated to her. The way her hips swayed to the sounds of the music floating through the air. The moon light danced in her hair, the fire played in her eyes. Unable to tame my thoughts and feelings any longer, I grabbed her by the wrist and guided her down the beach away from the crowd.

She giggled at my urgency as I pulled her into my chest. Her large coffee colored eyes glistened under the full moon's light. "Thomas, what is it."

"I love you Charlotte." I pressed my lips into hers. "From the moment I laid eyes on you, I knew it, with every inch of my being. The only thing that kept me going, was I couldn't die before I told you."

His words paralyzed me as I was lost in the stormy abyss of his soul. His anchoring rod of a brown freckle in his sea of green kept me from floating away. I couldn't find the words to tell him I felt the same. I did the only thing that made sense at the time, the only thing that felt an appropriate response, the only thing my body allowed, I dove into his mouth, pushing my tongue through his parted mouth and our bodies crashed against the sand.

CHAPTER 86
Charlie Modern Day

THE FINAL BEATS OF THE song played and the four wood paneled walls of The Rip Tide returned. A round of applause filled the room. I felt my skin flush and the urge to flee. I exited the floor, quickly slinking to my table.

En route, I passed a woman similar in age to Kennedy but her dress and appearance gave her a much older feeling as she complimented, "I wish I could dance like that."

I felt my skin flush two shades redder than it was already. "Thank you." Was all I was able to spit out. Not only was I horribly awkward with any sort of attention or compliments, I had lost time, so I had no idea what I actually did out there. I could have given that woman a lap dance for all I knew.

I squeezed Thomas' shoulder as I circled round him, returning to my seat. He startled as if he's been waken from a dream. "Are you okay?"

His puzzled dreamy expression was one all too familiar. "What do you know about Nassau?"

The euphoric tingling of the vision still lingered through my body. I cooed, "You saw it too?" In that moment I realized we had shared the same vision; one of our stories from long ago.

"Is it always like that?" I searched his copper green eyes. The brown freckle, my heart's compass looked a darker shade of green in this light, but was still very much there. He was was not fearful or dismissive, he wanted to understand.

"Not always." I softly answered as I sat my hand on top of his on the table. "Let's go for a walk. Get some air." I suggested as I stood up and gathered my things.

He laced his fingers through mine as we walked through the sand back to our motel. A million thoughts raced through my mind. Thousands of questions I wanted to ask, but he seemed peaceful in our quiet moonlit stroll.

Thomas squeezed my hand. My eyes glued to the path ahead. "You don't have to be telepathic to hear your mind racing a million miles a minute." He playfully poked, pulling me to his chest, wrapping his arms around my shoulders. "Penny for your thoughts?"

Words fell uncontrollably from my mouth, "I'm so sorry. I had no idea I could project-"

"Wait. Wait. Wait." He interrupted. "You don't think what happened back there is your fault? Or something to be ashamed or afraid of? Do you?"

"I just feel horrible. I can barely control what I see. And to be honest, some of it is awful. I would hate for you to have-"

Thomas delicately massaged my temple with his thumb as he comforted, staring deep into my eyes, like he needed my soul to feel his words. "Lifetimes of our love have haunted my dreams my entire life. Tonight I got to experience an extraordinary moment from one of those lives with you. Life is messy. I can deal with the ugly parts that tormented me for so long because now I know you're real. I know it all happened, all the lives and deaths I've seen, it was real, and knowing the mistakes of the past, makes me love and appreciate you that much more."

CHAPTER 87
Charlie's Journal–Modern Day

If perfect existed,
he could be it

But perfect is an illusion
lies sold to the world

To make us crave and covet false idols
and not appreciate
blessings bestowed
and loves that are true

Because it does not measure up
to what we've been conditioned to want

So I dare not sully a love profound
with labels and constraints
of what society says to be

For once in this life,
we shall simply exist,

he be he
and I'll be me
because it's more than enough to fill the need.

It was never happenstance
or accident.
It was always by the design Ananke's hand.

CHAPTER 88
Charlie Modern Day

THOMAS SURFED THE MOTEL'S TV six channels as I watched myself pull and pin my wild curls out of face into a nub of a ponytail. I shimmied on a pair jogger's shorts over my hips then pulled Thomas' Sex Pistols shirt, I had stolen and slept in religiously since, over head. I wonder if he'll not-

"I knew you stole it!" interrupted my thought. I guess he did notice."Dirty little thief!" He played.

"But look." I pouted as I turned to the side. "It's has the most perfect side boob cut out ever." I cradled myself into his lap, wrapping my arms around his neck.

He slid his tattooed hand into the shirt's oversized cut outs and massaged my bare breast. I swung my hips around, straddling him and inched my lips closer to his as he panted, "Keep the shirt." and pulled it overhead.

The sounds of waves crashing on the beach and smells of salty night air bled through the screens. I nestled in to Thomas' bare chest as he played with a loose curl at the nape of my neck. I was trying to stay awake as long as possible to savor every second of this moment but my eyes were heavy and fluttering in and out of slumber.

Thomas' breath changed. I could feel him trying to find the words. "You suppose Nassau was a good life." I felt his eyes on me.

I leaned deeper into his chest, hugging him tight as I search for an answer. "I suppose." Looking into his haunting hazel eyes, I continued, "It did not end in tragedy, but there were some rather ugly bits."

"That's rather dark." I know he meant it as a light hearted comment. But the mood had turned, his timing was off. I shot him a nasty look. Trying to recover his flub he added, "And beautiful. Just like there is genius in madness. I totally get it." His smile melted the glaciers building around my heart.

I gave him a playful shove calling him out, "You think you're pretty charming or clever or something, don't you?"

Thomas leaned in, his lips hovered above mine, leaving me twisted with anticipation. He was so close I could feel his face crack into a devious smile. I opened my eyes. "Actually Love," He pulled away and ran his fingers through his dirty blonde tresses. "I am pretty, charming, and clever or something."

CHAPTER 89
Charlie Modern Day

I FOUND IT INTERESTING HOW Dahlia seemed to take more interest in Phillip's newest trollop than Liv. There had been several in the months since Thomas and I found each other. I hadn't committed this one's name to memory yet, as it was sure to fizzle out at any given moment.

She was the GM of a cantina in Walnut Creek. Which provided a weekly venue for the band. They had been playing there most Friday night's as of late. It was a relationship of amenity, but you could see the boredom brewing in Phillip.

It had proven convenient, as going into Contra Costa County was always a more enjoyable than driving into The City. Kennedy and Dahlia were in tow most nights to keep me company. This week, they had managed to drag Greyson and Finn along. This meant two things. One; Greyson or Finn would be driving home. Two; Kennedy and Dahlia planned on getting annihilated, dragging me along with them.

The air was electric, the band on fire; I had never heard them so precise. They even played one of my co-writes, which was terrifying and exhilarating all at the same time. It was the kind of night that you knew in your bones magic was possible.

Half way through the set and two and a half pitchers of sangria later Thomas' mates took a breather. He sat on a stool, tooling with the keys of Charlotte, strumming *When You Say Nothing At All*, and spoke into the microphone. "So my girlfriend is here tonight." A mix of applause and sighs filled the room. He points over to my table. I slink into my chair feeling my skin flush red. "Give 'em a wave Love." I reluctantly waved and he continued, still strumming our song, "She once told me something, That I didn't quite understand till recently." I might actually keel over and die of embarrassment. I will be the first documented case of death by mortification. "I took her to my favorite music store and we were playing around, because what else do you do in an instrument store?" There was a roar of giggles, but not so much because Thomas was funny, but because his smile transforms even the strongest of women into giddy teenage girls. "That performing for a crowd was an intimate affair. Then a few weeks later she said I would never be able to get her on a stage although she has the loveliest voice." He paused for a breath. "Like she was challenging me or something." the audience giggled and swooned at his smiling face.

I had sunk so deep in my chair, I was almost under the table. I felt Kennedy's hand along the collar of my shirt as she yanked me into my seat like she was correcting a child.

Phillip took his seat behind the drum kit. Olivia crossed the stage and picked up her bass.

"What do ya think Charlie?" Thomas pressured with a wink. "This is a cozy little crowd. I'm sure they'll be kind."

My face felt hot. I shook my head no as my body radiated Abso-Bloody- Lutely Not Thomas Black! You needn't be psychic to hear it.

Olivia started plucking the base cords from a familiar tune. I thought we were friends?! Thomas added to the melody. "Come on Babe. I know you know this one."

Then he began to sing Van Morrison's words and continued to play, "Come on Babe. Don't leave me hanging here."

The crowd was chiming in now. Peer pressure is the worst. Kennedy pushed my chair forward, spilling me from it's lap. The audience applauded. I mouthed I hate you to Kennedy as Thomas grabbed my hand, dragging me on stage and continued singing.

By the time the song had ended, I was so lost in the music, I couldn't see past the end of the microphone. The roar of applause brought me back to the moment. "She's spectacular. Isn't she?" Thomas coached the audience, I unconsciously curtsied.

Thomas presses his lips to the mic. "What do ya say Darling? You got another one in ya?" He starts to pluck the cords of the Melissa Etheridge.

I spoke into the other, "Did you plan your set to purposely ambush me?"

Phillip stood over his kit, answering for Thomas. "Yes, yes we did." Before I could protest Greyson had let out one of his obnoxiously loud whistles, riling up the crowd once again.

"See they want you. They need you." Thomas egged plucking his electric guitar's strings. "Peer pressure. Peer pressure." He was relentless. "Come on Babe. You mop-sing it so beautifully."

Everything fell away. All I could see was Thomas and all I heard was the music. The way I sang to him and the way I let the moans of his guitar move my body reminded me of Santa Barbra beach, but instead of feeling someone else's moment, we were making our own. It marked my heart; maybe one of our future selves will dream of this very moment. It was dizzying to think about.

The song ended and the room filled with applause, but I was still kind of lost in the haze. "Fuck me." I heard Thomas' gravel voice through the speakers. "That was steamy Doll." I felt my face flush.

I couldn't handle anymore. I was not used to use this kind of attention. Every nerve ending shrieked 'run' as I darted off stage, Thomas grabbed me by the wrist, "Now where do you think you're going. We're not done with you yet."

"Thomas, no," I protested. "I don't have another one in me."

I froze as Thomas dropped to one knee. His playful light-hearted mood shifted to bumbling and nervous. He pulled a small velveteen box from his pocket and presented me with an oval shaped emerald set in a delicate gold band.

The room was spinning. "You are the love I have waited for my entire life." The collective awe had no idea how literal he was being. "I can't imagine spending another day without you. Charlotte, will you share this life with me, be my wife?"

Shock paralyzed my vocal cords, actual words could not escape my mouth. I mouthed, "I love you" as tears welled in my eyes and he leaned his to kiss me, sliding the gemstone promise onto my left ring finger while I nodded yes.

When his lips touched mine, flashes of our lifetimes passed raced through my mind. A stormy Kentucky night. A bonfire on a Caribbean beach. All of it.

"All right you two." Phillip interrupted. "Congrats and all, but this is family place."

I regained my composure but not my breath. Thomas ran his fingers through his messy locks, effortlessly placing each stand in its place. I somehow appeared more dis-shelved, quickly harnessing my medusa curls in a pony.

CHAPTER 90
Charlie Modern Day

I SQUEEZED THOMAS' WAIST TIGHT as we leaned into each bend and turn of treacherously windy route leading into Berryessa. He was right. It was a gorgeous day for a ride but I think I might have preferred to take Scout.

I was beginning to think he was enjoying giving me a scare, because we approached each bend slightly faster than the last. Causing an equivalent affect on my clench. On the back of the Ducati down 121 was a much different ride than in a vehicle with four wheels. I wonder if he'd be mad if I Ubered home?

Thomas finally scouted a spot to pull off. In all fairness I was no help, my face had been buried between his shoulder blades. Relief instantly washed over me as I heard the motor cut out and felt the kick stand touch the ground. I dismounted and ripped the helmet off my head.

He dismounted, removing his helmet all in one sweeping motion. It was effortlessly sexy. I subconsciously bit my lower lip. Before I knew what was happening, Thomas had grazed my bottom lip with his teeth as he pushed his tongue into my mouth. I melted.

He pulled his lips away just far enough that when he spoke I felt them tickle mine. "Sorry." His breath was heavy. "You just looked like you needed a proper kissing is all."

I looked up into those stormy green eyes as I uncontrollably bit my lower lip again. "Is that right?"

Thomas wrapped his arms around my waist, pulling my hands behind my back, lacing his fingers though mine. The motion automatically straightened my posture and pushed my neck up to meet his gaze met. "That's right." His lips lingered, teasing me.

I caved first, breaking away. Distractedly, I pulled the blanket from my backpack, spreading it underneath a shady oak. I pulled out my copy of 'The Symposium' from the bag as Thomas removed his leather motorcycle jacket making himself a pillow against the tree.

We ate our deli sandwiches overlooking the lake before reading four chapters aloud. He laid next to me with his hand firmly placed on my three month bloated belly.

It was a familiar moment of comfort. I found myself having one of those moments where you find yourself inexplicably happy. Where everything is right with the world. Every step I had taken had been to get to this moment now.

CHAPTER 91
Thomas 2132

THE BLOOD CURDLING SQUEAL OF brakes and violent shriek of metal twisting force me awake as I dart straight up drenched in sweat and tears streaming down my face. The smell of burning rubber and coppery blood coat my lungs.

This was the third dream in as many nights, each more intense than the last. The dreams were tortuous, but the questions they raised terrified me.

What happened?

To her?

To me?

Our baby?

Did I kill us?

Get it together Thomas, it's just a dream, a nightmare.

A dream where I could taste the apple linger on her tongue, smell the flowers in the air. I dreamt her in color, and still feel the lines of her smile beneath my fingertips. A dream where all my bones ache from a crash that didn't really happen. A dream where the best bits of me ripped away, leaving a painful hallow.

"Vital scan initiate; Patient, Thomas Walker. Time, two hundred hours, thirty four minutes. Date; fifteenth of November, twenty one thirty two. Elevated heart rate. Staggered breathing. Increased body temperature."

"That's enough." I cancelled the computer's programming as I hopped from bed.

"What is it Tom?"My wife, Kennedy, groggily asked as she rolled over reaching for me. "Are you okay?"

I made my way to the window's bay, staring down at that water covered rock we orbited. She was calling to me, her pull tighter than ever.

"Nothing, just a dream." I lied.

About the Author

Bay Area native, KD Hart, enjoys cuddling with her bully breed mutt, herding cats, and sipping locally roasted coffee while watching dusk become dawn. If she's not feverishly scratching away in her journal, she can be found immersed in the diverse landscape and culture of Northern California. She fills her days bucking traditional gender roles as a successful project manager in the male dominated world of construction and her nights, teeing up for a successful writing career. As she methodically builds her platform; samples of her passion for the written word and flirtation with photography can be found on her website, www.authorkdhart.com, Facebook and Instagram. Her work has been featured as a Top 20 book idea for ten weeks with Something Or Other Publishing and with nearly 400 followers on Twitter including; Denise Landis and The Mindy Project, she is definitely the up and comer you'll want to proudly boast, "I read KD Hart was before it was cool."

www.ingramcontent.com/pod-product-compliance
Lightning Source LLC
Chambersburg PA
CBHW030547310726
48979CB00010B/2067/J

9781732098817